"In today's world of very early identification of deafness, surgical implantation of cochlear implants and endless wireless technology and downloadable apps, *Painting Bridges* is magnificent in presenting a sensitive and accurate depiction of the 1970s. The novel presents a time when late identification of deafness was the norm, resulting in limited language and speech development, amplification equipment that was rudimentary and bulky, and deaf educators were at war with one another in pursuit of parents' hearts and minds. Patricia Averbach has written a great historical novel documenting a contentious period in deaf education."

—Beverly A. Goldstein, Ph.D

PAINTING BRIDGES
A NOVEL

PATRICIA AVERBACH

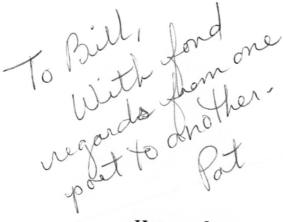

To Bill,
With fond
regards from one
poet to another -
Pat

HARMONY SERIES
BOTTOM DOG PRESS

HURON, OHIO

ISBN 978-1-933964-69-0
Bottom Dog Publishing
PO Box 425
Huron, Ohio 44839
http://smithdocs.net
e-mail: Lsmithdog@smithdocs.net

CREDITS:
General Editor: Susanna Sharp-Schwacke
Layout & Design: Susanna Sharp-Schwacke
Cover Design: Susanna Sharp-Schwacke and Larry Smith

ACKNOWLEDGEMENTS

This book would not have been written without Adele Ward, who encouraged me to turn a short story into a novel and who provided ongoing guidance and support over the three years it took to complete the project. Adele, a London based poet and novelist, is a true friend who I met in the virtual world called Second Life.

I am profoundly grateful to The Chautauqua Writers Center and Chautauqua Writers Festival for helping me, as well as many other aspiring writers.

Particular thanks are due to Sherra Babcock, Clara Silverstein, Phil Terman, Diana Hume-George, and George Looney for assuring the ongoing quality of literary life at the Chautauqua Institution.

I would also like to thank my early readers for their insight and encouragement. They include members of an online writers group that met for several years in Second Life, and members of my hybrid Sarasota/Chautauqua writers' group: Pam Beck, Chalise Bourque, Georgia Court, Monica Gardener, Carma Lloyd, Susan Nusbaum, and Aina Segal. Additional early readers who offered support and advice include Julie Aarons, Leatrice Abrams, Elana Averbach, Mark Averbach, Kathleen Bennett, Gwen Cooper, Jean Cummins, Roxanne Miller, Barbara Rose, and Gladys Yanow.

Particular thanks to Jean Cummins who spent hours double-checking the manuscript for typos and other gaffs.

Finally, I want to express my gratitude to Larry Smith and Susanna Sharp-Schwacke of Bottom Dog Press.

DEDICATION

For Mark, Ann, and Elana
With all my love

CHAPTER 1

Spring didn't bring the sense of renewal she'd been waiting for. Daffodils, ravaged by a late April blizzard lay on the grass, their heads stretched out on scrawny necks like butchered chickens. Melting snow collected in the ruts that ran from Edison up the unpaved drive to the old farmhouse. The forsythia's yellow blooms called out the only hopeful note in a landscape exhausted by the winter. Sam's denim jacket hung open, flapping in the wind as she slogged up the drive juggling three heavy bags of groceries. She heard a farewell toot as Sheila drove off and turned to see her mother-in-law's blue Bonneville pull away in a spray of muddy water.

Sam kicked off her wet sneakers, dumped the groceries on the table, and clicked on WHUG, a popular country music station. Walter Chapman, Trucker Joe, and Vera Brag were her best friends now. Their slow, kind radio voices and *Top Twenty Country Favorites* followed her from room to room as she went about her day. Two years ago the sentimental twang of country music made her teeth hurt, but now her radio stayed tuned to *Huggin' Country*. Rhinestone cowboys had played no part in her old life, so they didn't bring back painful memories. Blue eyes cryin' in the rain and lonely hearts were no longer the sole province of men with bad teeth and women with too much hair. They'd become her heart's home, her comfort and consolation.

The house itself was cold and damp. She and Ben had conquered the musty smell that once permeated the floors and carpets, but the windows still had leaky sashes, and the frames were so rotted that the old wavy panes of glass sometimes fell out, crashing to the floor if jolted open or closed too hard. Ben had nailed plywood over the missing panes to keep out the elements until they could afford new windows. Now, Sam couldn't deal with broken glass or wood or nails, so she left them as they were. They'd been nailed shut when a disoriented trucker had swerved in front of Ben's car on a cold October morning, and they could just damn well stay closed forever.

She knew that she should put the milk and frozen beans away, but why? How much easier to sink into the sagging sofa, a hand me down from Sheila, and float off into that half awake-half asleep fog where she'd spent the greater part of winter. The radio hummed between stations. *Why is it that nothing, not even the airwaves, stays put?* Sam fiddled with the dial until she locked in WHUG again. The news was almost over. The Khmer Rouge had installed Pol Pot as the new prime minister of Cambodia and New York State was funding some new program to educate the handicapped. She waited impatiently until the familiar voice of Walter Chapman, welcomed her to *Catawba County Count Down*. That meant it was only six o'clock, but she couldn't keep her eyes open another minute.

When she woke it was already dark and the temperature had plummeted. Pulling her denim jacket close, she made her way to the kitchen where her grocery bags, now limp and soggy, sat waiting on the table. The irregular old glass in the wooden cupboards distorted her reflection making her forehead oversized and bulbous, her eyes too small, her mouth twisted and off center. She used to be a pretty girl, not movie star material, but she'd had a decent figure and thick brown hair that she'd worn parted in the middle and feathered into soft layers that high-lighted her high cheek bones and long lashes. No telling what she looked like now, faded and pasty she imagined, and she should probably wash her hair. She'd been avoiding mirrors for some time.

Switching off the overhead light she sat down in one of the ladderback chairs that ringed the kitchen table, trying to muster the will to empty her shopping bags and heat up a can of minestrone soup for supper. She didn't cry. The crying had stopped some months ago, but sometimes she would just freeze up staring at nothing for an hour.

A ringing phone startled her back to her thawing groceries. It had to be eight-thirty. Her mother called every evening at exactly half past eight. Pushing back her chair, Sam lumbered toward the phone determined to sound cheerful. Sure enough, there was her mother's perky voice, upbeat as always "Hi sweetie, how did your day go?"

Ten minutes later she was rummaging through her gadget drawer looking for a can opener while once again promising her mother that she'd think about going back to school next fall. A flash of something white darted past her window. A moment later there was a crash followed by metallic clatter that might have been two small cars colliding in the dark. Sam's heart missed a beat. Visions of broken glass and crumpled metal made her grab the counter for support. Taking a deep breath, she opened her eyes and lay the phone down beside the sink. Cautiously peering out the back door she saw that a ladder had fallen upsetting two large metal trash bins. The back end of a white cat disappeared into the bushes.

She stepped back inside and picked up the phone. Her knees felt a little wobbly, yet she kept her voice from quavering. She was in no mood to put up with her mother's incessant prodding and probing. "It was nothing, just some cat making a mess of my trash. I'm going to eat supper now, so how about if we talk tomorrow?"

While her soup was heating Sam went outside, picked up the ladder and gathered up scattered cans, banana peels and egg shells. She'd often get these little bursts of energy at night when she could do her laundry or wash the dishes piled up in the sink. Sometimes she'd take out her old Singer sewing machine and make small patches out of Ben's jogging shorts, his ties, his underwear, his socks, his swim suit, even his baseball cards and album covers. Eventually, she would cut up his pajamas, his bathrobe, the flannel shirt he wore on weekends, but not yet. When she had enough patches she'd make them into a quilt or something. Maybe she'd reassemble all the pieces into a young man with wide shoulders, bushy eyebrows, a childlike sense of humor, and an encyclopedic knowledge of native plants, the man who had been her husband for two years, four months and sixteen days.

At the same time, she knew that she would never take a pair of scissors to the baby blankets, the bonnets, the flannel sleepers, or the small ruffled dresses that had belonged to her beautiful wise-eyed daughter. Converting Ben's clothes into a quilt seemed sanctification, while cutting her baby's things felt just the opposite, a desecration as unthinkable as cutting into her very flesh. There was absolutely no logic to her feelings, only a deep, irrational conviction about what she could and could not do.

The house had been a wedding present from Ben's mother. Sheila had grown up on the farm back when a family could support itself on a few acres of corn, a couple cows, maple syrup in the spring, and cider in the fall. This hard, spare life offered few inducements to a young woman whose head was filled with Hollywood images of Lauren Bacall and Katherine Hepburn. As soon as Sheila married she'd fled to the relative glamour of a modern tract house in the suburbs, and she'd never thought of moving back, not even after her parents died and left the property to her. Occasionally renters moved in for a year or two, but eventually the cost of repairs outpaced the rent and the house stood empty. Untilled acreage was gradually sold off, and the farm was almost forgotten until Ben and Sam drove out to the property and stood with their arms around one another's waists, envisioning a gracious home with a large barn on the remaining fourteen acres. Sheila had gladly given them the house and land as a wedding present, and they'd immediately set to work on renovations. By the time June was born, the bathroom and plumbing were up to code, and the derelict old structure was showing signs of renewed life.

Sam had been happy on that October 15th, sitting at her desk at the *Seneca Sun Journal,* theoretically writing an article about the Rotary Club's Haunted Hayride, while actually thumbing through the new Penney's catalog, when Joyce came over and stood beside her desk. Her boss was a large, confident woman who ordinarily commanded attention by virtue of her loud voice and even louder wardrobe. But on that day she'd been so quiet, so shrunken, that Sam hadn't been aware of her presence until she'd felt a cold hand trembling on her shoulder. Sam hadn't been able to make out what Joyce was saying, but she'd allowed herself to be led down the hall and pushed, uncomprehending, through the doorway into Joyce's office. The Sheriff had sat Sam down and closed the door.

Her parents stayed with her for two weeks after the funeral. They'd begged her to come back home to Cleveland, but she'd refused. Ben's clothes still hung in the closets, the baby's toys were still in her crib, *Pat the Bunny* and *Goodnight Moon* were tucked into the bookshelf beside Ben's old biology texts. Back issues of *Scientific American* were piled on the floor beside Ben's chair, and Nolly, the stuffed monkey, still slept on her baby's pillow. This was still their home, and she would stay here with them, even if they were dead. Rather than disappearing, Ben and Baby June had become ubiquitous in death. Yes, they were in the small family plot at the back of the property where Crawfords had been buried since the 1840s, but they were also at the school, in the fields, at the hardware store, in the barn, in the kitchen, in her bed. But, she was afraid they might not be in Cleveland and she couldn't take that risk.

Sam had kissed her parents goodbye and promised that she'd be okay. She'd get a new car and go back to work and maybe she'd find someone to finish shingling the roof. But after her parents left, Sam had found that all she could do was sleep. When her boss called to ask how she was feeling and when she'd be coming back to work, Sam told that her she needed more time off. She'd call when she was ready. After three more months Joyce called again. "Still not ready," Sam had said. "Maybe you'd better hire someone else. It might be a while."

On that day, their car had been totaled when it slammed into the side of a Ryder's rental truck. The truck driver, a student from

Detroit, had barreled across the right hand lane toward the exit ramp cutting off their new 1974 Chevy Nova, the proudest purchase of their married life. It was all in the hands of lawyers and insurance adjusters now. Sam wasn't interested. Her father would handle all of that. The insurance company had sent a check to cover the cost of a new car months ago. It was in the bank waiting for her, along with the money from Ben's life insurance. She let it all just sit. She'd planned to buy a car once her nerves had settled down, maybe in the spring. But that first spring had come and gone. Now April had rolled around again and the idea of car shopping was no more appealing than it had been a year ago.

Ben's mother came every Friday afternoon to drive her to Bell's Grocery and the library. Just this afternoon Sam had watched Sheila turn up the gravel drive and park below the muddy ruts that had been hollowed out by winter's ice and snow. Sam knew that she should run to the door to wave a cheery greeting, grab her purse and coat, and head out the door like a good daughter-in-law. But the very thought of making small talk while navigating brightly lit grocery aisles festooned with pastel Easter bunnies and oversized bouquets of cardboard tulips sapped her strength. So she'd peeked out between the slats of the venetian blinds while Sheila picked her way through the mud and icy puddles. Even when Sheila was standing on the front step knocking loudly Sam found she couldn't move. Only after Sheila had begun jiggling the doorknob and shouting for her, had Sam finally sighed and headed toward the door.

"Sorry," she'd said, "I didn't hear you. The doorbell's broken."

"We need to get that fixed." Sheila eyed Sam appraisingly, "Good girl, you're wearing your new sweater." Sam looked down; she had no idea what she was wearing. It was the blue turtleneck from Bigelow's that Sheila had given her for Christmas. Suddenly she was smothered in Sheila's good wool coat, having her back patted and her head kissed just above the hairline. "What do you say we hit the road?" Sheila blew her nose, stuffed the tissue back into her pocket and headed toward the car.

Sheila used these outings as an opportunity to reminisce, and Sam knew it was her duty to smile and nod at stories she'd heard a hundred times before.

"You know Ben was a champion swimmer back in high school." Sheila's cheeks flushed, and her eyes sparkled like a teenager's whenever she mentioned Ben or Joe. "His team won the district, and then took regionals. There wasn't another team in Western New York that could touch them. They went all the way to Albany." Sam heard this story every time they drove past Kleiner High School. "Did I ever show you his trophy? It's still in the bookcase in Ben's room."

"I know, I've seen it." Sam bit her tongue and didn't add, "about a thousand times." *Had Sheila loved her husband, the balding man with bushy eyebrows in the photo beside her bed, as much as she'd loved her sons?*

"And he was a born scientist. He didn't just play outside like other boys, he studied things; he knew the Latin name for every plant and animal." Then she warmed to her favorite topic as Sam slouched lower in her seat. "Ben claimed to be agnostic, but he had a truly spiritual nature. He didn't go to church, but I know that he experienced God in the miracles of creation."

Sam rolled her eyes, but didn't say a word. There was no reason to remind her mother-in-law that Ben had claimed membership in the Church of the Wholly Grossed Out. Sheila took a long drag on her cigarette, exhaling with a sigh. "And he was a wonderful student. I bet he would have gone on and gotten more degrees if he hadn't ..." There was a moment's hesitation, "but what would another degree have meant if he hadn't found you?" Sheila turned and beamed at Sam affectionately.

Sam had been staring out the window as they drove past Branson's Orchard; she turned to Sheila, pointing out the trees. "The late freeze probably killed off the new buds on those peach trees. Ben used to call April the killing time. He said birds are the hungriest and weakest in the early spring."

"Do you know what else he said?" Sheila turned her gaze on Sam who was pretending to watch the passing landscape, her forehead pressed against the glass. "The unselfish effort to bring cheer to others will be the beginning of a happier life for ourselves."

"Ben never said that."

"Well someone did. Maybe it was Helen Keller."

A week later, the weather hadn't changed. The fields behind the house, fragile in the spring, were swollen by melted snow and heavy rains. Spongy earth sank under Sam's feet, so that a trail of muddy footprints sprouted behind her as she cut through the new grass and clover toward the woods. She should have put on boots; her Nikes would be ruined. Her socks were already damp, and she hadn't even reached the pond and its surrounding marsh. In a normal state of mind she would have returned to the house, put on dry socks, thick soled rubber boots, a warmer coat, but she was in no mood for turning back. She trudged forward clutching a pot of daffodils from Bell's Grocery. Sheila had bought them for Sam as a gift, but Sam thought, *Too bright, too loud, too yellow for the house.*

An old logging road ran through the forest which began just beyond the fields. This had been a working farm; the fields had sprouted soybeans, corn, timothy and rye. Sam had inherited the stories with the house. Black and white Herefords had grazed in the adjoining pasture, the orchard had produced heavy crops of apples, northern spy and golden russet. Sheila claimed to remember teams of oxen, then big Peterbilts, hauling timber from the woods. Of course, that had all been history by the time that Ben was born. Now there wasn't much but mud and weeds, thorny brambles and wild ramps that smelled like onions. The blade of an ancient plow rusted beside an outcropping of glacial rock just beyond the field where it had sat for untold years.

It had all looked so different through Ben's eyes. When she had stood in this very place beside her husband, she'd only seen the future. Once the house was finished, they were going to hire a backhoe to dredge the pond, clear the brush and cattails. She had looked beyond the algae clogged surface of the water, the overgrown weeds, the decaying stumps and seen a grassy slope, a willow tree, and children splashing in a clear pool. Fungus had destroyed the northern spy trees, but the golden russets were still strong. She and Ben planned to bring them back, and they were going to rebuild the barn, and buy a couple goats and maybe a pony for June when she was older. Her eyes followed the property line to the north where she'd planted a hedge of blueberries that last September. They weren't there anymore. Deer had eaten the young bushes to the ground.

Slogging forward she continued into the wood, past the pond and across the ravine, ignoring the water sloshing in her shoes and the mud weighing down the bottom of her jeans. Where the road forked, she headed north until the trees came to an abrupt end, and she stepped into a clearing marked by thin gray stones etched with the names of Crawfords dating back a hundred years. In fact, most of the deceased had been laid to rest before the Second World War, since the more recent dead generally chose to be buried at South Shore Cemetery with its views of Lake Erie to the north and endless rows of Concord grape vines to the east. But even so, there were two new graves. Sam took a small trowel from her jacket pocket and began digging in the soft mud. Tipping the flowers from their pot, she gently divided the bulbs and planted a few on each mound. Patting the earth smooth, she sat back on her heels, satisfied that the flowers looked lovely beneath the simple headstones. The smaller one read:

June Crawford
June 1, 1973 – October 15, 1974

Engraved on the larger headstone just beside it:

Benjamin Lee Crawford
January 12, 1951 – October 15, 1974

Sam had insisted they be buried here in the old family plot. South Shore Cemetery was miles away, too far from home, too far from her. She wiped off the trowel, stuck it in her pocket and turned back the way she'd come. Just at the point where the path disappeared into the woods, Sam turned for one last look then blinked in disbelief; a little girl was standing on her baby's grave picking the newly planted daffodils. For the briefest moment Sam had the irrational thought that her daughter had somehow risen from the dead to accept her mother's gift. But no, this child was old enough to be at school and she was wearing a dirty pink parka that was a size too small.

"Hey!" Sam shouted. "What do you think you're doing?" The child tore the last daffodil from the ground and added it to her bouquet. Sam ran toward the child. "Hey, look at me. Turn around and look at me. Don't you know better than to steal flowers from a grave?" Sam was standing right behind the child who continued to ignore her. Exasperated, she grabbed the girl's arm and whirled her around so that they faced each other. A look of abject terror crossed the child's face. She let out a wild, bestial grunt and struggled to get free. Sam recoiled as if she'd seen a ghost. The child's almond eyes, her thick brows, the contours of her face were exactly like her daughter's. "June?" She said softly, illogically, not a question but a prayer. Sam didn't want to frighten her, but she held tight. "It's okay, please, I'm not mad, just tell me your name. Do you live around here?" The little girl began kicking and emitting strange yipping sounds. Sam let go and the child fled into the forest still holding tight to the stolen flowers.

Why was her heart pounding and her hands shaking so badly that she had to cross her arms and hug herself to keep them still? *They're just stupid flowers,* Sam kept repeating to herself. *I can plant some more tomorrow.* Her eyes followed her feet all the way back through the woods, never glancing to the right or left. *I must be going mad, imagining the child looks so much like June.* As she cut across the lawn toward the house, she looked up to find a note taped to her side door. *Damn.* She'd promised Sheila she'd drive with her to Erie for lunch and shopping and now she'd probably stood her up. What

time was it anyway? Sam didn't wear a watch, so she left her muddy
sneakers in the hall and headed for the kitchen stove where the clock
told her that it was half past time to be washed and dressed and
waiting in the drive. She sat down on the one good chair that didn't
rock on uneven legs and opened the note. *Samantha—Where in the
world are you? Call me when you get back. If it's not too late, we could still do
lunch. Love, Sheila.*

Sam dialed Sheila's number, noting the mud she'd dripped across
the kitchen floor. She'd definitely have to mop it up tomorrow.

"Hello, Sam? Where are you?" Sheila was her usual abrupt self.
Sam could picture her mother-in-law's graying hair pouffed up in a
sort of loose bouffant, her body squeezed into the tweed suit she
saved for trips to the city. She was undoubtedly pacing impatiently in
her immaculate kitchen with its cheery wallpaper and coordinating
curtains, and probably stubbing out her tenth Kent of the morning
in the flower pot beside the sink. "Are you alright? I worry myself to
death when I don't know where you are?"

"For God's sake, where could I be? I just walked out to the
cemetery to plant some flowers and I forgot about the time."

"It's a swamp out there when it's this wet. What were you thinking?"

"It wasn't that bad." Sam bent down and swiped at a muddy
footprint with a paper napkin, but only succeeded in leaving a smudgy
smear on the linoleum. "But the weirdest thing happened. This little
girl, she was maybe six or seven years old, appeared out of nowhere
and made off with all the flowers I'd just planted. She went all to
pieces when I tried to talk to her. She wouldn't say a thing, just made
these weird little sounds then ran off. I think there was something
wrong with her."

"There aren't any young children on Edison. I wonder who
she belongs to."

"Well, they must be idiots, letting a little thing like that wander
off unsupervised." Sam wasn't going to say a word about the child's
uncanny resemblance to her daughter. Sheila was already convinced
that she was losing her mind.

"The world is full of idiots, not much we can do about that.
Have you eaten yet? Are we still on for lunch?"

"Sure, it's only twelve o'clock. If you give me half an hour to
clean up, we'll still have time for lunch."

"Good girl. Put on some make up and don't wear that denim
jacket. You're such a pretty girl when you make a little effort."

"Please, Sheila, don't push me. I'm doing the best I can."

*   *   *

The next morning Sam woke to the sound of Loretta Lynn's voice on the clock radio. Her heart was pounding and she felt agitated and confused. She'd had that dream again, the nightmare that had been plaguing her sleep for weeks. It was always night in the dream, and she was always driving down Route 17 in the new car she and Ben had purchased. Suddenly, two police cars come up behind her, sirens blaring and lights flashing. She becomes frightened, and her mind begins to race, *My God,* she thinks, *I've been driving too fast, I must have killed someone.* Convinced she's murdered someone and that the police are going to arrest her, she drives faster and faster, trying to escape. A huge green exit sign looms in her headlights, and she tries to evade her pursuers by turning off the highway. A moment later she's on a strange uninhabited road speeding past empty fields with no buildings or familiar landmarks, but she isn't safe. They're still behind her. The sirens grow louder and louder, even as she goes faster and faster trying to outrun them. The noise increases, wailing, pulsing in her head. Confused and disoriented, she stops the car and turns around. No police cars are in pursuit, only a small child in the back seat crying and crying.

Sam reached out and clicked off her radio. Loretta Lynn fell silent and a hazy light sifted through the dirty bedroom windows. *Only eight o'clock and I'm not ready to face another day.* Sheila was arriving at nine with a painter from Seneca Rocks, so she'd better pull herself together and be up and dressed when they arrived. Most of her clothes were in the laundry hamper, so she pulled on the same underwear she'd worn the day before, fished a pair of jeans off the floor and found a clean sweater in one of her drawers. She probably should have taken a shower, but she wasn't about to get undressed again. She splashed some water on her face and pulled her hair back with a rubber band. Sam hadn't had a haircut since last autumn and her long brown hair reached to the middle of her back. Sheila said she was turning into a regular hippy. Sam didn't know what she was turning into.

She filled a bowl with cornflakes and carried it into the living room where she turned on *The Today Show.* There was that new girl, Jane Pauley, who'd replaced Barbara Walters. She was cute and bubbly, but Sam didn't like her. Probably she wouldn't have liked anyone new; she'd used up whatever tolerance she had for change and separation. The station abruptly cut from Jane flirting with a crowd of New Yorkers wearing Groucho Marx moustaches to Tom Brockaw sitting behind a desk grimly citing the death toll from another leaky ship crammed past capacity with South Vietnamese trying to escape the Communists. She was treated to footage of emaciated bodies being plucked out of the water by the Australian Navy. Sam put down her corn flakes and turned off the TV. *So that's what my brother-in-law died for.*

Sam wasn't political herself, she'd never attended a march or a rally, although she'd certainly been ecstatic when the draft ended and she knew that Ben was safe. She'd secretly sided with the protesters, but not vocally, not in public. She knew she would start her own civil war if she breathed an unpatriotic word around Sheila, who'd sacrificed her first born son to that bad cause.

A solid rap on the door announced Sheila's arrival. Sam left her cereal bowl on the coffee table beside the remains of last night's Spaghettios and grabbed her denim jacket before opening the door. "Hi, up and dressed as promised." She slipped outside and shut the door behind her hoping that Sheila had been spared a view of the kitchen. A lanky man in blue jeans and a paint stained sweat shirt stood beside Sheila. Sam was surprised to see that he was black. She'd practically been raised by a succession of black housekeepers, but Sam had rarely seen a black man in Catawba County.

"Sam, dear, this is Billy Crabtree, the painter I told you about. He's going to take a look around and give us an estimate on repainting the house. Billy, this is my daughter-in-law, Samantha."

Billy nodded in her direction, and then went back to scribbling something in a small spiral notebook. Sam followed his eyes up to the second story windows where she'd begun scraping away at the wooden casements eighteen months ago.

He finished writing, then turned toward Sheila. "No sense painting those windows. The wood's rotted; bet I could stick my finger right through the frames, and those plywood boards aren't giving you a bit of insulation. You must have had some heating bills last winter. How about if I include a quote for new windows as part of the job?" His voice was deep and gravely, his accent unexpected. He must have been from Boston or somewhere in New England.

"You know, I was going to paint the house myself," Sam said. The guy looked okay, but Sam wasn't sure she wanted him hanging around, getting chatty, making small talk. "I already bought the paint."

"So what happened? You did a great job prepping the siding over there," he pointed his pencil at the wood scraped raw under the eaves, "but you should have put some paint over it before the weather turned."

Sheila gave Billy a warning look and shook her head. Without missing a beat he snapped his notebook shut and said, "Well, I guess I'll take a walk around the property and see what else needs doing, then you can tell me about that paint you bought." He walked up the drive past the back of the house and disappeared behind a large honeysuckle.

Sam crossed her arms and glared at Sheila "You knew I was going to finish painting the house as soon as the weather got better, and I don't have money for new windows." The money sitting in her bank account flashed across Sam's mind, but she continued to stare defiantly at Sheila.

"It's a gift. You have enough on your mind without worrying about the house."

"I'm not worrying about the house. I don't think about the house at all."

"Good, then let me worry about paint and windows. It's what Ben would have wanted. He worked so hard to fix this old place up for you."

"Actually, I was the one who was painting the house. Ben wasn't into painting."

"Well, you can't install new windows. How about if I hire Billy to replace the windows and patch the roof? Then maybe he could just help with the painting if it's too much for you to do yourself."

"What can I say? It's your house."

"It's not, it's your house." Sheila was hurt, "I gave it to you and Ben when you got married and all I want is to make it nice and comfortable so you'll live here a long, long time." Sheila reached out to squeeze Sam's hands, but Sam's hands had disappeared into the pockets of her jacket. Sam loved Sheila, but her kindness was sometimes a burden.

"Hey there!" Billy was striding toward them and waving his hands above his head. "You know what you've got out there in that barn?"

Sam and Sheila turned toward him blank faced. "No," they shook their heads in unison.

"Well, you better come take a look. I had a feeling you didn't know what you had in there." Billy's eyes gleamed and his face lit up with excitement. Sam noticed that his cheeks crinkled and furrowed when he grinned. The man was older than she'd thought, maybe as old as Sheila.

They followed him back to the barn where he'd moved several tires, ropes, chains and the frame of an old bicycle to reveal the rusted hulk of a tractor that hadn't seen daylight in years.

"How long's that been out here collecting dust?"

"Oh, for Heaven's sake, my father was the last person to drive that tractor and he's been gone since 1955." Sheila clearly couldn't imagine anyone getting so excited about a heap of rusty metal. "We just left it out here because it was too much bother to sell it or give it away."

"What you've got here is an original Model B Allis-Chalmers, a really early one, probably from the thirties."

"But it's in terrible condition. Look at the rust on the front part over there. If you have an old Allis-Chalmers I suppose you could use this one for parts."

"I do not have an old Allis-Chalmers, but I sure have been looking for one. This is the very model my granddaddy used to ride when I came out to visit him summers as a kid. I learned to drive on one of these things."

"Maybe it has some sentimental value, but I'm sure it can't be worth anything." Sheila was doing a little two-step, torn between the impulse to take a closer look at the old tractor and her repulsion at the thick layer of oily dust, cobwebs and dead spiders that encased it.

"That's just surface rust. You could buff that right off." Billy ran his hand along the filthy hood uncovering a swath of orange paint." Was she still working when your daddy died?"

"I don't remember. No one's worked the farm for years, so we just left it here. It wasn't worth much even back then."

"Well, it's worth something now. I mean it could be, if someone fixed her up and got her running. There're people who collect old tractors, I've got four of them myself. Of course none of them are this old; this one here's a genuine antique, almost as old as I am." He chuckled as he reached up to pat the old bench seat. His longing was palpable. Sam watched as Sheila did a quick calculation.

"I'll tell you what; you can have the thing in exchange for cleaning out the barn and giving me a good deal on helping Sam paint the house. How about that?"

Billy pulled a package of Marlboros and a lighter from his shirt pocket. He took his time tamping a cigarette from the box, putting it between his lips, and lighting it. Exhaling a small cloud of smoke and still staring at the tractor he asked, "What about the windows?"

"You get back to me with a price for the windows, and I'll think about replacing them. We might want you to do some work on the roof too, but this is just about paint and cleaning out the barn. Have we got a deal?"

"I don't know." He inhaled deeply and let out another mouthful of smoke like a sigh. "I'd love to fix her up and get her running like I said, but I've already got four tractors. My wife would have me skinned alive if I came home with another one."

"Oh, well. All right then," Sheila flushed, embarrassed that she'd misread the man. "Why don't you just go ahead with your estimate and then we'll talk."

"Tell you what," he brushed the dust off the motor and studied the serial number a moment then wrote down some numbers in his spiral notebook. "What if I clean out the barn and help with the painting, but we just keep the tractor right here for the time being. But you've got to give me enough work so I have an excuse for hanging around here without the wife wondering what I'm up to. I'll tinker with Allis on my own time."

"Well, if the windows don't cost too much, I guess that would be fine with me. I mean that tractor's sat here all these years; it can sit here a little longer. But if you do the work, it's yours; you can take it whenever you want. I'd sign over the title to you if I knew where to find it. Did tractors even have titles in those days?"

"They did. But we can work that out with the BMV when the time comes."

"Well then, it's a deal, Mr. Crabtree." Sheila held out her hand.

Billy flicked the ash from his cigarette, "Deal," he said and shook her hand.

Sam stepped forward and crushed the ember under her tennis shoe. "You shouldn't smoke in here. This barn is nothing but dry timber, plus there are eight gallons of oil paint stored in the loft."

"You're the boss," Billy pinched out the business end of the cigarette between his thumb and index finger then placed the butt in his pocket with a sly wink in Sheila's direction.

As Billy's truck backed down the drive, Sam turned to Sheila, "Why'd you just give him that tractor? I bet it's worth a lot of money."

"Well, if it is, good for him. I don't want the old thing, and I do want the barn cleaned and the house painted." Sheila was heading back to the house, hopping between rocks and grassy patches in an effort to keep her loafers dry.

"Does it matter what I want? Do I even get a vote around here? Is this my house or isn't it?" Sam splashed through the muddy water soaking her own jeans and spattering Sheila's legs.

"Of course it's your house, but we can't let the place go to pieces while you're getting your head together." *Getting your head together. When did Sheila pick up that expression?* Hearing Sheila use trendy slang was as jarring as progressive rock blaring from an old Victrola. Sam paused as her mother-in-law, one hand resting on her heaving chest, hurried to catch up with her. "Now don't give Billy a hard time. He's a good guy and it'll perk you up to see the house with fresh paint and new windows."

"I don't want a strange man crawling all over my house. Where did you find him anyway? He doesn't sound like he comes from around here."

"Billy? I think he grew up in Boston, but he's lived here forever. You don't have to worry about him; he's practically an institution in Catawba County. He does everything, carpentry, painting, plumbing, electrical. Everybody uses him."

A flash of white darted behind one of the overgrown Yews that passed for landscaping beside the house. "Sam, did you get yourself a cat?" Sheila parted the branches and stuck her head into the foliage trying to get a better look at the animal.

"It's not mine; it just hangs around out here. It knocked over a ladder the other night and scared me half to death."

"Oh, what a pretty kitty, aren't you a pretty kitty. Come here, darling, don't be afraid. That's a good pussy cat." Only Sheila's posterior was still visible, the rest of her had disappeared into the hedge. Sam heard a hiss and a yowl and the cat streaked past them toward the barn.

Sheila straightened up and tried to smooth what was left of her bouffant back into place. "What a beautiful animal. I don't think it's feral, someone's been looking after it."

"Well, it isn't me."

"Maybe you should think about getting a cat or a dog. They're great company, and it would be good for you to have something to look after."

"Sheila, please. I can't be responsible for a pet. What if I move somewhere they don't allow animals?"

"Now why would you move and give up this house just when we're fixing it up?" Sheila turned her face away, but Sam could hear a slight quaver in her voice. "I'm sure *The Seneca Sun Journal* would be happy to take you back whenever you're ready or you could work for Alan Siebert; a law office can always use a good secretary with your typing skills. If you decide to go back to school, Fredonia is only half an hour away. We have everything you need right here, so please stop talking like that."

Sam nodded noncommittally. Her head hurt and she felt chilled. "I want to go inside and take a shower. We'll talk later, okay?" If her kitchen had been cleaner, she would have invited Sheila in for coffee, but she couldn't do it, not this morning with a week's worth of dishes in the sink, books and clothes piled on the table, and a thick slick of dirt across the floor. Worse than scolding her, she was afraid that Sheila would take one look at her wrecked kitchen and start pulling out buckets and mops to set things straight.

Sheila smiled affably, although she was clearly disappointed. As a wave of guilt unsettled Sam's stomach she offered up a little apology. "I'm sorry for being so touchy, and thanks for bringing Billy over. You're right, the house does need work. I don't know what I'd do without you." She leaned forward and gave Sheila a kiss on the cheek, inhaling the familiar smell of powder, rouge, and tobacco.

Sheila cheered slightly, "Alright, dear, I'll give you a call right after lunch. There's a rummage sale at the church, maybe we could go together."

There was no fight left in Sam for now, she smiled weakly as she turned to open the screen door.

"And I think I saw a sign at the church advertising free kittens; maybe we could take a look at them later in the week." Sam closed her eyes. Sheila was just like her mother. Neither one could ever give up or let go.

CHAPTER 2

The white cat had taken up residence beneath the back steps ever since Sam had made the mistake of tossing it some table scraps, but its heart was clearly set on cushier digs inside the house. The determined ball of fur spent hours yowling by the door demanding to be let in. As Sam cut Ben's swim trunks into neat six inch squares of red nylon she found it increasingly difficult to ignore the caterwauling. Her concentration was so rattled she slammed her pinking shears onto the table and stormed into the kitchen. Grabbing two large pot lids she opened the back door and began banging them together in the direction of the cat. Unperturbed by the racket, the cat saw its chance, slipped between Sam's feet, and streaked through the open door. A moment later Sam returned to the living room to find a ball of white fluff curled up in the warm spot on her vacated chair.

"Oh, for Heaven's sake." Sam and the cat eyed each other warily. "Don't get too comfortable, Buddy, I'm afraid this is going to be a short visit." Dropping the pot lids on the sofa, Sam slowly removed her denim jacket, and held it in front of herself while inching closer and closer toward the chair. Just as she was about to pounce, the cat jumped onto the table scattering squares of fabric over the floor then bounded to the top of the flimsy Masonite bookcase. The bookcase teetered a moment then fell face forward with a dull thud like someone who'd been shot in the back. *Peterson's Field Guide*, *The Complete Jane Austen*, Asimov's *Foundation Trilogy*, *The Norton Anthology of American Poetry*, *The Bridge* by Hart Crane, *Pat the Bunny*, *Mother Goose*, several old biology texts, and an ancient portfolio of Sam's artwork landed in a jumble on the carpet. Long forgotten water color landscapes and charcoal nudes flew across the room. Water from a green vase seeped onto the cover of *How to Draw and Paint* by Henry Gasser. The cat had disappeared under the sofa.

"That's it, I've had it." Racing back to the kitchen Sam returned with a broom and swept madly under the couch, violently dislodging the cat that was cowering in a corner. "You're out of here. Out! Get Out!" She opened the front door, then swung and batted her weapon at the terrified animal until it beat a retreat just ahead of the broom.

Sam slammed the door shut, and then locked it. Picking her way across the room, she did her best to avoid stepping on the papers strewn across the floor. The lightweight bookcase was easy to stand on end without its contents. She shoved books and bric-a-brac back onto the shelves, then gathered up the remnants of her high school art portfolio. She meant to stuff the old art class exercises back into their manila folio and dispatch them to the top of the bookshelf where they'd sat for years, but they refused to go. Their clarity and strength surprised her, awakening memories of a time before Ben and the baby.

She sat down on the sofa and began to sift through the tattered remnants of three years of high school art. There was an architectural rendering of the Tudor style house where she'd grown up, a portrait of Galen—the golden retriever who'd died the week she'd graduated from high school—a life study of a classmate in a bathing suit. She studied a charcoal rendering of an oak tree, remembering how she'd almost thrown it away thinking it looked crippled and off balance. The drawing struck her as expressive and showing promise. But it was the portrait of a girl whose piercing gaze stared out from beneath neatly cut bangs that riveted her attention. Sam looked into her own younger eyes amazed to see such confidence, almost an expression of defiance, looking back at her.

Leaving the stack of drawings on the coffee table, she bent to pick up the sodden book that had promised to teach her how to draw and paint. Dye from its mustard colored binding stained her hands and left yellow fingerprints as she turned the pages.

Sam had bought the book the summer before high school and spent her entire vacation methodically going through each lesson. By her senior year she was winning awards for her art and had plans to paint the historic bridges dotting the Cuyahoga River. A smile crossed Sam's face as she remembered her AP English teacher insisting that Hart Crane's long poem, *The Bridge*, had been inspired by his time on Cleveland's waterfront. That had given her the idea to illustrate Crane's famous poem with her own paintings of Cleveland's Detroit-Superior Bridge, the Lorain-Carnegie Bridge, the Main Street Bridge, the Eagle Street Bridge, and the old Center Street Bridge. Sitting on the sofa, she recited their names under her breath.

But there had been a fight, a loud, hysterical, door rattling, battle with her mother. Sam shook her head mystified by the conflict. It seemed crazy now. Her logical, cerebral mother had totally lost her cool. Adamant that the lakefront was dirty, dangerous, and a magnet for the worst element, she swore no daughter of hers was going near the place. Equally passionate, Sam was determined to paint those bridges and nothing else. They had screamed, made threats, and carried on until Sam tearfully packed her suitcase and moved to Ithaca, New York eight weeks before Cornell's fall term was scheduled to begin.

At the time, Sam had felt that she'd stood firm, taken a stand for her independence, but the reality was that her mother had won that battle, the same as she'd won all the others. Sam never painted the bridges; in fact, she never took a single art class during her three years at Cornell. Pre-med students didn't have time for frivolous electives and she'd been promised to medicine the way the prophet Samuel had been promised to the priesthood. Her destiny had been predetermined *in utero*, probably before that.

Sam snapped the book shut. *Well, I burned that bridge, so to speak.* She'd never even completed her bachelor's degree, although her mother reminded her almost daily that it wasn't too late. Sam laid the volume on the coffee table beside the crinkled pastels and watercolors then set to work picking shards of green pottery from the carpet.

A blizzard of heavy wet snow stopped traffic, closed the schools, and brought down power lines the second week in April. Six o'clock news anchors trotted out every superlative in the weather lexicon to describe the storm. It was the latest, the coldest, the deepest, and the most destructive. The phone rang and it was Sheila calling, worried and apologetic, to cancel their weekly shopping expedition. Sam had to assure her that she still had a pantry full of soup, and noodles, and canned tuna.

That night the sun set on a landscape muffled by mountains of tiny crystals, each reflecting the dying light in its own way. Sam put on a jacket and stood on her back porch staring past the lawn toward the barn and past the barn toward the trees and past them toward the cemetery where June lay small and unprotected in the snow beside her father. Tears welled in Sam's eyes. The moon radiated an opalescent fog that pulsed within a wavering pink halo. First one star blinked on and then another until Sam could make out the Big Dipper directly overhead, then Arcturus, the brightest star in the eastern sky. Gradually Virgo, Leo, and Cassiopeia appeared, and then, below Regulus, in an empty expanse of sky, Alphard, the star whose name means lonely in Arabic.

The night sky had been Ben's second home. He knew the stars by name, and he knew where to find the constellations as they moved across the heavens month by month. She used to lie beside him on the grass and listen, mesmerized, as he told her the myths and legends of the Greeks, the Chinese, and the Aztecs, those great watchers of the sky. She smiled remembering how they'd sat out expectantly every August to watch the great Persied meteor shower and how they'd been thwarted year after year by rain or clouds or the ambient light of a full moon. "Look," she'd say pointing, hoping to console him. "There's one over there, and is that another?" Ben would be so disappointed. "Yeah," he'd concede, "That's one, but I didn't want to show you one. I wanted a fuckin' light show. I wanted the whole sky to light up for you." He'd loved her that much. He'd wanted the whole sky to light up for her.

"Look Ben," she whispered to the night. "The stars are still there, right where you left them. I still remember all their names. I still remember everything. Do you remember? Do the dead remember?" Some of her words were spoken aloud and drifted off in a visible fog of breath; others were thoughts that resonated in her mind.

A cloud blew past the moon and she could no longer make out the silhouette of the barn or the distant trees. She laid her head against one of the columns supporting the porch roof and closed her eyes. The wind ruffled her hair and froze her face and hands. Then, without explanation, a warm breeze touched her cheek like a lover's breath. She leaned against the column and sighed, she could almost feel Ben standing close beside her, his familiar arm twining around her shoulders, pulling her into an embrace. Sam's head rolled toward the imagined warmth and nestled in the crook of a young man's neck. She wanted to turn, to throw herself sobbing into her husband's arms, but she didn't move. Experience had taught her that the slightest movement would wake her from the dream. She didn't know how long she'd stood immobilized by longing and memory when a barn owl screeched somewhere in the distance and she realized that her teeth were chattering, and her fingers had gone numb.

The next morning Sam felt woozy, as though she had a hangover, although she hadn't had a thing to drink the night before. A dull headache pounded its slow rhythm at the back of her skull. Cross and out of sorts, she headed downstairs without bothering to dress. When the gas refused to ignite on the stove's front burner, she slammed down the cast iron frying pan so hard the salt shaker jumped from the ledge and skittered across the floor. Giving up on eggs, she decided on cold cereal. But the milk, left out on the counter, had gone sour.

She finally managed to assemble a couple slices of toast and a cup of black coffee. She was carrying them into the living room when the cat started yowling outside her door. Sam turned on the television and turned up the volume to drown out the beast, but her head threatened to split open and explode from the noise. Clicking off the set, she looked out the window trying to gauge her chances of hitting the thing with an old boot. Before she could locate the white cat against the white landscape, she saw a child in a bulky snowsuit come lumbering up her unplowed drive.

Sam squinted into the early morning sunlight. The puffy pink jacket was unmistakable; it belonged to the little girl who'd stolen June's daffodils. Her little rubber boots plodded through the snow with unswerving determination. The child was following a set of paw prints to her kitchen door. To Sam's astonishment, the cat emerged from its hiding place to greet the child and began rubbing its back against her leggings. The child reached down, scooped up the animal, and started back down the drive hugging the cat to her chest.

Sam ran out her front door and stood on the front step in her night shirt. "Hey, is that your cat? Does it have a name?" The child didn't even look up, so Sam called after her, "Sorry if I scared you the other day." The child, who looked uncannily like June, didn't turn or run or change her pace but simply continued slogging her way back toward the street. "Do you live around here? Hey! Hello there! Did you hear me?" She disappeared just past the stand of silver birches that stood along the road. Sam kicked the snow from her slippers and went back inside to finish her cold toast and coffee.

The art book was still on the coffee table where she'd left it the day before. The book exuded the fetid odor of mold when Sam turned back the cover. The water logged paper had discolored and begun to curl. Feeling a surge of compassion for the book, she took it on her lap, riffling the pages, trying to air them out. *How old had she been when this book had been her Bible? Thirteen? Fourteen?* She remembered working her way through the first units on shape and composition and the next units on tone and color. In high school art had always been an easy 'A' and had contributed to her outstanding grade point average. Mrs. Marks, the art teacher, had tried to convince Sam to apply to the Rhode Island School of Design. *Was I really that good? Could I have gotten in?* Sam rose slowly from the sofa and headed toward the downstairs closet. Somewhere behind all the coats and boots was a small suitcase full of oil paints, watercolors and pastels that had followed her to Dickson Dormitory, to a student apartment, then to marriage and to this house. But it wasn't there.

In all that time she'd never once opened the suitcase, but always kept it with her. Now when she wanted it, the thing had disappeared. She pushed the coats and jackets back in place. The suitcase couldn't be in the cellar; there was nothing down there but rusty buckets and left over building supplies that could tolerate the mildew and the mice.

The suitcase finally turned up in the attic, stashed behind a crate of old clothes. When she unpacked it on the kitchen table, she found everything just as she'd left it almost seven years ago. The tube of burnt sienna still carried the warm scent of linseed oil and earth. Sam closed her eyes and inhaled. *Burnt sienna.* She loved the names, the scent, the feel of the tubes and the brushes. Picking up a size six filbert, she gently brushed the soft hairs across her lips. She loved this stuff; she wanted to eat it, to fill herself with color.

The back of her wood cutting board would do for a palette, but she needed canvas. There were yards of fabric in her sewing basket, but they were useless. She'd have to improvise. Heading back to the attic, Sam pulled out rolls of wallpaper left over from when she and Ben had decorated the dining room and downstairs hallway. She cut a large square and turned it upside down on the table, pinned the corners with soup cans from the cupboard, and turned on the radio. Dolly Parton belted out *The Seeker* as dabs of titanium white, burnt sienna, burnt umber, cadmium yellow and Prussian blue appeared on Sam's palette. Most of them were a little thick and gummy from years of neglect, but she thinned them with a few dabs of turpentine and within minutes she was lost in a meditation on the forsythia bush outside her window, its yellow blooms a rebuke to the late snow. Her hands were magically busy and her headache had completely disappeared.

When the doorbell sounded, Sam had no idea what time it was. No one but Sheila ever stopped by, and she always phoned ahead. Sam stood at the table, her brush poised in mid air, waiting to see if the ringing would stop. It persisted, almost rude in its rapid repetition. With a sigh, Sam dropped her brush into a cup of paint thinner and went to the door. She was alarmed to see a young man in a police uniform standing on her doorstep. Even more disturbing was the fact that he looked vaguely familiar. Sam stared at him through the small window in the door, riffling through her mental Rolodex, but she couldn't place him. She opened the door a crack.

"Excuse me for bothering you, but I was wondering if you'd seen my daughter, she just turned seven. She's wearing a pink snowsuit."

"Yes, I think I did see her." Sam opened the door a bit wider; this was apparently not official police business. "She was chasing a cat over there by the side of the house, maybe two hours ago, maybe a little longer. I tried talking to her, but she wouldn't say a word. She just picked up the cat and headed off that way." Sam pointed down Edison toward Grant Street.

"Two hours? My God, that Gordon woman is an idiot."

"Do you mean Ina Gordon, the woman with the chickens?" Ina Gordon lived in a brown clapboard house about a quarter mile down Edison. Her chickens were always running into the road and annoying the neighbors.

"Yeah, that's her. She doesn't have the brains of a pet rock. She can't get it through her thick head that it's her job is to actually watch Tara, as in know where my daughter is at all times. Every time I go to pick Tara up after work, that woman starts running around looking for her like she's a set of misplaced car keys. The lunatic just called me at work to ask if I'd seen her. How could I have seen her? I work in the county building on Grant and Erie for God's sake. She's an idiot." His eyes darted about wildly as he talked; his words were coming too fast, his nose and ears were tipped red from the cold.

Sam felt a pang of sympathy, although there was something comical about a uniformed policeman on the verge of hysterics. "Why don't you just fire her?"

"I intend to fire her. I'm dying to fire her, but I can't find anyone else, and I can't afford to lose my job."

"Couldn't the other policemen help you find her?"

"I'm not a policeman. I work in the Sheriff's office, but I'll call out the whole National Guard if Tara doesn't turn up before dinner."

"Well, I don't think it will come to that. Tara looked fine when I saw her. I think she was just out looking for her cat." Sam scanned the road hoping to spot a small figure dressed in pink.

"That white cat? That's just some stray that hangs around the Gordon house. Which way did you say she went?" The man was already heading back toward his car. Sam was surprised to find that the tall, well built man in uniform walked with a decided limp.

Sam pointed to where the road veered to the left at the bottom of her drive.

"Thanks, Sam, I'll let you know when I've found her."

Sam did a small double take, startled that he knew her name. "Sorry, I know that we've met, but I don't remember how I know you."

"I'm Jerry Doyle, I was friends with your husband. Well, actually I was more friends with his brother, but we all went to school together. We met at the Seneca Rocks Winter Festival a couple years ago." He lowered his voice, "and I was at the funeral."

Sam nodded, not really remembering, "Well, good luck finding your little girl." She was about to shut the door, but Jerry kept talking.

"She's deaf, can't hear cars coming or anything." His hands moved toward his ears in case Sam didn't know what it meant to be deaf. "She can't talk either. That's why she didn't answer you. Well, thanks again."

"Good luck." Sam watched as Jerry Doyle confidently navigated the ruts and potholes despite his bad leg. She stood a moment watching his red Camaro head off toward Grant Street. *So*, she thought, *the little girl's name is Tara Doyle and she's deaf.*

Sam went back to her makeshift canvas and again lost herself in her work. A cloud of yellow was taking shape in the foreground of her painting when she heard the sound of a truck rumbling up the drive. *What is going on? The place is suddenly Grand Central Station.* Could Sheila have sent a plow? Not likely, the temperature was approaching fifty degrees and great swaths of grass had begun to reappear. Still wearing the stained apron she'd been using as a smock, Sam stuck her head out the door as Billy Crabtree clamored out of the cab of his venerable Ford pickup.

"May I park here? I won't be blocking you in or anything will I?"

"I don't know. How long will you be here?"

"Maybe a couple hours. Thought I'd get started on that barn. I need the truck for hauling out trash."

"All right, but I need to see everything you cart out of there. Some of that stuff is valuable."

"Nothing goes without your say so." He didn't seem offended, in fact he smiled at Sam approvingly. "You look real sweet in that apron. I didn't take you for the domestic type."

Sam bristled slightly, everything irritated her these days. "It's a smock. I've been painting."

"Hope you're doing interior work, otherwise the paint will just peel right off. We've got to wait until things warm up a bit to work outside."

"Not that kind of painting, I'm... I've got to go, the phone's ringing. Remember nothing goes until I've checked it out."

Sam picked up the phone, thinking it was probably her mother. Instead, a male voice said, "Just wanted to let you know that Tara's home safe. She was practically back at the house by the time I found her. She walked all the way down Edison up Grant and turned at Hiawatha. Can you believe it? Nearly two miles with that cat following her the whole way. I had no idea that she even knew her way back here. I didn't want you to worry."

Sam hadn't been worried, but now she felt guilty for not worrying. "Well, it's a relief knowing she's back home. You and your wife must have been scared to death."

"Tara's mother took off a couple years ago, so I guess she wasn't worried, but I was scared enough for the both of us."

"Well, thanks for calling, but I've got to go. I'm glad to hear Tara's home safe."

"Say, you wouldn't want a cat would you? I'd keep it myself, but they make my eyes itch."

"No thanks, I don't want any pets right now. Anyway, I'm more of a dog person."

"Too bad, it's a really nice cat and it needs a home."

"Sorry, anyway I've got to get back to some work I'm doing. Good luck with the cat."

"Wait, don't hang up," there was a pleading tone in Jerry's voice. Sam opened the fridge and took out a carton of orange juice, her ear still to the phone. "Listen, if you have time I was hoping we could meet for dinner sometime."

Whoa, that came out of left field. Was he asking her out on a date? Sam shook her head in disbelief. "Thanks, but I don't go out much. I'm just not ready to start socializing again." She picked up a glass from the sink, rinsed it briefly under the tap, and then filled it with orange juice.

"Just something casual, we could meet at the Lighthouse Diner. I could tell you stories about what Ben was like in high school."

"I can't meet you. I don't have a car." What a stupid thing to say. Her social skills were beyond rusty.

"No problem, I'll pick you up and we can drive together. How about tomorrow at seven?"

Sam took a swig of the cold juice. *What the hell. It would be good to hear stories about Ben's early life from someone who wasn't Sheila.* "Sure, seven would be fine."

Before the phone's receiver had even hit the cradle she was verbally kicking herself. "You idiot," she said out loud, "you moron." Violently swishing her brush through the turpentine, she accidentally let it splash onto her painting smudging a carefully rendered branch. "Shit," she took off her smock and threw it over a chair, too agitated to paint any more that day. Throwing on her denim jacket, she headed out to the barn to see what Billy Crabtree was stealing from her.

CHAPTER 3

"This pile goes to the dump, this pile we burn, and this pile I guess you better take a look at." Billy was tearing through generations of accumulated trash with the experienced eye of a collector. It all looked like junk to Sam who couldn't tell the piles apart. She kicked at a large piece of corrugated tin that vibrated with the sound of rolling thunder. *Is it valuable? Would someone want to buy a thing like that? What about the mason jars half full of nails and bolts and screws?*

"Take a look at this, would you?" Billy waved an old bottle in front of her. Sam jumped back and turned her face away in disgust. A moment later morbid curiosity made her turn back for a second look. The skeleton of a rat, as white and finely rigged as a ship in a bottle, stood on its hind legs in a one gallon mason jar. "The poor little fellow must have fallen in and couldn't get back out. That's sure no way I'd want to go." Billy put the jar on the window sill, and Sam didn't ask which pile it was destined for.

"What do you want me to do with those?" Billy pointed the handle of a broken rake at a stack of two-by-fours sitting beneath tangled coils of chicken wire.

"I don't know, aren't they all warped and rotted?"

"Nope, I checked them out, and most of them are still solid. I could build you a chicken coop with that stuff if you wanted to keep chickens."

With a clarity that Sam had not felt for some time, she answered, "No, I do not want to keep chickens. Thanks anyway." A grin lit her face. She now knew something for certain about her future. She would not be keeping chickens. The revelation cheered her. She surveyed the barn with fresh eyes.

A thin shaft of light slipped through a crack high in the ceiling illuminating half of Billy's face and leaving half in shadow like a Rembrandt portrait. An idea, half in light, half in shadow, began to emerge from the back of Sam's mind. "Actually, I don't think I'm going to want to keep any of this stuff."

"You sure? Some of this trash is worth something as salvage, and a couple things, like these old pickle jars and that radio," he pointed toward them with his foot, "would bring money at a flea market. A lot of people collect that kind of stuff."

"I don't want it. Keep anything you want. Just get it out of here." Sam was giddy with her sudden change of heart. "Take it all. I want to clean this place out and turn it into an art studio." *An art studio?* She'd never even thought of a studio before the moment the words left her mouth.

"What about the tractor? I need a place to keep her until she's up and running. That was part of our deal."

"That's not a problem; just keep all your parts and tools and everything in the back. I'll work up front where I can keep the doors open and let in some light. Are there any electric outlets in here?"

"Nope, no outlets. You want me to run a line from the house so you can plug in a couple lamps? I wouldn't mind having some more light out here myself."

"What would that cost me?"

"Oh, let's just say it's a fair trade for the old lumber and these other doo dads."

"Yeah, thanks. I'd love to have electricity out here. That would be great." Sam turned and looked Billy in the eye for the first time since they'd been talking. He was probably her father's age. In fact, he was tall and thin like her father and had the same salt and pepper hair. Although Billy's hair was coarse and thick where her father's was fine and beginning to thin. They even wore the same old fashioned wire rimmed glasses.

"So, what kind of artist are you? Do you paint landscapes or still lifes or what?" He was smiling at her.

Sam felt embarrassed, as though she'd been caught in a lie. She looked away to survey the barn for its studio potential and to formulate some new definition of herself. "I paint a little, and I can draw, and I work with textiles. I'm experimenting with a couple different things at the moment."

"I do some woodcarving and painting myself, mostly ducks and geese for decoys. Sometimes I do songbirds just for no reason."

"Do you sell them?"

"There's a guy in Warren with a gun and tackle shop. He takes the decoys, but the song birds just trash up the house and annoy my wife. They're pretty though. Would you like to see one?

"Sure, that would be great." Sam didn't want to hurt his feelings, but she had no interest in wooden birds.

"Well, I'd better get back to work. I want to load up the truck and get over to the Stillman dump before it closes. I'll pick up

some wire and start juicing up the barn as soon as it's cleaned out."
Billy reached into his pocket for a pair of work gloves and put
them on.

"Thanks. I guess I'd better get back to the house." As Sam
headed up the drive, she noticed that the sky was a clear shade of
cobalt blue. She inhaled a great breath of cold air that carried the
scent of wet earth and new grass, and then before she could exhale,
she was blinking back unexpected tears.

Nights were always hard for Sam, and something about the
clear skies and warmer weather made them even worse. She stood
outside on the back porch breathing in the cool night air. The lilac
bush that she and Ben had planted beside the kitchen door was in full
bloom and the scent of lilac blossoms nearly broke her heart. The
kettle whistled on the stove, so she shut the door and went back to
the kitchen and her tea. It was only eight thirty in the evening, but she
was already in her nightshirt. She had just curled up on the sofa with
a cup of Constant Comment when the phone rang.

"Hi, Sweetie, how did your day go?" It was her mother.
"Did the raincoat come yet, the one with the matching umbrella
that I sent you?"

"I think so. UPS delivered something yesterday."

"What do you mean, you think so? You didn't open it? It's one
of those pink and orange paisley things they're showing. I thought of
you as soon as I saw it."

"Mom, I can't wear a thing like that around here."

"Another good reason to come home. So, what have you been
doing with yourself? I hope you're getting out. It's not good to spend
so much time alone." Sam never went anywhere, and her mother
knew it.

"Don't worry so much, I'm fine. In fact, I'm going out for
dinner with a friend tomorrow night." It had been ages since she'd
been able to report a social outing, and so Sam threw out the news
like a rabbit to a hungry wolf.

Predictably, her mother pounced, "You are? I am so glad to
hear that. Who is she, a friend from college or someone local?"

Sam already regretted opening her mouth. Her mother read
too much into everything, "It's a friend of Ben's from high school.
He's a little older; he was actually in Joe's class."

"He? You're having dinner with a he? I am so glad you're
starting to get back into the swing of things. Put on something pretty
and knock his socks off."

"Mother! We're meeting at a tacky diner and he's going to fill me in on some of Ben's early history. That's all. I hardly know him. I don't want to know him."

"Well, after you have dinner together you'll know him better. Believe me, I'm not pushing you into anything. The last thing I want is for you to become involved with anyone from Catawba County, but I do want you to be the girl that I remember, someone who goes out and has a good time."

"I'm not the girl you remember, Mom. Things change. I've changed. How could anything be the same?"

"Sweetie, you've had an awful time and we understand that you needed to be alone to sort things out, but it's been eighteen months now." Her mother's tone was suddenly serious. "It's time to come home. Let us help you start looking forward again. You're so young, everything is still possible. You can put these last few years and all the pain behind you and get right back on track."

"What are you saying, Mom? Do you want me to pretend that I was never married, that I never lost a baby, that the two people I loved most in the world weren't...?" Her voice trailed off.

"No, no, of course not. But you can't live in the past forever. You need to put all that in a little box in the attic of your heart and start thinking of your future." Sam froze, seized with anger. *I don't need to listen to stupid platitudes. She's never lost a husband or a child. In fact, the only thing the woman really loves is her work as a pediatrician.* Sam wanted to slam the receiver down to shut her up. Oblivious to Sam's rage, her mother kept chattering.

"Listen, your dad ran into Mel Gladden at The Hampton Grill last week. Mel has a lot of pull at the university and he said that even though it's past the deadline for fall applications, he'd make sure they hold a space for you. All you have to do is send in a few papers."

"No, Mom. I'm not ready. I don't know what I want to do or where I want to be. Why do we have to have this discussion every time you call?"

"Because September will be here before you know it, and you'll lose another year when you could be finishing your degree. I predict that things will look a lot different by the fall and that you'll be chomping at the bit to get out of that God-forsaken backwater of a town. If I'm wrong, what have you lost, a couple minutes and a postage stamp?"

The tea was growing cold and the mug felt heavy in her hand. Sam put it down on the coffee table and stared at her own reflection floating disembodied just beyond the window.

"Samantha Cassell, are you listening to me?"

"My name's Samantha Crawford. I got married."

"Okay, Samantha Crawford. Listen to me. No one will ever care about you as much as your mother and father, and we can't stand to see your beautiful young life going to waste. I'm sending you the Case Western Reserve University catalogue and an application. All you have to do is fill in the blanks and put it in the mail. Promise you'll do that for me. Promise?"

"Sure, Mom, I'll fill in the blanks and put it in the mail."

"Now that's my baby. Believe me, you'll thank me in September. Let me know how you like the raincoat. Maybe you can wear it when you come to visit next month."

"Alright, Mom. I'll pray for rain."

"Your dad and I can't wait to see you. It's been so long since you've been home. Now don't stand us up. You're dad's going to meet you at the bus terminal."

"I said I'd come. I'll be there."

"And have fun on your date tomorrow night. I want to hear all about it."

"Goodnight, Mom." Sam hung up the phone. Her reflection stared back at her with a look that was something between resignation and disgust.

Sam sipped her cold tea and tried to remember the last time she'd visited her family. She hadn't been back since the summer before the accident when she and Ben drove in to celebrate her parents' anniversary. It had been an ordinary evening without the faintest hint of the apocalypse that was bearing down on them.

Aunt Janet had booked their usual table at the Mayfair Club, a place where the Cassell family enjoyed the status of minor royalty. Her paternal great-grandfather had been one of the founders back in the twenties and a succession of Cassells had sat on the club's various boards and committees ever since. No one in Sam's family ever cooked, so Christmas, Thanksgiving, birthdays, and graduations were observed in the Mayfair Dining Room, on the Wellerstein Patio or the more intimate Eaton Club Room.

It had been a warm evening in August, so they'd opted for the patio where they wouldn't swelter in the jackets and hose required in the more formal dining rooms. Sam had arrived in a cotton peasant blouse and gathered skirt, gifts from her mother. The skirt swayed as she walked. The top hung loose and cool beneath its embroidered bodice. She stepped into the room feeling pretty, feminine, and a bit bohemian. Baby June, who was just learning to walk, toddled beside her, holding Samantha's hand and wearing a little embroidered smock that matched Samantha's blouse. Ben followed behind them in plaid pants, a wide belt, and a polyester shirt with a wide collar left open to expose a hint of hairy chest. Sam had bought this outfit for him thinking it would overcome his country boy persona and help him fit in at the club. Sensing his discomfort, she wished she'd let him wear Levis and the Grateful Dead T-shirt that were his usual weekend uniform. She turned and gave him an encouraging smile as he brought up the rear carrying a diaper bag, Cheerios, two picture books, and Nolly, the stuffed chimpanzee.

Before they could make their way past the reception desk, Gladys, the dining room manager, fell on Sam with a big welcoming hug, demanding, "Why don't you come round to visit us more often? I like to keep up with all my kids." She stood back, her broad brown face beaming with delight. "Now aren't you one pretty momma?"

June grabbed her mother's skirt. "My mommy," she proclaimed.

Gladys bent down in front of June and took her hands. "Why you was tiny as a mouse's hiney last time I saw you, and just look at you now, talkin' and walkin' like a growed woman in business for herself. Aren't you going to give your Aunt Gladys a little sugar? Your momma always had a little sugar for her Aunt Gladys."

June turned toward her mother, confused and alarmed, but Sam just smiled and said, "Give Aunt Gladys a kiss, Junebug. Aunt Gladys wants a kiss." So June dutifully placed a little peck on Gladys' cheek and Gladys stood up smiling, "That is one sweet baby you've got there, one sweet baby doll, just like her momma."

There had been a succession of club managers over the years, but each one had been wise enough to retain the core group of waiters, cooks, and maintenance personnel that the members regarded as extended family. These kind and capable employees knew everyone's name, kept track of where their children went to school, where they'd traveled on their last vacation, their special dietary needs, and whether they preferred to be seated in the sun or in the shade. Gladys had known Sam since the first day her perambulator had been wheeled through the club's grand foyer. She'd looked after the member's children while their mothers lunched or played golf, and she'd been there for most of their holidays and celebrations. She'd arrived from Alabama, a raw, uneducated girl of sixteen, and worked her way up the staff hierarchy from general cleaner and playground supervisor to waitress, then banquet services assistant, and finally to dining room manager.

"Walter," she turned to the waiter who was standing patiently beside her, "Would you escort these young ladies to their table—and this gentleman." She seemed to notice Ben for the first time.

"Good evening, sir. You are one lucky man, dining with two pretty ladies. Enjoy your dinner." Ben smiled back then hurried after Sam looking ill at ease in his new clothes. The anniversary had been her parent's thirtieth, a milestone, but they'd invited only the immediate family. Uncle George, her mother's older brother, must have come straight from work since he was wearing a seersucker suit and an unfashionably narrow tie. Uncle Allen, by contrast, was wearing a leisure suit in an odd shade of green that made him look slightly bilious. Aunt Janet was playing hostess, telling everyone where to sit and ordering extra baskets of the club's signature pecan rolls for the children, even though Spencer, the youngest of the children, had just celebrated his eighteenth birthday.

Sam's mother jumped up from the table as soon as she caught sight of her daughter, greeting her with a big hug and swooping baby June into her arms. Sam's dad was right behind her demanding his turn. Amidst all the hugging and kissing and shrieks of delight, Ben stood stoically bearing his burdens and smiling at no one in particular. Seeing his discomfort, Sam wrapped her arm around his waist.

"Guess what? Ben just got some fantastic news. They're promoting him to assistant head of Life Sciences at Kleiner High School, and he's only been there two years. I am so proud of him."

"Why, that's just wonderful, Ben." Sam's mother smiled as she turned back toward the table. Sam could hear her muttering *sotto voce*, "...assistant head of Life Sciences, imagine that."

Sam stiffened; her parents blamed Ben for the fact that she'd dropped out of college, nipping their hopes for her medical career in the bud. Ben grinned, too polite or too oblivious to respond. Sam's jaw was clenched as she eyed them all warily. Her father returned to his seat without noticing.

"This family is just full of glad tidings," he said as he lifted his water glass. "To Stephanie, who's just been accepted at Wharton and to Allen, the new chief of Gastroenterology at the Clinic."

Sam turned her gaze to Uncle Allen, wondering if he'd earned his position as head of gastroenterology based on the size of the gut that hung over the elastic waistband of his leisure pants. He was whispering something to Alice, the long-time girlfriend he was never going to marry. One of her false eyelashes had come unglued and was drooping at a weird angle; she was patting his knee with one of her soft, pudgy hands, and beaming in response to the announcement. Allen's daughter Stephanie, who was struggling to load a small camera on her lap, looked up briefly when she heard her name, and then went back to threading a fresh roll of film onto the spool.

"And to Ben," Sam chimed in, "who's been promoted to assistant head of Life Sciences at Kleiner High School," Sam, busy fitting June into a booster seat, turned to stare defiantly at her mother.

"Sam, my promotion's no big deal. It's not the sort of thing you brag about." Ben was clearly embarrassed.

"No, it's not something to brag about. It's respectable, it's even commendable, teaching children in that rural backwater, but it's not particularly ambitious. You've hit a target that was hung too low. A young man of your obvious talent should aim higher." Great Aunt Harriet spoke through a fog of cigarette smoke. She often talked about kicking the dirty habit, but Sam knew she'd never give it up since smoking provided the perfect opportunity to show off the enormous rings and red lacquered nails adorning her arthritic fingers.

Great Aunt Harriet, who'd gotten an early start on her "martoonies," was even less reticent than usual. "You are a fine young man with an obvious gift for science. Why waste it teaching children who won't even go on to college?"

Passionate about his kids, Ben was suddenly animated. "You're wrong about that. Over half of our graduating class continues their education. Not many of them go to fancy private schools, although some do." He pointed to himself, "Case in point. But, a lot of them go on to good New York State universities or junior colleges. But it doesn't matter whether or not they go on to university; everyone needs a basic science education."

Harriett nodded, conceding the point, but she wasn't letting him off the hook. "Yes, but you must realize that Samantha's going to tire of playing Daisy Mae in a few years. She's going to want the symphony, theater, decent restaurants."

"That's not true. How do you know what I'll want?" Sam was indignant. "I love living in Kleiner. It has fresh air, beautiful scenery, and some really nice people. What makes you think they're all idiots and bumpkins? A lot of the teachers at Ben's school have advanced degrees, if you think that's so important." Sam knew she'd flown in the face of her family's ambitions for her, but she hadn't expected a frontal attack. "I'm not like you. I don't need all that stuff. I don't need all *this* stuff." She gestured expansively toward the canopied patio, the tables with their elaborate settings, the exquisite landscaping, the swimming pool and the golf course in the distance.

"Perhaps *you* don't need all this stuff, but what about June? Doesn't she deserve the advantages you had, good schools, piano lessons, travel? I mean, what if she gets sick? What sort of care would she receive in a rural clinic? I did a rotation through one of those clinics when I was in medical school and I know what those places are. You may not need all this now, Samantha. But take it from an old lady, there will come a time." Harriet finished her martini then sucked the olive off the furled toothpick.

Everyone at the table sat staring into their water glasses. Alice picked up her camera and said, "Smile." Everyone ignored her.

"Aunt Harriet," Ben said with that slow, gentle cadence that captivated his students and thrilled Sam when he called her on the phone, "things have improved a lot since you were in medical school. We have electricity and indoor plumbing now, and we make all the kids wear shoes in class." Sam knew Ben was trying to defuse the tension, but no one laughed.

"I think what Aunt Harriet meant to say is that we don't want to see Sam or the baby limited in any way." Sam's mother leaned forward and directed her words to Ben. "You know that Sam is a bright girl. She was well on her way to medical school when she got sidetracked by love and marriage. We'd pay for nannies, tuition, whatever it takes to get her back in school." She rested her hand on Ben's arm. "We understand that you're happy teaching high school in the town where you grew up, but we want you to understand that our daughter was pre-med at Cornell."

"For God's sake, I met Ben at Cornell! He's every bit as smart as you are. He knows what he wants and it's not a lot of money and a big house with fancy cars, and summers traveling through Europe." Sam rose from her chair and looked as if she might bolt, but then she lost her nerve, reached across the table, snagged a pecan roll, and sat back down.

"Hey, wait a minute. I definitely want to spend summers traveling through Europe." Ben took her family's abuse with such good natured equanimity. Sam's heart melted. Whatever her family said, she'd never regret her choice.

"What about Samantha, Ben? What about her career?" Sam's mother never blinked, she was determined to win this point.

"Mom, I have a job. I'm the feature editor for *The Seneca Sun Journal*," Sam protested.

"Oh, for Heaven's sake, writing about Cub Scout field trips and Rotary Club picnics is not a career. I'm talking about doing something meaningful, something worthy of your talents." Her mother continued, looking at Ben, challenging him with her eyes.

"Sam's going to finish her degree as soon as June starts school. There are two good state colleges within an hour of our house and she can go to either one and study anything she wants." Ben squeezed Sam's hand. She squeezed his back hard.

"Neither of those colleges has a medical school. She won't be able to study medicine." Sam's mother refilled her water glass. The table was so quiet that the clinking of ice falling from the pitcher resonated like the sound of distant artillery. "But if you moved somewhere near a large university, I'm sure you could find a teaching job and Sam could get herself back on track. Think about it. Please, tell me that you'll think about it."

Sam burst in, "Do I get a vote? What if I'm not sure that I want medicine anymore? You know, not everyone wants to be a doctor." June had started to fuss and Sam was holding her in her lap, rocking her back and forth.

"Some people just aren't cut out for medicine. I guess that's why I'm going into business—no blood, no emergency calls in the middle of the night." Stephanie pushed her long blonde hair back behind her ears and smiled reassuringly at Sam. At one time Sam and Stephanie had been rivals, competing to see who could bring home the highest grades, the most trophies, and acceptances to the most prestigious schools, but Sam had ceded the contest to her cousin when she'd married and dropped out of the race. Despite that, they still weren't close, so Sam was surprised by her support.

"Yeah, maybe I'd rather be a commodities trader, or a cowboy, or a stone mason or an astronaut, or an actuary, or..." Sam stumbled, running out of unlikely professions and looked at Stephanie for help.

"Or a ballerina," Stephanie finished Sam's sentence. "You'd be a lovely Swan Queen. I think you should definitely give it some thought."

"Nope, not a ballerina, I'd have to give up the pecan rolls and there's no way. In fact, pass me the basket, maybe I'll be the fat lady at the circus."

The tension had been broken and the rest of the evening progressed without further conflict, but as much as Sam knew her parents loved her, and as thrilled as they were with their adorable grandchild, she still felt the chill of their disapproval. The last thing her father said as he helped load their car for the trip home was, "Anytime you kids decide to come back to civilization we'll be there to help, whatever you need. Don't worry about the money, it would be our pleasure."

"Thanks, Dad, we'll keep that in mind," She smiled, but her chest felt heavy and every breath ended with a sigh until they were well past Ashtabula. *I should have told him what he could do with his money. What the Hell does he mean by civilization?* They'd been to her home. It might not be a Tudor mansion, but it sure wasn't a thatched hut in the middle of some jungle. "They're idiots. I was raised by a bunch of pompous idiots," she'd finally said aloud.

"They're not so bad. I mean, parents always want their kids to be like them, that's normal. Actually, they're kind of funny. We live two hours away and they think you've been abducted by aliens from a distant planet. I must look like some sort of Martian."

"Like I said, they're idiots." Sam turned to check on June who'd fallen asleep in the backseat. She'd kicked off her pink and white coverlet and Sam tucked it back around her.

"Okay, they're idiots," Ben agreed. Sam pursed her lips, but didn't say anything. She didn't like Ben badmouthing her family. She didn't know what she wanted.

"Come here, Pumpkin," Ben put his arm around her and she scrunched over so she could lay her head against his shoulder. Their car didn't have air conditioning, but the temperature had fallen with the setting sun and a cooling breeze wicked the sweat from her skin. There were few lights on this stretch of road, just the head-lights of the occasional passing car and the white line in the road that blinked hypnotically before them. With a sigh, she realized that she already had just what she wanted; she wanted to drive home through a summer night with Ben at the wheel and June asleep in the back seat.

They didn't go back to Cleveland again that summer. The small vegetable garden Sam had planted in the spring overwhelmed her with such an abundance of tomatoes, cucumbers and squash that Sheila had to help her can them for the winter. June cut two new teeth, and *The Seneca Sun Journal* asked Sam to write a special fall edition featuring local farms and wineries.

Sam and Ben had been happy, busy with their lives and, de-spite what Sam had promised, neither of them gave a moment's thought to living anyplace but where they were. With the bad taste of the last trip still in their mouths, they hadn't gone back to visit that September. Then, that terrible October, after the crash, Sam no longer saw any point in going anywhere or seeing anyone.

For a year and a half Sam had locked herself in the house, admitting no one but immediate family through her door. When her parents visited, she allowed them to drag her, zombie-like, to some local restaurant, but she never accepted their offers to stay the night, and she never visited them in Cleveland.

But something had changed in the past month; her circle of acquaintances had expanded almost against her will, and she had amazed herself by promising to go home for a week at the end of May. Whether she was going to Cleveland to see her parents or to escape the sudden and unwelcome presence of all the new people arriving at her door was a question she couldn't answer. Whatever the reason, she'd promised her parents a Memorial Day visit and she was going to keep that promise.

CHAPTER 4

The menu at The Lighthouse Diner was exactly like the menus at all the other restaurants in Catawba County: fried fish, fried chicken, burgers and fries. She'd even seen French fries served on top of salads. Sam ordered the haddock and nervously played with one of the little dinner rolls the waitress left in a red plastic basket on the table. Jerry was telling her something about how he'd gotten his job with the sheriff's office after training to be an MP in Vietnam.

What made a man volunteer for military service during a war? She searched his face for clues, but he was pretty much like the menu, just what you'd expect, a good-natured country boy with a bad hair-cut and crooked teeth. If he'd grown up in her neighborhood, he'd have worn braces and had his hair styled at one of the new unisex salons. But, she had to admit, the gap toothed smile didn't detract from his basic good looks. In fact, apart from his limp, he was a little taller, straighter, and more confident than most of the boys she'd known. He looked younger out of uniform. A beaded choker on a leather cord was tied around his neck. That surprised Sam; he didn't seem the type.

She looked around to see if anyone she knew was watching them. Her husband had been dead a year and a half, but she couldn't get over the feeling that there was something illicit about sitting here with another man. How had she been maneuvered into accepting this invitation anyway? Jerry was nice enough. He hadn't brought her here at gun point, but she still felt a smoldering resentment as though she'd been taken into custody against her will.

Sam tried to size him up. He looked normal enough; in fact he looked abnormally normal. She blushed, realizing that she was in-dulging in her exceptional family's tendency to judge normal people as deficient. He'd been her brother-in-law's best friend; he'd known her husband. He was probably a nice guy. Well, in for a dime in for a dollar as her grandmother used to say. As long as she was sitting here she might as well ask, "What made you volunteer for Vietnam? Weren't you afraid of getting killed?"

Jerry held her gaze a full minute without saying a word. Sam was becoming afraid she'd offended him when he finally said, "I didn't have money for college, and I probably couldn't have gotten in anyway. It's not like I was all gung ho to go over there and start killing commies; but there was a war on and it seemed like the right thing to do. My uncle said they'd teach me a trade, make a man of me." He snorted a wry half-laugh into his beer. "It kind of worked out that way for me, apart from my leg. It didn't work out that well for most of the guys. It sure didn't work out that well for Joe."

"No, I guess not," Sam stopped fiddling with her spoon and stared at the table.

"Ben was smarter than the rest of us. I mean that. He really was. He stayed in school, got an education, kept his socks dry. It's just weird that he's gone. Me and Joe, we put ourselves in the line of fire, but Ben should have died in bed an old man." Jerry shook his head then shrugged philosophically. "I guess a lot of things happen that shouldn't happen."

"Yeah, I guess they do." Sam looked out the window so that Jerry couldn't see the pain she knew must be visible in her eyes. She turned back to look at him, "What happened to you? Is your leg a war injury?"

"Yep, a souvenir of my time in the service. It got crushed under a jeep a couple days after Joe got himself blown up by a grenade."

"That's awful. How did it happen?" Sam leaned forward, genuine sympathy in her eyes.

"Let's talk about something else."

"Sorry." Sam flushed. She hadn't meant to pry. She of all people should know better than to intrude on other people's pain. There was a long silence while they pretended to read their menus, although both of them had already ordered.

Finally Jerry said, "Bottom line, they sent me home with a gimpy leg. The sheriff's office had a position open, a desk job really, not what I dreamed about. But it's a good job and the leg doesn't matter. Mostly I'm in charge of investigating vacant and delinquent properties, enforcing eviction notices, that sort of thing."

Sam was anxious to change the subject. "You said you were going to tell me about Ben, what he was like in high school."

"Let's see, Ben was quiet, kind of a brain. Everyone liked him, but he didn't have a lot of friends. I guess he was a loner."

"He was on the swim team though, wasn't he?"

"Maybe, swimmers aren't exactly high profile. He definitely didn't hang out with the jocks. I think he ran track one year, but I don't remember him winning any trophies."

"He won a swimming trophy and another one for science, for a biology experiment. His mom told me about it." Samantha looked over at the clock behind the counter. How much longer would she have to sit here? This guy didn't seem to know anything about Ben. She tried another tack, "Did Ben date? Did he ever have a girl friend?" Sam swished the end of a French fry through a pool of ketchup then used it like a brush to paint scallops around the edge of her plate.

"I don't know much about Ben's love life, but I can tell you he took Margo Michalski to his senior prom."

"Ben never mentioned a Margo Michalski." A little furrow appeared between Sam's eyes. "I wonder why I never heard about her."

"Probably there wasn't much to tell. She was Ben's prom date. That's all I know."

"What was she like? Was she pretty?" Sam's interest was piqued.

"Yeah, she was beautiful, a big, beautiful red head. I had a crush on her all through high school. She never gave me a second look though, but she must have had a thing for Crawfords, because she dated Joe too, back before he enlisted." Jerry produced a twisted sort of half smile, "Joe was in the marching band and all the musicians wore their uniforms to Homecoming. I can still see her hanging on Joe's arm like she'd just snagged herself a general. My God, I was jealous seeing the two of them together."

"Really? She got turned on by a band uniform? Was she some sort of idiot?"

"I suppose so. She lived with me for almost six years."

Sam dropped her French fry and stared at Jerry. "The girl Ben took to his senior prom is Tara's mother?"

"Yeah, funny how things turn out." He took a long swallow and finished his beer.

"What happened with her and Ben? How long did they go together?"

"I can't say. I was overseas at the time. I only know about the prom thing because Joe showed me a letter from his brother with a couple photos in it. By the time I got back to the States, Joe was dead and Ben was off to college. Margo must have been lonely because she practically threw herself at me when I got back from Nam. It was probably the uniform." He put down his glass and picked up his cheeseburger. "So, what have you been doing with yourself? Are you working, or what?"

"Wait a minute, what happened to Margo? Where is she now?"

"She is far, far away." It was the waitress who answered as she refilled Sam's coffee, "So, you two want dessert? We have strawberry pie." Even after three and a half years, Sam was constantly startled by what it meant to live in such a small town.

"How far? Where did she go?" Sam addressed the question to the tired looking blonde who stood over them with a pot of coffee.

She shrugged, "Beats me, and if he knows, he's not talking," she indicated Jerry with a toss of the long, thin hair that had been feathered and bleached in a failed attempt to make her look like Farrah Fawcett. "None of us heard a word from Margo after she left."

"That would pretty much include me." Jerry reached over and grabbed one of Sam's fries. "Do you mind?" Sam shrugged and pushed the whole plate toward him.

"Some of us think he has her buried in the basement. Not that anyone would blame him."

Jerry gave Kathy a look that said he was not amused, "Margo skipped town owing Kathy something like two hundred dollars, and she's still pissed."

"Two hundred twenty bucks and change, but it's not the money. We were friends. At least I thought we were friends. She hurt a lot of people when she left."

"Kathy, let's not go into all that. This isn't the time or place."

"I'll drop it, but you're not the only one who got hurt. That's all I meant. Margo just wasn't the person that we thought she was."

"No dessert for me, what about you, Sam?" Sam shook her head no. "Well then, I guess that's all for now. Thanks, Kathy. How about if you go wait on the Harrisons?"

Kathy stood her ground, refilling their coffee cups, "I just wanted to say that Margo did a terrible thing and everyone thinks you're a hero raising that baby by yourself. That's all I wanted to say."

"Let it go, Kathy."

"Okay, I'm going, I'm going," and she was gone.

"Well, now you know the story of my life. How about telling me what you've been up to." Jerry fixed his eyes on Sam's and waited expectantly.

This was just the moment she'd been hoping to avoid. She couldn't exactly say, "I sleep until ten most mornings and then I watch a little TV. I finally clipped my toenails last Tuesday because they were starting to tear holes in my socks." Then she remembered, there was something, "I've started painting again. I'm thinking of turning the barn into an art studio."

"Far out. What sort of stuff do you paint?"

"I don't know yet. I haven't done much of anything since high school. I probably can't draw a straight line anymore."

"You studied art in high school?"

"Yeah, I was pretty good, but I haven't picked up a brush since I was a kid."

"You're still a kid, and I bet you're still a great artist."

Sam wasn't in the mood to be patronized. It was time to wrap this up. "Look, I have to be up early, so would you mind if we headed back home?"

"No, of course not, just let me pay the bill and we're out of here." Jerry pulled out his wallet. "But before we go, there's just one thing I want to ask you. I had an ulterior motive wanting to talk with you tonight."

Sam was already standing up and putting on her coat. She'd fished a five dollar bill out of her pocket and handed it to Jerry. "This should cover my dinner and the tip."

"I asked you out. It's my treat."

"This isn't a date. I just wanted to hear what you knew about Ben. I can pay for myself," Sam's voice went up a notch in pitch and volume.

"Sorry, I didn't mean to offend you." He took her money and headed to the register.

As they crossed the parking lot she could see bands of pink and purple clouds streaking the sky above the lake. She paused to watch the lights blink on in the houses and trailers that dotted the shore.

Jerry fumbled with his key, trying to unlock the passenger side door for Sam. As she slid into her seat, she turned to look at him, "So, what did you want to ask me?"

"What?"

"Your ulterior motive, you said you had an ulterior motive for asking me out."

"Well, I was hoping you could save my life. I can't leave Tara with that Gordon woman any longer; I might as well leave her home alone. The woman hasn't a clue. She's a menace, and I'm probably guilty of criminal negligence for leaving Tara with her as long as I have."

"Aren't there any day care centers that would take her?"

"First Baptist runs a day care center, but they don't take deaf children. St. Anthony's won't take her. Sunny Days won't take her. No one will take her. Everyone's afraid of her, like deafness is contagious or something. I mean, she's just a sweet little girl, for God's sake."

Sam saw where this was headed, and it made her a little queasy. "And you couldn't help but notice that I'm home alone all day doing nothing, so how about if I look after her? Was that the question?"

He turned to look at her with a sheepish expression, "Not permanently, just until I find a regular situation for her. I'd pay you whatever you want."

Something about Tara had been bothering Sam, and now she realized what it was. "If Tara's hard of hearing why doesn't she wear hearing aids?"

Jerry rolled down the driver's side window and let the cool evening air waft through the car. Sam could smell the lake and the odor of cooking meat as they sped passed a burger joint. It was the place she and Ben had stopped for lunch the day they'd taken June for her first dip in Lake Catawba. Sam closed her eyes.

"Tara was fitted for a body aid when she was first diagnosed, but she hated it. It was this big box that she had to wear strapped to her chest with cords going up to her ears. The ear molds were so tight that we needed Vaseline to get them in. My God, that child would throw a fit whenever we made her wear it."

"Where is it now? Why doesn't Tara wear it?" Sam was appalled that Tara wasn't following doctor's order.

"Margo pitched it. Tara didn't seem to hear any better when she wore the damn thing, and she hated it—constant tantrums for almost two years. One day Margo just said, 'Fuck it!' and tossed the thing out."

"Wow." Sam didn't know what else to say.

"Anyway, will you help us out, at least until I find a school or a program for her?"

Sam watched telephone pole after telephone pole whiz by as they sped down Grant Street. Every few seconds a car's headlights raced toward them, illuminating their faces for a moment, then disappeared, leaving them in shadow once again. If it had been any other child, her answer would have been an easy no. But there was something about Tara, something that reminded her of June. Sam mentally played back a snippet of conversation from the diner and did a quick calculation in her head. "If Tara's seven, she must have been born in 1969.

"You're good at math. She was born April 12, 1969."

Sam counted back nine months. Margo got pregnant the summer after Ben graduated from high school, the summer before he started Cornell. The sun was no more than a thin red line marking the horizon. Sam watched it fade then disappear into the lake. "I see," she said at last. "Give me a couple days to think about it. I'll let you know."

*   *   *

"Of course I knew Margo Michalski.," Sheila answered. "Well, I didn't know her personally, but everyone knew Margo, or at least they knew *about* her. You couldn't miss her with that red Bozo hair and potty mouth. She was popular though. She had a way of rounding up all the lost lambs, the kids with no backbone or conviction, and twisting their little minds around. She had them marching around with cardboard signs, protesting the war and picketing the ROTC recruiters. I'll tell you that child was a piece of work." Sheila was steering with her left hand while gesturing with a Kent held between the fingers of her right. Periodically, she'd turn her head to blow a mouthful of smoke out the driver's side window.

"Did you know that Ben took her to prom? Was she his girlfriend?" Sam had never seen Sheila express such a visceral aversion to anyone.

"Of course she wasn't his girlfriend. What would he have to do with a girl like that with his brother in the army? He went to homecoming with a nice bunch of kids from the swim team. Who told you such a thing?"

"Jerry Doyle." Sam lowered her voice as though she was revealing a secret. "He's the father of that little girl I was telling you about, the one who stole the daffodils."

"So the little girl is Jerry's kid? He used to be good friends with Joe back in high school. He's a nice guy, but who knows if he's really the father? Margo had the morals of an alley cat. No wonder that child's a little off with a mother like that. Now *that* was a scandal." Sheila pounded the steering wheel for emphasis. "Imagine running off and abandoning your own baby."

They were beyond the range of WHUG and the music had turned to static, so Sheila reached over and turned off the radio. "Jerry's got his hands full raising that child by himself. Still, I don't know why he'd tell you that Ben had anything to do with Margo. He probably didn't want you thinking he's the only fool in Catawba County."

"Did you know that the little girl is deaf?"

"No, I didn't know that." Sheila snuffed out her cigarette in the car's ashtray. "Well, that's a pity. The poor thing, no mother and she can't hear. Does he have her at a special school?"

"She doesn't go to school. Normal nursery schools and day care centers won't take her, so she just stays home with baby sitters. She's supposed to start first grade in September. I didn't think to ask about special schools. Are there schools for the deaf around here?"

"I don't know. I was blessed with two perfect little boys. Come to think of it, I don't think I've ever met anyone who was born deaf. That's odd isn't it? I wonder where they keep themselves." Sheila turned off Interstate 90 and headed north toward Erie.

"Does anyone know what happened to Margo, where she went?"

Sheila put a fresh cigarette between her lips and lit it with her free hand. She took a long draw and exhaled slowly. "Well, I certainly don't know. From what I hear, she turned into a full-fledged hippy and went off to live in one of those free love places, some kind of commune. I don't know any details, just the stuff that everyone knows, that she disappeared and left Jerry with a baby. But I hadn't heard the child was deaf. Isn't that just the icing on the cake?"

They rode in silence for a few minutes. At last Sam said, "Jerry asked me to babysit for Tara, that's the little girl's name, at least until he can find a regular sitter or a school. The lady he has now just lets her run wild."

"That was a lot of nerve; of course he must be desperate. That's the last thing you need, responsibility for a handicapped child. How did you meet him anyway? You never leave the house."

"He just showed up on my doorstep a few days ago. Tara had run away from her babysitter and Jerry was going door to door looking for her. I wonder how he communicates with her."

"Oh, they probably talk with their hands, you know," Sheila waved her right hand around and wiggled her fingers attempting to imitate sign language. A hot ember fell from her cigarette and landed on Sam's sweater.

"Hey!" Sam brushed the ash onto the floor where it was extinguished by the wet rubber floor mat. The car smelled of smoke, vinyl, gasoline and wet wool. Sam hadn't eaten breakfast, and she felt nauseous and headachy. "You know, you ought to quit smoking. The whole car smells like an ashtray."

"I'll quit when I'm ready, just like you'll go back to work when you're ready."

"Oh, that's good. Let's equate recovering from losing your whole family in a car crash with giving up cigarettes."

Sheila swerved to the side of the road and hit the brakes. She turned toward Sam and grabbed her wrist, "Samantha Crawford, how dare you? You are looking at a woman who has lost her husband, her granddaughter and both her sons. Believe me, I know a thing or two about grief and if these cigarettes give me a few minutes of comfort and relief then I'm going to smoke. Like I said, I'll quit when I'm ready just like you'll go back to work when you're ready."

"I'm sorry," Sam blushed, genuinely chastened. Sheila put up such a good front that Sam frequently forgot that her mother-in-law's losses more than equaled her own. She wanted to reach out and put her hand on Sheila's shoulder, but she'd gone rigid, frozen with embarrassment.

"Alright, then," the car resumed its course toward Erie. "Everyone's cutting you a lot of slack, but there's a limit. You need to start thinking about getting back into the world. You can't let this tragedy destroy your life."

"I know. That's why I told Jerry that I'd think about the babysitting job. It would help him out and it would give me something to do. You've been encouraging me to go back to work."

"That's not a real job, Sam. You need to do something where you'll meet new people, make new friends, get out of the house."

"It would only be for a few weeks. Anyway, it might be interesting to work with a deaf child."

"Suit yourself, but I wouldn't put my money on Jerry finding someone else anytime soon. Why take on his problems when you've got plenty of your own?"

Sheila pulled into the parking lot of Seraphini's Restaurant where the smell of garlic bread and marinara sauce diffused the tension between them. The sun was shining and the temperature had climbed into the high sixties. Sam took off her denim jacket and tossed it onto the backseat, flashing Sheila a conciliatory smile. "I just told him I'd think about it," she said as the two women disappeared into the comfort of the lunchroom where all dissention disappeared in a fragrant cloud of olive oil, grated cheese, and ground beef.

CHAPTER 5

The sun was doing its best to penetrate the dusty film that coated the large window looking out onto the side yard where Billy's truck had been parked since breakfast. Sam was sitting at her sewing machine doing battle with squares of brown suede and thinking it was about time to get out the Windex and let some light back into the room. She turned the squares like puzzle pieces, trying to make the suede fringe lie flat. The fringe had always hung straight down across Ben's chest, but now, no matter which way Sam turned it, the fringe poked out at odd angles.

Country Gold with Vera Brag blared from the radio, but the music was lost in the high pitched wail of an electric drill emanating from the roof. Irritably, Sam turned up the volume just in time to hear Vera wishing all her listeners a golden afternoon and reminding them to stay tuned for the twelve o'clock news. Sam clicked off the radio and poked Tara gently with her slipper. The child had been pasting scraps of fabric onto a cardboard box. The effect was more paste than pattern, but at least the project kept her occupied and happy. Sam had been looking after Tara for only two weeks, but they were already establishing little rituals and patterns. The large white cat had arrived in Tara's arms that first day. With Sheila and Jerry as allies, Sam's protests had been useless, and so the cat had finally insinuated itself into the house. Content in its new home, the cat stretched out on top of Sam's quilting material and batted at the leather strings.

"Hey, cut that out." Sam picked the cat up and set it on the floor. Less than a moment later it was back on the table rubbing its head against Sam's shoulder. She scratched it absentmindedly behind the ears, ignoring the white hairs shedding on her navy pullover.

Tara turned and looked up at Sam with those strangely familiar eyes that made Sam melt. If it was noon that meant it was time for lunch. Sam rubbed her stomach and pointed to the kitchen. Tara shook her head, "No," and went back to daubing gobs of glue on a strip of red corduroy while watching Cookie Monster and Big Bird argue in pantomime on the silent TV.

Sam held her hand up, palm facing forward, hoping that Tara would recognize this as the signal to stay. Tara didn't know formal sign language, and she couldn't read, so the only way to communicate was through facial expressions, pointing, and improvised gestures. Sam backed out of the room, never taking her eyes off the child. When she got to the foot of the stairs she called up, "Billy, could you come down here a minute? I need some help." The drilling continued without a break so she let Tara out of her sight just long enough to climb a few stairs and shout, "Hey, Billy. Can you help me out here for a minute?"

The drilling stopped and Billy called back, "Sorry, what was that? I couldn't hear you."

"Could you keep an eye on Tara for a couple of minutes while I make a sandwich? She runs off if no one's watching her."

"Sure, give me a second, I'll be right down."

"Thanks, we'll be waiting downstairs." By the time Sam descended the few steps back to the living room the fabric covered box sat abandoned, the television flickered silently in an empty room, and the back door stood wide open. The cat had jumped to the back of the sofa where it was staring out the window, flicking its tail. Sam raced back up the steps.

"Too late, she's taken off again. Would you help me find her? She hasn't been gone a minute." Sam ran back down the stairs and out the door. On a hunch, she headed toward the road remembering how Tara had walked all the way home a few weeks ago, but no small figure was visible hiking along the street in either direction. These escapes were almost daily events, but they unnerved Sam. She turned back, deciding to search the barn and then the fields behind the house, but that proved unnecessary. Billy was standing by the side door holding Tara by the hand.

"I found this little chickie hiding in the bushes. Maybe we better shake some salt on her tail." Tara was staring defiantly at Billy, but didn't struggle or try to pull away.

"Why does she keep running off like that?" Sam exclaimed. "I'd love to know where she thinks she's going, but she can't even tell me what she wants for lunch."

"Cute as a button, though, aren't you, sweetheart?" Tara had no idea she'd just received a compliment and continued digging a hole in the grass with the heel of her shoe.

"She's cute enough, but I have a feeling that she's also really smart. She learned to print her name in only one day, and when we go on walks she always notices stuff: bits of eggshells, pinecones, and unusual rocks. She was decorating a special box to hold her rock collection just before she ran off."

"You don't say?" Billy smiled indulgently, but he was clearly unimpressed.

I just found out my husband used to date her mother." Sam blushed, embarrassed. Why had she blurted that out as though the handyman would care?

"Small world, I guess. Who's her mom?"

"Margo Michalski. I never met her, but she was in my husband's high school class."

"No kidding? This is Margo's daughter? I should have guessed, same red hair, same independent streak. My wife worked with Tara's grandma when Margo was just about this size. That child could throw the most God-awful fits." He handed the child back to Sam who held her tightly by the hand. "I always liked her though. I heard she'd gone off to college somewhere."

"Oh, she went off somewhere. I understand that she got into the whole counterculture thing and split. She left this baby high and dry without a mother."

"That's too bad." He started to put his hand on Tara's head, but she jerked away. He and Sam exchanged looks that said, "Well, what can you expect?" Billy looked toward the barn where a new electric wire bore through a hole just beneath the roof into a new fuse box. Sam followed his eyes upwards and to the north where a bank of dark clouds was beginning to gather. "I'll have that line juiced up this afternoon if the rain holds off, then you can start plugging in lamps, or anything you want. I'll probably be back tomorrow morning to work on the tractor. Hope you don't mind if I bring my grandson, Marcus. I promised I'd teach him how to fix a motor if he'd help out with the painting and keep his mouth shut about Miss Allis-Chalmers back there."

"Sure, no problem. I didn't know you had kids."

"Two sons, Douglas and Earl. Marcus is Earl's boy. He and his mom have been living in Buffalo while his dad's away for awhile, but he's staying with us for the summer."

Sam wanted to ask why Marcus was already in Kleiner for the summer when school wouldn't let out for over a month, but she bit her tongue and didn't pry. Instead, she just said, "Sure, you can bring him, and thanks for finding Tara."

"No problem. I'm going to head into Kleiner to grab a sandwich and pick up some supplies. You keep an eye on that young lady, now."

"I do watch her. I watch her like a hawk." Sam thrust out her chin defensively, afraid she was being accused of negligence.

"Hey, I didn't mean anything. Take it easy. I'll see you later."

"Come on Tara, time for lunch." Sam tugged on the little arm and pointed at the door for emphasis. Tara resisted the tug and pulled away to pick up a piece of shale that she'd unearthed with the heel of her shoe. The rock contained a cluster of fossilized mollusks. Tara held it up to show Sam who stared at it, stunned. Fossils were common in the area, but Sam accepted the smooth gray stone dotted with the indentation of ancient shells as though it were the Hope Diamond. "Did you see that?" she asked Billy. "She's a born naturalist. They say my husband was just like that at her age."

Billy wasn't able to complete work on the barn that afternoon, or the next; the rain didn't let up for three days. Fierce wind and heavy rain troubled Sam's sleep Sunday night, but when her alarm sounded on Monday morning she was greeted by sunshine streaming through her window. Climbing out of bed, she pulled back the curtains and opened the window to let in some fresh air. She blinked, suddenly confused. Something was radically different, the sky was too big, the unbroken expanse of blue too vast. It took her a moment to realize what had happened. The pair of old maples that towered above the weathered barn, softening the horizontal line of its roof, was gone. The soil had become so saturated with accumulated rain and snow melt that the venerable old trees had lost their grip and toppled over in the night.

Sam raced downstairs, slipped her bare feet into a pair of fleece lined boots, threw her new paisley raincoat over the sweatshirt and pajama bottoms she slept in on chilly nights, and ran outside. A sucking sound accompanied every step she took as the mud reluctantly released its hold on the boot's rubber soles. She looked up, trying to adjust her gaze to the altered landscape. Without the trees, the barn looked exposed, somehow newer and more vulnerable. Sam walked around to the back where she found the fallen pair, their branches tangled together on the ground. She was lucky they'd fallen away from the barn and hadn't ripped a hole in the roof. Mucking her way back to the house, she saw a pair of headlights turning into her drive. "What the Hell?" she muttered under her breath. Jerry wasn't due to drop Tara off for another hour.

Jerry sounded his horn, a pair of friendly beeps, as his formerly red Camaro came to a stop in front of her side door. The car, already white with road salt, now sported an additional coat of splattered mud making it the same indiscriminate dirt color as most of the cars in Kleiner.

"Hey," Sam called over to him. "What are you doing here so early? I just got up. I haven't even brushed my teeth." Sam was in a sour mood and pissed that she wouldn't get to eat her breakfast and watch the morning news by herself.

"I'm not early. You forgot to set your clock ahead." Jerry flashed a broad smile as he helped Tara out of the backseat. *Why is Jerry so damned cheerful so early in the morning?* Sam vaguely remembered hearing something about daylight savings time, but she'd become accustomed to disregarding news from the outside world as though nothing that happened out there applied to her anymore. It was irritating to realize that the world still had her in its grip and could still intrude on her private domain.

"So it's eight o'clock already?"

"Yep," Jerry concurred.

"Your car's a mess." Sam wrote her name with her finger in the dirt clinging to the driver's side door.

"You're right." Jerry wrote his name beneath hers. "By the way, I love your outfit. Is that what they're showing in Paris this season?"

Sam rubbed the two names out with the side of her fist then wiped the dirt off on her raincoat. "Cut it out. I ran out here before I got dressed because those two big maples toppled over last night. I'm lucky they didn't fall on the barn." Sam pointed to the expanse of sky visible above the barn's roof.

"Which trees?" Jerry scanned the horizon for fallen trees, but all he saw was grass and a few scrub bushes.

"They fell behind the barn. You can't really see much from here." Sam pointed to a spot where gnarled roots poked out from behind the building like the twisted feet of the Wicked Witch of the East. "Come on, I'll show you." She led Jerry and Tara around to the back of the barn where they stared down at the fallen maples with something like reverence.

"That's too bad. They were beautiful trees. They look like old lovers who died in each other's arms." Sam looked at him surprised. He'd never struck her as the romantic type. Embarrassed by his own sentimentality, he went on quickly, "We've sure had a stretch of freak weather and weird things happening. Do you want some help clearing them away? I could split them into firewood for you." Tara was squirming and trying to escape from Jerry's arms. He'd been carrying her to keep her out of the muck. He put her down, but held fast to her hand.

"I don't know. Maybe. Do you have a chain saw?"

"I do. I'll bring it over Saturday morning. With a little luck the ground will have dried out by then."

"I guess Saturday would be all right."

Jerry carried Tara back to the house where he handed her over to Sam. Before stepping over the threshold into her small hallway, she turned to watch Jerry back down the drive in a fine spray of muddy water. *Sheila's right, Jerry is a nice guy.*

The week progressed seamlessly. By the time Friday rolled around, Sam realized that she would miss Tara's company over the weekend. Caring for a deaf child made her forget herself for stretches at a time. More than once she looked up from tying a small shoe lace or brushing a tangle of long red curls, to realize that she was unexpectedly at peace. The child's silence resonated with her own. Tara seemed delighted to do whatever Sam was doing, although she continued to wander off if left alone for any length of time. They both enjoyed long walks through the woods, baking, drawing pictures, and cutting fabric into little squares. Just as Tara's presence gave order and purpose to Sam's day, her home began to recover from its long lapse into chaos and neglect. For the first time in ages the floors were clean, the sink and counters clear, and the art and sewing supplies organized in baskets.

The first morning that Jerry dropped Tara at Sam's house he'd also brought a set of workbooks titled *Lip Reading for Children*, volumes I and II, and *Learning to Talk, the Oral-Aural Path to Natural Speech*. Sam had picked them up and riffled through the pages. Jerry had shrugged apologetically, "The school loaned those to me a couple months ago, but I'm not much of a teacher. Maybe you can get her to do some of the exercises; I haven't had much luck with her."

Judging from the books' pristine condition, Sam figured he hadn't tried very hard. "Sure," she'd said. "I'll give it a try." So every morning Sam tried to teach Tara how to read lips, and every afternoon they looked at picture books and did formal exercises to develop Tara's speech and language skills. Twice a day, at eleven and four o'clock, Sam switched on *Sesame Street* and let Tara sit mesmerized by the Muppets while she took a break, listened to the radio, and hoped that Big Bird was teaching Tara her numbers and the alphabet. Actually, Tara was a sponge, and quickly learned any lesson that could be taught by example or imitation. Speech was another matter.

It was Friday morning and Sam followed her regular routine. She sat Tara down at the kitchen table and kneeled beside her face-to-face. "Tara, what do you want for breakfast?" she asked, holding up two boxes. "Puffs?" She raised the box of Cocoa Puffs, "Or Flakes?" She raised the box of Corn Flakes.

Tara pointed to the Cocoa Puffs. Sam shook her head. "No, tell me, Puffs, say Puffs," and she refused to fill Tara's bowl until Tara pressed her lips together as though she were forming the letter "P." Tara was becoming very good at this game, pointing less and mouthing sounds more frequently. She pressed her lips together to indicate Puffs or bit her bottom lip if she wanted flakes and was rewarded with her morning cereal. Sam felt they were making progress and was proud that she was finally teaching Tara how to talk. However, no matter how often they played the game, Tara never emitted a sound. Why would she? She had no idea that a complex system of buzzes, hisses and pops accompanied the strange mouth movements that other people made when they spoke to one another. *How do real teachers of the deaf teach that?*

After breakfast Sam cleared away the dirty dishes and laid out a big sheet of white paper on the kitchen table. She gave Tara a box of pastels and set the child to work. While Tara was occupied with her creation, Sam set up the easel she'd purchased on her last trip to Erie and began mixing her own colors.

Painting beside Tara, who attacked each sheet of paper with absolute joy and a total lack of self-consciousness, made Sam feel looser and more experimental about her own work. She wasted paint and canvas, dabbing, swishing, and smearing color to her heart's content. This was her only indulgence and she had the money. Not every canvas was destined for the Louvre. The child worked alongside Sam for two hours without a break except to demand more paper.

Eventually, they both grew restless and Sam knew it was time to go outside. She waited patiently as the little girl carefully signed her creations, each letter in a different color, then they put on light jackets and headed out of doors.

Tara carried a paper bag to fill with the pretty stones, leaves, and flowers she found along the way. The company of the quiet child trudging along beside her felt perfect, like a gift. In fact, she sometimes felt guilty for the joy she took in the child's silence.

Tara raced ahead of Sam, past the barn, past the open pasture and into the woods, stopping occasionally to put something into her bag while Sam maintained a steady pace, enjoying the smell of the wet earth and the new grass whose green fragrance had finally asserted its dominance over winter. Yellow buttercups and purple phlox bloomed wherever there was sun, while Mayapples and violets grew thick in the shade of newly unfurled leaves. Patches of blue sky were visible through a canopy of branches overhead as Tara bent to pick the dandelions and wild geraniums blooming along the path through the woods. With the sun on their backs it was too warm for jackets, so they took them off and Sam showed Tara how to tie the arms around her waist. The day and their moods were both so fine that neither of them wanted to turn back when they reached the rear property line that bordered Whiskey Road. Taking Tara's hand in hers, Sam crossed the street and continued along the old logging road that cut through her neighbor's property. Sam thought it might connect with Morley Road where there was an elementary school and a small playground.

Tara had collected a blue feather, three rocks, a small bunch of wild flowers, and a Budweiser can and placed them in her bag. Something shiny caught the sun and glinted from a pile of moldy leaves. Sam watched indulgently as Tara trotted over and retrieved a small transistor radio from where it had been lost or discarded beside the path. As far as Sam could see, there was nothing unusual about the radio. It was just a bit of electronic trash, a small red square with a corroded metal face and a small leather strap, but the moment she touched it Tara began to crumple. Her lips trembled and tears poured down her face. When Sam went to comfort her, Tara pulled away dissolving into a hot, red, squealing ball of inexplicable misery. Helpless and utterly confused, Sam watched the child cry herself out. She would have given anything to trade all those lovely moments of companionable silence for the ability to ask Tara, "What is it? What just happened? What can I do?"

When they returned to the house, Tara wouldn't touch her soup and took only a few perfunctory pecks at the grilled cheese sandwich Sam placed in front of her. Instead of spending the afternoon looking at picture books, or matching printed words with objects, they curled up on the sofa with the cat squeezed in between them, and watched one stupid cartoon after another. Sam often wondered what Tara got from watching television; she couldn't possibly follow the story line or understand the dialogue, or could she? Whatever the answer, Tara sat quiet and transfixed with her thumb in her mouth until her father came to pick her up at six o'clock.

As soon as Jerry walked through the door, Sam told him about the incident with the transistor radio.

"Do you have any idea what happened? A radio of all things! What can an old transistor radio mean to a deaf child? Why did Tara dissolve into tears? She's still not herself." Jerry shook his head. He couldn't imagine what triggered such an outburst.

Just then Tara looked up and, seeing her father, ran to him with her bag of treasures. She pulled out the small radio and held it out to him, her eyes welling with tears, as though it was the body of a small dead bird. Immediately Jerry's face caved in and he gathered his daughter into his arms. Seeing Sam's puzzled face, he said, "It was Margo's. Or at least Margo had a radio just like it. She carried it with her everywhere she went."

They looked at one another with solemn expressions until Jerry said, "I guess we'd better head home. See you tomorrow." As he gave Tara one last hug, Sam could hear him whisper into the child's hair, "Who would have guessed you'd remember a thing like that?"

The next day dawned warm and sunny; the previous week's rain already a distant memory. Sam lay in bed, snug beneath her comforter and warmed by the sunlight pouring through the window. Suddenly she shot up, *Shit! I did it again!* Jerry was on his way over to cut up the fallen trees at the same time Sheila was picking her up for lunch and shopping.

It was too early in the morning for her brain to concoct a plausible lie, but she had to act fast before Jerry and Sheila collided in her driveway. She was simply going to have to worm her way out of one or the other of her commitments. A few implausible scenarios presented themselves as excuses to cancel lunch with Sheila, but they all ended with her mother-in-law tearing up the drive with chicken soup, the fire department, or the National Guard.

Jerry then... but what could she tell him? At last she decided to simply own up and apologize. She felt unexpectedly irritable and disappointed as she picked up the phone beside her bed and dialed his number.

"Jerry, I'm not usually such a twit, but I'm afraid I've double-scheduled myself this morning. I forgot that I had a date to go shopping and out to lunch with my mother-in-law. It's a regular Saturday thing we do. I just wasn't thinking when you offered to come by."

"I could stop over later, when you get back. I've got the old chain saw cleaned up, full of gas, and raring to go."

"That's okay; the handyman who's been doing some work around here probably has a chain saw. I'll ask him to clear the trees later in the week. Thanks for the offer, though. See you Monday."

"Wait a minute," Jerry interjected before she could hang up. "I wanted to talk to you about Tara. The trees were sort of an excuse. Can I come by later—with or without the chain saw?"

"Is there a problem with Tara?" Sam was trying to dress as she talked, and was stretching the phone cord to the point of almost pulling it from the jack as she struggled to reach her underwear drawer. "Hold on a minute, I'll be right back." She tossed the receiver onto the bed and grabbed a pair of underpants and a bra from the top drawer of her pinewood chest.

"I'm back. Actually, there are some questions I've wanted to ask you too, about Tara." Sam had the phone pressed between her shoulder and chin as she tried to fasten the bra behind her back.

There was a catch of desperation in Jerry's voice, "No, there's no problem with Tara. I mean there's nothing new, but I have a lot of decisions to make and I really need to talk to someone."

"Why not? How about three o'clock?" Sam stood at the window in her underwear staring at the empty expanse of sky above the barn.

"Thank you," Sam heard a note of relief in his voice. "Three it is. See you then."

"And you may as well bring the saw." Sam felt oddly buoyant as she walked over to her closet and pulled out a pair of Calvin Klein skinny jeans she hadn't worn for quite a while.

"Well, look at you," Sheila beamed as Sam climbed into her car.

"Why, what's the matter with me?"

"Nothing. You look adorable. I forgot what a cute little figure you were hiding under that denim jacket."

"It's too hot for a jacket, so I put on some summer things. It's no big deal."

"And lipstick, when's the last time I saw you wearing lipstick?"

"It's not lipstick, its lip gloss. My lips were dry. Can we drop it?"

"Well, forgive me for noticing that you look nice."

"You're forgiven. How about lunch first, then shopping? I didn't eat breakfast."

"Let's go to Svenson's for fish. We haven't eaten there in ages." Sheila was looking in her rear view mirror as she maneuvered down the long, narrow drive and into the street. Sam noticed a cigarette butt smoldering in the ashtray and wondered if Sheila had snuffed it out on her account. Suddenly, without warning, the car came to a screeching halt throwing Sam forward so violently that she nearly banged her head on the dashboard. Two motorcycles, blurs of chrome and rubber, veered around them, barely avoiding a collision. A moment later only the smoke from their exhausts lingered on the quiet country road.

Sheila gripped the steering wheel with her foot still on the brake. "My God, I think I'm going to have a heart attack. They came out of nowhere like bats out of Hell. Would you give me a cigarette?"

Sam fumbled in Sheila's bag for her package of Kents and handed her the box. "How fast do you think they were going? It's a miracle you stopped in time." All the color had drained from Sam's face.

"I don't know. Could they have been doing a hundred miles per hour? Do motorbikes go that fast?" Sheila put a cigarette between her lips and lit it with the red hot coils of the car's cigarette lighter.

"I don't know, but those guys were flying. They could have killed us." Sam realized that her whole body was shaking.

Sheila exhaled a great cloud of smoke, took another long drag on her cigarette before straightening her car and continuing down the street. "And this was the day I was going to give you a big pep talk about driving again."

"I am not driving again! I don't even want to *sit* in a car. I'd get out right now if I didn't need groceries," Sam could hear the irrational edge of hysteria in her voice.

"We won't talk about it now, but you know you've got to start driving eventually or move to someplace like New York. You can't live in a place like this without a car."

"The Amish do." Sam knew she was being stupid and belligerent but she couldn't help herself.

"Wouldn't it be nice to just go to Bell's Market, the bank, the beauty shop, or wherever, without asking me for a ride?" Sheila paused almost a full minute at the intersection, looking in every direction, before turning onto Grant Road.

"What are you saying? Are you tired of driving me places? You don't have to drive me anywhere if you don't want to. I'll get a horse and buggy."

"I don't mind driving. In fact, I look forward to our Saturdays together, but you know this can't go on forever." Sheila was using the same voice she'd use to coax frightened cats from trees. "Eventually, you're going to have to face down those fears and get on with things.'

"Or I could just move back to Cleveland. They have a great bus system and a rapid transit. I wouldn't need to drive if I moved back there." Sam blew her nose in a Kleenex she'd pulled from Sheila's purse.

Sheila stiffened and her face froze. "You have a beautiful house and everything you need right here. I don't want to hear another word about you moving. I'm sorry I brought it up. Do you want to stop at Cavanaugh's after lunch to see what they got in for spring?"

Sam shook her head, "I have to be home by three. Someone's coming over to remove those trees that fell behind the barn."

"Really? I figured Billy Crabtree would take care of them when he came to work on the house."

"Well, someone else offered to do the job and they're coming at three." Sam stared out the window, avoiding Sheila's quizzical gaze.

"That was awfully generous of someone." She smiled slyly in Sam's direction. "Is it anyone I know?"

"Okay, it's Jerry, the guy I work for. I guess he figures that he owes me for taking care of Tara."

"Jerry? Isn't that nice? Well then, we'll be sure to get you home by three." All the tension dissolved from Sheila's face and the shadow of a grin played along her lips.

CHAPTER 6

They were home before two-thirty and Sam had already un-loaded her groceries when Jerry's Camaro turned into the drive. The car had been freshly washed making its shiny red exterior look garish against the pastel landscape of a world awash in pink and yellow blooms. She'd been looking forward to a cup of coffee and a quiet chat with Jerry, but there was Tara sitting beside him in the passenger's seat. *What is the matter with the man?* It was irresponsible to let a child run around while he worked with a dangerous power saw. But of course, she reminded herself, leaving Tara at home wasn't exactly an option. Her head was throbbing and the morning's surge of energy and optimism had burned itself out.

Sam turned from the window and began filling the auto-matic coffee maker with water. Maybe caffeine would get her through the afternoon. To her surprise, there was no knock at the door and the doorbell didn't ring. She could see the red Camaro glowing in the drive, but Jerry and Tara were nowhere in sight. Eventually, the coffee stopped dripping and she poured herself a cup. Curious, Sam stepped outside and looked around. She couldn't see anyone, but the thrum of a chainsaw was clearly audible work-ing away behind the barn. She was tempted to go back inside and take a nap. Did she have an obligation to play hostess to someone who didn't ring the bell? Yes, she probably did, but she'd need a minute to brush her hair and freshen her lipstick. Somewhat re-vived, Sam braced herself with another swig of coffee then headed toward the barn.

While Jerry systematically sawed large limbs off the fallen trees, Tara was at work, some distance away, gathering up small twigs and branches. Sam watched them for several minutes before Jerry looked up and turned off the saw. "How long have you been working?" Sam called over to him. "I didn't hear you drive in."

"Half an hour, maybe. I thought I'd do this first, then come in and talk to you."

"There's no way you're going to finish this afternoon. That's going to take hours."

Sam was suddenly aware of the enormity of the task Jerry had undertaken on her behalf.

"Well, I'll get a good start today and finish up tomorrow. Will that be a problem?"

"Not for me. Won't it be a problem for you? Honestly, I didn't realize how much work was involved." She took another sip from the mug that she'd carried out from the kitchen

"Nope, no problem. I like working out of doors. I do too much sitting on my butt during the week. I thought I'd be chasing bad guys all over the county, but with this bum leg it's mostly sitting at a desk pushing paper." Although his face was smudged with dirt and patches of sweat stained his shirt, he looked happy.

"Do you want some coffee? I just made a pot."

"Sure, cream, no sugar."

"Cream no sugar," Sam repeated. Jerry nodded, turned the saw back on, and went back to dismembering the trees.

"You don't have to do this, you know," Sam shouted over the saw.

"What?" Jerry switched the saw off again.

"I said you don't have to do this. You can just come in if you want to talk."

"Thanks, but I finish what I start and I'm going to cut these suckers down to size."

"Okay, then, thank you," Sam said, but she doubted he could hear her since the saw had resumed roaring at the fallen maples.

By the time Sam returned with the coffee, the largest limbs had been sawed off one tree and Jerry had begun cutting them into neat three foot logs. "Where's Tara?" Sam asked as she handed him the mug.

Jerry, who was bent to the task of cutting wood, suddenly shot up to his full height. "Damn!" He craned his neck to scan the yard. Sam realized that he was even taller than Ben who'd stood six feet tall. "You can't take your eyes off her for one minute."

"No, you can't," Sam agreed. Anxious though she was for Tara's safety, she was aware of a guilty pleasure in knowing that even Tara's father couldn't keep her from running off.

Alarm, irritation and embarrassment played over Jerry's face as he ran his fingers through his hair. "Why does she do this? Where does she think she's going?" Sam stared back at him saying nothing.

"You check the front of the house and along the road. I'll look behind the barn and in the woods. She's only been gone a couple of minutes." He was in police mode, taking control, snapping orders.

"No, that doesn't make sense," Sam snapped back. "I know the trails and terrain on my own property and you don't. You check the road and I'll head back toward the pond." Her coffee mug sat abandoned on a tree stump as she rushed toward the woods, but she could hear Jerry mutter, "Yes ma'am," under his breath as he hurried off on the task that she'd assigned him.

Sam raced down the same path she'd taken a month earlier when she'd brought daffodils to her daughter's grave. It was difficult to stifle the urge to call for Tara, to scream her name across the fields. But shouts would only startle wrens and finches from their nests, so Sam raced on in silence, scouring the landscape with her eyes, searching for rustling branches, for a tell-tale flash of pink. How did Tara do it? How could such a little thing cover so much territory in a flash?

Sam smiled remembering Gomer, the pet gerbil she'd received for her eighth birthday. He'd turned out to be a gerbil genius, an escape artist, who had outwitted every attempt to keep him caged. She and her father had spent the better part of a year crawling under beds and emptying cupboards searching for him. Each time they found him, heavier and more draconian hardware was added to his cage, and always, a few days later, he'd be gone again.

"Tara's probably part gerbil," Sam started to chuckle, then stopped abruptly, remembering that Gomer had ultimately drowned in a washtub full of dirty socks.

Leaving the path, Sam ran full-tilt toward the pond, trampling Mayapples, wild geraniums, and fiddlehead ferns underfoot. Breathless, she scanned the sloping banks of the pond for any trace of Tara without success. As she returned toward the path, intending to head back in defeat, Sam saw a small footprint in the mud pointing toward Whiskey Road. She shifted into racing mode and sprinted toward the street hoping to intercept Tara before she waded into traffic on her own. She reached the end of the trail without catching a glimpse of the child, but she knew which way she was headed. Three cars and a truck raced by in fast succession before Sam could cross the street. Her stomach churned and her heart lurched as she caught sight of a fawn half eaten by maggots lying on the berm.

Finally catching up with Tara, Sam grabbed the child by the arm and stupidly started scolding her. "What the Hell's the matter with you? Are you trying to scare us half to death? Can't you to stay put for two minutes without an armed guard? You're deaf, you're not stupid. You know you're not supposed to run off like that." Tara struggled to pull away, startled and confused. She began producing the small mewling sounds that were her only audible sign of distress.

"Oh for God's sake," Sam looked down at the small, uncomprehending child. *What am I supposed to do with a child who can't hear a word I say? How can I explain things to her? How can I keep her safe?* Gripped by remorse and melted by Tara's pale upturned face, the face that so resembled June's, Sam knelt down and kissed her curls. "I'm sorry. I'm so sorry, Tara." The child watched as tears welled up in Sam's eyes then overflowed when she could no longer blink them back. Tara reached out and touched one of the tears with a small finger, tracing its course down Sam's cheek.

Tara allowed Sam to lead her back toward the house where they met Jerry loping down the path in their direction, moving fast despite his rocking, unbalanced gait. "Thank God, you've got her. I was going to ask the office to send out a search team if she didn't show up in another couple minutes. Where did you find her?" Beads of sweat ran down his forehead and he was breathing hard. Sam wondered if moving so fast made his leg hurt.

"She took herself for a walk across Whiskey Road, back to the place we found the radio. Do you think she's looking for her mother?" Both she and Jerry turned and looked at the small figure trotting along between them.

Jerry stared at the ground, speaking in a low voice as though he didn't want Tara to hear what he had to say, "I've wondered that myself. Margo and Tara were inseparable. I'll never understand what happened. Margo had her faults, but she adored this child. Then one day, out of the blue, she was gone. Just like that. No note. No warning. Nothing. I mean, we all knew she had problems, but no one ever thought she'd leave Tara. It's never made any sense."

"And there wouldn't be any way to explain it to Tara anyway because she can't hear," Sam added, comprehending the child's confusion.

"Explain it to Tara? I can't explain it to myself. You can't imagine how disorienting it is, thinking you're part of a happy family one day then being all alone the next."

"I can imagine it," Sam answered.

"Of course, I'm sorry. Of course you can. It's just so hard, suddenly being a single parent, not that Margo was ever what you'd call a responsible adult."

"Didn't you say she'd gone off to join a commune?" Sam was curious about a woman who could walk out on a husband and small child. Nothing like that had ever happened to anyone she knew.

"Yeah, a couple weeks later I got a letter from Santa Fe saying not to worry. She was living on the Moonbeam Commune, or whatever its name was. Doing fine, nothing personal, no hard feelings, give my love to Tara, bullshit. Like I said, it didn't make sense. I could have put a trace on her, but what the hell? What would I do if I found her? I mean, if she doesn't want to live here I can't bring her back in chains."

They made their way back to the barn where Jerry picked up the saw and went back to work while Sam led Tara into the house and kept a close eye on her for the remainder of the afternoon. It was almost seven o'clock when Sam looked out her kitchen window and saw the sun drifting toward the western horizon. The early evening sky had the pearly opalescence it acquires before fading into twilight. The air glowed; it almost seemed to hum a chord that resonated feelings of wholeness and content. Something in her itched to capture the moment, to pin it down on canvas, but what colors could replicate the light of a luminous spring evening?

Sam had given Tara a large bowl and a selection of raw veggies from the fridge. Tara was assembling them into a large salad as Sam supervised her progress. Not long ago June had sat at this table in her high chair struggling to master the intricacies of a spoon. She remembered Ben beside her, the two of them smiling fondly as their baby gurgled up at them, her face covered in peach yogurt. As though waking in a lucent dream, she was aware of two worlds at once, the dream world of her lost family and the reality of this particular spring night. She was so lost in her meditation that she didn't notice when Jerry walked through the kitchen door without bothering to knock.

For a moment the two worlds converged and she thought Ben was standing by the door, but the voice wasn't her husband's. "Do you mind if I use your bathroom to clean up? I'm kind of a sweaty mess." Sam had to concur; sawdust clung to the mud and oil that coated his hands and face. He unlaced his shoes and left them in the hall.

"It's upstairs. These old houses don't have downstairs powder rooms." Sam pointed to the stairs, "First door on the right." As Jerry headed toward the stairs, Sam caught a whiff of sweat, fresh wood, and gasoline emanating from his body. His shirt sleeves were rolled back, revealing muscles that Sam hadn't suspected beneath the neatly pressed uniforms he wore to work.

"Is it alright if I take a quick shower? I'll clean up after myself."

Sam looked away, discomfited by his presence in her house. She hadn't been with a man for a year and a half. The thought of his naked body in her shower evoked feelings she didn't want. "Use the old blue towels, not the white ones," she called after him in a peevish tone, but her eyes followed his wide shoulders up the stairs.

Tara stood at the kitchen table tearing lettuce leaves and dropping them, one by one, into the large wooden bowel. She turned toward Sam, a puzzled expression on her face, when she saw her father going up the stairs. Sam looked away and focused on the cutting board, chopping a carrot into smaller and smaller pieces.

Jerry came back downstairs smelling of Ivory Soap and Clairol Herbal Essence. Three place settings waited on the kitchen table and a pot of spaghetti sauce bubbled on the stove. "It's past seven, so you may as well stay for supper." Sam threw a dash of oregano into the pot, and busied herself at the kitchen sink.

Jerry stood by the table watching her work while Tara sprawled on the kitchen floor playing with a set of wooden blocks that had once belonged to June. "I found this shirt hanging on a hook in the bathroom. I'm really sorry, I didn't want to take it, but mine was soaked through with mud and sweat."

The shirt had been hanging in the bathroom for eighteen months, just where Ben had left it. Sam turned and saw Jerry in the frayed blue flannel shirt that her husband had worn to putter in the yard. It fit Jerry pretty well, but it looked wrong on him, very wrong. Her mouth went dry and pasty. She wanted to say, "How dare you?" or "Oh, my God!" or more bravely, "Sure, no problem," but not a word emerged. Ultimately, she produced a guttural sound, something Tara might have said, as she dropped handfuls of pasta into the pot of boiling water.

Dinner was quiet, awkward and uncomfortable. It wasn't until Tara went off to play in the living room that Sam and Jerry finally started to relax. "Cream, no sugar, right?" Sam carried two mugs into the dining room and set them on the table beside a plate of Oreos. "So, what did you want to talk about?"

Jerry twisted one of the cookies apart and stared at the two halves without answering. "Well, as you know I've been having a hard time finding the right situation for Tara. Everyone I talk to has a different idea about her education. The Kleiner Public Schools don't have a Deaf Ed program, but there's a new law going into effect this year that says they have to either find a school for her or provide a private speech pathologist and tutor. If I go that route she could live at home and the speech pathologist could teach her how to talk. But her doctor thinks I should send her to a boarding school in Buffalo where she'd live with other deaf kids and learn sign language."

"Why would you do that? You don't know how to sign, so you'd never be able to talk to her. Besides, she's way too little to go to boarding school." Sam was outraged by the very idea.

"Yeah, but her doctor tells me that even with the best therapy, profoundly deaf kids like Tara almost never learn to talk or read lips well."

"The workbooks say that every deaf child can learn to talk. Give the local school a chance. You can't just send her away. Tara won't understand that she's at a boarding school; she'll think you've abandoned her. She's already lost her mother, what happens when she thinks she's lost you too?"

"But the doctor says she might never learn any language at all if she doesn't learn sign language. He said she could grow up stupid and empty. Those were his words, stupid and empty. Frankly, he thinks I've already wasted too much valuable time."

"That's just his opinion. I don't have any special training or qualifications, but I've been reading books on deaf education." Sam got up from the table and ran into the living room where she pulled two volumes out of the bookcase and dropped them on the table.

"Look at these. They both say that learning oral language is Tara's only shot at living a normal life."

"Her doctor scared me, but I agree with you, which brings me around to what I wanted to discuss. First, I still haven't found anyone to take care of Tara while I'm at work. Second, I know that you've been working with Tara, and really trying to help her." He pointed at the books she'd just brought him. "You're teaching her things and I'm really grateful for that. Also, she likes coming here. She hops in the car without the tantrums she used to throw when I took her to that other woman. So, I have a proposition for you."

Sam braced herself. She knew what was coming. Jerry took a sip of coffee and leaned forward in his chair. He looked like a guy applying for a job he really needed. "If I keep Tara at home for the next year, and get tutors and therapists to work with her, would you be her babysitter and help with her homework and speech exercises? I'd pay you for your time. What do you think?" Exhausted by this little speech, Jerry dunked the Oreo into his coffee and popped it into his mouth, chewing and swallowing, as he waited for her reply.

"I can't make that kind of commitment." Sam spoke softly but deliberately as she sipped her coffee. "I hope you keep Tara at home and find someone to work with her, but I have no idea what I'm going to be doing a year from now. I don't know what I'm going to be doing in six months. My mother wants me to go back to school in September. I might do that, or I might..." Sam's voice drifted off into silence.

"Or you might what?" Jerry watched as Sam's confidence evaporated and she seemed to shrink in her chair.

"Or, I don't know what. I have no idea. To be honest, there's absolutely nothing I want to do."

"Well then, that's perfect. You can look after Tara while you figure things out. I won't hold you to a full year commitment. Help me out for as long as you can, and we'll deal with later later." Jerry looked confident that Sam would accept his offer.

"I'm not a teacher. I've never wanted to be a teacher. I'm supposed to be a doctor." Sam felt herself shrink even smaller. She half hoped she might disappear altogether.

"A doctor? Really? What kind of doctor?" Jerry looked surprised. He'd clearly never imagined Sam as anything but a widowed housewife and Tara's babysitter.

"I don't know. It's what I'm supposed to do. Everyone in my family's a doctor."

"No kidding? That's impressive. Everyone in my family's an alcoholic." Jerry gave Sam a wry smile. "No one in my family's ever gone to college; they thought I was a genius for passing the military police exam. I've never known anyone who could get into medical school."

"You knew Ben. He could have gotten in, he just didn't want to. To tell the truth, I don't know if I want to either. It's just what I'm supposed to do. My parents can't imagine why anyone would want to do anything else."

"Well, I guess that explains these books. I should have figured Ben would marry a brainiac. But you're going to be around for awhile, so what about my proposition?" Jerry's blue eyes crinkled at the corners when he smiled.

Sam sat up straight and looked away from him. "Give me a few days to think about it. It's a big decision." She stood up abruptly and began gathering the dirty dishes from the table.

"Let me give you a hand. I'm chief cook and bottle washer at my house." Jerry picked up a couple water glasses and started to follow Sam into the kitchen.

"No! Put those down. Don't do that. Please, don't touch them." She'd raised her voice, she was actually yelling at him. He stared at her, bewildered, but he put the glasses back on the table. Sam turned red and stammered, "I'm sorry, I just meant don't bother, you're my guest. Why don't you gather up Tara's things and we'll call it a night."

"Sure, I'll get our coats," Jerry replied, but he and Sam stood facing each other across the table without moving. "Are you alright?" he asked. "You seem to be on edge."

"I'm okay." She swallowed hard and kept one hand on the table. "The truth is that Ben always helped me with the dishes, and you're wearing his shirt. It's stupid, but seeing you clear the table was too much. It brought back memories."

"Yeah, it's funny how ghosts creep up on you sometimes. Don't worry about it."

Sam nodded, knowing that Jerry had his own ghosts to contend with, "Well, thanks for tackling those trees. I really appreciate it. I guess I'll see you tomorrow."

"I'll stop by sometime after lunch to finish up. In the meantime, think about my offer."

"I'll think about it." Sam turned and carried the dishes into the kitchen by herself.

CHAPTER 7

Billy Crabtree didn't usually show up on Monday mornings, so Sam was surprised to see his truck clamber past her kitchen window on its way toward the barn. Normally she would have run outside to investigate, but Tara was in the middle of a full scale, no holds barred temper tantrum because Sam couldn't understand something about her shoes, or maybe it was her feet, or her socks. Sam was exhausted from trying to decipher Tara's gestures and facial expressions, while Tara, in utter frustration, finally threw one shoe into the cat's water bowl and the other on top of the stove. She then pulled off both her socks and pounded her bare feet on the floor, squealing with red faced indignation. Sam, who'd been squatting in front of her with a picture book in one hand and a box of Legos in the other, had taken a direct kick to her left shin. She was standing against the kitchen sink, rubbing her leg, when she caught a glimpse of a boy with brown skin and a funkadelic afro sitting beside Billy as his pickup truck rattled past her window.

By the time Sam had finally settled Tara and a bowl of Frosted Flakes in front of the television, she was too exhausted to do anything but watch cartoon mice wreak havoc on a cartoon cat for the better part of an hour. Guilt finally trumping fatigue, Sam rallied sufficiently to take Tara outside for some fresh air and exercise. It was a fine morning in late May. Swallows swooped in and out of the barn carrying grass and twigs for the nests they were building in the rafters. Sam closed her eyes and inhaled the smell of new grass and the resinous odor of pine. When she opened them she saw Tara chasing a baby rabbit across the lawn. The sun illuminated Tara's red curls making them look like a halo. The demon child of early morning had been transformed into an angel who might have stepped out of a painting by Fra Angelico. Sam hurried toward the barn where pads of drawing paper, water colors, and pastels were waiting. *Would Tara sit still long enough for me to sketch her portrait? How in the world can I capture that electrified hair?*

The central part of the barn had been divided in two, the back half for Billy and the antique tractor, and the front half for Sam and her art studio. The four stalls that had once housed the Crawford family milkers had been converted into storage bins for everything Billy had deemed too valuable for the dump. Eight gallons of blue house paint were neatly stacked in the stall closest to the door. Now that the weather was warm, Sam had no excuse for putting off painting the house. She vowed to start next week as she headed toward the work table Billy had made from a solid pine door he'd found abandoned in the loft.

At the back of the barn, Billy and a smaller figure were half hidden in shadows, their arms and faces a study in chiaroscuro. They were probing the tractor's innards with flashlights and wrenches beneath a single light bulb dangling from the ceiling. The older man was lecturing the boy about something, and from the sound of his voice the subject wasn't tractor maintenance. He fell silent as soon as he realized that Sam and Tara were headed toward them.

"Hi!" Sam called over to them. "Beautiful day, isn't it?"

"Sure is. You want to meet my grandson?"

"Sure," Sam called back, although she was anxious to start drawing before the sun shifted, erasing the soft morning shadows. Taking Tara firmly by the hand to guard against any sudden disappearances, she headed over to where Billy and the boy were standing.

"This is Marcus." Billy pointed to the boy Sam had seen sitting in the pickup truck. "He's going to be helping me out for awhile." Marcus didn't look up, but continued to probe the engine with his flashlight. He looked about twelve years old, making Sam wonder why he wasn't in school on a Monday morning. *Schools in Catawba County won't let out for another month. Is the school year that much shorter in Buffalo?* Marcus stood with his back to her and didn't turn around when he was introduced, so Sam couldn't see his face. What she saw was an enormous afro, a black thundercloud of hair that bristled like live nerves around his head.

As if in response to her unasked question, Billy added, "Marcus here's kind of under house arrest. The Buffalo Public Schools sent him home for the rest of the semester to meditate on his sins. His momma works during the day and can't keep her eye on him, so he's going to be staying with Grandpop for a while. But summer vacation hasn't come early for this boy. He is *not* on vacation. He's going to be finishing his school work and working his butt to the bone as my assistant. Isn't that right, Marcus?" The boy's shoulders rolled into a sort of shrug, but he didn't turn his head. "So, Mrs. Crawford, you've got yourself an extra pair of hands at your disposal. This young man is going to know the right way to paint a house before the summer's over, and he's going to know a thing or two about getting an old tractor up and running."

"They suspended him to the end of the term?" Sam eyed the boy suspiciously.

"They did, but if he turns in his final papers and passes his exams, he gets to start eighth grade with a clean slate." This little speech was clearly for Marcus's benefit. As he talked, Billy was wrestling with a rusted nut somewhere inside the engine; his face growing red from the exertion. There was a long silence while Billy gave his full attention to the petrified piece of metal, alternately banging it with a hammer and putting his full weight into turning a lug wrench. When the nut finally rolled off into the palm of his hand he stood up smiling, "Got it. The trick is you've got to be more stubborn than the tractor, isn't that right, Marcus?"

Marcus shuffled his feet and pretended he couldn't hear. "I said, isn't that right, Marcus?" Billy repeated the question in a louder voice that carried a hint of warning.

"I don't know," Marcus raised his head and risked a quick glimpse at Sam and Tara. He was wearing a skin tight black T-shirt and Kelly green pants that flared at the ankle. The handle of a hair pick stuck out of his afro like an ornament.

"Well, I know. And you know what else I know? I know this boy's going to turn himself around and get his head screwed on straight if I have to keep banging on him 'til he's a grown man."

Tara was pulling on Sam's arm, anxious to go back outside and Sam was glad for the excuse to leave. "Nice meeting you, Marcus, but Tara and I have to get going." She gave Billy a sympathetic look.

"We'll be moving along too, just as soon as we finish up in here." Billy was gathering his tools and handing them to Marcus who placed them in a large metal box. Tara waved goodbye as they left and Marcus flashed a sweet and unexpected smile in her direction.

The perfect ruse for getting Tara to sit for a portrait was to keep her busy with art supplies of her own, so Sheila had the pleasure of finding two heads bent over drawing paper when she arrived to drive them to the library. Tara had a pile of completed work stacked on the picnic bench she was using for a table, while Sam had a small sea of crumpled papers lapping at her feet, evidence of her frustration with her limitations as an artist. "Now isn't that pretty?" Sheila asked in a loud clear voice with exaggerated lip movements for Tara's benefit. The little girl, seeing a Sheila shaped shadow fall across her paper, looked up and smiled. She liked Sheila, who spoiled her with toys and sweets whenever she came over.

"There's no point in raising your voice, Sheila. She couldn't hear you even if you screamed in her ear." Sam spoke under her

breath, as she added another few lines to her drawing, tore it from
the pad, then started to crumple it up like the others, but something
about the tilt of Tara's head caught her eye and she decided to spare
it, leaving it inside the tablet.

"Are you sure? Did you see how she just turned to look at
me?" Sheila gave Tara a little kiss on top of her head.

"She looked at you because she's deaf, not blind. Trust me, she
doesn't hear a thing. Give me a minute to put this stuff away before
we leave," Sam gathered up all the papers, scraps, discards and small
masterpieces and headed to the barn.

"Well, how will she ever learn to talk if no one talks to her?
Anyway, she should be at school by now. There's a new law that says
public schools have to educate children with handicaps. They don't
have a choice." Sheila had Tara by the hand and was trotting along
beside Sam as she spoke.

"You're right. Jerry's been working with people at the school
to figure something out, but it's complicated. Everyone has a different theory about what he should be doing. Her pediatrician thinks he
should ship Tara out to a boarding school in Buffalo to live with a
bunch of other deaf kids and learn sign language."

"Boarding school? She's only seven years old. That's ridiculous," Sheila put a protective arm around Tara.

"That's what I said. But there's no program for deaf kids in
Kleiner, so the alternative is private speech pathologists and tutors.
The school would pay for most of it, but someone would still have
to stay home to look after her." Sam added several of Tara's newest
creations to the corkboard gallery where she displayed their work.

"Has he found anyone yet?"

"Yeah, me," Sam said, sticking a pin through the sketch she'd
just completed of Tara sitting on the lawn. She stabbed it with more
force than was absolutely necessary.

Sheila pursed her lips as she sorted out this new turn of events.
At last, with a long sigh, she said, "Well, isn't that just what I predicted? I knew he'd never find anyone as good or competent as
you to look after her. What did you tell him? He'd have to pay you
a real salary."

"He'd pay me. It's not the money, it's the commitment." Sam
was combing her fingers through her hair as they headed back toward Sheila's car. "I only promised to do this for a few weeks to
help him out. I may be back in Cleveland by September, or I might
join the Peace Corps or move to Paris. I don't have a clue. Frankly,
nothing appeals to me. I don't want to do anything."

"Then the job might be perfect, it would give you another year to figure things out." Sheila climbed into the driver's seat while Sam settled Tara in the back.

"No, it wouldn't be perfect. Perfect was living here with Ben and June. Everything else is crap."

No one spoke another word as the car eased backward down the long driveway. Just as they were about to back into the road Sam yelled, "Stop!"

Sheila slammed on the brakes and swung her head around expecting to see a pair of Harleys zoom into view.

"Sorry, I forgot the library books. I'll be right back," Sam bolted from the car and headed toward the house. It took only a moment to scoop up *Harold and the Purple Crayon, Curious George* and several other early readers that were supposed to stimulate Tara's language development. Like a race horse going through its paces, she sprinted upstairs, grabbed *Watership Down* and *Breakfast of Champions* from her night stand and was bounding back down the steps when the phone began to ring. Sam slowed, hesitated a moment, then changed course and headed toward the kitchen.

"What took you so long?" Sheila demanded when Sam finally plopped herself back down in the passenger seat.

"Jerry called. He wanted me to be on the lookout for Margo. Someone called to tell him they saw her in the parking lot behind Yoder Hardware, at least they think they saw her. They weren't positive." Sam twisted around to hand Tara Richard Scarry's *Best Word Book Ever.* "He's terrified that she's going to come back and cause trouble, maybe try to take Tara away. If we see her we're not supposed to say anything, just grab Tara and head home."

"He's right to be scared. Margo's a wild woman, unfit to raise a child. But honestly, if anyone had seen Margo, they'd be positive. The woman is five foot ten, weighs maybe two hundred pounds, and has flaming red hair. She's not someone you think you maybe, might have seen. If they'd seen her, they'd know it."

"My God, she's an Amazon. I never pictured her like that." Sam and Sheila turned toward one another grinning like Cheshire cats.

"Oh, and she has a tattoo, a big peace sign on her upper arm. Did I mention the tattoo?" The grins had turned to giggles, "And you wanted to know if Ben had taken her to prom. Believe me, she wasn't his type."

"But I can't imagine her with Jerry either. He's so ordinary and conservative. I can't put them together in my mind. What was the attraction? I mean if a guy like Jerry could fall for Margo, then why not Ben?"

"Why not Ben? How can you ask such a question? I'm sorry, I need a cigarette." Sheila dug a pack of Kents from her handbag and managed to extract one, put it in her mouth and light it while keeping one hand on the steering wheel.

"Five foot ten, two hundred pounds with red hair and a tattoo? Are you serious?" Sam was still trying to assimilate this new information.

"One hundred percent," Sheila relaxed as she inhaled the nicotine and smoke.

"But why would Jerry tell me that Ben had dated Margo if he hadn't? Why would he make that up?"

Sheila shrugged her shoulders, "I never knew Jerry that well. He came over once in awhile to shoot baskets with Joe and he seemed like a real nice kid, but boys that age don't talk much, at least not to middle aged mothers." Sheila paused to check on Tara in her rear view mirror. "My guess is that Jerry got Margo pregnant. She was part of the hippy crowd and into all that free love stuff. Then, since Jerry was basically a good guy, he decided to do the right thing and marry her, but then Margo took off and left him with the baby. That's my guess, anyway. It's the only thing that makes sense to me."

"They never got married." Sam felt a pang of guilt, as though she were betraying a secret.

Sheila rolled her eyes and shook her head as if to say, "Of course, what else would you expect from such people."

As they pulled into a parking space at the library, they heard the roar of motorcycles approaching at high speed. Turning toward the sound, they saw a blur of black and chrome whiz past the library, slow slightly, then careen south onto Seward Street toward Sherman. "Someone should arrest those guys before they kill somebody." Sam looked after them in disgust as she helped Tara from the car and waited while Sheila took a last puff of her Kent then crushed it beneath the heel of her penny loafer.

The Kleiner Public Library was a small two room affair. Adult books were shelved in the first room just past the entry hall with its messy jumble of pamphlets and public service announcements. The children's room was at the back. A large counter, dividing the two rooms, served as a desk for the librarian and her two assistants. Tara immediately ran to the children's section while Sam dropped the books she was returning into the bin and picked up a copy of *Centennial* by James Michener. She was weighing it in her hands, deciding whether or not she had the fortitude to slog through a thousand pages when the librarian tapped her on the shoulder. She wasn't the regular librarian; Sam had never seen her before. She was about Sam's age, but seemed older and more sophisticated in her striped blouse, flared trousers and platform shoes. Her blonde hair was cut into a page boy that swung, when she turned her head, like hair in a shampoo commercial. Sam ran her fingers through her own mousy brown hair. It was flat, straight and parted in the middle, the same way it had been all through college. She was wearing the blue jeans and denim jacket that had become her second skin.

The librarian was smiling. "You've got to see this, it's so cute. Is that your daughter?" They both turned to the children's section where Tara was sitting next to a little girl of nine or ten who had a big picture book open on her lap. The older girl was reading out loud to Tara who appeared to be listening with rapt attention. "Isn't that sweet?" the librarian beamed.

Sam nodded, but the lump in her throat prevented her from answering right away, "She can't hear. She can't hear a thing. She's deaf." Sam's voice was just above a whisper.

"But she's hanging on every word." As the young woman shook her head in disbelief her blonde hair swung back and forth like drapery being drawn back.

"I think she's pretending to hear so the other girl will play with her. She won't be able to fool her for long." Both women watched the girls in silence until the librarian asked, "Where does she go to school?"

Sam shook her head, "Nowhere. There are no deaf education programs around here. No one knows what to do with her. She'll probably stay at home with private tutors and a speech therapist."

"But then she won't have any children to play with." A furrow appeared between the young woman's eyes. "What will she do for friends?"

"I don't know, but you're right. She never plays with kids her own age." Sam watched as Tara grinned at the other child who was turning a page and chattering on, oblivious that her prattle was literally falling on deaf ears. "I don't know how she'd get along with other children. She hasn't learned to talk or read lips yet."

A born librarian, the woman rose to the challenge, certain that the solution to every problem could be found in the library." There are a lot of activities for children her age. There's a Brownie troop that meets in our recreation room on Thursday afternoons, and— wait a minute," she held up her index finger indicating that she'd be right back. She returned riffling through a catalog from a pile on her desk. "She's about seven, right?"

Sam nodded, "You're good. She just turned seven last month."

"Alright then, the recreation board offers T-ball, swimming lessons, ballet–I guess she couldn't do ballet, but what about gymnastics, or Make it and Take it Art? What do you think?"

"May I have copy of the catalog? I'll need to show it to her father. I'm just her babysitter, but you're right; she needs to get involved in one of these programs. I had no idea all this was available. Do you think they'd accept her? She couldn't follow instructions like the other children; they'd have to take extra time to show her what to do."

"I don't know. Give them a call and explain the situation. Maybe you could go along as her interpreter. Does she use sign language?" The librarian had perked up, her glossy pink lips beaming a broad optimistic smile.

"No, we're teaching her oral language, but we've just started. She doesn't know much yet."

"So how do you talk with her?" The librarian still looked confident that Sam must certainly have some means of communicating with a child who couldn't hear, sign or read lips.

"We just point and gesture a lot. It's sort of an endless game of charades, and I feel like most of the time we're losing." *Why am I confessing this to a librarian I just met? I've never said anything this pessimistic or honest to either Jerry or Sheila.*

"Well, I think you're wonderful for working with her and teaching her to talk. You're a lot more than a babysitter. If I found some books about teaching deaf children, would that help you?"

"I've already checked. You don't have anything on deaf education at this branch, but I found a couple books at the main library in Jamestown. Basically, they say we've started too late. She should already be talking and learning how to read by now." Sam was appalled to realize that two huge tears were rolling down her cheeks. She wiped them away, hoping the librarian hadn't noticed.

"It can't be too late; she's still just a little thing." *She'd noticed.* "Just look at her, she's adorable." The librarian patted Sam on the shoulder trying to console her.

"My goodness, what's the matter?" Sheila hurried over carrying an armful of books. "Are you alright?"

Sam nodded, "I'm fine, go ahead and check out your books. I'll be right with you." Sheila paused, uncertain for a moment, and then headed for the counter.

Sam turned back to the librarian who was still hovering beside her. "My name's Samantha Crawford, but everyone calls me

Sam. We come here pretty often, but I don't think I've seen you here before."

"Sarabelle Peterson. I just graduated from Syracuse. This is my first job. I started here last Monday." The new librarian held out a perfectly manicured hand.

"Well, welcome to Kleiner and thanks again." Sam shook her hand then hurried off clutching the Recreation Department catalog. She was about to join Sheila at the checkout when the sound of scuffling, yelps, and whimpers resonated through the quiet room. Sam raced to the back of the library where Tara was gulping for air as tears streamed down her cheeks. The ten year old who'd been reading to Tara was huddled in a corner with another girl, probably one of her classmates. They were pointing at Tara and rotating their fingers beside their ears to indicate they thought that she was crazy. Sam raced over and took Tara by the hand. "Is she retarded?" one of the girls wanted to know.

"No, she's not retarded. She's deaf. She just wanted to be friends and you made her cry. You should be ashamed of yourselves." The girls giggled and ran off leaving Sam to console Tara who had no idea why she'd been taunted and rejected.

"How about stopping for a Dairy Queen on the way home?" Sheila asked once they were all back in the car.

"The Dairy Queen's closed for renovations." Sam was looking through her purse for some Kleenex because Tara was still whimpering and kicking her feet against the front seat.

"Then how about The Lighthouse? They serve ice cream." Sheila was pretty sure that ice cream would solve most problems involving children.

Sam turned and pantomimed licking an ice cream cone. "Ice cream," she said, trying to get Tara to watch her mouth, "ice cream." She pretended to lick an ice cream cone again, but Tara wouldn't stop crying.

"What's the matter with her, what happened in there?" asked Sheila. "Make her stop kicking, my kidneys can't take it."

"She's upset because a little girl in the library stopped playing with her once she figured out that Tara couldn't talk. In fact, she was pretty mean." Sam hung over the back seat, trying to hold Tara's legs while shaking her head, no. "We don't realize how lonesome Tara must be without any kids to play with. Ouch! Cut that out!"

"I'm sure you're right," Sheila arched her back away from the angry feet pounding on the seat behind her. "So, is The Lighthouse okay?"

CHAPTER 8

Kathy seated the three of them in the same booth by the window where Sam and Jerry had met for dinner little more than a month ago. Tara was quiet again, drawing on her paper placemat with a little box of crayons while Sheila and Sam discussed books and waited for their ice cream. Suddenly, the roar of revved up motorcycles drowned out their conversation. Unperturbed, Tara continued to work on her drawing of a large purple house without windows or doors. Sheila and Sam, however, both whipped around in time to see two bikers wearing black jackets, helmets and goggles screech into the parking lot, turn and brake just short of hitting the building. The taller of the two dismounted and took off her helmet releasing a cascade of flame red curls that tumbled below her shoulders.

While Sam sat transfixed with her eyes glued to the window, Sheila had already grabbed Tara, the crayons, and the unfinished picture. "Pay the waitress. I'll meet you in the car," Sheila ordered as she headed toward the rear exit. Sam stood up shakily and began fumbling for her purse. She pulled out a five dollar bill and was headed toward the register when the red haired woman strode in through the front entrance, making it to the counter in three long strides. She stood there a moment taking inventory of everything and everyone in the room. Apparently not seeing what she was looking for, she called out toward the kitchen, "Hey, Kathy, are you back there? It's Margo. I want to talk to you."

Sam hurriedly slumped back into her seat, feeling pale and puny as Margo looked in her direction. A stocky young man with dark hair that fell just below the collar of his leather jacket, and the slow, bowlegged gait of a cowboy, walked in behind Margo. He also looked around; he appeared to size up the place, then stopped, crossed his arms and waited by the door.

"Kathy! Hey, Kathy are you back there?" Margo shouted a second time with no regard for the customers seated at the booths and tables. "Is anyone working here or what?" Her voice was as loud and riveting as the rest of her. Not wanting to attract Margo's attention, Sam pretended to be absorbed in the menu that trembled in her hands. A moment later Kathy emerged through the swinging kitchen doors carrying a tray with three small sundaes, all topped with chocolate sauce, whipped cream and maraschino cherries. She froze, dumbfounded by the sight of Margo decked out in her full cycling regalia, but only for a moment.

"Well, if it isn't Miss Congeniality," Kathy said dismissively as she swept past Margo and continued toward Sam with the tray of ice cream.

"Where's Tara? I know she came in here with two women. I saw Tara get out of their car at the library and now that same car's in your parking lot."

Kathy stopped short of Sam's booth, put the tray down on an empty table and turned to Margo, hands on her hips, and beamed a supercilious smile. "Nice to see you too. Yes, it has been a long time. My goodness, has it been two years? Time sure flies, doesn't it?"

"Cut the crap, Kathy. I just want my daughter."

"Excuse me, it's not Miss Congeniality, it's Mother of the Year. What do you care where Tara is? You're late for her doctor's appointment? Her ballet lesson? What? What business do you think you have with that child?"

Sam had counted on the bikers coming in, finding seats, and reading the menu while she surreptitiously paid the waitress and made her get away. Now she was trapped. She eyed the sundaes melting on the table and realized she could no longer simply pay the bill and slip out unnoticed. She stood up slowly, her heart pounding so hard she held her sweater against her chest to muffle the sound, and attempted to walk nonchalantly toward the ladies room. If she could just make it to the back door, she'd make a run for it.

Without a word passing between them, Kathy pivoted to the right and stepped closer to Margo, obstructing her view of the young woman trying to walk nonchalantly toward the exit, her eyes riveted on the ground.

"Hey, you. Where are you going? Don't you want your ice cream?" Despite Kathy's best efforts, Margo had spotted her. Pretending not to hear, Sam continued heading toward the back door, but Margo moved faster and had longer legs. "Wait a minute; I need to talk to you." A wall of black leather suddenly stood between Sam and the parking lot. Sam's gaze rose slowly from Margo's black buckled boots, to her black leather chaps, past a black jacket spiked with metal zippers, to a wide, open face unexpectedly lit by Tara's blue eyes, and a complexion like roses on porcelain china.

"I'm sorry, I've got to go," Sam sputtered. Margo didn't move. "I can't talk now; I'm late for an appointment." Burning with fear and shame for telling such an obvious lie, Sam tried walking around Margo, but found her path blocked again. "Really, I've got to go. I don't know who you are and I've got an appointment." Sam barely kept her voice from shaking.

"Well, I think I know who you are. You're one of the women who came in here with Tara, aren't you? You don't know me, but I'm Tara's mother and I want to see my daughter. Kathy, tell her I'm Tara's mother and that I'm entitled to see my daughter."

"You're a mother all right, but I don't know that you're entitled to anything." Kathy leaned forward with her feet spread apart like someone looking for a fight.

"That's not true; I'm legally and morally entitled to see my own daughter. Please, just tell me where Tara is." Margo lowered her voice, "I've come a long way and I'm not leaving without her. I really need to see my daughter."

Sam tried sounding conciliatory, "Why don't you just contact Jerry and set up an appointment to see her? I can't make those sorts of decisions. I'm just the babysitter."

"And I'm the goddamned mother and I want to know where the Hell my daughter is." Margo turned the volume back up. "I know she came in here with you and some old lady. Now, where the fuck is she?" Margo's complexion was undergoing a transformation from petal pink to fire engine red. The few customers seated in the restaurant hunkered down in their seats, trying to become invisible.

Sheila's face suddenly appeared at the back door. She stood outside, looking through the glass, apparently deciding whether to jump into the fray or hightail it back to the car. Sam sent her a silent message with her eyes, "Go, go," they begged Sheila. "Take Tara and go home."

But the message must have zinged past her head and evaporated in the hot air rising from the asphalt parking lot, because a moment later Sheila bustled through the door and grabbed Sam by the elbow. "Why there you are. What's been keeping you? Come on now, we're running late." She pulled on Sam's arm and began dragging her toward the door.

"Cut the shit. Where's my kid? Where's Tara?" Margo was pacing in circles, swinging her arms, and scaring Sam half to death.

Sheila stopped tugging at Sam and turned to stare coldly at Margo, "I'm sure I don't know. But if your child is missing, why don't you call the sheriff's office?"

"Bitch!" Margo ran full tilt toward the two women who jumped out of her way only to see her fly past them and out the back door. The bowlegged biker, who'd been standing like a statue up to this point, unfolded his arms and sauntered out slowly behind her. They felt a split second of relief as they found themselves alone in the restaurant, but their calm was quickly shattered by the sound of a car door slamming. The women looked at one another in alarm, then Sam, Sheila, and Kathy all raced for the parking lot. They arrived just in time to see Margo pulling Tara from Sheila's Bonneville.

The child was clinging to Margo's neck, her face buried in her mother's hair. Sam watched, her guts twisted in a complex maze of emotions, as Margo sat on the hood of Sheila's car, rocking Tara in her arms while the child heaved and gurgled and yelped her grief and anger and happiness. Sam hadn't imagined that Tara would recognize her mother after all this time.

No one moved for ten long minutes as Margo and Tara clung to one another, staring into each other's eyes, the child's red curls intermingled with her mother's. A few customers stuck their heads out hoping to catch a cat fight in the parking lot. Instead they saw three women and a man standing silently, a respectful distance from the foul mouthed woman who was covering a small girl with hugs and kisses. They had no idea what had happened, but they could feel the air crackle with high-voltage emotional energy. The onlookers stood watching a moment then slipped back inside to finish their burgers and fries.

When Tara had finally cried herself out, Sheila stepped forward and said quietly, "Okay, you've seen her. Now it's time for everyone to go home." She reached out her arms to take the child, but Margo pulled back, hugging Tara more closely.

"You have to let her go, Margo," Sheila said more firmly.

"Like Hell I do, she's my daughter." Margo didn't raise her voice, but she gave no hint of relenting. Her biking companion moved closer and stood beside her, his hand on her shoulder. Margo looked at him beatifically, Madonna of the Lighthouse.

"What's your plan? Do you think you can just throw Tara onto the back of one of those motorcycles and ride off with her?" Sheila was trying to lift Tara from Margo's arms but the two were clamped together so tightly that she didn't have a prayer.

"Maybe. You know kids can ride on motorcycles. Do you want to go for a ride, baby?" Margo pointed at her bike then at Tara then back to the bike, then pantomimed holding the handle bars with

a manic, "vroom, vroom" look on her face. Tara smiled and nodded, her eyes wide with anticipation.

"That's it. You're crazy. Sam, call the police." Sheila still had
hold of Tara even as Margo stood up and headed for her bike with
the result that Sheila was jogging along beside them, hanging on to
Tara's little legs.

"Where's a payphone? I don't have any change." Sam was
rummaging through her purse for a quarter. "Kathy, is there a phone
I can use in the restaurant? Kathy?" Sam looked around for the waitress, but Kathy had disappeared. Panicked, Sam raced back toward
the restaurant calling over her shoulder, "Don't let them take Tara.
Hang on to her until I get back." Sam ran back toward the building
and was about to open the door when a red Vega emerged from
behind the building, cut across the lot, and stopped dead in front of
the motorcycles, blocking them against the building. Kathy jumped
out, grinning with satisfaction at her little maneuver. "You're not taking Tara anywhere. She belongs with the people who take care of
her. This car isn't moving until you hand her back to Sam and this
lady here."

"For God's sake, Kathy, did you really think I was going to go
roaring off with Tara on the back of a bike? Do you seriously think
I'm that crazy?" Margo seemed genuinely insulted. "You really don't
know me, do you?"

"I know that I wouldn't trust you to look after a geranium, much
less this child. Why don't you hand Tara back to this nice lady, put your
ass back on that bike and just disappear like you did last time."

"Excuse me? I could swear you were the one arrested for
possession and driving under the influence. And you sure look like
the broad with more hair than brains who collapsed in tears on my
living room sofa because, 'Oh my God I think I'm pregnant and I
don't know who the father is.' Or am I confused? Maybe that was
some other whoring little..."

"Stop that. Stop screaming and using language like that in front
of this child. Can't you see you're scaring her? What's the matter with
you two?" Sheila was rubbing Tara's back and patting one of the
small legs that dangled from Margo's arms.

"Hey, I was only trying to help. If you want, I'll just move my
car and she can take the kid back to her commune or wherever she's
living these days." Kathy opened her car door, as a demonstration of
her willingness to back off, if her services were no longer required.

"Wouldn't it be just peachy keen if we had to worry about
Tara picking up my bad language? I mean I'd love to hear her say,

'Go fuck yourself.' That would be the happiest day of my life, but she can't hear, so don't worry about it. Also, I only lived on a commune for maybe two months. I have a regular apartment, I make decent money, I'm not on drugs, I don't drink, and I want my daughter. What's so hard to understand about that?" Margo was still holding Tara, kissing her hair and hugging her when she wasn't throwing barbs and curses at the women gathered around her. Tara began to struggle to be let down. She wanted her ride on the motorcycle.

"Really? You're not on drugs? Since when?" Kathy turned to Sheila, "Back in high school Margo was always what you'd call a chemistry major."

"She couldn't have been a chemistry major. They don't have majors in high school." The conversation had taken a sharp turn and Sheila had fallen off.

Sam watched and listened from a safe distance. There no longer seemed to be any urgency about calling the police. Clearly, Margo and the biker weren't going anywhere while their motorcycles were blocked by Kathy's car. Besides, Sam didn't want to let Tara out of her sight, even if she was intimidated by her big, brash, beautiful, foul-mouthed mother.

"Be careful now, hold on to her." Sheila was still hovering over Tara and barking instructions to Margo who'd placed Tara on the seat of her motorcycle as though it were a pony at the county fair. Biker boy had put his helmet on Tara's head so that almost nothing could be seen of her tiny face but a wide grin just visible under a dome of black plastic.

Things had quieted down for the moment, but Sam's nervous system was still vibrating from the screaming commotion that had just played out. She hated noise and overwrought emotion. When her parents had fought—and they'd never once used the profanity that seemed to be Margo's native tongue—Sam had fled from the house and sat in a little grassy patch behind the garage until things quieted down. She'd always given people like Margo, the rabble rousing, sex, drugs, and rock and roll crowd, a wide berth. Of course that hadn't always been easy.

Her freshman year, the student body had been feverish with anti-war sentiment that had culminated in shutting down the entire university for three days after the Kent State shooting. All discipline had broken down; the smell of pot drifted through the hallways, the cafeteria, and even the teacher's lounge. The Beatles, Dylan, Joplin, Led Zeppelin, and Pink Floyd blared from every door and window. The pill, spring, and the possibility that the world really was coming to an end had given uncensored license to carnal appetites. She remembered picking her way over bodies entwined in various stages of sexual congress as she cut across the quad to class or passing through the dorm to her room. It wasn't her scene.

Student organizers had designated her dormitory a field hospital in case the National Guard fired on protesters camped out in the administration building and hanging out the windows of the library. When a graduate student asked Sam if she knew first aid, because she might be called upon to dress wounds or administer CPR, Sam packed up her books and virtually moved into the McDonalds Restaurant a few blocks off campus.

She hadn't left in fear of physical danger, and she hadn't left because she supported the war. She'd left because she simply didn't like conflict, not personal, not political, and certainly not violent. She just wanted to study for her exams, drink coffee, enjoy the spring weather, and daydream about Ben, who'd finally asked her out. Now here she was eight years later, still cowed by the rabble rousers, still recoiling from the fray. She studied the large woman who Sheila said had a peace sign tattooed on her arm. There was no doubt about it, if Margo had been at Cornell in those days, she would have been leading the parade.

Sam looked at her watch, four o'clock. They should have left an hour ago. Tara needed to go home, to rest and recover from the emotional upheaval of the afternoon. *Grow up*, she told herself. *Do your job.* Mustering all of her strength and courage, she waded into the tight little circle of bodies surrounding Tara who was still perched on her mother's motorcycle.

A momentary détente seemed to have been reached as the entire group watched with delight as Margo's biking companion made quarters magically appear from behind Tara's ears, and then just as magically, made them disappear again. He gave Tara one to hold, but when she opened her palm it was gone, only to reappear a moment later in Margo's hand. Sam stood watching just outside the circle, trying to figure out the most painless way to extract a pearl from an oyster. She stared at Margo, trying to read what made her tick. *If she just wants to visit Tara, why not phone Jerry and make a date to see her like a normal person? If she wants to kidnap Tara, why show up on motorcycles? Why create all this havoc and commotion? What does she want? What is she really after?*

"You used to have a little transistor radio didn't you?" Sam had found the courage to address Margo directly.

"Everyone used to have a transistor radio. What about it?" Margo was helping Tara down off the bike.

"Tara found one in the woods and she takes it with her almost everywhere. She thinks it's yours. At least we think she thinks it's yours."

Margo's face lit up with an unguarded expression of delight. "We used to listen to a transistor radio when she was little. I'd put one side of the headset in my ear and one side in hers and I'd hold her and we'd dance together." Margo took Tara's hand and held it firmly in her own.

Sam cocked her head to one side, "But she's deaf."

"Yeah, well, we didn't know it then." Margo was glowing, "When she got bigger, I'd play my tapes and we'd dance around. She used to crack me up, imitating all my moves."

Sam had to bite her tongue to keep from asking, "So why did you leave? What made you do it?" Instead, she said, "Tara seemed very happy to see you, but she needs to go home now. I think all this must have exhausted her. Do you plan on being in Kleiner long?" Sam offered her most charming, least threatening smile.

"As long as it takes. You can tell Jerry I'll be here as long as it takes. Nice meeting you." She bent down and gave Tara another long hug and a kiss, but didn't put up a fight when Sheila led her back to the car. "Hey, Kathy, you can move that junker now, Tara's going back home to her daddy."

Kathy was standing next to the car with her hand on her hip, "You know, I think the car just ran out of gas. Maybe if you paid me back the two hundred bucks you owe me I could get it moving again. What do you think?"

Margo didn't say a word; she turned to her partner and performed an intricate series of quick, graceful hand gestures, her face alive with expression. He looked at her quizzically, and then gestured back. Margo nodded, signing back to him. He pulled two hundred dollar bills out of his wallet and placed them in Kathy's outstretched hand.

"Thanks," she said staring at Margo, and then at the money.

"Yaaw Wekhum," said the deaf biker.

CHAPTER 9

The whir of something mechanical, a drill or a saw, was coming from the barn. Billy was working on his tractor and his delinquent grandson was probably helping him. Her home had been invaded by people constantly going in and out: painting, puttering, repairing, installing. It was ridiculous. She wouldn't care if the whole house came crashing down on her head as long as everyone just left her alone. The end of May had arrived sooner than she'd expected. She didn't feel ready to go home, but she'd promised her parents that she'd visit them. Besides, why not go back to Cleveland for a few days? It wasn't as though there was any peace and quiet in the country.

Sam threw two pair of pants, a sweatshirt, T-shirts, and toiletries into the old duffel bag she'd used since she was a kid. It was an ordinary green army surplus bag that had taken her to camp when she was twelve and then gone on with her to college. She stared at it sitting on her unmade bed. The canvas was a bit scuffed, but it hadn't faded much. It was the same bag filled with basically the same stuff she'd taken home on school vacations, as though nothing had happened, as though nothing meant anything at all.

Sam mentally cringed as she visualized carrying the bag into her old bedroom and plopping it onto the Mexican Serape that had served as her bedspread since an eighth grade trip to Acapulco. She could see herself folding her clothes into the maple chest that was part of her childhood bedroom, the initials of a high school crush still engraved inside the top drawer. Then, already feeling as though she were fourteen again, she'd go downstairs to find her parents waiting in the kitchen with a plate of sugar cookies from Hough Bakery.

"Isn't this lovely," she could see her mother saying with a smile as she poured herself a cup of coffee. "Here we are, all together again, just like old times. Tell me, dear, what do you plan to do now?"

It was too much. She couldn't bear it, and collapsed on her bed and stared out the window. There was no way she was going back to Cleveland as if nothing had changed, as though she were still the innocent child who'd left home eight and a half long years ago.

Her sewing basket lay open on the floor beside her bed. She pulled a pair of eight inch sheers from the jumble of spools and tangled thread. They were stainless steel and razor sharp. Standing in front of the mirror she raised them to just below her ears.

When Sheila came to drive her to the bus station at a little past ten, Sam was waiting outside, looking drawn and jittery as though she hadn't slept much the night before. The look on Sheila's face as Sam opened the car door didn't make her feel any better.

"My God, what have you done to your hair?" she asked, gaping at Sam's appearance.

"I cut it." Sam was in no mood for long narratives.

"I can see you cut it. What did you use, a lawn mower?" Sheila reached out to touch the ragged bangs hanging limply across Sam's forehead.

Sam jerked her head away, "I know how it looks. I'll get someone to fix it when I'm in Cleveland."

"We have beauticians here, you know. I would have been happy to take you for a haircut." Sheila was shaking her head as she stared at Sam's shorn head. "You look about twelve with your hair like that."

"Well, fantastic then, that's just the look I was going for." Sam reached forward to turn on the radio and got Tammy Wynette, her voice full of tears. Sam wasn't in the mood. She flipped the dial and got one of the Jesus stations, tried again and got a local announcer inviting her to the grand opening of a Super Duper on Fluvanna Street in Jamestown. She clicked the radio off. "At least they have decent radio in Cleveland."

"What's wrong with our radio stations? We have great stations here, in fact on good days I can pick up channels all the way from Buffalo." Sheila knit her brow and looked worried. "Once you feel better and start going out more you'll remember what a great place this is. You were happy here for a long time, Samantha. You could be happy here again."

"I really don't see myself being happy here, but if it's of any comfort to you, I don't think I'd be any happier in Cleveland. I guess it doesn't much matter where I am at this point." Sam turned her face to the window. She didn't want a few stupid tears to unleash a flood of sympathy and advice from her mother-in-law.

"Well, if it doesn't matter to you, why not stay here and make me happy? You know I love you like a daughter, Sam." Sheila looked tired. She'd stopped dying her hair after Ben died and she looked a little older and grayer every time Sam saw her. She ought to be kinder to Sheila; Sheila was certainly good to her.

"I'm only going to be gone a week." Sam was surreptitiously wiping her wet cheeks on the shoulder of her windbreaker. "And don't forget to feed the cat. He gets a bowl of dry kibble and a couple tablespoons of canned food every morning. If you have the time, stay and visit with him awhile, he gets lonely."

"I know how that is." Sheila set her jaw and concentrated on the road until they arrived at the Jamestown bus station. The station consisted of two benches and a wooden sign that listed the schedule and prices. It hadn't been changed in awhile so most of the information was out of date, but Sam had called ahead and knew her bus was supposed to arrive in fifteen minutes. She leaned over and gave Sheila a kiss on her cheek, "Don't forget to pick me up next Saturday. It's a long walk home."

"I won't forget. Give your parents my best. Call if you have a change of plans."

"There won't be any change of plans." Sam gave Sheila another quick kiss, carried her duffel bag to one of the vacant benches, pulled a paperback from her purse, then settled down to wait for the bus.

The trip that had taken about two hours when she and Ben had driven in their own car, now took four hours on the Greyhound since it made stops in Erie, Conneaut, Ashtabula, Geneva, and Painesville before rolling into the Cleveland terminal. She sat with her eyes glued to the window, barely glancing at the succession of passengers who occupied the seat beside her. There was something soothing about feeling anonymous and invisible as she watched the flat, monotonous fields and strip malls, warehouses and parking lots come and go as the bus sped down Interstate 90. Lunch had consisted of a small bag of chips from a vending machine in Ashtabula, but Sam felt more nauseous than hungry as she stepped off the bus.

Entering the station was like stepping into a black and white movie, something Deco from the thirties. Wooden benches were lined against walls of no discernible color. Fluorescent lights hung from the ceiling overexposing the scene, making the weary people who slouched and shuffled across the scuffed tile floor seem pale and insubstantial.

Sounds reverberated against the room's hard surfaces and Sam's head began to throb. The building smelled of urine, tobacco, old magazines, hot nuts and stale coffee. She clutched her duffle bag with both hands and squinted across the terminal looking for her father. When he didn't appear, she found a seat at the far end of one of the wooden benches and sat down, her bag safely on her lap.

She noticed a tall, lanky man in an oversized suit who appeared to be working the room, approaching each traveler in turn. At first Sam thought he might be an employee of the bus company, but she quickly ascertained from the icy stares and shaking heads that he was some sort of beggar. She ducked her head and pretended to search for something inside her bag, hoping he would pass by without noticing her. Instead, he headed straight in her direction. He smiled an engaging smile as he pushed a small card into her hand. It read, "I am a deaf and mute. Your purchase of this card will help to support me and my family. Any amount you can spare will help. May God bless you." On the back of the card was the deaf alphabet with small pictures of hands illustrating the manual sign for each letter.

What is the matter with this guy? She didn't usually stare at strangers, but he confused and upset her, and she wanted to figure him out. Her eyes did a quick inventory: probably in his mid forties, two good arms, two functional legs. He didn't appear feeble minded, although his suit was worn thin and a size too big. Her heart contracted, thinking of Tara. She refused to believe that this was all the future held for her. There had to be jobs that didn't require hearing. She couldn't be sure, but she had a feeling this guy was a con. *Why can't a strong, healthy man be productive and self-sufficient even if he can't hear?* Despite that, she wanted the little card with the deaf alphabet. She dug a quarter out of her wallet and handed it to him. He smiled his thanks and moved on to pester a rotund black man rolling a cigarette on the other side of the bench.

By the time her father strode into the terminal looking like an emissary from a brighter Technicolor world, Sam could finger spell her entire name. As soon as she saw him waving his arms and grinning broadly, she tucked the card into the inside pocket of her purse and ran to greet him. Her father's idea of cheering someone up was to talk loudly, smile a lot, and tell jokes, so she braced herself for the onslaught.

"There's my girl. Can a father get a hug around here? Let me take that," he grabbed her duffel bag with one arm and threw the other arm around her shoulders, drawing her to him and kissing her with a loud smack. "How was the ride? We've got to get you driving again; I wouldn't like to think of you in a place like this at night."

"It was alright, there wasn't much road construction. I think we got in early."

"Your mother's got a great dinner planned. We're going to Giuseppe's for veal and pasta. They're offering a deal where you can mix and match any veal and pasta dish for eight dollars. How's that sound?"

"Honestly? I just want to go home and chill out. Could we just make sandwiches or open a can of soup or something?"

"Sure, the special runs all week. Maybe we can go tomorrow. Say, how many real men does it take to change a light bulb?"

"Oh, my God, light bulb jokes?" Sam grimaced, both appalled and amused. For a middle-aged doctor with Ivy League credentials her father could be such a child.

A low throaty chuckle made the arm he'd thrown across her shoulders shake. "None. Real men aren't afraid of the dark." Sam smiled indulgently, the joke wasn't even funny. "Okay, I've got another one. How many librarians does it take to screw in a light bulb?"

"I don't know, Dad. How many librarians does it take to screw in a light bulb?"

Her dad answered in a high falsetto, batting his lashes, "I don't know, sir, but I can look it up for you." Sam rolled her eyes and leaned into him as they walked toward the new Lincoln Town Car parked by a meter two blocks away.

By the time they'd pulled into the familiar drive on Morrison Court Sam had begun to relax and was telling her dad about the renovations to her own house. She was explaining about the problem of finding irregular sized windows to fit the old window frames as they walked in the door. Her mother was sitting on the leather sofa in the living room, eyeglasses pushed up on top of her head, a pen in one hand and a sheaf of paper in the other. She threw them down on the coffee table as soon as she saw Sam. "My God, where did you get that haircut?" She gave Sam a big hug then drew back to assess the damage. "Whoever did this to you? They should be tried for assault."

Her father looked at her, noticing her hair for the first time, "Your hair used to be a lot longer, didn't it? I think you look cute with short hair."

"Lloyd, for heaven's sake, this isn't short hair it's...the Texas Chainsaw Massacre. I don't know if there's enough here for Richard to work with." She ran her fingers through what was left of Sam's long, straight, chestnut colored hair. "I'm calling Richard and we'll see if he can fit you in as an emergency first thing tomorrow. You'll have to go by yourself. I'm at the clinic in the morning and I'm booked solid."

Sam nodded her agreement. Cutting her own hair had been a bad idea. She knew she looked awful, but at least no one would mistake her for the long-haired flower child who'd gone off to college without an inkling about the dark places love could take you. Her mother was still talking, but Sam had momentarily tuned her out, so she was surprised when she heard her mother say, "Sam, I asked if you could be ready by eight?"

Sam tried to cover her momentary lapse, "For the haircut tomorrow? That's awfully early."

"No tonight—for Giuseppe's. We have eight o'clock reservations. Dad says you're tired, but you could take a nap. I don't think we can get another reservation this week. They're having their veal and pasta special and they're all booked up."

"I'm not that hungry and I feel tired and kind of woozy from the bus trip. Could we just eat in tonight?" Sam was dreaming of a shower, her nightgown and her bed even though it was only four in the afternoon.

"You always loved Giuseppe's and you'll perk up in a few hours. I say, let's go. I want to celebrate having you back home." Her mother didn't like having her plans changed.

"Sure, that would be fine," Sam acquiesced. It was too early in the visit to start going head-to-head with her mother and she didn't have the will or the energy for a battle.

"I have a beautiful Courreges scarf you can tie around your head like a turban. That should cover most of the damage, now go take a nap." She kissed Sam on the cheek and pointed her in the direction of the stairs. "I have to finish rewriting my bit for a study we're submitting to the *Journal of the American Medical Association*. I haven't had my name on a paper since I collaborated with the Gensen group seven or eight years ago. I'll tell you all about it at supper, very exciting stuff."

Sam picked up her bag and headed for her room.

Her mother was right. By eight o'clock she was hungry and looking forward to veal piccata and penne pasta with creamy vodka sauce. Giuseppe's was a special occasion restaurant that demanded a level of clothing she hadn't stuffed into her duffel bag, so Sam found herself wearing a black midi skirt borrowed from her mother and a white cotton blouse that had been left in her closet when she packed for college. The Courreges scarf was such a disaster that her mother had relented, admitting that Sam's hair was less conspicuous than the jury-rigged turban. Ultimately, she was seated at Giuseppe's staring across a candle lit table at her mother and father, her hair chopped to pieces and sporting the blouse from her high school uniform.

"You've lost weight, Sweetheart. What have you been eating? Or rather, what haven't you been eating? I can't wait to put a good meal into you."

This was new. Sam's mother, who could still wear the Balenciaga sundress she'd taken to the Costa del Sol on her honeymoon, had always worried about Sam's weight. "A moment on the lips, a lifetime on the hips," had been her mantra—and now she wanted her daughter to eat more? Sam wondered if she looked even worse than she imagined.

Her mother was effortlessly elegant, as always. Her thick black hair was lightly streaked with silver that she never thought of coloring. It had been cut and feathered into a modified shag that softened her strong chin and aquiline nose. Sam resembled her father, with his straight brown hair, green eyes and pale skin that turned lobster red if he played golf or sat by the pool too long.

"I eat three meals a day. I'm fine." Sam buttered a warm roll and took a big bite. "I don't cook much, but I eat."

"Good, I hope you do. When you've suffered an emotional trauma, you need to take extra good care of your body." Her mother was giving her a clinical once over and Sam could tell that she didn't like what she saw.

"Are you getting out? Seeing friends? Exercising? I never feel as though I'm getting the whole story when we talk on the phone." Great, her mother was going for a full case history and medical workup.

"I'm doing the best I can, alright? I mean, what do you expect me to be doing? I'm breathing. That feels like a real accomplishment some days."

"Maybe you should talk to someone." Sam's mother had been making the same pitch since the accident, but now Sam could see the lines of pain and worry in her face. With a pang of guilt, Sam found she didn't care. What made everyone else think they knew how she felt and what she needed?

"I don't want to talk to anyone. I just want to be left alone to work things out by myself. Do you really think some shrink could make it better? Do you really think a little mental tune-up would get me out of the shop and back on the road?" The words sounded sharper than she'd intended, but the small whiney protestations she'd been making over the past few months hadn't done the job.

Her father's head was bobbing in the affirmative, "Yes, that's exactly what I think a therapist could do. I think he'd help you get over your driving phobia for starters." The waiter brought their salads and the three of them sat silently with fixed, bland expressions on their faces until he was out of earshot.

"I do not have a driving phobia. I'll drive again when there's somewhere I want to go."

Sam was shaking olive oil from a cruet over her mixed greens and speaking in a lowered voice through clenched teeth.

"They probably don't have real therapists in a town like Kleiner. Please, move back to Cleveland where there are people who love you and some of the best doctors in the world." Her mother actually looked as though she might cry. "It just doesn't make sense for you to be all alone in the middle of nowhere at a time like this."

Sam put down her fork. She was beginning to lose her appetite. "Can we please change the subject? I thought you were going to tell me about the study you're getting published. Wouldn't you rather talk about that?"

"Okay, but the subject is not closed." Her mother took a sip of the Chianti they'd ordered for the table. "Oh, and you're going to have to live with that haircut for another three days. Tomorrow's Saturday so Richard's booked solid and the salon is closed on Monday. He doesn't have an opening until Tuesday morning."

"Got it, Tuesday morning, now tell me about your research."

"Well, it's fascinating really; we're studying the ototoxicity of various classes of myacins on fetal development." Her mother leaned forward, her face lit by the passion she always brought to her work. Sam smiled back encouragingly; it was so easy to distract her mother with any question related to medicine. "An ototoxin is any chemical that causes deafness or hearing loss. We've known for a long time that drugs like neomycin, and quinine and streptomycin are ototoxic to adults, but there hasn't been much work done on what those drugs do to a fetus *in utero*."

Sam looked up, suddenly interested in earnest. "So, if a mother takes the wrong drugs while she's pregnant her baby might be born deaf?"

"Well, that's what we wanted to find out. As I said, there aren't many studies addressing the issue so the field is wide open. To answer your question—and you're hearing this pre-publication—the old placental barrier concept seems to be a fallacy." Her mother glowed with the flush of success. "With few exceptions, if a drug is in the mother's system, it's going to show up in the baby's." Her mother looked so pleased with herself that Sam thought she might take a victory lap around the restaurant.

Sam nodded, "Poor babies."

"Exactly. Now we're trying to pinpoint the stage of development when the fetus is most vulnerable. It looks as though the earlier the exposure the more harm, since the fetus can't cleanse toxins from its system until its liver and kidneys are up and running."

Sam's dad hadn't participated in the study, but he'd read it over more than once so he chimed in, "But even in the last trimester, it turns out that a dose that's safe for the mother can still be ototoxic to the fetus."

Her mother sighed and nodded. "That's exactly right. We were looking at streptomycin, in particular, hoping to find a window of opportunity when it could be safely prescribed to pregnant women. It's a good drug; unfortunately, I don't think anyone's going to be prescribing it to pregnant women from now on without extreme cause."

"Do you see a lot of deaf babies in your practice?" Sam wanted to know.

"There's been a rubella epidemic, so I see a lot of deaf babies, but they're mostly the victims of German measles. Very few cases are related to the use of streptomycin. That's fairly rare."

"But it could be from other drugs: acid, speed, meth, dex, all that stuff?" Sam could feel her jaw clench. She knew she was overreacting.

"Since when did you become a walking pharmacopeia of controlled substances?" Her father studied her with a look that was not entirely amused.

"Dad, I just want to know if those kinds of drugs can make a baby lose its hearing. My interest is purely scientific."

Her mother responded, "As I said, this is a new field. Our study only looked at streptomycin, but it's certainly possible that some of those other drugs might affect aural development." The waiter, dressed in black pants, a tuxedo shirt and bow tie, cleared the salad plates as her mother talked.

Sam was appalled to find her eyes tearing up again. *Why can't I get through a simple conversation without being overcome by emotion?* She excused herself to the ladies' room where she splashed water on her face. She leaned forward, staring into the sink to avoid catching sight of herself in the mirror. *It isn't fair.* She'd taken her vitamins, eaten her vegetables, gotten enough sleep, and her beautiful, perfect baby had died anyway– while women like Margo who used all kinds of shit, didn't give a damn, and messed their kids up, still had their children. *It doesn't make any sense. Is God crazy?* Even as she washed the tears from her eyes, Sam had the sense that her logic might be a bit askew, but her feelings were clear. She felt cheated, betrayed, alone and adrift. Cupping a drink of cool water in her hands, she took a series of gulps, dried her face with a paper towel, and then went back to her parents and the veal piccata.

CHAPTER 10

It was almost ten o'clock when Sam finally wandered downstairs the next morning. The house was empty since both her parents had left before sunup to do morning rounds at the hospital. Once, Sam had assumed her life would replicate her parents, but now the thought of waking before dawn to poke and probe a succession of broken and diseased bodies had lost its charm.

The coffee maker was waiting on the counter, still half full of the fresh ground coffee her mother bought from a special shop on Coventry. At home in Kleiner, Sam had mostly reverted to stirring a teaspoon of powder into a cup of hot water as though she were still in college. Brewed coffee was something else entirely. The intense aroma awakened memories of leisurely Sunday mornings with Ben, memories of their first year in the farm house when she'd boiled coffee in an aluminum pot because they didn't own a coffee maker. She remembered snuggling into his bare chest on cold mornings, the smell of coffee and toothpaste on his breath. How many times had they wound up back in bed leaving their cheese omelets and fried potatoes uneaten on the table? Sam realized she'd gotten lost in one of her staring spells again, and forced herself to focus on the immediate task of locating a mug and a slice of bread for toast.

She poured herself a cup of black coffee then sat down at the kitchen table to examine a note written in her mother's careful, undoctor-like handwriting.

Good morning Sleepyhead,

We've left you coffee and the paper. Make yourself a good breakfast then give Aunt Harriet a call. She's expecting to take you shopping and out to lunch. Tell her you want to eat at the Geranium Room, it's her favorite. Dad and I will both be home by seven. Think about where you'd like to go for dinner. Pizza? Deli? The Club? I'll give you a call this afternoon.

Love, Mom XXX

Sam found the *Cleveland Plain Dealer* on top of the bookcase in the hall and settled down to enjoy a leisurely morning, but she hadn't gotten through Dear Abby and the comics when the phone rang.

"Aunt Harriet? I was going to call as soon as I finished my coffee. Yes, yes, I'm looking forward to seeing you too. No way! I can't be ready that fast. Look, I'd love to see you but I just woke up. I'm still working on breakfast, and there's nothing I need to shop for anyway. Why don't we just meet for a cup of tea at the Geranium Room? No, really, I don't need a thing. That is so sweet of you, but I don't need a pant suit. Nope, I've got enough shoes. Hey, if you really want to buy me a gift, how about some art supplies? I just found a box with all my old stuff and most of the paint is dried out and the brushes are stiff and balding. What?" Sam found herself giggling uncontrollably for the first time in ages. "Aunt Harriet, you didn't just say that. Oh, my God, stiff and balding? Please, I don't want to hear another word about the old geezers who are asking you out."

It turned out that Aunt Harriet didn't want tea at the Geranium Room after all. She picked Sam up at four o'clock and drove directly to the Lion's Den to get a head start on the cocktail hour. The restaurant was dark and her eyes hadn't quite adjusted, but she could see that the room hadn't been redecorated since the fifties. The Lion's Den had been an odd choice. It catered to businessmen who wanted a place to escape the office for a quick meal and a stiff drink, not to ladies who lunch. Harriet was leaning back in her chair, appraising Sam through squinty eyes. "You don't have to wait for Richard. I know a place that's open until eight tonight. They could see you right now. Whatever made you think you could cut your own hair?"

"Please, Aunt Harriet, let's just forget about it. I can wait another couple of days." *Why is everyone so involved with my hair? It's my own goddamn hair after all.*

"Pay attention, I'm telling you something important." Sam's mind had wandered off again and Aunt Harriet was having none of it. She was using the imperious tone that had frightened her students at the medical school. "You're in a great deal of pain at the moment, but you are going to survive." Sam had heard this speech before. It was the essence of virtually every condolence call she'd received. She picked the orange slice out of her whiskey sour before taking a long swig of the drink. It was so sweet she could feel the enamel on her teeth recoil. "I've seen people live through horrendous losses. It's a mystery how they do it, but they usually do." Aunt Harriet was warming up for a long lecture. "Let me tell you a story," she began. Sam snuck a peek at her watch, barely four thirty. She might try an actual martini next.

"As you probably know, my husband died in the flu epidemic of 1918. The disease was particularly hard on the poor souls living in slums and tenements, but of course no one was immune. I remember seeing quarantine notices on some of the finest houses in the city, but by and large our circle escaped unscathed. What I'm saying is that Edgar had survived the war, and he probably would have survived the epidemic, if he hadn't been a doctor.

"He'd just returned from a field hospital in France where he'd treated men who'd lost their limbs, lost their senses, lost their lives. In those days, men never talked about the war or what they'd seen, at least not to the women, so I never heard the whole story, but it must have been horrific. I remember how pale and thin he looked the day we met him at the train station. Frankly, I think he was a bit shell shocked, but that didn't matter. We had one week, that's all the army gave us once he got back to the States. He was ordered to report to the hospital at Fort Devens. The army was that desperate for doctors. Our boys were dropping faster from influenza than they had in combat. Edgar was a good soldier; he didn't even blink. He just put his uniform back on, picked up his little black bag, and marched into battle with this new enemy."

Harriet leaned forward and lowered her voice, "I've never told this to a living soul, but the night before he left I had a dream. It was actually September and hot, but in my dream it was snowing. I was dressed in a white nightgown with calla lilies in my hair. I was standing outside a stone cottage waving at a figure receding in the distance. Cold wind and snow were swirling around my gown and Edgar, I knew it was Edgar, was disappearing into the blizzard." Aunt Harriet smiled a bit sheepishly. "In the dream, he looked just like Charlie Chaplin with a funny little hat and a bow legged walk and he was swinging a cane. I just kept waving and waving, and he kept walking away, getting smaller and smaller until he disappeared. That's all I remember, but I knew I'd never see him again."

Aunt Harriet was a great storyteller. If she hadn't become a doctor she could have gone on the stage. She certainly had a flare for the dramatic. Sam raised her eyebrows, "You had a prophetic dream? I thought scientists didn't believe in that sort of thing."

"That's why I never told anyone. They'd think I'd lost my marbles, but it's the truth. You don't forget a dream like that."

"Did you try to stop him?"

"I did. But the screams and histrionics of his young bride made no difference—and he understood what he was doing. Doctors understood the basics of germ theory. They were already growing the deadly bacilli in their Petri dishes, but treatment was another matter. Are you paying attention? I want you to hear this."

Sam nodded that yes, she was listening. Her aunt continued, "Even with no cure to offer, he battled the fevers and pain with the few drugs doctors had in their arsenal back then: aspirin, epinephrine, and salicin. It wasn't much, but he soldiered on fighting the influenza just as he'd fought the Germans. He was working sixteen hour days and still losing a hundred young men each shift. In his last letter Edgar wrote about inoculating the worst cases with antibodies from recovering victims. I didn't understand how remarkable, how advanced, that was at the time. I was only twenty-one, and an aspiring pianist. Blood and gore terrified me. I actually felt superior because I was an artist with a more refined soul. Can you imagine being such a ninny? Of course later, when I was in medical school and understood what he'd done, what he'd been part of, I realized that his was the greater soul. There now, that's what I wanted to tell you."

Sam held her glass without taking a sip, imagining her aunt as a frantic young wife trying to prevent her husband from going off to a plague ridden hospital because she'd had a portentous dream. The image was too romantic and improbable, her aunt too cynical and pragmatic, but she sure could tell a good story. Sam was pretty sure Aunt Harriet had embellished the tale a bit for effect.

"I thought it might comfort you." Harriet looked at Sam kindly, but there was something like a challenge in her gaze.

"And why would a world pandemic that killed millions of people comfort me?" Sam was full of her own sadness and couldn't imagine why her aunt wanted to burden her with more.

"Not the pandemic, dear—Edgar. The thought of Edgar has always been a comfort."

"You must have really loved him."

"Yes, I suppose so. Of course, I was very young and we were married such a short time. In retrospect, I didn't know him all that well, but I admire him to this day." Aunt Harriett finished her martini and looked around for the waiter to order a second. "Are you ready for another whiskey sour?"

"No thanks, this should hold me." Sam hadn't been serious about ordering another drink, but clearly Aunt Harriett was. *For an old lady, Harriet can sure put them away.* "And that's why you never remarried?"

"No, that is why I became a doctor. I moped around for a year or so, like another young woman I know, and then I decided that that the best way to honor Edgar would be to finish his work. Ah, thank you." She took a second martini from the waiter. "And could we have a couple shrimp cocktails? You do like shrimp, don't you Samantha?"

Sam nodded her assent, "You became a doctor to complete Edgar's work?"

"Well, that was the idea at the time. I was going to find a vaccine for Spanish flu and complete all the things that Edgar meant to do. Of course, that was ridiculous. Edgar was dead and no one could change that or live his life for him. But, as it turned out, medicine became my life. That was the gift he left me."

"Are you telling me that I should become a teacher because that's what Ben did?"

"No, not necessarily. I'm just saying that Ben left you gifts, and that you can't enjoy them locked away by yourself."

Sam folded her cocktail napkin in half and then in half again. She'd turned all the corners inward before she realized that she was making an origami fortune teller. It was a game she and her friends had played in grade school. Numbers were written on each of eight folded triangles and behind the numbers phrases like *he loves you, don't do it, don't wait, old maid.* She crumpled up the paper and tossed it into the ashtray.

"Did you ever regret not marrying again?" Sam's voice was barely more than a whisper.

"I never made a decision not to remarry; it's just that over time I lost interest in the institution. In those days a woman doctor was a freak of nature, a two-headed dog. I had to work night and day to prove myself. By the time your mother went to medical school things were just starting to change. Even now the female students get a bum deal." Harriet was fishing around in her shrimp cocktail, but apparently not finding what she was looking for. "I think there's time for one more round before we head home. What'll it be?"

"Aunt Harriet, you're driving. I think you've had enough." Sam was skittish enough about cars without an inebriated chauffeur.

"I'll be fine. You know for such a young woman you're a bit of a tightass." Harriet pushed the mostly uneaten shrimp toward Sam. "Do you want this? I'm not that hungry."

"No, thanks. Mom and Dad are taking me out to dinner, so I'd better save my appetite." Sam watched as Harriet began to work on her third martini. "Shouldn't you be putting something in your stomach besides alcohol?"

"Don't worry about me." She pulled the olive out of her glass and waved it around on the tip of its little plastic sword before popping it in her mouth. "Olives are vegetables. These are very nutritious." Harriet was having a wonderful time pulling Sam's chain.

Sam wasn't amused. There was nothing funny about a car wreck. "I'm not getting into the car with you if you have another drink."

"You're right. I've had too much to drink. Would you mind driving home? It's only a couple of miles." Harriet purred over her martini glass.

Why that sly fox, Sam thought to herself. *This whole martini thing has been an act to trick me into driving.*

Sam was not getting behind the wheel of a car, and she was not subjecting herself to a white knuckle ride home. She ignored Harriet's question as she calculated her options. "So, you gave up everything for your career?"

"I gave up nothing. I loved what I was doing. I had exciting work, friends, travel, and men. I did not live without men, you know; I just lived without their laundry." *Whoa, now this is a three martini confession.* Sam remembered overhearing gossip at the club when she was younger, something about Harriet and a married man. She raised her eyebrows but held her tongue, doubting that Harriet's life decisions had been as easy as she made them out to be. After a silence that began to grow uncomfortable, Sam asked very softly, "Did you ever want children?"

"Oh, there was a time in my thirties whey my hormones were still raging that I thought I needed children. But motherhood would have meant giving up everything else that I wanted for my life. I was always close to your mother and your Uncle Allen and that's been enough for me. But Samantha," Harriet reached out and took Sam's hand and held it tightly between her gnarled fingers. "That wouldn't be enough for you. I saw you with June. I know what you have to give a child. You have the generous, unselfish nature of a born mother, and it is my sincerest hope that you eventually remarry and have another child."

Sam snatched her hand away from Aunt Harriet's. "More children? I don't want more children. I want June. You never had children so maybe you don't get it. Babies aren't interchangeable. They're not replaceable." She stood up, wanting to bolt from the table, but caught her breath, and eventually sat back down.

The outburst had taken them both by surprise. Harriet eyed Sam with a combination of sympathy and a clinical detachment born of years in medical practice. Sam reddened and grew even angrier beneath her aunt's cool gaze. She wasn't one of her patients; there was no reason for Harriet to look at her like that.

"Of course, dear, that was tactless of me," Harriet began cautiously. "We all adored June, she was just the breath of fresh air this family needed. The child was a pure joy and none of us will ever fully recover from her loss. Losing her hurt all of us, and yet we all have to go on and live the rest of our lives somehow. For me, at my age, that's not a great problem. I've made my choices, but you're still so young, barely more than a child yourself. So, the question is, what do you want? What are you going to do?"

Always the same question and she never had an answer. There was a knot in the back of Sam's neck that was making her head throb. "I'm going to go home for supper. Mom and Dad will be home soon, so I think it's time that I headed back. Thanks for the drink." Sam took one last sip of her whiskey sour, picked up her purse, and headed for the door.

"Wait a minute dear, not so fast. I need to pay the waiter." Sam turned, taking a perverse satisfaction in seeing Harriet so flustered and trying to move faster than her age and three martinis allowed.

"Take your time. I'm going to walk." Sam called back to her. "I'll probably see you at the club later in the week." Then she pushed through the tavern's heavy oak door onto the sunlit pavement leaving her aunt fumbling for her wallet.

Sam's parents were standing in the garden deciding whether or not to have the lawn service mulch the flower beds when Sam arrived home an hour later.

"Well, there you are," her mother greeted her. Aunt Harriet just called to see if you'd gotten home all right. She said you decided to walk all the way from the Lion's Den. What inspired you to hike all that way in this heat?"

"I needed the exercise." Sam sat down on the lawn and removed one of her shoes, examining a blister on her big toe.

"So, how was the shopping? Did you get to the trunk sale at Gina Benita's?"

Sam sighed, why did every conversation with her mother feel like an interrogation. "We didn't go shopping. We just stopped for martinis at The Lion's Den."

"Martinis in the middle of the afternoon? What happened to lunch and shopping?" Sam's parents exchanged a concerned glance.

"We got off to a late start and I didn't want to go shopping anyway, so we just stopped for drinks. Aunt Harriet told me a very romantic story about how her husband died of the Spanish flu."

"And just how many martinis did Aunt Harriet have? I bet it was more than one if you wouldn't get into a car with her." No wonder her mother finished first in her class. She didn't miss anything. "I'm starting to worry about your Aunt Harriet and her martinis. They had to call a cab to drive her home from the club twice last month."

"She's fine. I just wanted to walk. It's no big deal." Sam was surprised to find herself taking Aunt Harriet's side.

Sam's mother shook her head, "She was supposed to take you out for lunch. She promised to put a good meal in you."

"We had shrimp cocktails." Why did her parents think it was their business to supervise what she was eating and drinking? "In fact, I'm not hungry. I think I'll just go inside and lie down."

"But we're going to The Golden Dragon for Chinese. Mr. Han was looking forward to seeing you again. You haven't seen him since..." Her father stumbled over his unfinished sentence. "You haven't seen him in a long time."

"Go ahead without me. I'm taking a nap." Sam limped toward the house carrying her shoes.

"Do you want us to bring you some take-out?" her mother asked.

"Sure, whatever, I don't care," Sam shrugged. "Say hello to Mr. Han for me."

"Will do, and we'll bring something back in case you're hungry later. Are you sure you don't want to join us?" Her dad was clearly disappointed, but Sam didn't have the energy to sit through another meal warding off questions and enduring her parents' anxious scrutiny.

"No thanks, Dad. I'm just going to watch TV then turn in early." She was just about to step through the front door when her father called her back.

"Wait a minute. How many Chinamen does it take to change a light bulb?"

Sam paused, half in and half out of the house. "I don't know, Dad, how many?"

"Thousands, because Confucius say many hands make light work."

When Sam finally wandered downstairs in her pajamas the next morning she found coffee and the newspaper waiting, but no sweet note from her mother. She should probably call to apologize for standing them up last night, but she wasn't ready to talk to anyone yet. Talking and answering questions and being normal and sociable were hard and she was out of practice.

It was strange to think that only nineteen months ago she'd reveled in noise and activity. She remembered singing to her daughter, squabbling with her husband, gossiping with the girls at work. Now all she craved were privacy and quiet. She'd actually duck and hide if she ran into old friends on the street or at the library. People made jokes about watching the paint dry, but she could probably do that. She knew she could watch shadows moving back and forth across the floor and dust motes swimming in sunbeams for an entire afternoon because she'd done it more than once. She also knew she'd have to pull herself out of this morass. She couldn't sit around counting the squares in her linoleum floor forever.

Just as Sam was getting comfy on the sofa, the phone rang. Sighing, she put down the carton of moo goo gai pan she'd found in the refrigerator and picked up the phone. "Aunt Harriet, I'm glad you called. I wanted to apologize for walking out on you yesterday. It's just that I'm touchy around cars. Nope, I'm not doing much, I haven't even showered yet. Honest, yesterday was fine, better than fine. You don't have to get me anything, but sure I'd love some new art supplies. If Slater Graphics is still around they'd have everything I need. I could be ready in an hour. I'll get moving. Bye." Sam shoved one more mouthful of cold chicken and green peppers into her mouth, returned the box to the fridge, and then hurried upstairs to get dressed.

When Sam's parents got home later that evening they oohed and aahed over each item she pulled out of her new artist's supply chest. They examined each tube of paint, beamed over the brushes, and even asked to try out her new pastel sticks. Her parents had never taken much interest in her art before, not even when she'd won juried competitions back in high school, so Sam regarded their sudden enthusiasm with a jaundiced eye. They undoubtedly saw art as a sort of therapy. They suggested she set up the new easel and begin work while they watched, but that wasn't going to happen.

Sam packed as much as she could into her duffel bag and put the paper and canvases into the large portfolio that Aunt Harriett had generously included in her gift. There'd be plenty of time to paint when she got back home. Home? Where was that? When she'd left Kleiner she'd told Sheila she was going home for a visit, and now she was telling her parents that she would paint when she got home to Kleiner. Sam lay down on her bed and fell into a stuporous sleep that would have lasted until morning if her mother hadn't knocked on her bedroom door to say she had a visitor.

"Shit, who is it?"

"Don't talk like that. It's Ellen Berman. Come down and say hello. She's been at Brown working on a master's in Education, but she's in town visiting her parents for a few days and she wants to see you."

"Who told her I was here?" Sam was sitting on the edge of her bed still only half conscious.

"I did. I ran into her mother at the grocery and told her you'd be in this week. Don't be such a curmudgeon, Samantha. Ellen's one of your best friends. She misses you."

"Okay, I'll pull myself together." Sam's hands suddenly flew to her head. "How do I explain this? It looks like the haircut they gave Marie Antoinette on her way to the guillotine."

"She's your friend. She doesn't care about your hair. Now come on downstairs, Ellen's waiting for you."

Sam looked at herself in the mirror above her dresser. She brushed her hair back and clipped it with a pink plastic barrette that had been sitting in her dresser since she was nine years old. It didn't help. Nothing helped. She changed into a fresh T-shirt and rearranged her face into a pleasant expression. She wasn't sure the phony smile would fool Ellen, but it was the best she could do.

Ellen ran toward Samantha with open arms as she saw her coming down the stairs. Hugs and kisses were mandatory under the circumstances. Samantha braced herself for the assault. "I've been so worried about you. You got my letters didn't you? I talk to Laurel and Lizzy all the time and they always ask about you, but I never know what to tell them." Ellen was wearing a long batik skirt made of Indian cotton, an army surplus jacket and tennis shoes. Apparently word still hadn't reached Brown that the sixties were over.

"Hi, Ellen. You look great. I didn't know you were in Cleveland." Ellen did look great. The past two years had evidently been good to her. Her acne had cleared up and she'd dropped at least one dress size. Her long brown hair hung in a thick braid down her back, a style that hadn't been fashionable in the sixties and wasn't in style now. Sam was surprised to find she was genuinely glad to see her old friend. "My mom tells me you're at Brown now. Your folks must be ecstatic."

"Totally, and I mean after four years at Oberlin I needed to be in a real city. Providence is fantastic, a ton of young people and a great arts scene." Ellen took a breath and grabbed both of Sam's hands. "My God, no one's seen you in almost two years. Do you know how much we've missed you?" "We" referred to Ellen, Laurel and Lizzy. They'd dubbed themselves the Fab Fems in high school and had been inseparable until graduation scattered them across the continent. "I cried my eyes out when I heard what happened, and you were so far away and you wouldn't talk to anyone or answer my letters." As evidence, Ellen's eyes welled up and she blinked back tears as she talked. "It's so good to see you. Can I give you another hug?" Ellen flew at Sam again, wrapping her arms around her and rocking her slightly as though she were a child. Sam waited a decent interval before extricating herself from the effusive embrace.

Ellen had been a good friend in high school, bright and funny, but their paths had parted years ago. Ellen had never had a serious boyfriend, much less a husband and a daughter. Her life was still about school work and going out on dates. It was as though Ellen belonged to a younger generation that Sam couldn't quite relate to. But Ellen was right; there was no excuse for the pile of unanswered letters on her desk.

"I'm sorry. I just wasn't ready to talk to anyone. I'm still pretty much a hermit. How about some coffee? No, I remember you only drink herbal tea. I'll see if my mom has any Red Zinger." Sam headed toward the kitchen.

"Forget the Zinger, I've become a caffeine fiend. Hey, guess who Lizzy's dating?" Ellen followed Sam into the kitchen. For the next hour Sam caught up on the lives of friends and classmates she hadn't thought of in ages. It was strange to realize how little their lives had changed. It was as if their life clocks were stuck at half past high school, while hers had spun through love, marriage, motherhood, widowhood and loss. She'd lived an entire lifetime while Ellen, Laurel and Lizzie were still choosing majors and waiting for the cute guy in English Lit to ask them out. The stories about Lizzy's boyfriends and Laurel's trip to France, seemed surreal and bizarre, tales from another planet.

When Ellen finally asked what she'd been doing, Sam had an answer. She was learning the deaf alphabet because she'd gotten a job working with a deaf child. She even showed off the finger spelling she'd learned from the card she'd gotten at the bus terminal.

But when Ellen enthused, "Maybe you should go to Gallaudet. I hear they have an absolutely rad Deaf Ed program," Sam quickly put her fingers in her lap.

"No," she'd said. "I'm just working with this one little girl. It's not a career thing." Wanting to change the subject she'd added, "And I'm doing some painting again. In fact, I've converted the old barn on my property into an art studio."

"Way to go!" Ellen shot up, practically bouncing on her chair. "That's what you should be doing. You're work is awesome. Everyone thought you'd go to New York and starve in a Soho loft, and hang out with Andy Warhol and that crowd."

They did? Sam felt an electric shock run up her spine. *People really thought I'd be an artist?* She brushed Ellen's compliment off with a joke. "So what are you saying? You figured I'd have pink hair and be strung out on heroin by now?"

"No, we thought you'd be famous, that we'd be reading reviews of your work in *Mother Jones* and *Rolling Stone.*"

"Ellen, I won a few prizes in high school. I wasn't that good." But she remembered her art teacher, begging her to apply to The Rhode Island School of Design. Why hadn't she even considered the idea?

"You *were* that good. Your stuff was out of sight. I don't know why you stopped. Did you ever finish the Hart Crane illustrations of Cleveland bridges?"

"I never even started them. It was just a thought."

"Honestly Sam, you should come to Providence and look around. We have some great bridges and Brown has an absolutely awesome art program, or maybe you'd rather go to The Rhode Island School of Design. I can really see you at RISD." She pronounced it *Rizdee.* "We could get an apartment together next year. That would be so cool. You should do it."

Ellen would be a great teacher. She obviously had a talent for telling other people what to do. Her eyes were shining and she was beaming with pleasure. Sam was so horrified that she only stared back, dumbstruck. Ellen took her silence for encouragement. "I'll send you brochures and an application. Just take a look at them. My God, it would be wonderful having you in Providence."

"I don't think so," Sam finally stammered. "This wouldn't be a good time."

Undaunted, Ellen repeated her invitation as they hugged goodbye.

Sam replied, "Thanks, but like I said, I'm not up for traveling and meeting new people right now." Ellen's disappointment was palpable, so Sam added, "But let's keep in touch."

"One hundred percent." Ellen perked up immediately. And I don't care what you say; I'm sending you applications for every art program in the area."

CHAPTER 11

Aunt Harriet picked Sam up early Tuesday morning to drive her to the beauty shop.

"This is ridiculous; you should be driving me around. I'm the old lady. When are you going to start driving again?"

Sam bristled at the question. She sat in silence beside her aunt, still stinging from the rebuke, while her aunt chattered on about the Republican primary. "I just can't accept the idea of an actor running for president of the United States. TV has ruined politics. Reality and fantasy are getting blurred together in people's minds. You have to look like a movie star to get elected dog catcher these days." Sam felt herself relax. How could anyone stay angry with Aunt Harriet? By the time they arrived at Bella Donna's, she and Harriet were engaged in an animated discussion of the upcoming election.

"I'd never get elected with this haircut. That's for sure." Sam caught her reflection in the window as they entered the shop.

"Tell Richard you want a pixie cut. You'd be adorable in a pixie." Aunt Harriet was riffling through a stack of fashion magazines trying to find something to read. She finally found an old copy of *Look* and made herself comfortable in a chrome and leather chair near the reception desk.

"*Oy, Gottenyu!* What has she done to herself?" Richard raised his hands in mock horror. "Sit here. Let me look at you." He directed Sam to one of the high swivel chairs. Sam cringed as Richard ran his fingers through her shorn locks, clucking and muttering as he sized up the damage. "Thank the Lord for small mercies, you left something on top, in fact..." He eyed her critically. "Have you heard of an ice-skater named Dorothy Hamill?"

Samantha walked out of Bella Donna's an hour later with a short wedge cut with bangs that moved and bounced when she turned her head. It was only a new hairstyle, but it made her eyes look bigger and her cheekbones more pronounced.

"Richard's a genius," Aunt Harriet said, stealing glances at her as they drove home. "You're absolutely gorgeous; he's turned our duckling into a swan. We need to take you to the club and show you off. Did you bring something to wear?"

As Sam shook her head, "no," she could feel hair sway above her bare neck.

"Well then, we've got some shopping to do," Before Sam could protest that she had no interest in going to the club, Aunt Harriet had already turned down Chagrin Boulevard and set their course for Gina Benita's.

Two hours later Samantha stepped out of Harriet's car buried beneath a small mountain of bags and boxes. While Gina and Harriet conferred about her wardrobe, Samantha had allowed herself to be pushed and prodded into slacks, T-shirts, and sweaters as though she were a school girl being decked out for the new semester. The *piece de resistance* was an emerald green dress that wrapped around her hips and tied at the waist. The neckline dipped lower than Sam's usual dresses, and it hugged her waist, showing off her slim figure. Definitely not a school girl's dress, but Harriet and Gina had agreed that it was perfect, that she couldn't leave the shop without it.

Back in her room, Sam put on the new dress and studied herself in a full length mirror. She looked good, practically beautiful, but instead of giving her pleasure this unexpected loveliness made her collapse on the side of her bed with her head in her hands. *What is the point of being attractive if Ben will never lean against the door jam and whistle at me? What is the point if June will never hug my knees and say, "Pwitty mommy."*

She took off the dress, hung it on one of her mother's monogrammed hangers, and then slipped back into her jeans and tank top. The graceful silhouette of the wrap dress was visible through her open closet door. Sam stared at it as though it was someone she used to know, an old friend whose name had slipped her mind.

Sam had to snap herself out of this funk. Maybe she could call Jerry to see how he and Tara were getting on, but what business was that of hers? *Jerry's a nice guy, but is he my employer, or a real friend?* She could call Sheila, maybe ask how the cat was doing or how the renovations were progressing, but then she'd have to sound upbeat and chatty so Sheila wouldn't worry about her, but not too cheerful so she wouldn't scare Sheila into thinking that she was moving back to Cleveland. In the end, Sam got out her new art supplies and drew dresses, wild, extravagant, improbable dresses: dresses standing serenely before open windows, dresses waltzing, dresses riding bicycles, dresses preparing to dine.

"Whatever are you drawing? Why, aren't those imaginative? I don't know where you get that creativity. Not from me or your father, that's for sure." Sam had been so engrossed in her work that she hadn't heard her mother come home. She snapped the tablet shut and stood up blushing as if she'd been caught sneaking into the house past curfew.

"I was just doodling around, it's not anything,"

"Well, I'm glad to see you drawing again. People don't realize it, but the ability to draw is a real asset in medical school. I never had the skill, but doctors who do can visualize anatomy much more clearly than the rest of us. It's a real gift." Her mother took a sip from the high ball glass she was holding. It looked like a cocktail, but Sam was pretty sure it was her mother's usual tonic and lime juice.

"Why weren't you happy to see me drawing back in high school?"

"What do you mean? We always encouraged your art work. I remember you won a prize for one of your paintings." Her mother looked hurt.

"It was an important award, The Juliette Skidmore Young Artist Prize. It was a big deal, a national competition,"

"I remember. Your father and I were very proud of you."

"Yeah, right. You never even came to see the show."

"Samantha, has that been bothering you all these years? I was covering for two other doctors and working incredible hours or I would have been there. Your father went to the exhibit, and even if I never saw the show, I saw the painting and thought it was wonderful. It's still hanging in your father's office."

"Do you remember the summer after I graduated from high school? You sure didn't seem very supportive then."

"That wasn't about your art work. That was about keeping you safe. What mother would let her daughter set up an easel in the seediest part of town? I was afraid you'd get raped or murdered under one of those bridges."

"The area isn't that bad. If I'd wanted to go down there to do medical research you'd have packed my lunch."

"Please Samantha, be fair. We were very proud of you for winning that prize. You're an amazing young woman. That's why we can't bear to see you wasting all that talent."

"By which you mean talent for science and medicine."

"And art. A lot of doctors paint. Admittedly, medical students don't have much time to spare, but once you've graduated there will be plenty of time to develop your other interests."

"And by other interests you mean hobbies, don't you?"

"I don't have time to stand here debating this with you. We have reservations at the club for seven o'clock. Do you want to look through my closet for something to wear?"

"No, I have something. Aunt Harriet bought me a new dress. It's a little low cut, but I guess I'll wear it."

"Nothing was ever too low cut for Harriet in her day. She was quite the act. By the way, that haircut is spectacular. I don't know how Richard does it. He's made a new woman of you. Be downstairs by six-fifteen, we're picking up Harriet on the way." She ran her hand over Sam's hair, "If they gave Nobel Prizes for haircuts, I'd have to nominate Richard. You're absolutely transformed. Who knew my daughter was such a beauty?"

The club never changed. Every few years old carpet would be replaced with new or the chairs in the grand foyer would be reupholstered, but these minor alterations only served to maintain the illusion that the club was ageless. If her long dead great-grandfather strolled into the Mayfair Dining Room in the spring of 1976, he could sit at his favorite table by the window, order a sidecar from an obsequious black waiter, and admire the Charles Sheeler painting he'd donated in 1934, without ever suspecting that forty years had passed.

Certainly, the club had not changed in Sam's memory, and yet, entering the grand foyer that evening, nothing looked the same. The polished walnut paneling and crystal chandeliers that had always exuded elegance and comfort suddenly looked tired, dated, and quaint. The ornate furnishings and deferential staff had the air of museum pieces, relics from an age long past that the future could only gaze upon with bemused nostalgia or contempt. She followed her family down the hall, smiling and nodding at familiar faces with an odd detachment.

"Well, aren't you a sight for sore eyes? Have you still got some sugar for your Aunt Gladys?" There was nothing deferential in the enveloping hug that wrapped Samantha close. As Gladys held her tight, she whispered in Sam's ear, "We were all so sad to hear what happened; it all but broke our hearts. But you're a strong woman. You're going to be okay, you hear me? You're going to be okay."

Sam stiffened slightly and took two deep breaths, "Thank you," she gave Gladys a kiss. "I hope you're right."

"I'm right alright. Do you remember when you were on the club swim team; you must have been what, maybe nine years old? You're the girl who slammed her hand against the side of the pool and finished the race with a broken wrist. You're tough stuff."

"Thank you," Sam gave Gladys another squeeze.

Gladys didn't let Sam go, "And you're a beautiful young woman. Just look at you. I'm telling you, the good Lord's got some big plans for you."

"If he does, I haven't gotten the memo."

"God won't be sending memos, but He'll let you know. He's got his eye on you."

Sam blushed, embarrassed but touched, then hurried off to join her family.

"So, what were you and Gladys chatting about?" Sam's mother pushed her chair to the left to give Sam more room. "I bet she was giving you an earful about her granddaughter getting into the University of Chicago."

"The University of Chicago?" Sam did a double take. "No, she didn't say a word. Wow, that's news. I knew she had grandchildren, but I don't think I've ever met any of them."

"Apparently Carmen is her daughter's oldest child." Sam's father stayed current on club gossip. "She took a first in debate at the state level, has straight As, and intends to be a civil rights lawyer. How about that?"

"In another few years Gladys will be seating her own granddaughter in this dining room. Now won't that be awkward?" Aunt Harriet was grinning wickedly at the image.

"No, that would be wonderful. That's what they've been marching for." Sam was suddenly animated.

"I wouldn't be surprised if you're right. But I don't expect to see anything like that in my lifetime. The country just isn't ready for it yet." Harriet was snapping a fluorescent pink disposable lighter at a cigarette. "These little plastic things are an abomination. Does anyone have a proper lighter or a match?"

"Do we have any black members now?" Sam realized that she'd never even thought of the possibility before. "There isn't a rule against black members is there?"

"There's no rule, but new members have to be sponsored by existing members. I can only think of one time the issue ever came up. Marvin Bradley got chummy with a black dentist he met at the Play House. I think they were both on the board. Anyway, he proposed the guy for membership, but then he withdrew the application before it ever came to a vote. Hey, look at this." Sam's Dad was reading a card with the evening's specials. "They have soft shell crab tonight."

"Why did he withdraw the application?" Sam was watching Gladys help an elderly member with a walker to her seat.

"There were a couple different rumors flying around at the time." Her father continued to speak as he leaned over and lit Harriet's cigarette with the silver lighter he'd received for his fortieth birthday. "But the one I like the best is that the black dentist told Marvin, thanks but no thanks. He didn't want to hang out with a bunch of stuffy old WASPs."

"He made a terrible mistake." Harriet exhaled a cloud of smoke. "Old WASPs are a lot of fun."

"It's more likely that someone on the board read Marvin the riot act and forced him to back off." Sam's mother had been reading the menu, but she put it down now and looked around the room. "This isn't a crowd that exactly embraces change. The idea of a colored face on the golf course would be enough to make some of these old codgers hang up their clubs. They still haven't recovered from the fact that a couple Weinsteins and Shapiros made it through the front door."

"This place is a mausoleum. Why do we even belong here?"

"Because it's our mausoleum, dear, but we bequeath it to you. If you want to fill the place with—what's the polite term—minorities? You go right ahead. Your great-grandfather will be spinning in his grave, but it's going to be your club. Your generation can invite whoever it wants." Harriet raised her martini glass, "To Gladys's granddaughter."

"Well, as far as I'm concerned, if Carmen wants to join, she's in. But I wouldn't be surprised if she didn't want any part of this place. In fact, don't expect to see me here."

"Come on, where else could you get soft shell crab this early in the season?" Sam's father stuffed a large piece of pastry into his mouth. "And warm pecan rolls?"

"That black dentist was right," Sam considered the large number of elderly diners, the white haired men in navy jackets and plaid trousers, their bleached blonde wives sporting suntans and tasteful jewelry. "This place is full of stuffy old WASPs."

"Say, how many WASPs does it take to change a light bulb?" Her dad was smiling, delighted that he'd remembered another joke.

Samantha rolled her eyes. "How many?"

"Two. One to call the electrician and one to mix the martinis." Harriet raised her glass a second time, "I'll drink to that."

Sam's duffle bag, art supplies, and portfolio case were already packed and waiting by her bedroom door when the alarm woke her at eight o'clock the next morning. She threw on a pair of jeans and a

T-shirt, grabbed her things, and then ran downstairs to find her father pacing in the front hall jingling his car keys. "Come on Sweetie, your bus leaves in fifty minutes and it's a thirty minute ride."

"We're okay, I already bought my ticket." Sam raced past him into the kitchen and poured herself a glass of orange juice. "Give me a minute to chug this down and we're out of here."

"Not before I get a goodbye kiss." Her mother stood in the kitchen doorway with her arms outstretched; she was wearing an old flannel nightgown and floppy slippers. Sam gave her a quick hug and a kiss on the cheek. Her mother patted Sam affectionately on the bottom. "You look great. All you need to do is fill out that application and you can get yourself right back on track as though the last few years were just a bad dream."

Sam took a step backwards as though she'd been struck. "What? You think my marriage, my husband, and my baby were some sort of nightmare I want to forget? Well, they weren't. They were everything that meant anything to me in this life and I can't just get back on track, because I don't know where I am, much less where I'm going. You lost your grandchild. Didn't June mean anything to you?" Sam was suddenly in a rage, she couldn't stop herself. "Didn't you love your own granddaughter?"

Her mother was standing with her hand over her mouth. The cheery atmosphere had turned toxic. "I adored June. She was my beautiful little grandbaby. How could you ever think such a thing?" This early in the morning, without her make-up, Sam could see the first signs of old age in her mother's face. "Losing June broke my heart, but you're my baby too, and I'm afraid of losing you." Her mother stepped forward tentatively, reaching out to stroke Samantha's hair. "We want to see you healthy and productive and moving forward with your life. What's wrong with encouraging our daughter to finish her education?"

Sam jerked backward, beyond her mother's reach, "What's wrong is you don't just want me to finish my degree. You want me to be head of neurosurgery at some major teaching hospital, you want a Nobel Prize in Medicine."

"Well, of course that would be great, but we'd be happy with a bachelor's degree for starters. You can work up to the Nobel Prize gradually." Sam's Dad was tapping his watch, "There's no time for this right now, we've got to go."

"Bye, Mom, nice seeing you." Sam turned to leave.

"Wait a minute," her mother blocked the doorway. "Listen, Sam, all I'm saying is that sometimes good can come, even from a terrible tragedy. You've suffered, we've all suffered a horrible loss, but it's also given you an opportunity for a fresh start. That's all I'm saying."

"All you're saying is that Ben and June dying wasn't such a bad thing because now you have another shot at making me a doctor? Is that all you're saying?"

"No, of course not." Sam saw tears welling in her mother's eyes.

"Well, that's what it sounds like to me." Sam pushed past her mother, picked up her bags and headed to the car. She climbed into the passenger's seat and shut the door hard. A moment later she turned to find her mother, still in her nightgown and slippers, standing in the driveway and tapping on the window.

"What?" Sam reluctantly rolled her window down.

"I love you. That's all. I just wanted to say I love you. Do whatever you want. Go wherever you want. Just be happy. That's all we want from you."

Sam's lips began to tremble and her eyes burned. Reaching through the open window she gave her mother's hand a long squeeze. "It's so hard and I don't know what to do."

"You'll figure it out, baby. You'll figure it out, and when you do, whatever you do, your father and I will be behind you one hundred percent."

Sam wasn't able to think straight on the bus back to Kleiner. Her mind felt like an aquarium full of strange, exotic fish endlessly circling the inside of her head. She could almost feel the water sloshing against her skull. She took a small notepad from her purse and began drawing. By the time the bus stopped in front of the bench where she'd first boarded in Jamestown, the pad was covered with fanciful sea creatures swimming through a dark sea.

The bus arrived ten minutes ahead of schedule, so Sam was seated on the bench, still sketching fish with long ruffled fins and heavy lidded eyes, when Sheila's car pulled up beside her. "Welcome home, stranger. How was the trip? Love your hair." Sheila was beaming, clearly delighted to have Sam back.

"It was okay. Cleveland's still Cleveland. Mom and Dad said to say hi." Sheila came around and unlocked the trunk of her car. An Amish family passed them in an open carriage pulled by a sleek black horse. The smell of the horse's sweat and the sound of its hooves lingered in the air, even after the carriage disappeared around the corner of West 6th and Main. Sam took a deep breath. She could smell the blossoms from an apple tree in full bloom beside the post office. It was good to be back in Kleiner. Sam threw her things into the trunk and climbed into the passenger seat beside Sheila.

"What are you working on?" Sheila wanted to know.

"What?"

"You were drawing something. I was just curious. You looked so intent." Sheila smiled encouragingly at Sam.

"Oh, that was..." A fleeting Mona Lisa smile crossed Sam's face, "a self-portrait."

"Really? I'd love to see it."

Sam shook her head.

"Sorry, they're just preliminary sketches, but I'll let you look if I ever finish them. Say, I'm famished. Could we stop somewhere for lunch?"

CHAPTER 12

Weightless specks of white fluff floated past the barn door and hovered over the grass like white stars drifting through a green sky. Submerged in the half dream state where she did her best work, Sam sat at her easel with a brush motionless in her hand. The specks didn't fly or fall, but seemed to swim through space at a leisurely pace, sometimes dipping toward the clumps of tiger lilies poking up along the drive, sometimes wafting skyward above the mock orange that was perfuming the air with a heady scent. She sat mesmerized watching them for several minutes, then hurriedly grayed down a dab of Titanium White, warmed it with the smallest drop of Cadmium Yellow, and began dabbing fluffy poplar seeds onto the landscape emerging from her canvas. Perfect, the seeds gave the static painting a sense of life and movement that had been missing from her work. She stood up, took a few steps back to get a better perspective, and collided with a small, muscular body.

"For Heaven's sake, Marcus, what are you doing here?"

Marcus was wearing a striped T-shirt, shorts, and sneakers without socks. He was standing behind her, studying the canvas intently. "That's the tree over there, ain't it?" He pointed to a large fir tree with drooping branches that stood along the property line.

"Yep, it's a Norway spruce," Sam concurred.

"That's one sad looking tree."

"Sad looking? You mean you don't like it?"

"No, I mean it looks sad, like it just got some bad news."

Sam regarded Marcus with surprise. "I chose that tree because it looked sad to me too. Not everyone would see that. You've got a good eye."

Marcus grinned a big toothy smile, delighted with the compliment. "And I know what its problem is. The two big that trees used to be right there," he pointed to the space behind the barn. "They're gone now so that one's feeling lonesome."

This kid could be a charmer. "You might be right," she agreed.

"You know what you should do?"

"No, what should I do?"

"You should paint a forest, give that tree some friends." Suddenly Marcus was an art critic.

"No way! That would completely change my painting."

"So? It's your picture. You can change it if you want to."

Sam went back to filling in background shrubbery. Marcus stood at her shoulder watching. After another few minutes passed, Sam said, "Marcus, I've been wanting to ask you something. You don't have to tell me if you don't want to, but what happened at your school? How'd a nice kid like you get suspended to the end of the semester?"

"I put a white boy in the hospital."

Sam felt her breath catch, but she continued dabbing green paint on her canvas without turning around. "That's pretty serious. What happened?"

"The white kids didn't want us at their school, but we had to go there 'cause of busing making the black kids go to white schools and the white kids go to black schools. Seems like every day these white kids be throwing trash at us, tripping us in the hallways, saying stuff."

"Did the teachers know what was happening?"

"Sure they did. They kept having pow-wows where we'd sit in a circle and talk about respect and not being prejudiced, but that was just stupid. The shitheads were still shitheads. Sorry, Mrs. Crawford, but they just kept throwing stuff and talking trash. Mostly they threw stuff that didn't hurt like pens or erasers or balled up bread, except for this one guy, Gary. He especially hated me cause of my father. He was chief shithead. He'd make slingshots from rubber bands and zing Hickory nuts at me and call my dad names you don't want to hear. So one day we're sitting on the bus after school waiting to go home and Gary throws a rock right through the bus window. There's glass on the seat. Kids are screaming."

"Oh my God. Did anyone get hurt?"

"Yeah, he did. I threw a full can of coke right back at him through that window like to bust his head wide open. They suspended him too, but I think he should've got expelled."

"What did he say about your father?"

"He called him a nigger commie and other stuff I can't even say, really ugly stuff."

Sam had stopped painting and was listening intently. It turned out the boy could talk when he wanted to. "That's a terrible story. I hope things are better for you next year."

"There's not going to be a next year. I've had it with that school." He suddenly looked years older, angry and a little world-weary.

Sam ached for him, but didn't know what to say. "Shouldn't you be helping your grandfather or something? Where is he, anyway?" Sam brushed a strand of hair back from her face, leaving a green streak across her forehead.

"The hardware store. He needed some stuff." Marcus was picking at a scab on his elbow. "Is Tara here? Can I play with Tara?"

Sam concealed a smile, glad to find that there was still a child inside the belligerent little man. "Sorry, Tara's with her mom today. Anyway, what are you supposed to be doing right now? Aren't you supposed to be working?"

"I'm supposed to be scraping paint." He bent down to retie his sneaker. "But I'm taking a break. Can I go inside your house for a glass of water?"

"No way, I'm on to you. You just want to watch TV and goof off. You're grandfather would kill me if he came back and found you watching cartoons. You can go inside if you need to use the bathroom, but no TV. How about if I bring a pitcher of lemonade out to you? How would that be?"

"Okay." He was clearly not thrilled with the deal. "When will Tara come back? I have some stuff I want to show her. I know the signs for *show me, television,* and *stupid.* Wanna see?" His hands flew through some expressive maneuvers, accompanied by comical facial expressions.

"Are those real? Are you making this stuff up?" Sam stood with her arms folded, watching him with amused skepticism.

"They're real. Dan showed me. He's teaching me and Tara how to sign so we can talk to deaf people."

Sam was no longer smiling. "He'd better not be teaching Tara how to sign. Deaf kids who sign never learn how to talk. She's got to learn to read lips and use her voice so she can talk to everyone."

"But she can't hear anything," Marcus protested.

"Deaf people can learn to talk without hearing. They just have to watch people's mouths and figure out how to move their tongues and lips to make different sounds. If Tara's mom and Dan don't mess her up with all that sign stuff, she can learn to talk like a hearing person."

Marcus didn't look convinced, but he didn't say anything. Sam looked into his solemn little face and her heart melted. "Oh, alright, you can run into the house for a few minutes, but get back to work before your grandfather catches you." Once Marcus was gone she stood back from her painting and contemplated her work. It was a good painting, but Marcus was right. She could change it if she wanted to.

*   *   *

When the phone rang that evening, intuition told Sam that it wasn't her mother. Sure enough, the voice on the other end was Jerry's sounding more stressed and wired than she'd imagined possible. "I called Alan this afternoon. He says Margo's going to take Tara."

"Alan Siebert, your attorney?"

"Yeah, he says I've really fucked things up."

"No way. You've been a great father. You've got a responsible job, a house; you love Tara and you take good care of her. What more could you do? Margo's the unstable druggie who abandoned her baby. What's he talking about?" Sam had begun pacing like a large dog on a short leash, taking three steps to the end of the phone cord then three steps in the opposite direction.

"As far as the law is concerned, I barely exist. Margo and I were never legally married and I never got legal custody. How do I prove that I'm her father? As far as the law is concerned I'm just her babysitter, same as you."

"But you *are* her father, aren't you? There isn't any reason to think there might be someone else—is there?" Sam stopped pacing. In fact, she stopped breathing as she waited for Jerry to answer.

"Who knows..."

"What do you mean, who knows? Don't you know whether or not you're her father?"

"Not really. When I got back from Nam, Margo threw herself at me like I was Robert Redford or some war hero. She was living in my house before I had my duffle bag unpacked."

"Wow, you were a real pushover. A girl's got to learn to say no."

"Or at least take precautions. Tara was born eight months later. Either Tara was a little early or I was a little late. I've never known and I've never asked. I guess I never wanted to know." Jerry lowered his voice. "The thing is, I was in love with Margo. I had a crush on her all through high school. She was the woman I fantasized about when we were rotting in Con Thien. She was the only person I wanted to talk to after Joe got killed, and I couldn't believe that she suddenly wanted me, too."

"So why didn't you marry her?"

"I proposed as soon as I knew about the baby. But that was too bourgeois for Margo. She didn't want the government in our bedroom, a marriage license is just a piece of paper—you know how that goes."

"Is your name on Tara's birth certificate?"

"Yeah, that piece of paper is the one thing I've got going in my favor, but Alan says it isn't enough, at least not in this county. Apparently the judge is a sexist prick. All the years I've spent taking care of Tara don't matter as much as a pair of tits. Margo's the mother; mothers get the kids, period."

"Could you take a blood test? Would that make a difference?" Sam's head was reeling. Ideas that had been no more than fanciful speculation or wishful thinking suddenly didn't seem so crazy. *Maybe a blood test could prove that Tara belonged to Ben.*

"Blood tests can only prove who *isn't* the father. If things went the wrong way, I could lose what little standing I have now."

Jerry was clearly concerned that someone else might be Tara's father. Suddenly, Sam visualized the little girl with Ben's eyebrows, his almond eyes, and grabbed hold of the kitchen counter to keep her balance as the world tipped and whirled as though she were riding the Flying Turns at Euclid Beach Park. If Tara were Ben's daughter then she still had a living connection to her husband. So much would still be possible. She filled a glass of water from the sink and took a long cold swallow. If the law might not acknowledge a man whose name was on Tara's birth certificate and who had cared for her from birth, what standing would she have as the widow of a man whose connection to Tara was pure conjecture? None, that was clear, and yet she was suddenly desperate to keep Tara in her life.

"So it turns out Margo was wrong about little pieces of paper. That birth certificate is my only shred of hope." Jerry was still talking, although Sam hadn't heard a word for the last several minutes.

Jerry was Sam's only legitimate connection to Tara, and it was immediately clear that if Jerry lost custody she'd lose as well. She knew whose side she was on. "You're Tara's father and it doesn't have anything to do with blood tests or birth certificates. You've loved her and taken care of her since she was born. I'd like to see someone tell Tara you're not her daddy."

"Here's the deal, Alan tells me that custody battles in Catawba County always end the same way. Mom gets custody; Dad gets visitation a couple weekends a month, plus a bill for alimony and child support. He figures, given the circumstances, I won't be stuck with alimony, but I'll have to pay child support and Margo will probably jerk me around about when and if I get to see my daughter, assuming she doesn't just take her back to California."

"That's not going to happen. Margo abandoned Tara and that changes the whole picture. No jury's going to give Tara to someone who might walk out on her again. And Margo was a known druggie. Who'd give a little girl to a woman like that?"

"I guess we're going to find out. I'm filing for legal custody. Apparently, that's what I should have done the minute Margo left town. Alan thinks it's hopeless, but he's down at the courthouse filling out the paperwork anyway."

"You'll have the whole community behind you."

"Maybe, but I'm no saint. I should have gotten Tara into some sort of school before this, done more for her. Like Alan said, I've probably fucked it up already."

"Don't be so hard on yourself. What's Margo done? Smoked weed? Learned to ride a motorcycle?"

"She learned sign language. She knows how to talk to deaf people."

"But you don't want Tara stuck in a deaf ghetto. You're teaching her oral language."

"Am I? I didn't teach her squat before you showed up, but that's going to change. I went back to the audiologist and he worked it out with people at the school to get her an auditory trainer." His voice sounded tight and strained. "She should have had one years ago."

"What's an auditory trainer?"

"I've never actually seen one." Jerry paused and Sam waited for him to begin again. "It's an electronic box that's supposed to transmit sounds better than a hearing aid. It's got a microphone that sends your voice over an FM channel directly to a special headset that the deaf kid wears. Tara wouldn't wear it all the time, just when we're teaching her how to make sounds and read lips. She still wouldn't hear much, but she might hear something. It might make a difference."

"That's fantastic! That's just what I mean; you're doing a great job."

"I hope the judge sees it that way."

"He will. He has to. But if you're worried, my dad knows a couple of hotshot lawyers back in Cleveland. Do you want him to set up an appointment for you?"

"I don't think so, not right now, but thanks for offering, and thanks for looking after Tara. She's a new girl since you've been around. You've made me realize how much more I could have been doing for her."

"I really enjoy working with her." Sam realized she was telling the truth. Even if she knew for sure that Tara wasn't Ben's daughter, she'd still enjoy showing the world to a child who was so bright, but also so isolated within the silence of her own head. She took another sip of water, "In fact, I've been thinking about your job offer. When you come to pick Tara up on Friday, let's talk."

"You bet. It's a date." An optimistic tone returned to Jerry's voice and resonated in Sam's ears long after she'd hung up the phone.

It was almost one in the morning, but Sam couldn't sleep. She sat at her sewing machine snipping and stitching one patch after another until it seemed that she might have enough squares to upholster the barn. Sam closed her eyes and let a strip of blue flannel fall to her lap. "Enough," she whispered to herself, "enough." Simply making the patches, reshaping and reimagining anything and everything that had touched her husband had been sufficient for all the months following his death, but now something inside her said it was the time to stop cutting and to start stitching it all back together.

She picked up a black nylon square shot through with red embroidery, part of a swimsuit from Ben's high school days. Next, she touched a nubby patch of wool cut from an argyle sweater, her first Christmas gift to Ben. She brought it to her cheek, remembering how he'd been embarrassed, since all he'd bought for her was the new Bob Dylan album.

That memory sent her digging through the pile until she unearthed a stiff and shiny patch, a pink cardboard rose cut from a Grateful Dead cover stitched onto a square of faded denim. Ben had surprised her with a pair of tickets to hear the Dead play in Cleveland. The tickets were a two month anniversary gift, the trip to Cleveland a last hurrah before Ben started his new job at Kleiner High.

The weather had been unusually cool and pleasant for mid-August, and the concert had been magic. Public Hall throbbed with good will and energy, the air thick with the scent of pot and patchouli. She'd felt self-conscious, but also pretty and uninhibited beneath strings of love beads and garlands of yellow chrysanthemums.

Later, back at her parents' house, they'd sat out on the patio scanning the sky for shooting stars. Ben pulled a small bag from his pocket. "Acapulco Gold," he'd said waving it triumphantly. "Look at this." He took a fat yellow bud and crushed it in the palm of his hand then turned his palm face down. It stuck to his hand. "How's that for fresh? Smell it; it smells like a new mown field." They'd handed the joint back and forth, talking and giggling, and searching for silver streaks across the sky. "Too much ambient city light," Ben had finally said with resignation as they headed up to bed. "The Perseid shower is spectacular. I used to look forward to it every August. It was like fireworks marking the beginning of the new school year. I promise, we'll see it next year when we're in the country." They never did see the falling stars, but Sam was pretty sure that June had been conceived that night. Sam traced the rose with her finger, over and over again. At last, she placed it back in the basket, turned off the light and went upstairs to bed.

CHAPTER 13

A few days later Jerry arrived with a large box and a triumphant grin on his face. Tara stood beside him looking happy and expectant. She clearly knew the box was for her, and seemed to be anticipating some new toy or plaything.

"Big news," Jerry exclaimed as he carried the box into the living room and set it down on the coffee table. Sam watched as Tara tore open the brown cardboard carton then dug through a mass of Styrofoam peanuts until she found a gray plastic case the size of an old fashioned radio. Tara unfastened the metal latches, pulled back the lid, then turned to Jerry with a puzzled expression. Still grinning, Jerry pulled out a child size headset and put it over Tara's ears. She immediately pulled it off, handed it back to her father, then sat down on the couch as far from the box as possible. Jerry was undeterred. His mood was still buoyant. "I guess we'll have to ease her into this slowly. Let's figure out how the thing works."

Sam pulled the instruction pamphlet from the box and read it as Jerry extracted the console, a compact unit with separate volume controls for student and teacher, and a few electronic outlets for the cords. It didn't look that intimidating. She reached into the box and pulled out a microphone attached to a coiled wire and stuck it into an outlet marked master mic. "Hello, hello. Earth to Jerry. Come in please."

"Hey, wait a minute. I don't even have the thing plugged in yet."

"This is so cool." Sam had caught Jerry's good mood. She spoke into the microphone again. "Come here, Watson, I want to see you."

Jerry looked up and smiled. "Who's Watson?"

Sam realized that Jerry had never heard the story of Alexander Graham Bell and the invention of the telephone. Jerry was a smart guy, but she was constantly being surprised by things he didn't know. "No one, I was just goofing around. Tell me your big news."

"I am officially Tara Michalski's legal guardian. The judge signed the papers this afternoon."

"Tara Michalski?"

"Margo used her own name on the birth certificate. It doesn't matter. Her name may be Tara Michalski but Jerry Doyle is her father and legal guardian." Jerry made a small bow in Sam's direction, and then dropped to the floor to search for an outlet behind a large arm chair.

"Congratulations, bravo, well done!" Sam clapped her hands enthusiastically. "How did Alan pull it off? I thought only mothers got custody in this county."

"Alan explained that the mother left town two years ago with no forwarding address." Jerry was still on his hands and knees trying to find the outlet. "What could the judge say?"

"But Margo's back in town."

Jerry's head popped back up from behind the chair. His face was slightly red, from either exertion or embarrassment. "Alan may have failed to mention that."

Sam set aside the time right after breakfast to work with Tara's auditory trainer. Tara had to be bribed and coerced into wearing the headset and then fidgeted and squirmed during the entire lesson. Even with the trainer, there was little evidence that she heard much of anything. The work was boring and frustrating for both of them, but it was absolutely crucial. If Tara could learn to distinguish even a few vowel sounds it would move her closer toward oral speech.

"Pea," Sam said into the microphone as she held up a small card with a picture of a pea pod. Did Tara recognize the picture? Had she ever seen a pea in a pod or growing on a vine? Probably not. Sam put down the card face up on the table. "Pie," she said, holding up another card that showed a slice of cherry pie. "Pie," she repeated, putting the picture of pie beside the picture of the pea. "Show me pie," Sam instructed Tara. "Show me the pie." She exaggerated all the sounds and the movements of her mouth. Tara squirmed in her chair and tried to pull the headset off her ears. "No!" Sam pulled Tara's hands away from her ears. "No, you've got to keep these things on." It was no use; Tara wanted no part of the squawk box, the wires or the electronic ear muffs. Sighing, Sam decided it was time for a break. Neither of them could stand much more of this battle.

Once she'd given up on Tara's language lesson, the morning passed more pleasantly. They walked out to the edge of the woods where small bittersweet strawberries grew wild beneath a tangle of grass and weeds. Tara fell on the patch and began picking the fruit. Berry after berry landed in her pot with a satisfying plunk, satisfying to

Sam. Tara, of course, couldn't hear a thing. Soon, even Sam could no longer hear the berries fall as their drop was cushioned by the soft sweet fruit that preceded them. Sam watched Tara working, her little hands amazingly deft for a child who'd just turned seven. Her concentration was absolute, quite a contrast from her earlier performance. Every so often Tara would stand up to survey her work, arms crossed and her head cocked slightly to the right, before bending back to her task. It was Ben's gesture exactly. Sam's heart lurched in her chest every time she saw it. What were the chances that Tara really was Ben's daughter? Probably not much, and yet she was so like Ben.

Once Tara's bowl was filled and her mouth and T-shirt sufficiently stained with red berry juice, they headed back to the house to lunch on cornflakes and fresh fruit. As Sam cleared away the dishes she gazed fondly at Tara, who was fishing around in her bowl for one last berry. The more Sam studied her, the more she looked like Ben. It wasn't her imagination. Tara definitely had her mother's coloring, her red hair and blue eyes. But her almond shaped eyes, thick brows, narrow nose, and dimpled chin all reminded her of Ben.

"Look at you, you're a mess," Sam kept up a running dialogue with Tara even though she knew the child couldn't hear a word. Talking was simply a reflexive behavior, and besides, how else would Tara learn to read her lips? Tara's T-shirt, already dotted with red spots, now had wet shadows where the milk had missed her mouth. "Let's get you into some clean clothes, sweet pea." Sam half-heartedly shooed the cat off the table where it was lapping at a white pool beside Tara's bowl. It settled on the kitchen counter watching, miffed and insulted, while Sam pulled off Tara's soiled shirt. Since Tara's shorts were torn and missing a button, they came off as well, leaving Tara in nothing but her underpants. Sam left Tara at the table as she made a wild dash into the living room to retrieve a scissors, needle and thread from her sewing basket. Relieved to find Tara still sitting in her chair when she returned, Sam decided to risk a quick trip to the basement to drop Tara's dirty shirt into the washing machine.

Sam wasn't gone three minutes, but in that short time Tara picked up the scissors that Sam had left on the kitchen table and cut the legs of her shorts with a series of small vertical slits. Sam grabbed the scissors and started to scold, but what was the point in yelling at a deaf kid? Storming past Tara with the angriest face she could manage, Sam grabbed an index card and a black Magic Marker.

"No!" Sam stood directly in front of Tara mouthing the words as clearly and broadly as she could while holding the index card with the word *NO* printed in large black letters beside her mouth. "For

God's sake, look at me will you? No. No. NO!" Sam threw down the card and picked up the ruined shorts, the legs fringed with small cuts. "What's the matter with you? Why would you do a thing like that?" Sam held the scissors up beside her mouth and pointed at them as she repeated, "No." Then she stopped herself, realizing she had to be confusing Tara. "Scissors," she corrected herself. Tara stared back at her belligerent and uncomprehending. "No scissors. No scissors," Sam repeated in exasperation before slamming the scissors down on the kitchen table. She grabbed a new index card and wrote SCISSORS on it then picked up the scissors, cut the card into a dozen tiny pieces, and tossed them all into the trash. This was beyond her. Tara was so smart, but she wasn't learning much of anything. She desperately needed to work with a trained teacher of the deaf, someone who knew what the hell she was doing.

Why was this so hard? Anne Sullivan taught a kid who was both blind and deaf how to talk. Why couldn't she teach Tara to point to a simple picture? She took a deep breath, counted to ten, ran the cord from the auditory trainer back to the outlet and picked up the pack of phonics cards. They might as well do something constructive while Tara's shirt was in the wash.

"Pea, show me pea," she began again. Sam was exhausted but determined. If this child was going to live in the hearing world, she had to learn to talk, but Tara would have none of it. She threw the card on the floor and began kicking the bottom of the table.

"No! No!" Sam forgot herself again and went on shouting as she dove under the table to retrieve the card. Blinking back tears of frustration, she pulled herself together and put the card back on the table. "Pea, please show me the pea." Her voice sounded whiney and defeated. It was just as well that Tara couldn't hear her. Stubbornly refusing to point, Tara pulled off the headset and threw it to the floor. "No, Tara. No." Sam picked up the headset and faced Tara, intending to wrestle the thing back onto her head.

"Oh!" said Tara glaring back at her belligerently. "Oh! Oh! Oh!"

Sam was stunned; *Tara is talking. She is saying, "No."* Tara's red curls bounced back and forth as she violently shook her head, "Oh!" she kept repeating,

"Oh!" A huge smile spread across Sam's face and the tears she'd been holding back pricked her eyes then rolled down her cheeks. "Oh," she said as she grabbed Tara and gave her the biggest, tightest hug of her life. "Oh."

The moment was interrupted by the doorbell, then three loud knocks, then two more rings. Sam gave Tara a quick peck on the top of her head, then went to see what was going on. "Hey, open up, I know you're in there." It was Margo.

"I'm coming," Sam called over the sound of more knocking. Margo couldn't even ring a doorbell like a normal person. As soon as she opened the door Margo burst into the house as though she were leading a commando raid, pivoting in all directions, surveying the room. "Where's my daughter. I want to see my daughter."

"She's in the kitchen. You know, it's polite to call before you come over."

"Hey, Baby!" Margo turned toward the small half naked child who raced full tilt into her arms.

"Why isn't my daughter wearing any clothes? It's one o'clock in the afternoon, for God's sake. I thought you were supposed to be taking care of her."

"I am taking care of her. Her shirt's in the washer, and I was just sewing a button back on her shorts." Sam winced, thinking of Tara's shorts snipped to ribbons in the kitchen.

"Anyway, what do you want? What are you doing here?"

"Jerry just found out I'm contesting that bogus custody ruling. I'm filing for custody myself and he's really pissed. My lawyer tells me that some people get so angry they panic and run off with the kid when their custody is challenged, so I just wanted to make sure everything was mellow around here. Isn't that right, petunia?" She planted a big kiss on Tara's neck making her gurgle and smile with joy.

"Margo," Sam didn't want to create a scene, not with Tara in Margo's arms; she'd have to choose her words carefully. "Tara's really happy with Jerry. He adores her and does everything he can to take care of her. Don't you think it might be best to just leave her where she is, safe and secure in her own home? I'm sure Jerry would let you visit all the time. You could still be part of Tara's life."

"He'd *let* me visit? Nobody *lets* me visit my own daughter, and what makes you think Tara's so happy? Did you ask her about it? Did the two of you have a nice little heart to heart? No, you didn't because Tara can't talk and the longer she stays with Jerry the longer it's going to be before she can communicate with anyone."

"Jerry's taken Tara to two different audiologists. We have workbooks and flash cards and an auditory trainer for her. I work with her five days a week and Jerry works with her on the weekends." This last statement was a bald faced lie. Jerry was an even worse teacher than Sam was, and had given up after his first few futile attempts.

"Really? The only thing I've seen her do is wave bye-bye, and I taught her that when she was two. Let's go put some clothes on this child. Where are her pants?"

"In the kitchen. What makes you think you could do any better? I mean, seriously, where do you get the nerve to criticize Jerry?" Margo and Tara followed Sam into the kitchen where Margo picked Tara's shorts up from the table, and saw the slits cut into the legs. She stretched the shorts out in front of her examining them. "What happened here?"

"That's Tara's work. I don't know what she thought she was doing."

"Well, I bet I do." Margo was suddenly beaming, clearly tickled pink by the ruined shorts. "I wore fringed cut offs when we went to Seneca Rocks on Saturday. I think she wants shorts just like her Mommy's."

"Did you cut the pants?" Margo signed toward Tara as she spoke. Tara watched her with rapt attention. "You cut," she repeated. The signs were self evident, a sort of pantomime. Tara froze and Sam could read fear in her little face. She must have thought she was in trouble.

"Oh," Tara shook her head, "Oh."

Margo looked flustered. "My God, she said no."

"I told you, we're teaching her to talk." Sam tried to act nonchalant, but she felt as though she'd just hit a ball out of the park. Tara's timing was perfect. Margo would have to see they were doing a superior job of raising her daughter.

"Well, good for you. Tara's a smart little kid and she's learning to use her voice, but don't expect her to carry on a conversation any time soon. If she was learning to sign she could be talking to people and making friends within a matter of months."

"Sign isn't talking. And who would she talk to anyway? Other deaf kids?"

"Yeah, she could talk to other deaf kids. She is a deaf kid, so maybe she'd like talking to other deaf kids. Ever think about that? And maybe Jerry could learn sign so he could talk with her, too."

"I know that Jerry hopes Tara will be able to talk with everyone." Sam could hear the priggish, self-righteous tone in her voice.

"Yeah right. Good luck with that." Margo turned back to Tara who'd been watching the conversation looking worried and confused. "Yes," Margo said to Tara. She smiled broadly and nodded her head up and down while making her right fist move up and down as though it were nodding too. "Yes, you cut." The signs were intuitive, easy to decipher. "Yes," she repeated out loud as she simultaneously repeated the signs. "Yes, you cut." She grabbed Tara and began tickling her while pretending to snip at her with two fingers. Tara began to giggle and started snipping back at her mother until they were overcome with laughter as their fingers clipped away at each other's noses, ears and hair.

Sam had never seen Tara laugh and play with such abandon. She watched them with a sullen expression on her face. She felt left out, the kid on the playground with no friends because she's too prissy and uptight. It wasn't fair. So much wasn't fair. She thought about transferring Tara's shirt to the dryer, but she was afraid to leave Tara alone with Margo, so she stood there staring at them until they'd laughed themselves out.

When Tara had finally collapsed against Margo's shoulder and begun braiding her mother's hair, Sam let out a little snort of air and pursed her lips, "I think it's time for you to go. Jerry's not kidnapping Tara, so don't worry about it." She was two years younger than Margo, but felt a generation older. "He's not the kidnapping type."

"So, you know what type Jerry is, do you?" Margo leaned back on her heels and gave Sam a long appraising glance. "Well, I know a few things about Jerry too, and you can tell him they're all going to come out in court if he gives me any trouble. Tell him the custody suit is dead serious. Things have changed and I'm getting my little girl back."

Sam opened the front door wide, "I'll be sure to tell him and you be sure to call ahead next time you visit."

Margo gave Tara one more quick kiss then headed toward the motorcycle parked at the bottom of the drive.

In the weeks following her breakthrough, Tara began to consistently vocalize, "Oh," whenever she was unhappy or wanted to refuse something and Sam and Jerry never ceased to be charmed and delighted, confident that this single vowel would soon be joined by a, e, i, u, and sometimes y, along with the host of fricatives, sibilants, plosives, and diphthongs described in the auditory training manual. In fact, Tara did begin to make progress. She learned to match scores of printed words to appropriate objects and pictures, and eventually added the word "pea" meaning please, not the legume, to her spoken vocabulary. However, the ability to connect spoken words to pictures remained illusive. Getting Tara to work with the auditory trainer was a constant struggle, and Sam would have surrendered the battle if it weren't for the small victories that continued to buoy her spirit and give her hope.

By contrast, every time Tara went out with Margo and Dan, she came back with a half dozen new signs and radiated joy with the pleasure of her new accomplishment. Sam and Jerry feigned disinterest in her new skill. All the experts that Jerry consulted, and all the books Sam read, insisted that sign was the kiss of death for a deaf child, a one way ticket to an isolated life with painfully limited social and career opportunities. They determined to stand strong against the temptation to take the easy road, the quick and dirty route of sign and gestures. Yet, Sam had to admit, she was jealous of Margo's growing ability to communicate with Tara. Worse, she felt mean thwarting the child's first successful communication with another human being. At first, she and Jerry pretended not to know what Tara was saying, even when her signs were patently obvious. However, it wasn't long before Tara's signs evolved beyond what looked like simple mime, and they really had no idea what she and Margo talked about. If this went on much longer, there wouldn't be a chance that Tara would ever learn to talk.

Sam begged Jerry to call Mrs. Panetta, the head of special education for Catawba County. He'd already met with her several times to discuss plans for Tara's education, in fact she was the one who had assured Jerry that she'd known many hard of hearing children over the years and that they'd all, well nearly all, learned to speak and live full lives in the hearing world. From what Sam gathered, Mrs. Panetta was a motherly woman in her early sixties who had been with the county for over thirty years. Sam was sure she'd take their side, maybe even do something to prevent Margo from using sign when she took Tara on their twice weekly outings. Of course, that would mean Tara wouldn't be able to see Dan since he was totally dependent on sign language. Too bad. He seemed nice enough, but he represented everything they feared for Tara. His voice, when he used it, sounded like a parrot squawking, and he couldn't read lips worth a damn. If you wanted to tell him something, you had to write it in a little notebook that he carried with him everywhere he went.

Since Sam was going to be Tara's home speech aid, Jerry suggested that she be included in the meeting and Mrs. Panetta gladly agreed. Kleiner was the county seat, so it was a short drive to the board of education where Mrs. Panetta had a small, over-furnished office on the second floor. In an attempt to create a homey atmosphere, she'd crammed the small space with furnishings more appropriate for an old fashioned parlor than a modern office building.

Sam could just make out a rug under the piles of books, boxes, and assorted papers. Navigating her way to the chintz love seat beneath the window was an awkward and somewhat treacherous journey. Philodendrons and spider plants covered the window sill and hung suspended on hooks from the ceiling. She tried to ignore the vines that tickled the back of her neck and gave her the itchy sensation that they might start twining around her ankles and growing up her legs.

Mrs. Panetta stood in the doorway, "Before we start, would you like a cup of tea or coffee? I always need something by this time of the afternoon." She was a tall, stout woman with a ruddy complexion and unruly hair that resembled a tangled network of silver wire spilling from her head. Earrings that looked like large purple orchids were clipped to each ear. The pink cardigan that she wore over a pleated skirt was buttoned improperly, so it bunched in the middle and hung at a strange angle across her belly.

"No thank you," Sam shook her head.

"Thanks, I'm fine," Jerry looked uncharacteristically anxious and impatient.

"Well, I won't be a minute then. I absolutely need a pick-me-up before we get going." She returned a few moments later with a steaming mug and a handful of cookies in a paper towel. "Look what I found in the teacher's lounge. They're homemade, would you like one?

"No thanks," Sam and Jerry said in unison.

"Oh my, they're delicious," Mrs. Panetta's eyes rolled upward in a swoon of ecstasy. "Oatmeal chocolate chip, you really have to try one." She held out the paper towel to Sam and Jerry who each dutifully took one of the cookies they'd just refused. Mrs. Panetta removed a large box from the chair behind her desk and sat down. She took a sip from the mug and smiled, "Now, what can I do for you?"

Sam had a laundry list of things she'd like from Mrs. Panetta and the school, but she sat silently waiting for Jerry to take the lead. After all, Tara was his daughter and she really had no business butting in. She was only there for moral support and to pick up any teaching techniques that Mrs. Panetta might provide. Jerry, a Vietnam vet and a deputy sheriff, looked like a boy who'd been sent to the principal's office. His usual air of competence and authority had abandoned him entirely.

"The problem is..." Jerry shifted uncomfortably in his seat, paused and began again. "You see, Tara's mother just came back to town and she learned sign language while she was out on the west coast so, of course, she's all gung ho to teach Tara how to sign, but we're trying to teach her with the auditory trainer and lip reading and everything like you said, and we're afraid that..."

"I see." Mrs. Panetta cut him off, her head nodding sympathetically. "Oh dear, we can't have that. We can't have you and Tara's mother working at cross purposes. Tara will never learn to talk if she's using sign before the speech pathologist has even started working with her."

"Exactly, that's why we came in. We didn't know what to do." Jerry put his cookie down on the end table beside his seat.

"Would the mother come in to talk with me? Maybe all we need to do is give her a little education about the importance of oral language. I'm sure she wants what's best for her daughter."

Sam looked at Jerry and shrugged, "You could try, but it wouldn't be easy. She's never been much good at following rules or taking advice. Also, I guess you should know, she's suing me for custody so we're not exactly on the best of terms."

"She's suing *you* for custody?" The accent was on the "you." She clearly knew the story about Margo running off without her daughter. "I wouldn't have expected that. That's really unfortunate. I'm so sorry."

"Yeah, it really complicates things. We don't know what to do." Jerry looked to Sam for help articulating his dilemma.

Sam brightened. She'd been perched on the edge of her seat waiting for an opportunity to chime in. "Here's the thing, the court has given Margo visitation rights twice a week while this thing is being settled and she has a deaf boyfriend who only talks in sign so they're signing in front of Tara the whole time that they're together. It just makes a mockery of all the hours we're spending with phonics cards and her auditory trainer. It's just so frustrating and I'm, I mean *we're* scared that she'll never learn to talk."

"I see," Mrs. Panetta had been listening sympathetically while nibbling on her cookie. "How has her home instruction been going? Is she making any progress?"

"She's brilliant. She can match dozens of printed words to pictures and she can even say a few words, but she's been losing interest in oral language ever since Margo started teaching her to sign."

"Well, of course, sign is so much easier. It gives deaf children instant gratification without asking them to do the hard work of learning to associate lip movements and whatever residual hearing they have with words and meaning. Unfortunately, that hard work is the only path to life in the hearing world. I don't want to think of Tara living her life trapped in the world of the deaf. I've seen that happen and it always breaks my heart." She took out a pad of lined notebook paper and started taking notes. "Let's give the mother a chance. I'm going to invite her in to discuss our plan for Tara's education. If she understands what we're trying to do maybe we can nip this in the bud. Now, her name is Margo. That would be Margo Doyle?"

"No, it's Michalski, Margo Michalski. We weren't married."

"All right then, Margo Michalski." Sam could see the grandmotherly woman struggle to appear professional and nonjudgmental in light of this news. "Do you have a phone number or address where I can reach her?"

Jerry flushed. This was not going well. "Not really. I've never called her. I think she and her boyfriend are staying at the Wee Wan Chu Trailer Park. I guess if you called their office someone could get a message to her."

"Well then, that's what I'll do." Mrs. Panetta wrote something on her pad, popped the last cookie into her mouth and smiled at them. "Don't worry, I'm sure this can all be sorted out. By the way, did Margo go to school in Kleiner? There was a Margo Michalski who used to be a student there."

Sam raised her eyebrows. *Who does this broad think she's kidding? She knows exactly who Margo is; everyone in Kleiner knows about Margo.*

"Yeah, she graduated in sixty-seven." Jerry, who also had to know she knew, was playing along.

"So, that's what became of Margo Michalski." Mrs. Panetta made little tisking noises with her tongue. "She was quite the rabble rouser in her day, nearly got the whole school shut down from what I remember. I'm surprised they let her graduate."

"They had to." Sam could hear the pride in Jerry's voice. "She was valedictorian and had a scholarship to Oberlin."

"Really?" Sam shot up straight in her seat. "I never heard about that." She was dumbstruck, but instantly realized that it all made sense. Ben wouldn't have dated a dimwit. But Margo at Oberlin? She couldn't picture it.

"Yeah, she's a brain. That's probably where Tara gets it from."

"But I hope Tara got her character from you," Two lines furrowed Mrs. Panetta's brow. "That Michalski girl was a menace. I think they finally arrested her."

"Not then, she just got suspended for a few days. The judge decided it was a freedom of speech thing and let her off." Jerry turned to Sam to fill her in on this bit of local history. "Margo tried to get all the kids at Kleiner High to go out on strike to protest the war. Maybe twenty students walked out, but the administration freaked and called the police because they were walking around outside the school with signs."

"It was more than signs, they were shouting horrible things at passing cars, and frightening people. Some of them threw things at faculty cars, and one of them slashed Mr. Garvin's tires. That's not free speech." Mrs. Panetta was becoming quite heated as she remembered the event.

"That wasn't Margo's fault. Margo was a hippy pacifist—make love not war, flower power, that sort of thing. The other kids didn't get what she was doing and used her strike as an excuse to skip school and cause trouble. But don't blame Margo for those idiots. All she wanted was to keep them from going to Vietnam and getting shot."

"But you were in Vietnam yourself. "

"Yes I was."

"Weren't you angry that she was so disloyal to our troops?"

"No, I wasn't. Look, I don't want to talk about Margo any more. Let's get back to Tara."

"Of course," Mrs. Panetta agreed, although Sam could read the reluctance in her face. She'd noticed that people in Kleiner loved trashing Margo. *Good,* she thought to herself. *There'll be a riot in this town if the court gives Tara to her mother.*

Mrs. Panetta went on, "The main thing is to keep Tara focused on oral language. That's her ticket. You know you're doing the right thing for Tara and that's what you must always keep in mind. Don't give up, and don't let anything or anyone get in your way. When will you be meeting with Dana Zelinsky again?"

Two small lines creased Jerry's forehead, "Dana Zelinsky? Sorry, I've never heard of a Dana Zelinsky."

"Of course you have. She's the speech pathologist. Aren't you meeting with her periodically to monitor Tara's progress?" When Jerry shook his head "no," Mrs. Panetta looked flustered and started riffling through the papers on her desk. Unearthing a large desk calendar she began turning back the pages, one after another. "You're right, you're right, I'm afraid I let that get away from me. Yes, here it is. Oh well, no harm done. I'll have her give you a call so that she can check in and see how Tara's doing. We want that little girl ready for school this fall."

"I thought we'd agreed to have her tutored at home. You said she should only go to school for her speech pathology and maybe gym and art, things like that, so she could meet other children." Jerry leaned forward, studying the sweet old lady with a look of suspicion, as though she were someone he'd taken into custody whose story wasn't quite holding up.

"Of course that's the plan. I have a memory like a sieve, but don't you worry. It's all written down right here." She pointed to the avalanche of paper on her desk.

Sam broke in, "How about if you give us Miss Zelinsky's phone number and we'll call her. I can see how busy you are."

"I'm so sorry. I can't give out a teacher's private number—that's against school policy. I'm afraid you can only reach her through my office. You could leave a message for her with Miss Hadley on your way out if you like. That might be the best way. Yes, I think that would do it."

As Sam and Jerry stood to leave, Mrs. Panetta walked toward them with a wide sympathetic smile on her face. For a moment Sam thought she was going to give each of them a hug. Instead, she held out her right hand to Jerry who extended his expecting to shake hands. She surprised him by clasping his hand firmly between both of hers and squeezing it tightly. "Now don't you worry about a thing. You meet with Miss Zelinsky and I'll have a little chat with Margo and we'll get this ironed out. I have a feeling that everything's going to be just fine."

"Thank you, I appreciate it." Jerry was trying to extricate his hand without offending the older woman. "I'm afraid we're running a little late, but I'll stop and leave a message for Miss Zelinsky before we go."

Once they were out of earshot Sam turned to Jerry, "You didn't tell me she was a fruitcake."

"I didn't know. She seemed alright when I met with her before. She gave me all those workbooks and arranged for the auditory trainer. It's probably no big deal. She said, no harm done."

"No harm done? She just said that to cover her ass because she screwed up. I bet that speech pathologist was supposed to teach us how to work with Tara and how to use all the materials that they gave you. Instead, that Panetta woman never made the arrangements and left us struggling to figure everything out by ourselves. Thanks a lot." Sam was spitting her words out under her breath.

"Calm down, we'll leave a message with the secretary and you can meet with whatever her name is…"

"Zelinsky. Dana Zelinsky."

"We can meet with Dana Zelinsky and make up for lost time. Anyway, you've been doing a great job without her. You figured everything out on your own." Jerry laid a reassuring hand on Sam's shoulder. He'd never touched her before; she froze, stumbled over her own feet and forgot what she meant to say next. She picked up the pace leaving Jerry and his hand a yard behind her. "I think I remember passing the secretary's office, it was just down this hall."

Later, on the way home, she sat beside Jerry with a new stack of workbooks and informative pamphlets in her lap. They'd left a message for Miss Zelinsky and made an appointment to meet with the audiologist. Sam was optimistic that with these professionals involved, Tara would soon be chatting away just as the books promised she would. "You were right about Tara being smart," she said. "I don't know where she got it, but she's sharp as a tack. Even though she can't hear she doesn't miss a thing."

"I know, and I meant it when I said she got her brains from Margo."

"Did Margo really go to Oberlin? I don't remember you saying anything about her going to college."

"That's because she never went. She got arrested the summer before college and that was the end of her scholarship."

"Arrested? That doesn't sound so smart." Would Ben have taken up with someone so sketchy? She thought of the sweet, super responsible man she'd married and had her doubts.

"Yeah, she decked a nurse in the emergency room of Lake West Memorial."

"She what?"

"She's smart but she does dumb stuff. I mean how smart was it to take off the way she did?"

"She decked a nurse? You're kidding."

"No, I'm not." Jerry clearly didn't see anything funny in the story. "The hospital called the police and they arrested Margo for assault. Mike Jersey went out on the call. He's still with the department, I see him all the time."

"Margo actually hit a nurse? Was she on drugs or something? That's crazy."

"She was just really angry. Her Grandma had a stroke so she went to visit her in the hospital. As soon as she got off the elevator, she could hear Grandma hollering all the way down the hall. When she got to the room there was a nurse bent over the bed trying to tie Grandma's arms to the rails. Grandma was cussing a blue streak and struggling to get loose. Of course Margo jumped in and started screaming at the nurse to get away and leave her Grandma alone. Actually, she went up behind the woman and tried to physically pull her away. That would have been enough for a charge of assault, but it didn't end there." Jerry was so wrapped up in his story that he missed his turn.

"Hey, back up. You sailed right past our street." Sam waited while Jerry turned into the drive of Dick's Bait and Tackle and headed back in the right direction. "So, what happened?"

"So the nurse wheeled around to tell Margo to get the hell out of the room, but as soon as she took her hands off Grandma the old lady yanked out her IV and a bunch of other tubes and wires. The machine next to her bed started beeping and flashing alarm signals and nasty stuff started spraying the sheets."

Sam put one hand over her mouth as though she were listening intently. In reality she was trying to stifle a laugh. *Sheila will eat this story up.*

"Then the nurse got angry and turned back around and started to throttle Grandma—at least that's how Margo tells it. My guess is the poor woman was just trying to reinsert some of those tubes. Anyway, Margo hauled off and decked her. The hospital called the police and Margo lost her scholarship, end of story."

"Oh, my God." Sam rolled her eyes and shook her head, but part of her was secretly impressed, almost jealous, of Margo's ability to come out swinging without a thought for the consequences. *The woman has balls.*

"It's sad really. Margo's a beautiful, talented woman, but she keeps shooting herself in the foot. Nothing about her makes sense. Think about it. She grew up in a trailer with a drunk for a mom who never gave her the time of day, but she's so smart that she wins a scholarship to a fancy private college. Then, just when she finally has her ticket out, she does something so stupid that she blows the whole thing." Sam had never seen Jerry so animated. His face was glowing and he was waving both hands as he talked—including the one that should have been on the steering wheel. "Next, she has a sweet little house, a beautiful baby, enough money for all the normal stuff, and a guy who's crazy about her, but she runs off and ruins that too. How does Margo's head work? Why would a woman do a thing like that?"

"I don't know. There's clearly something wrong with her." *And yet*, Sam thought to herself, *you're still crazy about her. What is it about Margo?* Out loud, she added, "Nothing in this world could have made me leave my daughter."

"Exactly, and I would have said Margo felt the same way about Tara. She was always dancing around with Tara, cooing over her, taking her places. I thought she was this great mom and then, bang, she's gone. Go figure."

They pulled up in front of Sheila's three bedroom bungalow with white siding and blue shutters on a large corner lot. Tara was playing with Mazie, the poodle pup who lived next door. They watched as Tara threw a bone for Mazie, who raced to fetch it and then dashed away with Tara in pursuit. When Mazie dropped the bone, Tara swooped it up, and then ran with the bone high above her head and Mazie yapping at her heels.

"She looks like any normal happy little girl," Sam said.

"She is a normal, happy little girl," Jerry sounded more irritated than pleased by Sam's observation. "That's what everyone needs to understand."

Chapter 14

Tara may have been normal, but Sam knew she wasn't really all that happy because normal little girls need friends. Sam did her best to keep Tara busy and occupied. The child was healthy and active, but who knew what was going on inside her head. The sight of Tara being rejected over and over again by children on the playground was breaking Sam's heart. What it was doing to Tara herself could only be guessed at.

Likewise, Sam didn't know what to make of Marcus who she regarded with mixed emotions. On the one hand, he'd been suspended from school for injuring another boy. He'd been provoked, more than provoked, but still, he could have killed the kid. On the other hand, the little juvenile delinquent who arrived most mornings with his grandfather was astoundingly sweet and patient with Tara. He taught her to throw overhand, jump rope, and balance a Frisbee on her head. In some ways Marcus was a perfect big brother, an older friend. But then again, Sam needed a third hand. He was so much older, and a boy, and... Sam had to acknowledge her own racism. He was black and from a rough neighborhood. They never discussed it, but she could see the worried look on Billy's face as he watched Marcus teaching Tara how to break dance or when he saw the two of them crawling across the floor examining bugs through a magnifying glass. Maybe he shared her misgivings about his grandson.

For her part, Tara lacked any reservations regarding Marcus's race or background and was infatuated with her gentleman caller from Buffalo's east side. She waited with eager excitement for Marcus to show up each morning and her look of desolation when he failed to appear was almost comical. Sam decided to let Tara have her little fling, but to keep a close watch whenever the two children were together.

Dan was the other thorn in Sam's side. He'd shown up with Margo one afternoon and wandered into the barn looking for Tara. His face lit up the moment he saw the stripped down Allis-Chalmers at the back of the barn. Billy had removed the wheels and a lot of other parts Sam couldn't identify, and was staring at the rear axle with a wrench hanging limply in his hands. Sam had no idea what the problem was, but it was easy to read defeat in the slump of the old man's shoulders. Dan waved at Tara as he breezed past her and headed straight for the old tractor. It only took him a moment to assess the situation. He found a jack and set it under the axle, took the wrench from Billy, picked up a hammer and crow bar, and set to work. Ten minutes later he lowered the jack and pulled the axle out from under the truck with the aplomb of an experienced professional.

Marcus and Tara, who'd stopped their game of cat's cradle to watch Dan work, applauded as he extracted the heavy metal bar. Billy slapped him on the back and shook his hand. Within no time the men's heads were bobbing at one another as they pointed out the tractor's defects and attractions while thumping each other's shoulders and writing back and forth in Dan's little notebook. By the time Margo showed up twenty minutes later, the two men and the tractor had bonded fast. After that, Dan became a frequent uninvited guest, regularly showing up without Margo to work with Billy in the barn. That, in itself, didn't disturb Sam one way or another. Her problem was that Marcus, fascinated by the competent deaf biker, had begun picking up signs that he used to communicate with Tara.

"It's hopeless," she whined to Jerry when he came to pick up Tara after work. "What are we going to do?"

Jerry smiled; he wasn't as worried as Sam was about Tara learning how to sign. "Maybe we should just relax about the whole sign thing. Why can't she learn both? I bet a lot of deaf people know both."

"That's not what the books say. They say that kids who learn sign stop trying to talk and never learn to read lips. They marry other deaf people and have deaf children and get cut off from the hearing world. That can't be what you want for Tara."

"Whoa there, take a chill pill."

Sam took a deep breath and looked up at Jerry. He was still in his work uniform, but he'd unbuttoned his collar and rolled up his sleeves since the temperature had soared into the upper eighties. There was something calming about the man. He just did whatever needed to be done without a lot of fuss or second guessing. Why in the world had Margo left such a great guy? That was another mystery.

"We're meeting with the speech pathologist on Thursday. After we've talked with her, we'll have a plan and know what we're doing. Until then, don't get your knickers in a knot."

"You're right. It's just that I'm so fond of Tara and I really, really want what's best for her."

"I know you do. You're the best thing that's happened to me and Tara in a long, long time." He reached down and touched Sam's face. "Have I mentioned that I love your new hair style? I don't usually like short hair on girls, but you look great." It made her feel uneasy, being touched by a man who wasn't Ben, but she stood still and let him stroke her hair.

Finishing the quilt was more complicated than Sam had imagined, but several good books and a knowledgeable clerk at Jo-Ann Fabrics finally saw her through to the end. The quilting had been long and tedious, but the result was remarkable. After sewing the pieces together on her machine, she'd hand stitched an outline of Ben's profile with black thread over a large central medallion, then added extra stuffing so his profile stood out in bas relief, trapunto, the clerk had called it. The night she completed the final step, binding the edges with striped silk cut from Ben's old neckties, she took the finished quilt upstairs and spread it on her bed.

From the beginning, she'd imagined sleeping beneath the blanket, being comforted by the bits of wool, terry cloth, denim and corduroy that held a lingering scent, an invisible imprint of her husband. She showered, slipped into a clean nightgown, and crawled beneath the covers expecting to feel Ben's weight, his warmth, his presence. At first she felt nothing except the weight of disappointment, and then the cold realization that nothing she could do would bring Ben back. Unable to sleep, she watched shadows play across the ceiling for awhile, then plumped her pillow and turned onto her side, but her eyes refused to close. As she lay still, staring into the dark, the silhouettes of her arm chair, her dresser, the blank face of her mirror, seemed to move and breathe. A chill spread down her spine and her heart began to pound. The squares that she had so painstakingly sewn and assembled felt as though they were crawling, ever so slowly, across her back, her chest, her legs. Sitting up abruptly, she turned on the bedside light. "Okay," she told herself. "That was a mistake." Sam got out of bed, folded up the quilt, and carried it back downstairs where she made a cup of tea and listened to the radio until her heart stopped racing, and she no longer jumped at her own reflection in the window. She'd give the quilt to Sheila, who had an affinity for ghosts.

The meeting with the speech pathologist was scheduled for two o'clock. Miss Zelinsky was going to meet them at Jerry's house so that she could observe how Tara functioned in her own environment. Sam was inside Jerry's house at his invitation, but something about being there made her uneasy and hyperalert, as though she was trespassing. Jerry showed her around, explaining how the Victorian era farmhouse had been really nice before one of his "stepfathers" had decided to update it in the early sixties. The out-of-work contractor had stayed just long enough to rip out decorative moldings, lay vinyl tile over the original oak floors, and wreak havoc with the heating system. The house had never recovered, and neither had Jerry's mother. She'd gone into a depression, and then died of breast cancer two years later. The house had been boarded up and Jerry was sent to live with his Uncle Skip and Aunt Bibi until he finished high school. Sam looked around the sparsely furnished rooms. The place was a mess, but she had no right to criticize on that front.

An Amish lady came once every other week to wash the floors, run a vacuum, and keep germs and mice from running amok in the kitchen and bath. Unfortunately, this was the other week, and the place was a disaster. Jerry and Tara were upstairs stripping the beds, hanging up clothes, and gathering up Tara's toys. Sam had been assigned the downstairs with orders to "do whatever you can to make the place presentable."

The walls in the living room were a shocking shade of orange that was slightly softened by floral curtains that appeared to be home-made. Magazines, paper, crayons, bits of dismembered Barbie dolls, puzzle pieces, and record albums were strewn about the floor. An empty Jiffy Pop container, stray popcorn kernels and an empty Budweiser can adorned the coffee table. There was an old fashioned sofa with grease stains on the seat and cotton batting pushing through holes in the arms. But someone had sewn throw pillows to match the curtains, and these sat in bright contrast against the tattered cushions. Sam thought of a poem by Elizabeth Bishop about someone who'd embroidered doilies to decorate an old filling station. She couldn't remember the whole poem, but it ended, *somebody loves us all.* She guessed that, in this case, that somebody must be Margo.

She'd only thought of the place as Jerry's house, so it surprised her to see signs of Margo everywhere she looked. There were candles and incense burners on the mantle, psychedelic peace posters on the walls, and several heavy novels in the china cabinet that could only have been Margo's. Jerry read nothing but the *Seneca Sun Journal*, *Time*, and *Sheriff* magazine, so it was a safe bet those books weren't his. Sam made a quick attack on the clutter, gathering up obvious trash and carting it off to a bin in the kitchen. Next, she reunited Kenny Rogers, The Oakridge Boys and Johnny Paycheck with their album covers and added them to the pile of records stacked beside the stereo. At the bottom of the pile she saw more evidence of the missing Margo: albums by Jefferson Airplane, Jimi Hendrix, The Doors, Dylan and Credence Clearwater Revival. The thought struck her that her own taste in books and music was a lot closer to Margo's than to Jerry's. *That's weird*, she thought, as she tidied up the pile of records then went to work reassembling two decapitated Barbies and fitting an alphabet puzzle back together. The place looked fairly presentable by the time the doorbell rang a few minutes before two.

"Good afternoon, I'm Dana Zelinsky. I hope you were expecting me." She had a British accent. *Of course she has a British accent. All speech pathologists probably speak with British accents—the rain in Spain, and all that.* Samantha felt her mouth go slightly dry with fear that her own speech would be judged inadequate. Fortunately, Jerry was all cordiality and good natured welcome.

"Of course we've been expecting you. In fact, we've been looking forward to your visit for some time. Please, have a seat. Would you like a cup of coffee or, maybe you'd, uh, rather have tea?"

"No, no thank you, nothing for me. I'm fine." She surveyed the room, finally selecting a straight backed chair. "May I?"

"Of course, allow me." Jerry moved the small desk chair closer to the couch so that they could all sit together. He was being too proper and correct. The woman had him flustered too. She was fiftyish, thin, and wearing a simple skirt and blouse. Her salt and pepper hair was cut short and her only jewelry was a gold ring on her right hand. She seemed perfectly nice, but Sam felt intimidated. Maybe it was the accent, or maybe it was the appraising way she looked at them.

"And this must be Tara. Come here, darling and say hello. I won't bite." Tara couldn't know what was going on, but Sam could see that she was picking up the strange vibe in the room and keeping her distance. She was bouncing on a rocking horse that she'd outgrown some years ago and looked as though she'd like to gallop away altogether. "Don't you want to come see what I've got in my bag?" Miss Zelinsky pulled a small doll with blonde hair from a satchel. Tara watched her, still bouncing, not ready to engage.

"Well, we won't hurry her. She'll come say hello when she's ready. Why isn't she wearing her hearing aids?"

"She doesn't have hearing aids. She had a body aid when she was about four, but she hated it, and it didn't seem to help." Jerry's voice sounded tight, but he looked at Miss Zelinsky with an earnest expression that said that if they'd made a mistake it was an honest mistake made with the best of intentions. "We read that with profoundly deaf children like Tara, hearing aids don't always help. Did you see her audiogram? She's profoundly hard of hearing. The school has all her records."

"No child is too deaf to benefit from amplification. Who told you that some deaf children don't need hearing aids?"

"Dr. Maxwell Crocker. He was the second audiologist we took her to. That is her mom and I took her. That was three years ago. He has an office in Erie. We were told he's really good."

"Well," Miss Zelinsky pressed her lips together and gazed at the ceiling for quite some time. "There is a difference of opinion in the field of deaf education. There are those people who feel that deafness is an untreatable disability and that we should not frustrate deaf children by putting unreasonable expectations on them. Then there are others, and I count myself solidly in their camp, who have absolute faith that even the most profoundly hard of hearing child can learn to talk using the natural oral-aural method."

"That's the system we've been using," Sam chimed in. "The school gave us some workbooks and an auditory trainer." She'd been sitting quietly, not sure whether she was entitled to participate. After all, she was only a babysitter cum teaching assistant, but she couldn't contain herself any longer.

"I'm delighted to hear that, but she still needs to be fitted with proper amplification, probably binaural body aids given the severity of her loss. Let me give you the name of an audiologist in Toronto. I know it's quite a drive, but you won't be sorry. He studied with me at the University of Manchester where this method was developed. Trust me, you won't find a better man." Miss Zelinsky pulled a pad of paper and a pen from her bag and wrote down the audiologist's name and phone number.

Sam and Jerry exchanged relieved looks that said, "Yes, this is what we've needed. Now we're finally making progress." Sam relaxed and decided that Miss Zelinsky might be just the savior they'd been waiting for.

"So, have you worked with many deaf children? How long does it usually take for them to start talking?" Jerry asked.

"To be honest, there aren't that many deaf children in the area, although I worked with quite a few when I was a student. There are deaf Amish twins out in Sugar Creek. The county had me do an evaluation on them a few years ago, but the Amish run their own schools so I don't know what's become of them. Oh, and there was a lovely little deaf girl living in Seneca Rocks. She wasn't totally deaf. Her hearing loss wasn't as severe as Tara's, but she used hearing aids and they helped her enormously. She was chattering like a magpie the last time I saw her. Her family's moved to Grand Rapids, but I can tell you that she was reading at grade level, carrying on perfectly normal conversations, and that she had a lot of friends when she left. Now that's what we want for your daughter."

Jerry and Sam were nodding in agreement, yes, that's exactly what they wanted. Tara watched them intently, a solemn expression on her face. She clearly understood that she was the topic of discussion. As she watched them, her red rocking horse slowed from a gallop to a leisurely trot. Miss Zelinsky made another attempt to lure her closer with the little yellow haired doll and three small stuffed bears, but Tara would have none of it. She held on tight to the short pole stuck between the horse's ears and wouldn't budge. Miss Zelinsky hiked up her skirt and knelt down on the floor beside the rocking horse. "Tara," she said, holding out the toys. "Can you show me the bear? Where's the bear?" Tara pointed at the Mama bear in Miss Zelinsky's right hand. Sam beamed. *Maybe all the time I've spent working with Tara is paying off—or maybe it's just a lucky guess. After all, there are three bears and only one doll.*

"Oh, isn't Tara the clever girl. Now show me the baby. Where's the baby?" Tara pointed to another bear. Sam's heart sank. "No, not the bear, show me the baby," Miss Zelinsky repeated.

Tara snapped her ring and index finger down against her thumb, "Oh," she said.

"What? What was that?" Miss Zelinsky turned to Jerry. "What is she doing?"

Jerry was smiling, "That's one of her words. When she says oh, it means no. Sam taught her how to say it."

"No, I mean what she was doing with her hand. That thing she did with her fingers. Is that sign? Is she using sign?"

Jerry's face collapsed, "Yeah, I think that's the sign for no. Her mother's been teaching her. We're afraid it might interfere with her learning to talk. That's one of the things we wanted to discuss with you."

"It will interfere, it absolutely will interfere. You have to get her to stop. Once deaf children start signing, they lose all motivation for oral communication. It's the worst thing her mother could do. I was under the impression that her mother was, that she'd..." Miss Zelinsky stood up and began putting the toys away. "I mean, I didn't know that she was still in the picture. I understood she'd moved out of town."

"She came back a few weeks ago. She just showed up one day. The thing is, she's got this deaf boyfriend and they communicate in sign. That's the only way they can talk, so of course when they're with Tara." Jerry shrugged his shoulders with his palms up, the universal sign for, "Life sucks, what can you do?"

"Unless we can get the mother to cooperate, I'm not at all sure that we're going to see the sort of progress that we're looking for, and that would be so sad. Do you suppose she'd meet with me so I could explain the situation to her?"

"Mrs. Panetta is going to talk with her, but I don't know whether it will do any good. I think Margo really wants Tara to learn sign. She doesn't seem to care whether Tara learns to talk or not." Jerry walked over to Tara, picked her up off the rocking horse and sat her on his lap.

"I don't mean to be intrusive, but who has custody of the child? If you can't agree on the best course for Tara's education, it's going to come down to a custody issue."

"The court's going to be making that decision in the next few weeks. I have legal custody at the moment, but Margo's got a lawyer and it could get ugly." Tara's red curls had slipped out of the pink elastic that had been holding them in a loose pony tail. Jerry was absent mindedly putting it back in her hair as he spoke. "My lawyer says Margo will probably win; mothers always win in Catawba County."

"Yes, I've heard that. It's really unfortunate. These things can get so messy and there's so much at stake for this child." Miss Zelinsky looked genuinely pained. "Please let me know if there's anything I can do to help."

"Maybe you could tell the judge that Margo's preventing her daughter from learning how to talk." It seemed possible that this nice English lady might be willing to testify on their behalf. "If you could convince the court that Margo's standing in the way of Tara's chance to live a full life in the hearing world they'd have to make Jerry the custodial parent."

"Well yes, that might work, but I don't know if the school would permit me to testify in this case. Tara's situation is a bit irregular, especially with that new federal law going into effect. Things have to be done differently now, but the school isn't quite in compliance yet. Someone should have tested Tara to determine her aptitude and skill level and then devised an individualized educational plan based on the results. I'm afraid we've put the cart before the horse. It seems that Mrs. Panetta was overeager and sent you off with materials before we had a plan. It would be difficult to testify without all the facts." Miss Zelinsky was clearly annoyed, but trying to put a good face on the situation. "Oh well, no harm done."

Sam caught Jerry's eye. "No harm done?" They'd heard that before. Sam had her doubts.

"Let's make an appointment for you to bring Tara to my office so we can get her tested and develop a plan. How does that sound?"

Sam was beaming, "That sounds great."

"I'm sure Tara is an excellent candidate for oral speech; she's so attentive and alert. Of course, she's fallen behind because she hasn't had the benefit of hearing aids, but she's still very young. You'll be amazed at the progress she'll make with proper amplification. Now, let's see what you've been working on." There were more questions, a review of Tara's workbooks, an exchange of pleasantries, and the promise to call the Toronto audiologist in the morning. A faint odor of soap and breath mints lingered after Miss Zelinsky left.

"Well, that went well, don't you think?" Sam was smiling up at Jerry. She felt vindicated in her adamant resistance to Tara's use of sign.

"I guess," Jerry was irritatingly noncommittal. "I was hoping she'd have more experience working with deaf kids."

"You can't blame her if there aren't more deaf children in Catawba County. She seems very knowledgeable, and she worked with deaf kids back in England. I thought she was great."

"I think you're great," Jerry reached out and put a hand on each of her shoulders, turning Sam to face him. "You really didn't know me from Adam, but you jumped in and taught Tara more in two months than I managed to teach her in the past two years."

His hands were large and warm. She imagined them moving downwards, unbuttoning her blouse. She shrugged her shoulders, trying to free herself from his gentle grasp. "That's not true."

"It is. You're amazing," he refused to let her wriggle away. "You got all those books, and you ask all the right questions, and you don't give up. I know that you might go off to New York or Timbuktu, but I just want you to know how grateful I am to have met you."

"I guess I've gotten attached to Tara. I can just feel all the wheels turning in her head, all the intelligence locked up inside her, but I've got to go now." Sam pulled away from Jerry's hands and headed toward the door intending to make her escape. She stopped abruptly, realizing that she didn't have a car. "Would you drive me home now?"

"Let me take you out for supper first. I owe you that much for helping me clean up the house."

"No, it was nothing. How about a rain check? I'm kind of tired and I want to get back to this project I'm working on, and what about Tara? You'd need to get a babysitter."

Tara was watching from the archway leading to the dining room and Sam was suddenly overcome with the desire to give her a big enveloping hug. She reached out her arms to Tara, who approached cautiously, as though she were meeting Sam for the first time. Sam swooped down and clasped the child in a tight embrace, kissing the top of her head, and whispering little endearments that Tara couldn't hear.

She couldn't see Jerry with her head buried in Tara's hair, but she could feel his eyes, solemn and disappointed, watching her. "Well, another time." Sam relaxed and let Tara go. Jerry pulled his car keys from his pocket, "Come on, I'll drive you home."

CHAPTER 15

"I think he should get a restraining order against her. Margo's fully capable of grabbing Tara and riding off with her on that motorcycle." Sam was putting in a border of salmon colored geraniums along the front of Sheila's house and her hands and nails were encrusted with loamy dirt.

"You've got them too close together. Give them room; they're going to be huge by the end of the summer." Sheila was standing behind Sam, smoking a cigarette and coughing.

"The woman terrifies me. I don't know where she gets the nerve to show up and start bossing Jerry around. Not only is she demanding to see Tara three afternoons a week and all day Saturday but, get this, she wants to use his extra car. I guess it was her car when they were living together, but Jerry paid for it. It's not her car anymore." Sam began pulling up the geraniums she'd just planted by yanking on the flower heads.

"Careful there, don't manhandle the poor things. Get the whole root ball. There you go." This was the first spring that Sheila hadn't put in her own annuals, and she didn't like delegating the job, but she'd recently developed a cough and was always short of breath. Sheila bent to tamp down the soil around one of the replanted flowers and stood up slowly, panting. Once she'd caught her breath, she said, "I warned you about Margo. I told you she was a piece of work."

"You sure called that one. She's all guts and no sense."

"So what did Jerry say? What's he going to do?" Sheila exhaled a plume of smoke then coughed again.

Sam gave her a look of disgust. "He said you should stop smoking."

"Seriously, what did he say?" Sheila persisted.

"He said sure, anything you want, like a total wimp. He didn't even put up a fight. Honestly, you'd think he's still in love with her."

"I can't believe he's letting Margo spend all that time with Tara. She really might kidnap her. That's just the sort of thing she'd do."

"The court order only gave Margo visitation twice a week, but he's letting her pick Tara up from my house every Monday, Wednesday, and Friday afternoon. It's not like I need the work, but it doesn't make sense. First he tells the school that Margo's ruining Tara's chance to talk, and then he lets her take Tara an extra day a week. Something about it creeps me out."

"Well, it's not your choice; it's up to her parents. Whether we like it or not, that woman *is* her mother."

"What do you want me to do with these extra plants? You have about five left over now that we've spread them out." Sam tucked the left over geraniums back into their plastic pots.

"Why don't you take them home? You could plant them around the lilac bush." Sheila suggested.

"No thanks," Sam surveyed her work, avoiding Sheila's eyes.

"Why not? It wouldn't take you a minute to plant them."

"I don't know. I'm just not in the mood for flowers." Sam could hear how petulant her voice sounded. "I don't know why I don't want flowers. I suppose I'm just being childless." The two women froze, the word *childless* resonating between them. "Sorry, Freudian slip," Sam said as she continued staring at the ground. "I meant to say childish."

Sheila put her arm around Sam's shoulder. "I know, I know, believe me I know." Sheila pulled Sam a little closer. "But it's time to put a little color back in your life. Please, take the geraniums and plant them around the lilac bush."

Sam didn't say anything, but she nodded her assent. Although it was late afternoon, the sun was still high in the June sky. The days were so long this time of year. "That's a good girl." Sheila was patting her on the shoulder. "I wish you'd go to church with me sometime. If you could hear Reverend Jollip preach, you'd see everything in a different light."

Sam wished she hadn't rewarded Sheila with that little nod. Her mother-in-law had evidently taken it as an invitation to push into forbidden territory. Sam stiffened slightly. *Why do I have to endure this on top of everything else?*

Sheila knew Sam was a confirmed agnostic, but every month or so she'd take another swipe at trying to convert her. Sam got it. The Grace Evangelical Family Mission had kept Sheila alive after the two uniformed men rang her bell with news of her first son's death. Sam had no idea what kept Sheila alive after she'd lost Ben.

Sheila, a lapsed Presbyterian, would never have gone near Grace Evangelical if it weren't for the AA meetings in its basement. But once she'd stepped inside the simple cinder block structure with its clear glass windows and promise of eternal life, it became her second home. Ben used to make fun of his mother's new found religiosity, although it had nipped her nascent alcoholism in the bud, and gotten her out of the house when he couldn't get her out of a bathrobe. Sam bit her lip and never mocked her mother-in-law for buying the Evangelical hocus pocus, but it took all her self-control to endure her uplifting little sermons.

Apart from its silver-maned minister, a Bible thumper of the old school, who looked like a cross between Mark Twain and the Wizard of Oz, the church's great attraction seemed to be its clear and unwavering view of the afterlife. The church's position on the hereafter seemed blasphemously close to that of Lily Dale's, the nineteenth century spiritualist colony an hour up Route 60. In fact, Sheila had made more than one pilgrimage to Lily Dale, unperturbed by the conundrum of her sons' souls residing simultaneously with God in Heaven and hovering inside an old wooden assembly hall in Western New York. She and a recently widowed friend from the church periodically went to consult one of the registered mediums to ask how their deceased loved ones were doing, and how the afterlife was treating them. Sam always refused to accompany Sheila on these trips. Nevertheless, it was strangely comforting to hear that both the boys were doing well and looking out for little June.

"I couldn't go on living if I didn't know I'd see my boys again." Sheila was looking deep into Sam's eyes with conviction and sincerity.

"Let's not get into this again." Sam pulled away from Sheila and began gathering up the left over flower pots. "I said I'll plant the flowers. In fact, maybe I'll put in a few tomato plants, cucumbers, and green beans. It would be good for Tara to see where her food comes from."

"That would be wonderful. I wish I could help you, but I can't with this infernal cough. Can you still work your garden or has it completely gone to grass and weeds?" An approving smile lit Sheila's face.

"It's pretty far gone, but I can probably dig up the weeds and get the soil turned over." Sam was visualizing Tara pulling beefsteak tomatoes off the vine and popping tender snap peas into her mouth.

"If you asked Billy, I'm sure he'd give you a hand," Sheila suggested. "It's already late in the season, so you'll need to start planting in a couple of days."

"I don't need any help. I can plant a garden by myself."

Sheila's grin grew even wider and her eyes rolled to the heavens. "Hallelujah," was all she said.

*   *   *

Sam set about reclaiming her garden the next afternoon. She wore an old pair of jeans and a red T-shirt that read *Cornell* in large white letters across the chest. The work wasn't difficult since Ben had thoroughly rototilled the plot two years earlier, and the unusually wet spring had left the ground moist and pliable. Still, the temperature was in the mid eighties, the garden was larger than she remembered, and her only tool was an ancient pitchfork that she'd discovered in the barn. She dug the fork into the dirt, stood on it a moment to push it deeper, then turned over a foot of earth. Extracting the loosened weeds and grass, she tossed them to the side before moving on to take another bite out of the overgrown garden. She'd been working like this since Tara had driven off with Margo two hours earlier, and she hadn't finished a quarter of the job. Her arms were sore and a blister had popped up between her thumb and index finger. Months of inactivity had left her weak and she felt daunted by the simple task. Leaning against the pitchfork, she was trying to decide if she had the energy to finish turning another row when she heard Billy's truck clatter up the drive. Sam dove back into her work with feigned enthusiasm so he wouldn't see her slacking off. *Why do I care what some old guy thinks?* she berated herself. Yet she mustered the last of her strength to attack the field with her pitchfork rather than risk hearing some stupid comment about sleeping on the job. She still felt a twinge of embarrassment about how readily she'd ceded the house painting to Billy after making such a fuss about doing it herself.

To her disappointment, Billy didn't wave or call out a greeting. Instead, he headed straight to the barn with Marcus right behind him. Although the new windows had been installed, the roof repaired, and the fresh coat of colonial blue paint applied weeks ago, Billy still stopped by to tinker with the Allis-Chalmers. Sam was accustomed to seeing him come and go at odd hours, and didn't think anything about him showing up this particular afternoon. She turned over another few forkfuls of dirt then stopped again because the blister on her hand was raw and she actually felt a little faint. A moment later Billy and Marcus emerged from the barn, each of them carrying a shovel.

"You look like you could use some help over there." Billy was smiling. Marcus was not smiling.

"No thanks, I'm fine. I was just getting started," Sam lied.

"Well, you've got two strong men to help you now, isn't that right, Marcus?" Marcus nodded, but his sour expression didn't change. "If you want, we could have this garden all dug up and ready to go before supper."

"How much would you charge?" Sam asked. She sure wasn't going to pay for two men when she was barely getting one and a half.

"It's been taken care of. Mrs. Crawford sent us over to help you out. You don't have to pay us anything."

"I told her I was going to do this myself," Sam grumbled, not wanting to admit, even to herself, how relieved she felt to hand the work over to the men.

"If you don't want us, we can pack up and go. Mrs. Crawford just thought you could use a hand, that's all." Marcus brightened at this, probably hoping that he could still get home in time to watch *Soul Train*.

"Well, since you're already here, I guess I wouldn't mind some help. The garden extends to those poles over there." She pointed to a couple pieces of lumber, salvaged from an old ladder that marked the perimeter of the plot.

"You go on inside now and we'll get this little garden knocked out in no time." Billy's eyes crinkled kindly. Marcus sighed and picked up his shovel.

True to his word, Billy and Marcus had the soil turned over with a nice clean edge in a fraction of the time it would have taken Sam. To her surprise, each time she looked out the window, she saw Marcus soldiering away in his plaid bell bottoms, trying to keep up with his grandfather.

They rang her bell before they left to let her know they'd finished. "Do you want something to drink? I have a couple of Cokes in the fridge." Sam offered.

"How about a coke for Marcus and a glass of water for his grandpop." Billy was sweating and out of breath. He wasn't a young man and he'd been pushing himself hard, maybe for the boy's sake, maybe to prove something to himself.

"What are you going to plant in that garden, flowers?" Marcus asked between long swallows of coke.

"Nope, it's going to be a vegetable garden." Sam replied.

"Vegetables, what are you going to do that for?" Marcus clearly didn't see the point.

"I like growing my own food. Everything tastes better when it's fresh out of the garden. What's your favorite vegetable?"

"Pea," Marcus grinned up at her, "tza."

Sam grinned back. *The kid isn't as dumb as he looks.*

The long days didn't seem to make the nights any shorter. Sam tossed and turned in bed, got up to open the bedroom windows, got up again to close them. The new windows slid up and down effortlessly in their vinyl coated sashes. Ben would have loved seeing how the house was being restored, but without him it didn't mean that much to Sam. She got up again to go to the bathroom. The cat swished its tail along her legs as she sat on the toilet, impatient for her to return to bed. It followed her from room to room like a dog, shedding white fur over everything it touched. But Sheila had been right; it was a comfort to have another living creature in the house. Sam scratched the top of its head and the cat leaned into her hand. *So, is this what my future looks like? Am I a woman who lives alone in a big house with a cat to keep me warm at night?* She was twenty-six. That might mean fifty or sixty years of staring out the bathroom window by herself, fifty or sixty years of sharing her supper with a cat.

Maybe she should go back to school and become a doctor. She could join the Peace Corps or Doctors Without Borders. Maybe she could go to New York and join some avant-garde quilting cult, or hole up in a garret with her paints. Maybe she could... Maybe she could...

She still had no idea. Sam padded back to bed followed by the cat. It jumped into bed ahead of her and nestled into Ben's empty pillow and, unlike Sam, fell instantly asleep.

Tara never knew when her mother would arrive, but as soon as she saw the familiar car pull into the drive she knew to grab her bag and race gleefully to the door. It annoyed Sam to watch the little ersatz family happily reconstituting itself with hugs and kisses and exuberant signs, so she usually retreated to the kitchen where she pretended to wash dishes or clean out the refrigerator until they left. Fridays weren't too bad since Sheila arrived shortly after Tara drove off to take Sam for an outing.

It was late June and Sam still hadn't gone to look at cars, still hadn't completed her application to Case Western Reserve University, and still had no plan for her future. Her parents and Sheila had all had it with her, but she still had no idea what she wanted to do. Her mother had actually yelled at her the last time they'd spoken on the phone, "Who cares what you want to do? Just do something." By which Sam surmised she meant, who cares whether or not you want to go back to school, just get the damn application in. Probably she should. Or not. Her mother said she could do whatever she wanted. Maybe she'd take a couple classes at Fredonia in the fall.

The sun was shining when Sheila picked Sam up on Friday afternoon. She was in a hurry and anxious to get to Erie because she had a doctor's appointment that couldn't be rescheduled. Sam didn't relish spending half the afternoon in a doctor's office, but she couldn't complain since Sheila was driving her to the grocery, the drug store, and the post office.

"Is Tara with Margo?" was Sheila's first question as soon as they were settled in her car.

"Yeah, I wonder where they go. Tara can't tell me and Margo and I aren't speaking."

"Jerry could ask her. He should ask her. She's his daughter and he still has custody." As always, Sheila was positive and uncompromising with her opinion.

Sam decided to risk sharing the story that had hijacked her imagination—or at least part of the story. "It's possible that Tara's not Jerry's daughter. I probably shouldn't be telling you this, but Jerry thinks that Margo might have been pregnant before he started seeing her. He's not sure. Everything happened so fast, but it's definitely possible that Tara isn't his."

There was a long silence during which Sam could hear the window wipers' rhythmic beating against the windshield. "Does he know who her father is?" Sheila finally asked.

"Well, he hopes it's him, but he's just not sure." She wanted to add, "Haven't you noticed how much Tara looks like Ben? What's the matter with you, are you blind?" but she held her tongue. She could only roil the water so much.

"That Jerry's a better man than I gave him credit for," Sheila spoke quietly, almost to herself. "Does anyone else suspect he might not be Tara's father?"

"No, I don't think so. He's never even mentioned it to Margo. He just lets her think that he thinks that he's the real dad—and maybe he is. He says it's possible either way. It's just that Margo would have had to get pregnant the first time they slept together and Tara would have to have been born early. Both things are possible, but he has his doubts."

"I'm sure he does, especially given Margo's history with drugs and free love and all that. You certainly don't see any of Jerry in the child; she's the spitting image of her mother."

"Yeah," Sam had said enough. Sheila was driving through an unfamiliar part of town, constantly checking directions scrawled on the back of an envelope. She seemed quieter and more distracted than usual.

"We need to turn left on Hedley. There it is. Now we need to look for North Chestnut. It should be less than a mile from here." It wasn't long before they'd pulled into the parking lot of a modern three story medical building. It was a pretty nondescript place that didn't seem to offer anything that Sheila couldn't have gotten from her internist in Jamestown. It was a new commercial structure, all brick and asphalt with a few small bushes planted as an afterthought beside the entrance. The windows were some sort of tinted glass that reflected the light so you couldn't see inside.

"What are we doing here? Is there something the matter? Are you sick?" Sam was concerned, but not too worried. Apart from an annoying cough, Sheila seemed to be her usual hale and hearty self.

"It's nothing. I just wanted a second opinion about something. Why don't you wait down here? I'd rather see Dr. Frankel by myself." Sheila pointed to one of the black leather benches in the lobby. "Or you could go into the drugstore for a Coke." There was a lunch counter visible through the pair of glass doors.

"Are you sure you don't want me to go upstairs with you?"

"Positive. I won't be long." Sheila got into the elevator and disappeared from view.

"Sam spent half an hour looking through an old copy of *Ladies' Home Journal,* and then another fifteen minutes reading funny greeting cards off a rack in the drug store. She bought a Mars bar, and was unwrapping it as she stood in front of the building directory, idly reading names off the list. She stopped when she came to Frankel, Marvin, Pulmonary Oncology.

Sheila grew irritated when Sam questioned her on the way home. "It's nothing. My internist wanted me to see Dr. Frankel, He was just being cautious. Don't worry about it."

When they got back from Erie, Jerry's second car was parked behind Billy's truck in the driveway. Tara, Marcus and Margo were sitting on the grass feeding left over bits of Kentucky Fried Chicken to the cat. The Allis-Chalmers had been pushed or driven out of the barn and into the sunshine where Dan and Billy were going at it with sheets of sandpaper.

"Do I still live here, or what?" Sam was livid. "Did I invite these people to move in? What do they think they're doing?" She reached across Sheila and hit the car horn hard.

Margo looked up at them, "Do you need us to move the car? Are we in your way?"

"No, you're fine. I was just leaving." Sheila smiled pleasantly, apparently eager to make a clean get away. Sam scowled at Sheila, "I never gave them permission to hang out in my yard. I don't want them here."

"Samantha Crawford, life is too short to get worked up about nonsense."

"But they've taken over my yard." Sam gave Sheila a kiss on the cheek as she got out of the car and headed for the little group sitting on her lawn.

Marcus turned and made a sign to Tara who erupted in giggles. This was too much. Not only was Margo teaching Tara how to sign, but now Marcus was in on the act. She had the feeling that she was fighting a losing battle. "Hey," she called over to them. "The cat's going to throw up if you keep feeding it that garbage."

"Well hello, nice to see you again too. Why yes, we had a lovely afternoon, so kind of you to ask—and why the hell did you honk at us like that? We're not doing anything." Margo was on her feet and towering over Sam.

"What are you doing here? Aren't you supposed to be off somewhere enjoying quality time with your daughter?"

"I thought that's what I was doing. I'm enjoying it here because Dan found an old Allis-Chalmers breathing cap or breather cap or something in Buffalo. He had me call Billy to meet him in your barn so they could install it. They've actually got the thing up and running."

"Look, I'm in a rotten mood. I'm glad they got it started." Sam rubbed the back of her neck. The muscles were stiff and her head was throbbing. "But could you just leave now?"

"I'm sooo sorry. We're just sitting here while the guys prep the tractor before they paint it. We aren't hurting your grass."

"I don't care. I'm telling you to get your ass off my grass. Pack up and leave." What was she saying? What was her problem? Her rational brain told her to get a grip. *No big deal, some people are sitting in my yard watching Billy work on a tractor.* But another crazy part of her was seething. *Why the hell are Tara, and Marcus, and even the damn cat sitting at Margo's feet, playing her games, learning her new language?*

Margo, the certified nut case, was looking at Sam like she was the weirdo. "Hey, calm down, we were just watching the guys work. We didn't touch any of your stuff."

"Well, the show's over, time to go home." Sam was waving her arms, shooing them off.

"Can you give us another minute? We're just finishing up here." Billy called over to her. She hadn't meant for him to hear the exchange with Margo. Sam blushed, not liking how she must have sounded to the kind, soft-spoken man.

"How much longer do you need?" Sam stared at the Allis-Chalmers. All the parts that had been spread out on the floor of the barn for weeks had been reassembled. Every nut, bolt, piston and doohickey had been repaired, refurbished and replaced. With a fresh coat of paint the tractor would look like new. "It looks good."

"I'm driving it when we get it back to Grandpop's farm. You don't need a license to drive on your own property." Marcus's eyes were glowing. *What was it with males and machines?*

"Good for you, Marcus." Sam struggled to keep any note of sarcasm out of her voice. She turned to Billy. "Are you taking it home today?"

"Not if you'll let me keep it in your barn a while longer. I fessed up to the wife about my little affair with Allis. She says I've got to get rid of one of the others before I can bring this one home. Apparently, our place has a four tractor limit."

"Of course you can keep it here as long as you want. That was the deal we made. Take it whenever you want." Sam was anxious to prove that she hadn't become a complete asshole.

Marcus smiled and signed something to Dan who shook his head and repeated the sign, apparently correcting his "pronunciation." Marcus tried the sign again and this time Dan gave him thumbs up.

"Okay, Margo. Did you see that?" Sam pointed at Marcus. "That's what's really bumming me out. Has Mrs. Panetta called you yet? Has she told you that learning sign will ruin Tara's chance to talk? Watching you teach these kids to sign just kills me."

Margo stared at Sam appraisingly. Sam stared back without flinching. "Really?" Margo finally broke the silence. "It kills you? That's awfully strong language from the babysitter. What's your deal here? What's really going on? Maybe you were thinking I wasn't coming back and poor little Tara needed a mommy and poor lonely Jerry needed..." Everyone was looking at them, even Dan and Tara, who couldn't hear a word they were saying, stared with rapt attention. Margo cut her sentence off short.

Sam flushed with some combination of anger and embarrassment. "You don't know anything about me, and that's just fine. But don't go making assumptions. All you need to know is that I was hired to look after Tara and that's what I do. Period."

"Mmm-hmmm," Margo was not convinced.

"My relationship with Jerry is completely professional. We're on friendly terms and I fully support his efforts to teach Tara oral speech, but that's all there is to it." Sam knew this would be a good time to shut up, but her mouth kept rattling on without her like a runaway lawn mower. "However, if I had a daughter like Tara, and if a decent guy loved me and trusted me, I sure wouldn't run off and leave them high and dry because I was too selfish and childish to work things out."

Tara had gotten up and gone over to lean against her mother while Marcus had moved over to stand with the men. Margo lowered her voice, "You don't know anything about me either."

"Hey, it's almost five o'clock. You're absolutely right. It's time for Marcus and me to be heading home." Billy had heard enough for one afternoon.

"And I think it's about time that Margo and Dan left too. Margo, you can leave Tara here. Jerry will pick her up after work." Sam's voice was cold.

"How about if we take her now and drop her off when we're good and ready?" Margo gave Sam a withering look before herding Tara into the car that used to be hers and that Jerry had practically given back to her. Dan followed quickly behind them, climbing into the passenger seat. The cat followed after Tara and stood weaving in and out between the front tires of their car.

"Here kitty. Here kitty, kitty." Sam crouched down and patted her leg trying to attract the cat.

Margo leaned out the car window. "Save your breath. He can't hear you. White cats with blue eyes are always deaf."

"Whoa, that was exciting." Billy was leaning against his tractor, wiping his hands on a dirty rag. "Margo's way out of your weight class, but you looked about ready to take a swing at her anyway. I didn't take you for such a feisty one. I thought I was going to witness an actual cat fight for a minute there. Don't take offence, nothing personal." The last sentence was directed not to Sam, but to the white cat she was holding in her arms.

"That wasn't like me. Margo just gets under my skin." Sam put the cat down and it scampered back to the spot Margo had been sitting to check for stray chicken crumbs.

"I can see that. What's going on between you two young ladies?"

"Margo thinks she can disappear for two years, abandon her daughter, and then roar back into town like nothing ever happened. She's just this sweet, concerned, responsible mother all worried about her baby. Spare me." Sam scarcely recognized herself. *Where did all this anger come from?*

"Marcus, why don't you finish sanding this fender while I chat with Mrs. Crawford for a minute?" He handed a sheet of sandpaper to his grandson then turned back to Sam. "I told you I knew Margo when she was Tara's age, but maybe I should tell you something about her momma. It might give you a different way of seeing things."

"I doubt it. An unhappy childhood is no excuse for what Margo did."

"No, it is not." Billy leaned against the tractor, wiping sweat from his forehead with an old fashioned pocket handkerchief. "I have no idea what made Margo run off like that and I'm sure she shouldn't have done it, not the way she did, but I also know where that girl comes from. You know, the French have an expression, *tout comprendre, c'est tout pardoner.*"

"I don't know what that means. I took German in high school."

"It means 'to understand everything, is to forgive everything.' I try to remember that."

"I'm not sure that's true. Maybe it is. I don't know. Where did you learn French?"

"I drove for the Red Ball Express during the war, World War Two, not Vietnam. I was stationed in France the better part of a year."

"Not many soldiers learn the language when they're in a battle zone. I don't know anyone who came back from Saigon speaking Vietnamese."

"Well, I learned a lot of things over there. It was a very educational experience. I learned people do things you could never understand if you hadn't been there yourself."

"So what's Margo's story?"

"Her mom tended bar at the Lost Angel Grill. She made most of her money in tips, but sometimes she'd take a customer home if she liked him and thought he might be the generous sort. It's not like she went home with a different guy every night, but still, there were a lot of guys and a lot of nights."

"And you know this how?" Sam leaned against the tractor waiting for the rest of the story.

"My wife, Louella, cooked for the Lost Angel back in those days. She knew Margo since before she was born. Her momma used to bring Margo in and keep her behind the bar when she didn't have anyone to look after her at home. She'd throw a bunch of coats on the floor and let her sleep in the closet until closing time."

"So?" Sam would need to know a lot more if she were going to forgive anything.

"So, more than once her momma forgot she had a baby sleeping on the floor. She'd just go off with some guy and leave Margo in the coat closet. Louella would have to call Jean at home to come pick up her daughter, and then Jean would start cussing at Louella like it was her fault. Jean never drank on the job, but she'd start in the minute she clocked out. Louella figured she kept a bottle in her car because she'd be drunk by the time she got home, and Jean was a mean drunk, not that she was all that sweet when she was sober. She'd stagger back in with no apology, start shaking and dragging that sleepy child like she was some sort of rag doll, yelling at her the whole time. It happened more than once, maybe four or five times, and Louella would be up half the night worrying about Margo every time it happened. We used to wonder if we should call someone and tell them what was going on, but what would we have told them exactly?"

"I don't know." Sam was getting the picture, but none of it excused what Margo did.

"But that child turned out to be tough stuff and she had a mouth on her. By the time Margo was six or seven, she was sticking up for herself. If Jean got out of line, that little one would give her what for, really let her have it, and Jean would back off. Well, sometimes she'd back off. Sometimes she'd lay into the kid and one of the customers would have to step in and tell her that she'd gone too far.

"Louella had an idea about who Margo's daddy was. There was a guy who showed up at the Lost Angel in a three piece suit, which made him pretty memorable. He was in town for a couple weeks on business and he took up with Jean right about that time. We used to laugh that he must have been a lawyer because Margo could argue her momma into a corner almost as soon as she could talk."

"That does seem to be her forte," Sam agreed. "So, what became of Jean? Does Tara have an alcoholic grandma lurking around somewhere?"

"Louella left the Lost Angel when Margo was about nine or ten. By that time, Margo was pretty much raising herself. I think she had a grandmother who used to pay some attention to her, but she was basically on her own. We didn't see her very often after that, maybe if we ran into her on the street or something. Then we read an article in the *Journal*, with a picture of this beautiful young woman that said Margo Michalski had won a scholarship to an expensive private school. Louella couldn't believe it. She was so tickled that she cut out that article and slid it under the glass on her dressing table. It's still there. I don't know if she heard that Margo never went to college. We never talked about it after that, kind of left it with a happy ending."

"What about Jean, Tara's grandmother? Is she still in the picture?" Sam persisted.

"The last we heard, Jean moved down to Florida with a retired serviceman she picked up somewhere. She fell in love with his pension and goodbye, tootsie, goodbye. Maybe Margo knows where she is, maybe she doesn't. Like I said, Margo pretty much raised herself."

"I'm done sanding. Can I drive the tractor back to the barn? I know how to drive it," Marcus interrupted. Sam wondered how much he'd heard.

"You know how to drive it, but do you know how to start it? It's not like starting a car. Let's see what you know. Tell me how you'd cold start this tractor up?"

Marcus was all smiles. This was a test he could ace. "First you get the crank." Marcus hoisted himself up and over the back of the tractor and pulled a thin metal rod from its housing below the steering wheel. "Then you set the throttle to the first notch." He adjusted a lever to the right of the driver's seat. "Then," he jumped off the tractor and ran around to the front. "You put the crank in here." He inserted the crank in a small hole. "Then you go over here and turn on the gas." He turned a tiny lever just visible beneath the engine case. "Then you got to muscle it."

"Whoa. Stop there young man. First, tell me which side do you stand on?"

"I know this stuff. I told you. I know how to do it." Marcus stood in front of the Allis-Chalmers to the right of the crank. "I stand here and I brace one leg against the tire. Right?"

"That's right, but don't bend over the crank too far. It can kick back and take your fool head off. Let's see what you can do."

CHAPTER 16

"Betsy Ross must have sewn herself into a stupor. I've never seen so many flags in my life." The country's bicentennial had been all over the national news since the first of the year, but Sam hadn't anticipated the way Kleiner would throw itself into the celebration. Banners and flags festooned every telephone pole, street light and store front. Tree trunks were wrapped in red, white and blue ribbon and even the curbing had been painted red, white and blue for the occasion. "Maybe we should paint your car red, white and blue and play 'Yankee Doodle' on the car horn."

"Oh, we should. Wouldn't that be fun? Is there some sort of paint that would wash off after the holiday?" Sheila had missed the sarcastic tone in Samantha's voice. Sam smiled back at her mother-in-law; the woman didn't have a cynical or ironic bone in her body. She was a true believer in her God, her country, her president, and her doctor.

After her consultation with the pulmonary oncologist, Sheila had been understandably jittery and out of sorts for a few days and then, remarkably, her good spirits had returned. When Sam pressed for Dr. Frankel's diagnosis Sheila told her not to worry. The doctor had assured her these things were usually false alarms, and there was no sense getting worked up unless the biopsy was positive. Apparently she'd done as she'd been told. If anything, Sheila seemed more energetic and optimistic than usual. It was Sam who'd become anxious and morose.

In fact, on that sunny afternoon in late June, Sheila was ebullient. "I'm so glad to see the country finally remembering what it stands for, what it represents in the world. This is how we used to celebrate the fourth of July when I was a girl." Sheila was probably remembering the hyperpatriotism of the Second World War. She remembered victory gardens, war stamps, and rationing, and could never understand why the country failed to support the Vietnam War in the same way. Maybe she was being patronizing, but Sam had stopped arguing the point. Sheila's world was painted with a limited palette. Things were pretty much red, white, and blue, or black and white, so Sam didn't say a word. Or maybe she held her tongue because Sheila had lost a son in Vietnam, and Sam, of all people, wasn't about to rub salt into that particular wound.

"Let's stop at the library first so we won't have to leave our groceries in a hot car while we look around." Sheila had already turned off of Grant onto Prentice and was slowing as they approached the library parking lot.

"That makes sense." Sam had a pile of overdue books on her lap that she was anxious to return. She and Sheila had been driving into Erie for their weekly outings, so she hadn't been to Kleiner for a while even though it was only a fifteen minute drive from her house. This was Tara's afternoon with Margo, so Sam and Sheila were on their own. A blast of air conditioning hit the two women as they walked through the library's vestibule. Air conditioning was a recent addition, installed the previous summer. The library's cool, dark interior, with its worn marble floors, high arched windows, and scent of furniture polish, library paste and old paper was a sanctuary from the heat. She took a deep breath and felt the muscles in her neck relax. She paused to take a drink from the old fashioned porcelain water fountain. Maybe she'd spend a couple of hours here, just reading and drawing in her sketchbook.

Before she could lift her head from the drinking fountain, a small child barreled into her at full speed and began hugging her around her waist. Looking down she saw Tara's little face beaming up at her. Sam's first impulse was to swoop Tara into her arms, but the sight of Margo bearing down on them made her freeze where she stood. She managed to give Tara a friendly smile and to nod approvingly at the book she held up for her inspection before Margo grabbed Tara's hand and pulled her away.

Sam's calm was shattered in an instant. She'd seen Margo less than two hours ago when she'd picked up her daughter, but running into her in public completely rattled Sam's nerves. Why did Margo get to her like this? *Behave like an adult*, she cautioned herself. *Just because Margo's an idiot, doesn't mean you have to be one.* She took another sip of water then looked up to face Margo, "Well, fancy meeting you here. You didn't mention that you were taking Tara to the library."

"Sorry, I didn't think you were interested, given the way you practically slammed the door in my face. You know, we could try being civil toward each other. Do you think we could manage that?"

"I'm sorry about the other day when Dan was working on the tractor. All of you being there took me by surprise. I think I may have overreacted." Sam was surprised to hear herself apologize, and yet relieved. Her bad behavior had been on her conscience.

"You think? We weren't doing anything but sitting on the grass."

"I know. I was in a terrible mood. I'd just gotten some bad news and I wasn't thinking straight. I'm not usually like that."

"So, is that an apology?"

"Yeah, I'm sorry." Sam looked right into Margo's blue eyes and watched them soften as she smiled.

"Apology accepted," she held out her hand. Sam hesitated awkwardly a moment before holding out her own hand in return. "So, what are you reading?" Margo looked at the books Sam was still clutching in her free hand.

"*Centennial* by James Michener," Sam shifted the books she was carrying against her chest. They were getting heavy.

"I read that." Margo eyed the eight hundred plus page book in Sam's arms. "Michener should sell his books by the pound. He'd be rich."

"I think he *is* rich."

"Yeah, I bet he is, must be nice. Check out *Ragtime* if you haven't read it yet. I just returned it. It's still in the bin.

"I will. I've been meaning to read it for a while."

"Well, we've got to go. I'm taking Tara shopping for some new clothes; she's outgrown most of her things."

"Alright, then. Have a nice afternoon. Bye, Tara." Samantha waved goodbye and Tara waved back at her, smiling broadly.

Sheila had been watching from the sidelines, but now she hurried up to Sam, "What was that? Did you know Margo was going to be here?"

"No way, it was pretty weird, actually. She took me completely by surprise. At least we didn't get into anything ugly. In fact, it went pretty well. She recommended a book for me to read. "

"Well, good then, let's check out a couple of things then finish our shopping, I'm starting to droop." Sheila was apparently not as enamored of the air conditioning as Sam was.

Sam kissed her vision of an afternoon relaxing in the library goodbye. "I won't be more than ten minutes." She dropped her old books on the return cart and began picking through the pile for Margo's copy of *Ragtime*. Sheila was standing at the counter talking with the clerk when Sam walked over to check out her new selections.

"It's called *Human Personality and Its Survival of Bodily Death* by F.W.K. Myers." Sheila was reading from a note card she'd pulled from her purse. "It's an old book, but I've been told it's still available."

Sam shook her head and smirked, *Survival of bodily death?* Sheila's obsession with ghosts and spirits was... She suddenly felt tears pricking at her eyes. The woman had lost her whole family and now she might be facing cancer. No wonder she was chasing ghosts. Sam swallowed hard and closed her eyes. Sheila could be annoying and pushy, but Sam realized how much she loved her. As soon as the clerk stepped away to check the card catalogue, Sam put her arm around Sheila's shoulders. "You don't need to worry about all that. You're going to stay right here with me in this plane of existence for a long, long time."

"Maybe, maybe not." Sheila sounded more cross than comforted. "Anyway, one of the women from Lilly Dale told me to read it. It's a very famous and well respected work."

The clerk reappeared, "It's available and in stock, but at the Jamestown branch. Do you want us to order it for you or do you want to drive over and pick it up yourself?"

"Please ask them to hold it. Tell them I'll pick it up tomorrow."

Sam and Sheila checked out their books and were about to leave when the new librarian that Sam had met on her last visit emerged from the "Employees Only' elevator coming up from the basement. Her face lit up when she saw Sam and she wheeled her book cart in her direction. "Hi there, I've been hoping to see you again. Isn't it wonderful about Tara? You must be so relieved."

"Relieved?" Sam knit her brow and cocked her head to one side. "Relieved about what?"

"Well, Tara's mom is back, and she has Tara enrolled in Mom and Me classes at the library, and she has her scheduled for an interview at St. Francis de Sales for the fall. It's more than we could have imagined just a few weeks ago. You must be thrilled."

"What are you talking about? Tara's not going to St. Francis de Sales. It's an old-fashioned boarding school for the deaf—and it's in Buffalo for God's sake. You don't send a seven-year-old away to boarding school. Did Margo really say that?"

"Yes, I'm sorry, I thought, I mean, we talked about Tara needing friends, and I thought you knew about the school. I shouldn't have sprung the news on you like that. Don't worry about St. Francis de Sales. It has a wonderful reputation. The people there really know what they're doing."

"I work with Tara almost every day. I talk with her father almost every day and...," Sam literally clamped her mouth shut so hard she could hear her teeth clink. *This is none of Sara Something-or-Other's business.*

She took a deep breath and plastered a neat little smile over her appalled expression. "Thank you for letting me know about Margo's plans. I guess we have a lot to talk about. And what about those Mom and Me classes, aren't those for much younger children?"

"They are, but Tara missed so much because she can't hear that her mom and I thought it would be a good idea to go back and make sure that she has the basics: colors, numbers, the names of animals, that sort of thing. Margo sits beside Tara and teaches her the sign for each word while the teacher holds up pictures or tells a story. It's so sweet. Some of the other children are even picking up some sign."

"How sweet." Sam flashed another disingenuous smile as the offhand phrase, "her mom and I thought," echoed through her mind. The nice librarian lady was in cahoots with Margo; she'd sold her soul to that red-headed devil.

"Well, thanks for everything. I'm sorry, but I've forgotten your name."

"Sarabelle Peterson."

"Well then, goodbye Sarabelle. Nice to see you again."

As soon as they were outside, and safely beyond Sarabelle's auditory range, Sam began to rant. "Did you hear that? Margo is absolutely determined to undermine everything Jerry's trying to do for Tara. I bet she never even talked to Mrs. Panetta. She thinks she's smarter than all the experts, smarter than Jerry, and I just apologized to her. Can you believe that? I just told her I was sorry for being rude and all the time she was plotting to ship Tara off to Buffalo. Why doesn't she give custody to Jerry if she doesn't want to take care of Tara? Why doesn't she just go back to wherever she was living before?"

"I don't know, dear. I really don't know. Frankly, I was relieved to find out that Margo's been taking Tara to the library. I had visions of Tara hanging out with Margo and that long haired boyfriend of hers, drinking beer and using drugs in their motel room."

"You thought Tara was drinking beer and smoking pot?"

"Well, I thought they might be doing those things in front of her. At least the library is safe. It's a good place for them to go."

"I'm not so sure. You heard Sarabelle. Margo takes Tara to the library because it's a good place to teach her sign language."

"Are you sure that's such a bad thing? The librarian seemed to think it was a good idea. After all, Tara needs to learn some sort of language."

"Of course she needs to learn a language. How about English? She needs to learn English, and the more she signs the harder that's going to be. You know what the experts say. Haven't we had this discussion?"

"Indeed we have, but at the moment I have other things on my mind." Sheila's earlier buoyancy had left her. "I just want to grab my groceries and some cigarettes then head home. I don't think I have the energy for anything else today."

"Sheila, please no cigarettes. You've got to stop smoking. Aren't you worried about what it's doing to you?"

"No, I'm not worried. That's where we're different, Samantha. I have faith, and having faith means knowing your life is in God's hands. At AA they used to teach us, "Let go and let God," and that's what I intend to do. It's His problem, not mine."

"Sheila, that's bullshit. It's not a breach of faith to take your hand off a hot stove. You might have cancer for God's sake."

Sheila sighed and shook her head as though she were registering indignation more from duty than conviction, "Samantha Crawford, I don't ever want to hear you use that word again."

Which word, thought Sam, *bullshit or cancer?* She hadn't used either one in Sheila's presence before this afternoon, but she didn't ask out loud. She could see that Sheila didn't have the energy for a fight.

Sam wasn't scheduled to see Jerry again until Monday morning. She'd been seeing less of him since Margo was taking Tara three afternoons a week and driving her directly home. That meant there were three fewer afternoons when Jerry appeared at her door to pick up his daughter, three fewer opportunities to talk with him about Tara's future, three fewer evenings when he and Tara might stay and have supper with her, and three fewer nights when his eyes would stalk her from room to room with a longing that she was still pretending to ignore.

She knew she was being stupid, but she'd made the rules. The first rule was that Jerry and Tara could stay for supper then spend the evening talking, watching TV, or playing silly games, but they could not go out to dinner or a movie. Going out would be a date, and Sam wasn't ready to admit that she was dating. The fact that she saw Jerry nearly every day and spoke with him on the phone twice as often did strike her as hypocritical, yet somehow the rule stuck. More problematic was the rule that said they could curl up together on the couch, play footsie during dinner, or lean against each other at the kitchen sink, but they couldn't kiss or share a true embrace. Permitted intimacies, she told herself, were just normal familiarities between friends; anything more would be too much. That's what she told herself, but she knew she couldn't duck the reality much longer.

It was seven o'clock on Friday night, and she'd just tossed the aluminum tray from a Swanson TV dinner into the trash. There was nothing on TV and she was too jumpy to concentrate on the copy of *Ragtime* waiting on the coffee table. She had to talk to Jerry and she couldn't wait until Monday. She had to tell him about her conversation with Sarabelle at the library, even if that meant breaking rule number three, no social visits on the weekend. *It's my own stupid rule for heaven's sake, and rules are made to be broken.* She mentally added a clause that said work related visits were perfectly acceptable, and since this was clearly a work related crisis she picked up the phone.

"Jerry, I'm sorry to bother you, but we have to talk. The weirdest thing happened at the library today."

"Let me turn off the radio. I was just listening to the game."

"Do you want me to call back later?" Sam had no idea who was playing or what team he might be rooting for.

"Nope, we were losing anyway. I'll be right back." He was gone for a moment during which time Sam realized how little she knew of Jerry's life.

"So, what's up?" His voice was upbeat. He was clearly glad she'd called, which made her more anxious. This was a business call and she didn't want him getting the wrong idea. Still, she could feel her own heartbeat quicken and she knew she wasn't talking quite normally, her breath and her words seemed out of sync with one another. Were these symptoms of her distress about Margo, or was she nervous and excited because she was talking to Jerry? She never knew what she was feeling anymore. Ever since the accident she'd felt as though she were living in someone else's body.

She took a deep breath and plunged in, "I heard something really disturbing at the library today and I thought you should know about it right away. Apparently Margo's planning to enroll Tara at that school for the deaf in Buffalo this fall. That's what she told the librarian."

"She can't do that. I still have custody."

"She knows that. She's not stupid. My guess is that she really believes that she's going to win the custody suit. It's a boarding school Jerry. She wants to ship a seven-year-old off to a boarding school. Oh, and all the kids there sign. I think they even have deaf teachers who use sign. Tara would never learn to talk."

"Are you sure? Who told you all this?"

"Sarabelle Peterson, the new librarian at Kleiner Library. She and Margo have gotten chummy. She thought I'd be thrilled with the news."

"Damn!" Samantha heard a plate crash. She didn't know if it had been dropped or thrown. "Damn Margo, damn, damn, damn." There was another crash and then just Jerry's heavy breathing.

"Jerry, Where's Tara? You're going to frighten her."

"No. She won't be frightened because she can't hear. My daughter's deaf, her mother's insane, and I'm falling apart."

Sam was no longer worried that Jerry thought she'd called to flirt. He was upset, and he had a temper. Sam used her most authoritative and reasonable voice. "Jerry, I want you to come over tomorrow so we can talk. We need a plan. There's got to be something we can do. I'm sure it's not as bad as it sounds. The court has to realize that you're the one who really loves Tara. What judge is going to take a child out of a safe, secure home and send her off to a boarding school with strangers, or to who knows where on the back of a motorcycle?"

"You don't know everything; there's more. I talked to my attorney again today. Margo's submitted all sorts of documents showing what a clean, upstanding citizen she's become." He dropped his voice, "and there are things she could say about me that wouldn't exactly help my case. Allen thinks the judge will probably give her custody."

"It won't happen. No one would do that."

"Don't be so sure. I've seen the court do some pretty ugly things. You don't work in the system like I do. Some judges are really stupid and pig-headed."

She switched to a soothing, almost cajoling tone. "So, why don't you come over tomorrow morning and we'll talk."

"Not until after I've taken out a restraining order against Margo. I still have custody and I'm not letting her take my daughter to Buffalo or anywhere else. She's not getting away with this."

"Do you have grounds for a restraining order?"

"Attempted kidnapping. I'll talk to you tomorrow. I'm too upset to talk anymore tonight. Thanks for letting me know what's going on." Jerry hung up the phone before Sam could say another word."

"Good night," Sam said to the silence inside her phone. *What am I doing, jumping into the middle of someone else's war?* The cat leaped up on the table and paced back and forth, rubbing himself against her sleeve and purring as she scratched his head.

"Hey cat, what do you think? I could really use some good advice about now. What should I do?" The cat began purring more insistently. "I don't want to hear about tuna fish, this is serious. Can you think about someone besides yourself for a change?" The cat, in its unmistakably feline way, said "no," so Sam got up to fill his food bowl.

The phone rang as the cat was watching kibble flow from the bag. For a moment Sam imagined that it was Jerry calling back, but then she looked at the clock and realized it must be her mother checking in.

"Hi, sweetie, how did your day go?" Her mother always started the same way. Sometimes this daily ritual seemed annoying and intrusive, but this evening Sam was glad to hear her voice.

"Not great. Tara's mother wants to send her to a boarding school in Buffalo."

"She's too young for that. I never recommend boarding school for children younger than twelve, and fourteen is better. Do you want me to talk to her?" Sam flinched; her mother was so used to being the pediatric expert that she assumed the seas would part if she said the word.

"I don't think Margo would talk to you, but I wish she'd listen to somebody. Tara's barely seven years old. It's criminal."

"It sounds as though something went very wrong with that mother-child bonding process. First, the mother abandons her daughter, and now she wants to put her in a boarding school. That's very abnormal, absolutely pathological."

"Exactly, and Jerry's lawyer thinks the judge is going to give Margo custody. Why does she even want custody?"

"I don't know Margo, but maybe it's a power trip. Maybe Margo just doesn't want her husband to have their daughter. I feel sorry for that child."

Sam was nodding her head in agreement, even though the gesture was lost on her mother back in Cleveland. "You're right, Mom. I think that's it. She's maliciously jerking everyone around for the hell of it. The whole thing makes me sick. I don't know if I'll be able to sleep tonight."

"Why wouldn't you sleep? It's a sad story, but it's not your problem. Your problem is figuring out what you're going to do this fall."

"I've gotten very attached to Tara. She means a lot to me." Sam wasn't going to say a word about her suspicion, her hope, that Tara was Ben's daughter. Her mother would ask her what she'd been smoking, what alternate reality she lived in. After all, there was no hard evidence, nothing to support her theory, except that Ben once dated Margo and Tara had his eyes.

It had been a long time since Sam had sat by the phone waiting for a man to call, but that's what she found herself doing on Saturday afternoon. Since there was no phone in the barn she was painting in the kitchen. Her easel was propped up in the middle of the room and angled toward the light. She was working on one of her "self-portraits."

They weren't physical likenesses, but rather a series of fanciful projections of her emotional state. She'd begun them on the drive back from Cleveland and had executed dozens of drawings on the theme. Now she was committing some of them to canvas. This particular "self-portrait" was a still life of cold toast, half a cup of coffee with lipstick stains on the rim, a melting stick of butter, and a jar of strawberry jam that had tipped over and oozed like blood onto an asphalt tabletop. A bird's footprints led from the jam to the edge of the table where they disappeared. There was no bird in the picture, but a dark shadow that might be wings danced against one wall. Sam's real talent was for drawing, but sometimes she wanted to work in a medium that felt bigger and more permanent than a pencil sketch, so she'd pushed herself to work with the paint Aunt Harriet had bought her.

She'd completed the cartoon, and was filling in some large background spaces when the telephone rang. Laying her palette and brush on the table, she grabbed for the receiver. It was Sheila. Sam tried to keep the disappointment out of her voice. "Hi Sheila, oh nothing much, I'm just messing around with my paints. Anything special? Jeez, I haven't been to a movie in ages. I don't know. What's playing? Yeah, I heard it was pretty good; at least it's not as violent and depressing as most of the stuff this year. All right, it's a date. I need to get out of the house; these walls are beginning to close in on me. No, I'll just make a sandwich for supper. I'll be ready at six-thirty. Thanks for calling. Bye."

The phone didn't ring again all afternoon. She almost called Sheila to cancel their plans so that she would be at home if Jerry called, but some wiser self prevailed and she ran out the door as soon as Sheila honked her horn. Sheila was dressed in a floral shirtwaist dress with coordinating pumps and purse. Sam had forgotten that Sheila dressed for movies and felt a little guilty for not changing out of her paint spattered jeans and T-shirt. If Sheila noticed, and of course she must have, she didn't say a word.

"Where's *Silver Streak* playing?" There were two possibilities, the new multiplex in Jamestown or the old Fillmore Theater in Kleiner.

"Jamestown, but we have plenty of time. It doesn't start for an hour. How was your day?"

"Quiet, too quiet actually. All the quiet is starting to get on my nerves." Sam found this a hard admission to make after insisting for more than a year that all she wanted was to be left alone.

"You're right. Too much quiet is bad for you, especially at your age. What's the expression; you'll have plenty of time to be quiet when you're dead?"

"I think it goes, you'll have plenty of time to sleep when you're dead," Sam corrected her.

"Yes, that's it. I wouldn't expect you to understand, but peace and quiet sound pretty good to me at the moment. Young people need noise and activity, but at my age a little everlasting peace sounds wonderful."

Sam had just gotten into the car. They were supposed to be going to a funny movie not a funeral, why did the conversation have to get so heavy so fast? She'd looked forward to the evening as an opportunity to spend time with Sheila, to take her mind off the biopsy, but that plan didn't seem to be working. Sheila was obsessed with her own mortality since she'd seen the doctor, obsessed but not depressed. In fact, if anything, she struck Sam as ebullient, or maybe the word was manic. Sam wanted to console Sheila, but her words sounded trite and not entirely honest.

"You're not old, Sheila. I know you're thinking about that biopsy, but the doctor said not to worry. It's probably a false alarm. You have miles to go before you sleep."

"I know. You're probably right. Still, I was making some notes this afternoon. If it turns out that I do have cancer, I want Reverend Jollip to conduct a Service of Celebration at Grace Evangelical Family Mission. He'll know what to say, he's known me for years now. I already have a plot next to my husband at South Shore Cemetery so all they'll have to do is add my name to the stone ...'

"Sheila, I'm not planning your funeral. You're going to be fine," Sam protested, but Sheila continued to talk right over her.

"And I don't want Myra Barlow singing. She thinks she's an opera star, but she sets everyone's teeth on edge. Get Tildy Rudolph if you can, or else Norm Watts." Sheila's eyes were shining and she looked more alive than Sam had seen her in awhile. She sounded as though she were planning a party. "They'll want to sing 'Amazing Grace' and 'Nearer My God to Thee' and that's fine, but I love Patsy Cline so be sure that they include 'Just a Closer Walk' and 'Life's Railway to Heaven'. I won't rest easy unless they play some Patsy Cline. Do you want me to give you my notes?"

"No."

"Well, okay then, but don't forget. Oh, and I want to wear the gray suit I wore at Easter last year with the cream colored silk blouse, but no jewelry." Sam must have looked stricken, because Sheila patted her hand. "Don't look at me like that. Just imagine that I've been on a long visit and now I'm going home. You'll be fine. I'm leaving my house to the church, but you get all the contents and whatever I have in the bank so you won't have to worry about money."

"I'm not worried about money, I'm worried about you." Sam felt confused. Sheila was playing this all wrong.

"I'm meeting with Allen Siebert on Thursday to write a new will. I've been in such a state that I haven't looked at it since Ben and June died, so of course it's all got to be changed."

"Sheila, I don't want any of your stuff, and I don't want to plan another funeral. Please, just be well and live a long time, and stop talking about dying. That's all I want."

"It doesn't matter what you or I want; it's in the hands of God. Nothing we do is going to change that." Large raindrops that seemed to have come out of nowhere began hitting the windshield. It was the end of June and the rain appeared to be falling through a bright, cloudless sky. Sheila switched on her windshield wipers. Something about the rain made the car's interior feel more intimate and cozy.

The two of them drove on a few minutes without a word, and then Sheila startled Sam by asking, "Do you think that soul's have forms that resemble their earthly bodies?" Sam was relieved when she went on, not waiting for an answer. "I hope they do, but that's probably just wishful thinking. Reverend Jollip preaches that souls are pure spirit and they have a whole different way of recognizing one another. It probably has nothing to do with our earthly senses. But I'd love to see my boys again, really see them, my boys and June. What do you think? Do you ever think about the afterlife?"

What could she say? She didn't want to lie, but she wouldn't hurt Sheila for the world. "I hope you're right and it's a big family reunion, just like you picture it, but I'm an agnostic. That means I'm just going to wait and let God surprise me." A loud crash of thunder rocked the car. For a moment Sam considered that the thunderbolt might be God's response to her lack of faith, but immediately dismissed the thought.

The drops had turned to a downpour, and rain was cascading down the window in sheets. Sheila turned on her headlights, but didn't slow down. The road curved and twisted past empty fields and intermittent houses, Memory Lane Antiques, Happy Hooker's Bait and Tackle, Dairy Queen, Levi's Fish Fry, a corn field, a Shell Station and then The Jamestown Regal Theater. The parking lot, already dotted with inch deep puddles, was packed with cars. Storms came on fast and with terrible ferocity this time of year, yet neither of them had worn a coat. Sam thought of Sheila's good leather pumps. "We may as well just turn on the radio and wait it out. We have time."

"There's an umbrella in the backseat. I'll park as close as I can, and we'll make a run for it."

"Sheila, the lot's full. There aren't any close in spots left. Why don't we just sit here and listen to the radio until it slows down."

"Don't be such an old lady. Let's go for it. You only live once." Sheila pulled into an empty space at the end of a long row of cars.

"Are you sure?" It's coming down in buckets and we're probably a hundred yards from the door."

"Last one in's a rotten egg." Sheila was about to bound out of the car.

"No, stop. Wait a minute." Sam fished around behind her seat and found an old umbrella with a curved wooden handle. She opened the car door and jumped out holding the umbrella in front of her as she ran around to Sheila's side. Sheila grabbed Sam's elbow and they headed toward the box office. Sheila's squeals and laughter quickly turned to gasps as the quick pace left her breathless. The umbrella blew inside out and offered no shelter against the wind and rain that sliced through their thin summer clothes. They slowed to a crawl, hobbling the last thirty yards, with Sheila panting heavily with every step. By the time they'd reached the lobby they were both soaked. The air conditioning had been cranked up to full blast, chilling them to the bone. Sam's jeans and T-shirt were soaked, but otherwise undamaged. Sheila's thin summer frock stuck to her body and the cheap floral print bled pink and purple dye.

"We should have waited in the car. This was stupid." Sam was trying to dry Sheila with a handful of wadded Kleenex from her purse. They headed into the lady's room where a quantity of paper towels did a more effective job.

"I thought it would be fun. I should have more sense at my age." Sheila was dabbing her face with one of the towels. Sam wasn't sure if she was wiping away tears or rain or both. "I was remembering walking home from school in the rain with my girlfriends, splashing and singing. My mother used to say I must be part mermaid." Sheila looked up, smiling at the memory. "I thought it would be like that. Isn't that silly? Maybe the cancer is rotting my brain."

"You don't have cancer. It's just a little rain water. We'll dry off in no time. I just hope you don't catch cold." Sheila had started coughing again and Sam watched her with a worried expression.

They wandered back into the lobby and were standing in line to buy tickets when Sam saw Margo walk into the theater dressed in a hooded parka and carrying an umbrella. She was all alone, which seemed weird to Sam who had never gone to a movie by herself. *Where is her boyfriend? Maybe deaf people don't go to movies.* To Sam's dismay, Margo walked over and stood behind them in line.

"Small world, huh?" Margo smiled as if they were old friends. If their places had been reversed and Sam had walked into the theater to find Margo waiting at the box office, she would have averted her eyes and waited in the lady's room until the coast was clear. Sam and Sheila were trapped into making small talk, feeling awkward and miserable. "Wow, you guys must have really been out in the worst of it. You're both soaked to the skin."

"We're fine, just a little damp," Sam turned away to hand a five dollar bill to the lady in the ticket booth. Pocketing the change, they were about to leave when Sheila had another coughing fit.

"That doesn't sound good. You need to keep warm with a cough like that. Here, why don't you take my jacket?" Margo took off her parka and draped it over Sheila's shoulders.

"Oh no, please, really I'm fine," Sheila managed to say between coughs.

"One adult for *All the Presidents Men.*" Margo handed over her money and took the ticket. "You can give the coat back the next time I see you. Stay warm," and she sauntered off without looking back.

Sam and Sheila stared at each other and then at Margo's retreating body as it disappeared into Theater Two. In a low voice Sam said, "We may have to mail the coat back. Jerry took out a restraining order against her this morning."

"A restraining order? Why?" Sheila wrapped the coat more tightly around herself like a cape, embarrassed that it was Margo's but grateful for its warmth.

"He's afraid that Margo will kidnap Tara and put her in a boarding school in Buffalo."

"Wait," Sheila held her hand to her chest as she struggled to catch her breath. "That doesn't make sense. Kidnappers don't tell people where they're going to enroll the child in school."

"She *didn't* tell him. The librarian told me, remember? Kidnapping's probably the wrong word, but he doesn't want Margo taking Tara to Buffalo without his consent. I haven't heard from Jerry today, so I don't know if he actually got the restraining order or not. How hard is it to get a restraining order against someone?"

"I have no idea, praise the Lord. I've never had to deal with such a thing." Sheila began another bout of coughing.

"Maybe we should go home. We can catch the film another time."

"We'd just get drenched again on the way out." Sheila's words came in raspy spasms between coughs. "But you'd better buy me some hard candy and maybe a hot drink. I don't want to get thrown out for causing a disturbance."

CHAPTER 17

It was late Sunday afternoon when Jerry finally called. Samantha was struggling to paint a realistic looking toaster on her canvas and was having a bad time. She'd never painted highly reflective metal before and none of her attempts looked right. Wiping her hands on an oily rag, Sam picked up the phone.

"Jerry? Oh good, I was hoping to hear from you. Guess what happened? I was at the movies with Sheila last night and Margo walked in. No, she was alone. She stood right behind us in line and I had to make pleasant chit-chat with her, and all the time I was thinking about you taking out a restraining order against her. It was awful. Oh, and Sheila was wet and coughing because we'd been caught in that storm so Margo gave Sheila her coat. She just put it around her shoulders and walked away. Yeah, it was nice of her, but we were so surprised that we just stood there. Now what do we do with the jacket? Good idea. I'll get it from Sheila and send it back with Tara, unless the judge issues an order tomorrow. How long does it take? Well, let me know if you hear anything. Say, if you want to pick up a pizza, you and Tara could come over here. I'll make a big salad and toast up some garlic bread. How's that? I'll see you and Tara around six. Bye."

Sam had the table set and a large tossed salad waiting in the refrigerator when Jerry and Tara rang the doorbell. It was raining again, but this evening the rain was just a soft drizzle that washed away the heat of the afternoon. The smell of butter and garlic wafting from the oven collided with the odors of pepperoni and melted cheese escaping from the large cardboard box in Jerry's hands. Sam was ravenous; she hadn't had anything to eat since her Corn Flakes and toast at breakfast. Jerry handed the box to Sam then pulled a wine bottle from his raincoat pocket, "Chianti," he waved the bottle at her with a flourish. "A day without wine is like a day in Catawba County."

Without another word Sam put two wine glasses on the table and a small glass for Tara's milk. "I'm so hungry I could faint. You two wash up then let's dig in."

Dinner was a happy interlude of sipping, slurping, munching and crunching until all three were sated and only a sliver of pizza was left congealing in the box.

"Anyone for ice cream?" Sam pulled a pint of fudge ripple from the freezer.

"Not for me. I can't eat another bite." Jerry was leaning back in his chair with his hands on his belly and a contented grin across his face.

"Pea," said Tara who was never too full for ice cream. Sam scooped a small portion into a bowl and carried it out to the living room where Tara ate her dessert while watching *The Muppet Show*.

"This was so nice, I'm glad you came by." Sam was scraping a few wilted lettuce leaves and some pizza crusts into the trash.

"It was nice, but it was also stupid. Why couldn't we eat our pizza at Figaro's and let them do the dishes? Eating dinner together in a restaurant isn't a sin. You're not a married woman." Sam sighed. *Why can't Jerry just accept things the way they are?* This conversation was getting old, but he persisted. "I'm sorry, Sam, but that's the truth. We're both free agents and frankly I don't know what you're waiting for. You have to start dating again sometime."

"Do I?" Sam began rinsing the plates in the sink.

Jerry got up from the table and stood behind Sam, standing so close she could feel his breath on her neck. Leaning down, he whispered in her ear, "Yes, you do. You're a beautiful woman, Sam." He ran a finger from her wrist to the tender flesh in the crook of her arm. "Your skin is as soft and warm as fresh baked pizza." He gently turned her head until she was facing him. "Your lips are as red as a fine marinara and your eyes..." He bent toward her until their heads were almost touching. "Your eyes are as brown as two pepperonis—and I just want to eat you up." With that he began tickling her under her arms until she shrieked and retaliated by whacking him around the head and shoulders with a pot holder.

"Stop, please stop, that's enough," Sam was laughing and batting at him, "Maybe you're right. I'll think about it."

"Don't think, say yes. 'Yes, I will go to the movies with Jerry Doyle on Saturday night. I'll put on a pretty dress, spritz myself with cologne, and wear stupid high heels I can't walk in because I've got a hot date.'" Jerry's arms were around Samantha's waist and he was looking at her with the expression of a man who is pretty certain he's going to get laid.

"Sorry, Charlie, you don't have a babysitter. Sheila's having her biopsy on Thursday so she won't be available for a few days. In fact, if the news is bad, I won't be up to it either."

Jerry's tone changed at once. *He really is a good guy.* "How's this? You put on a pair of comfortable slacks and sensible shoes and I'll drive you and Sheila to the hospital. She's not going to be in any condition to drive herself home after the procedure."

"One of Sheila's friends from her church is going to drive us, but that's really sweet of you." Jerry's arms were still around her waist. She tried pulling away but he held her tighter.

"But I get a rain check, okay? We're still going to that movie." Samantha nodded her head in agreement and then she was kissing him and her back was pressed into the sink as he pressed himself against her and she pressed back against him and his knee was parting her legs and his hand was inside her blouse and she heard herself moan. "How about the fireworks?" he asked as he nuzzled her neck.

"Tara's in the next room. We can't." The smell of his sweat and after shave was making her dizzy.

Jerry stepped back and grinned at her, "I meant the Fourth of July. Will you go with me and Tara to see fireworks on the Fourth of July?" Sam could feel her face turn red, white and blue as waves of embarrassment washed over her. Jerry's delight at her chagrin was evident in the smirk on his face. "They're scheduled for nine o'clock at the high school, but we should get there early if we want good seats." He gave her one more serious kiss. "I'd better go before this gets out of hand."

"Wait, we still haven't talked about the restraining order. Tell me what's happening."

"The judge recused himself because he's hearing the custody case so my request for a restraining order was passed on to Judge Fredman. We'll probably have his decision by Friday. It could go either way.

Two furrows creased Sam's forehead, "Tara's going to think Margo abandoned her again. Maybe this isn't such a great idea."

"What's the alternative? Letting Margo ship her off to boarding school? That's not going to happen, not while I'm alive and breathing." A moment ago he'd been a comic Don Juan, but now Sam glimpsed someone tough and immovable. She remembered the sound of breaking glass that she'd heard over the phone and realized again how little she knew about this man.

Jerry gave her a platonic peck on the cheek as he and Tara said goodbye. Once they were gone, the house settled back into its accustomed quiet and Sam was glad for the time alone to untangle her emotions. What was she doing? Jerry was a nice guy, but she'd never have dated him in college. He was attractive enough, more than enough, but he belonged to Sheila's world, not hers. *Sheila's world not mine. Interesting.* She'd never verbalized that thought before. Maybe her parents were right. The people she met in Catawba County were smart, hard working, and kind, but they weren't her people. Ben had bridged both worlds, but now that he was gone, what was she doing here? She could make her parents happy and return to the world of big houses, maids and country clubs, but that wasn't her place either. It wasn't her place, and she wasn't going back.

An invisible beating of wings fluttered inside her chest. Her body froze then jerked with a small palpable spasm and then, as though a flock of imaginary birds had taken flight, she felt lighter, less burdened by her sorrow. Going into the kitchen she made herself a cup of tea and called her mother.

"Mom, I've made a decision. I'm not going to Case Western Reserve this fall. Nothing's changed exactly, but I'm sure that going back to Cleveland right now would be a terrible mistake. I know you're disappointed. No, I still don't know where I want to be, but I'm starting to cross off places that I know are wrong. Let's not talk about it now. Yes, I'm sure. Thanks. I love you, too."

That night in bed she conjured Ben beside her. In her dreams she held him tight, safe in the comfort of his arms. They rolled together in a delirium of passion and abandon, her skin plastered against his skin, closer and closer until the thin membrane separating them dissolved. She spread her legs like wings and Ben was deep inside her, and the two of them were flying, flying, flying.

The first of July was so hot the asphalt paving on Edison seemed to ripple as if it were made of water. Sam opened her bedroom window, a smooth effortless operation now that the old sashes had been replaced, intending to let in a breath of fresh morning air, instead she was hit by a blast of heat. She quickly closed the windows and drew the blinds against the sun. It was already eight in the morning and Sheila and Grace would be at her door in thirty minutes. She'd have to move fast, although the heat and humidity begged her to move at the pace of melting tar. Shorts seemed too casual for an occasion as momentous as Sheila's biopsy, but Sam couldn't imagine wearing anything heavy or layered. At last she decided on a light cotton skirt, a sleeveless tank top and sandals. She was finishing a glass of orange juice when she heard two apologetic little honks that meant Grace had arrived.

"Good morning," Sam gave Sheila a quick kiss before crawling into the back seat.

"I wish I had air conditioning. This heat isn't doing her any good." Grace looked at Sheila who seemed to be struggling for every breath.

"Maybe I should go back and get a thermos of ice water. It would only take a minute."

Sheila shook her head, opened her mouth, gasped, and then held up a finger asking Sam to wait until she caught her breath. "I can't have water. They said no eating or drinking for twelve hours before the test." She closed her eyes. Her condition, whatever it was, plus the heat, plus her anxiety had exhausted her. They drove to the hospital in silence. Sam felt dread riding along as a fourth passenger, crowding between them, using up the air.

The biopsy was an outpatient procedure that would be completed by noon. Sam and Grace kept vigil under the wall mounted TV in the waiting room. It was tuned to Jack LaLanne who was on his hands and knees. He raised one arm and twisted his torso as he cajoled them through the television. "Come on, ladies, you can do it, one–two–three–four." Sam got up and switched off the TV.

There were only three other people in the waiting room, an elderly couple who sat whispering to one another in the corner and a middle aged woman who kept checking her watch. "God, I hope Sheila's alright." Sam was too nervous to sit, so she paced between the free coffee, the magazine rack, and her seat.

"The Lord is more likely to listen to our prayers if we don't take His name in vain." Grace smiled at her sweetly. Sam bristled, but didn't reply. Instead, she found a back issue of *Ladies' Home Journal* and pretended to be absorbed in an article. "You know," Grace went on, "Sheila and I have a little pact. We made it on the way back from Lily Dale last summer. Whichever of us passes over first is going to try to come back and give the other a sign."

This was a joke, right? No, it wasn't. Sam looked at Grace in her long navy shirtwaist, laced up Oxfords with a black plastic purse clutched tightly on her lap, and saw that she was a woman incapable of a joke. "Really? What sort of sign(s) do you have in mind?" Sam tried to keep her voice from sounding patronizing or sarcastic. They had at least an hour to kill, so she might as well hear the story.

"Well, it's hard to say. We know so little about the life to come, that's what makes it so fascinating. I know you're a skeptic. Sheila's told me all about you, but things do happen. There are people who can reach through the veil and touch us here on the other side. Do you want to hear a true story?"

"Sure." Sam nodded gravely, trying to suppress the expression of skepticism that wanted to play across her face.

"I don't think you knew the Carters. Harold was gone before you moved to Kleiner, but he'd been married to Marta for almost thirty-seven years when he passed. They were a wonderful couple, just wonderful, so of course Marta was devastated. It was a pitiful thing seeing how she suffered without him, but then a remarkable thing happened.

"There used to be a Cole Porter song, 'Begin the Beguine' that was very popular when Marta and Harold started going out. You know how some couples have a special song? 'Begin the Beguine' was the Carters' special song. It was the first song they danced to at their wedding and they just always liked it.

"Well, Harold died in October of 1971, so he'd been gone about eight months. This happened in late June, I forget the exact date, but it was their anniversary. Marta was so sad and lonely that she didn't know how she could go on. There she was sitting alone in her living room looking at the album with their wedding pictures. She told me all this right after it happened. It was the most remarkable thing. So, she was sitting in her living room crying up a storm, and wishing that Harold could send her a sign so she'd know he was okay, that he was waiting for her on the other side. Now this actually happened, right after she made that wish—it was a little prayer really—she turned on the radio and what do you suppose they were playing?"

"Begin the Beguine?" Sam ventured.

"Exactly! Doesn't that just give you goose bumps?"

"Yeah, wow. What an amazing story." Sam returned to her *Ladies Home Journal*, pulling the magazine up close to her face, to discourage any more revelations.

"Marta was a different woman after that. She found so much comfort in knowing that Harold was still thinking about her, that he still loved her. It made all the difference. We were all so happy for her."

Sam didn't look up from the magazine. "That's a lovely story. Is she a member of your church?" Sam was determined to be polite.

"Oh no, not any more. She remarried a few months later and moved to Baltimore. I haven't heard from her in ages."

"You'd think she'd at least send you a sign," Sam muttered under her breath.

The woman from the reception desk popped into the waiting room, "Mrs. Crawford is all done with the biopsy. It went very well, no problems. We just need another set of x-rays and then she can go home. We should have you out of here on schedule." The woman looked tired as though she'd been on duty all night. Her mascara was smudged and her platinum perm had turned to frizz.

"No problems? That's wonderful. So there's nothing the matter with her then." Sam was chortling with relief.

The receptionist shook her head, "No, I'm sorry. I just meant that there was no problem with the biopsy. It went smoothly without complications. The tissue has to be sent to a lab for analysis. We won't have the results for another five to seven days."

"Oh," Sam was glad her parents hadn't heard her gaffe. A doctor's kid should have known better. She did know better, but she'd been so anxious to hear that Sheila was all right.

On the trip home Sheila was less anxious and therefore breathing more normally. The sedative they'd given her hadn't worn off, making her slow and lethargic, but much more relaxed. Even though she hadn't eaten since supper the night before, she didn't want to stop for lunch. "I just need to lie down awhile. It's not every day that someone sticks a needle right through your chest all the way into your lungs. Can someone open a window? It's so hot in here." She was fanning herself with the information folder the hospital sent home with patients.

"I'm going to stay with you tonight." Sam put her hand on Sheila's shoulder. "You shouldn't be alone after an ordeal like that. Grace, can you stop at my house for a minute so I can pick up a few things?"

"I'm fine, just a little tired." Sheila laid her head on the seatback and closed her eyes. "You're a sweetheart, but you don't need to worry about me. They say it will be a week before they have the results. Waiting is going to be the hard part."

"You're fine. I just know you're fine. Are they sure it isn't bronchitis or pneumonia? You should probably be on antibiotics."

"It's not an infection. The doctors can see something on my lung in the x-rays, in the lower right lobe, but it's not pneumonia. We'll know what it is in a week."

"If it is anything serious I'm taking you to the Cleveland Clinic. My parents will refer you to the best specialists in the city."

"I don't want to talk about that now." Sheila seemed to fall asleep and no one said a word for the next ten minutes. She suddenly opened her eyes and turned to Sam, "How long does it take to die from lung cancer? Would you ask your parents for me? I was just wondering." Then she closed her eyes again and drifted off.

*   *   *

By the next morning Sheila was back in what Sam thought of as her manic phase. Despite her shortness of breath and constant cough, she'd decided to clean out all of her cupboards and closets. She'd started with her linens and Sam had come over to help with the project. Sheila's linen closet housed not only sheets and towels, but also boxes of expired medications, a tangle of electric razors, electric blankets, heating pads, hand embroidered place mats, boxes of soap, and handmade sachets that had lost their scent years ago. At the very top, wrapped in an old pillow case, was the veil to Sheila's wedding gown.

Sam emptied the shelves and piled the contents on the twin beds in Ben's old bedroom so Sheila could sort through them. Sheila picked out two sets of sheets and two sets of towels and carried them back to the linen closet where they barely filled one shelf. She surveyed the remaining stuff with a face void of emotion then waved her hand in a gesture of dismissal, "Take whatever you want, then bag up the rest. It's all going to Goodwill."

"You can't give it all away. You need a lot of this stuff. You need soap." Sam held up a four pack of Camay. "And you need the blankets and the electric stuff and your wedding veil." She started to gather up these items so she could return them to the closet.

"I'll keep the soap, but the rest of it goes. All this stuff is just weighing me down. I want it out of here."

"But your wedding veil?" Sam was holding the pillow case out toward Sheila who refused to touch it.

"Why don't you keep it? It's made from real Irish lace."

"But it's your wedding veil," Sam repeated.

"I've stored that veil long enough. If you don't want it, just put it in the bag with the other stuff." She crossed the room and lowered herself into the small maple desk chair where Ben had sat to do his homework as a boy. "As soon as I catch my breath, we can start on my clothes closet. It's chock full of things I'll never wear again."

CHAPTER 18

Kleiner loved the Fourth of July and always celebrated with an Independence Day parade that started at City Hall and marched straight down Grant Street to the Kleiner High School stadium. Children decorated their bikes with red, white and blue crepe paper. There were picnics, raffles, relay races, and then always, as darkness fell, crowds filled the bleachers around the ~~Kleiner~~ High School football field for a fireworks display, but all of this wasn't enough in 1976. The country's bicentennial demanded something more, so the town council had thrown open the city coffers and hired an old country western star to sing "The Star Spangled Banner" from the saddle of a big chestnut horse.

Jerry stopped for Sam and Sheila right after breakfast so they could set up their folding chairs along the parade route. They arrived early enough to get an unobstructed view of the marching bands, antique fire truck, Veterans of Foreign Wars, baton twirling majorettes, cheerleaders, Boy Scouts, Girl Scouts, Kleiner A Capella Choir, St. Stephan's Unicycle Team, Pooch Parade, Morning Glory Barber Shop Quartet, and Fraternal Order of Police. The Rotary Club handed out little American Flags to everyone in the crowd and Tara waved hers until the end of the parade when the mayor, and every member of the town council, drove by smiling and waving from the back of two white Cadillac convertibles that bore misspelled signs that read, "Complements of Jay Gratowski Cadillac, Jamestown, New York." They bought Eskimo Pies and Rocket Pops from a street vendor, and talked and gossiped with old friends. It was a wonderful event. Sheila said she'd remember it as long as she lived.

Sam was cooking hotdogs outside on the barbeque she'd bought Ben for Father's Day the year that June was born. She tried to see the grill as nothing more than what it was, a metal brazier on legs with a slightly dented lid. It was just an outdoor stove for burning meat, not a sacred vessel for preserving old memories. She opened a package of wieners and slapped them down on the hot metal rack. Coleslaw, potato salad and slices of watermelon were already on the picnic

she's changing

table where Tara sat coloring a paper plate. Sheila, exhausted from
the parade, had stayed home, assuring them she could see the fireworks from her front porch. So it was a small party, just the three of
them: Jerry, Tara, and Sam.

Although they finished supper early, and left an hour before
the fireworks were scheduled to begin, the bleachers were packed by
the time they arrived so they found themselves seated near the top of
the stadium.

"These are great seats. We're right up where the action is. We
can practically reach out and touch the fireworks from here." Jerry
was in an expansive mood. He put his arm around Sam who looked
around furtively as though someone might be watching them. He
drew little circles on the bare flesh of her shoulder and whispered,
"Relax, everything's fine. No one's going to report you."

Tara tugged on Sam's T-shirt and pointed into the crowd, a
big smile on her face. Sam strained her eyes to see whomever or
whatever was making Tara so excited. Scanning the horde of people
packed into the stadium, she hoped it wasn't Margo. At last she saw
the source of Tara's excitement.

"Look, over there." She nudged Jerry in the ribs and directed
his gaze to three dark figures making their way up the aisle in their
direction. Tara's joy was complete. Sam had to physically restrain her
so that she wouldn't rush down after them. Jerry put two fingers in
his mouth and let out a piercing whistle. Billy and Marcus looked up
and Jerry waved them over. A plump, motherly looking woman
followed behind them carrying a paper grocery bag. Billy made the
introductions, "This is my wife, Louella. I don't think you've met."

Jerry scrunched closer to Sam to make room for the new-
comers while Louella pulled a paper plate covered with aluminum
foil from the grocery bag. "Do you all like brownies? I made these
fresh this afternoon." They munched and chatted until the mayor
stepped into the center of the stadium trailing a long microphone
cord and the show began.

An hour later the five of them picked their way back down
through the bleachers. It had been a spectacular evening. Tara had
been able to fully participate and enjoy the fireworks display since it
was entirely visual, a rare event in her life. When Marcus had covered
his ears to dampen the noise, Tara had imitated him, making the
adults catch each other's eyes to share bitter sweet smiles. Tara had
finally wilted and was leaning heavily against her father. Marcus was
kicking stones impatiently while the adults said their last goodbyes
under one of the mercury vapor streetlights that skirted the unpaved

parking lot. "It was a great evening. I'm glad we ran into you." Sam smiled at Billy who nodded back at her.

Before he turned to leave, Billy said, "Goodnight now. Nice seeing you. Oh, and when you see Dan, thank him again for finding me those parts. I'd have never gotten that tractor running without his help."

Jerry shifted Tara's weight and lowered his voice. He didn't want Marcus to hear what he had to say. "It may be awhile before we see Dan again, Dan or Margo. You know we're not exactly on good terms."

"Yeah, I know that, but you've got that child between you. You have to keep seeing each other."

"Not really. They didn't see each other for two years after Margo disappeared." Sam wasn't going to let Margo off that easy.

"Well, that was wrong of her, but she was really confused at the time. I'm not saying she did the right thing, but she had her reasons and she meant well. Remember," he looked at Sam, "*tout comprendre, c'est tout pardoner.*"

Sam shrugged, "Yeah, but we don't know anything. Do you know something we don't know?"

"I might. This isn't the time to talk, but Margo's told me a few things. Let's just say that she did it for Tara. I don't know the whole story, but I know she thought Tara would be better off if she stayed away for awhile."

"Well then, we agree about something." Sam thought she was being funny, but Jerry didn't laugh. His face clouded and she could see his Adams apple bobbing in his neck as he struggled for composure.

"Billy, if you know why she left I need to know. I've asked her a thousand times and she won't tell me."

"She might've been in jail." Marcus, who seemed to be wandering aimlessly just beyond earshot hadn't missed a word.

"Marcus, go sit in the car. You had no call to say a thing like that." Louella fixed him with a disapproving stare, but he didn't move. "I know what you're thinking, but you go on now. We'll talk about this later." Reluctantly, Marcus headed toward their truck.

"I'm sorry, he shouldn't have said a thing like that, but it's natural that he'd think that way, what with his father being in jail and all." Louella seemed surprised when Sam and Jerry replied with blank looks. "Didn't Billy ever tell you what happened to our Earl?"

Sam shook her head. "We never talked about Marcus's father. You don't have to tell us, it's none of our business."

"Well, I for one am not ashamed of my boy." Louella threw a challenging glance at her husband. "Earl might have gone too far, but he was going in the right direction. You want to tell them, Billy?"

"No, you go ahead. You tell it."

"All right, then. Do you remember when all the letter carriers went out on strike back in 1970? Earl was out walking the lines trying to get raises for the workers. There were men, full-time employees of the US Postal Service, collecting welfare. Welfare, can you imagine? That's how bad they were paid. He helped shut down post offices in Cleveland, Akron, and Detroit. It was against the law, but he wouldn't have gone to prison for that. The problem was that President Nixon thought the army could deliver the mail so he sent soldiers into the post office to break the strike. My son got it into his head that he could shut down the operation and clear out the military by calling in a bomb threat. There never was any kind of bomb, but the government prosecuted him like he actually meant to blow something up." Louella hugged herself as though she were standing in a cold wind. "Everyone else went back to work with a twelve percent raise and benefits while Earl went to prison. He's going to be away until Marcus graduates from high school. It's been rough on the boy, I'll tell you that."

Jerry called from work at three o'clock the following afternoon. It was Monday, so Tara was with Margo, and Sam was in the basement transferring laundry from the washer to the dryer when the phone rang. By racing up the steps two at a time she managed to grab the phone before it stopped ringing.

Jerry sounded edgy and unnerved. Sam was afraid he had bad news, "What's happened? Is something the matter?"

"No, no, everything's fine. Judge Fredman just issued a temporary restraining order. My grounds for the request were kind of flimsy, but my boss called in a favor and I got it."

"You don't sound very happy."

"I'm worried about what you said, about Tara thinking her mom's abandoned her again. I want to do what's best for my daughter, not mess her up. I guess I'm having second thoughts."

"It's your call, Jerry. Do you want the judge to cancel the order?"

"Maybe, but my boss would kill me. He pulled a lot of strings to get this for me. Anyway, it's only temporary to keep Margo from taking Tara to Buffalo or anywhere else without my permission."

"My God, she's got Tara now. It'll be a disaster if she finds out this afternoon. She might never bring her back."

"I took care of that. She won't be served until tomorrow morning when Tara's out of harm's way. But when she opens that envelope I wouldn't want to be within two hundred yards of her. She's going to go nuclear."

"Yeah, she will." Sam looked around her kitchen then out through the window at clumps of wild lilies growing beneath a stand of black locust trees. Margo was going to explode and Sam would have to deal with the fallout. She dreaded the loud scenes and raw emotions that were Margo's stock in trade. But the problem wasn't just Margo, it was Jerry and Tara and Sheila. Sam's whole world was coming unraveled. The house had been her refuge, but it no longer felt safe, not in the same way. She'd let the world in, and the world was noisy, unpredictable, and dangerous. It was full of demanding, complicated people, and a host of choices that could take her anywhere. Part of her wanted to hang up the phone, lock the doors, pull the drapes, and return to the hypnotic sorrow where she'd spent the winter.

As predicted, all hell broke out the minute Margo had the restraining order in her hand. By nine o'clock the next morning Sam had received a phone call from Jerry warning her to call the police immediately if Margo showed up anywhere within a hundred yards of her property. "She's gone ballistic; she's absolutely out of her mind. I can be there in ten minutes if you need me."

Then, a moment later, the phone rang again. It was Margo. "Tell that bastard he can wipe his ass with these papers. That's what they're good for. He has no right to keep me from my daughter. I haven't done a goddamn thing to deserve this and I'm not taking it. I'm not taking it for a goddamn minute. He is going to be so sorry that he started this. And what's your deal? You've seen me with my daughter. Have I ever missed a visit? Have I ever been late? Who decided that you get to see her and I can't? Who the hell are you anyway?"

Sam put the receiver back down on the cradle as if she were switching off loud music or a bad TV show. Margo had asked a good question though. *Who the hell* am *I?* Tara was bent over an Etch A Sketch and Sam could see her red curls, exactly the color of Margo's, falling toward her lap. *No question that Tara is Margo's daughter, but is she Ben's?* And if Ben was Tara's father, had he known? *Impossible, Ben would never have abandoned a child.* It was much more likely that Margo didn't know who the father was herself. She'd simply foisted Tara off on Jerry because Ben was away at school while Jerry practically lived next door. More to the point, Ben was a kid living on a scholarship and his mother's savings while Jerry was a man with a well-paying job.

The rest of the day was spent in a state of heightened vigilance. Whatever else she was doing—practicing with the auditory trainer, drawing a new self-portrait, preparing lunch—one ear was cocked, listening for Margo's motorcycle or her knock on the door, but it never came.

When Jerry finally came to pick Tara up at six o'clock, he found her curled up on Sam's lap turning the pages of *The Very Hungry Caterpillar*. "It's been really quiet. Margo never showed up, no scenes, no police, just a normal day." Sam smiled at Jerry who was still wearing his uniform.

"Well, it wasn't normal at my end. Margo burst into the department screaming in front of everyone that I had no right keep her from seeing her daughter. It was awful. Everyone heard her, my boss, the other officers, the clerk, everyone." He sat down on the sofa, took off his shoes and started to rub his feet. Tara came over and began pulling on his sleeve. She was tired and ready to go home. Jerry reached out and pulled Tara onto his lap where she snuggled into him

"How are you feeling?" Sam moved her chair closer to Jerry's.

"Shell shocked." He bent to kiss the top of Tara's head. "I'm terrified that Margo will get custody and I'll never see my little girl again. That could happen. I thought I'd die when Margo left, but if I lose Tara too..."

"Yeah, I know." Sam stared at the bookcase, not wanting to meet Jerry's eyes. She knew all too well. When she turned back, Tara had climbed off Jerry's lap and was trying to put his shoes back on his feet. Sam gave him a sad smile that she hoped carried the right amount of sympathy without being overly dramatic, "Do you want to stay for supper?

"No, I think Tara's telling me it's time we hit the road."

"Maybe we could take her for a Dairy Queen."

"Thanks, but I want to get home. Tara and I need some time alone." Jerry finished tying his shoes and stood up. "See you tomorrow."

Sam gave him a kiss on the lips, "See you tomorrow." His kiss back was tepid and perfunctory. Margo had apparently damped that fire.

Once Jerry and Tara were gone the house closed in around her. She could hear the kitchen clock ticking, the electric buzz of the refrigerator, and the sound of small insects swarming inside her head. What was the matter with her? When the house was full of people and commotion she wanted to be alone, and then when they were gone she felt lonely and abandoned. She was turning into a nut case.

It was only six-thirty, but her mother might be home, but no one answered. Sam hung up disappointed on the sixth ring. After a moment's hesitation, she began searching through her closet for the purse she'd taken to Cleveland, unzipped an inside pocket, and pulled out a scrap of paper. She owed a phone call to her old friend.

"Ellen? Hi, it's Sam." Sam held the phone away from her ear until the shrieks and squeals died down. "I got that huge envelope you sent me a couple weeks ago. The postage must have cost you a fortune. I read through the brochures and you're right, the art programs sound fabulous. Do you remember Miss Marks? She wanted me to apply to The Rhode Island School of Design back in high school, but...well; I didn't take art seriously back then. Yeah, of course Providence sounds great, but I'm pretty settled where I am. Besides it's way too late to apply for the fall semester. What do you mean? Of course it's too late. Really? So, if I started as a non-degree student I could just waltz in at the last minute? Well, maybe in my next life, but thanks for going to all that trouble. I really appreciate it."

Sheila was still at work on Wednesday afternoon, sorting through a lifetime of accumulated bric-a-brac, gadgets, geegaws, and assorted kitchen paraphernalia. Sam had to admit that most of it would never be missed, but the toaster? The tea kettle? The Havilland china that had belonged to her grandmother?

"Are you sure, Sheila?" Once you give this stuff away you can't ever change your mind." Sam was appalled at the growing mountain of stuff heaped on the dining room table.

"Don't be silly. If I ever want more junk I'll just go to Goodwill." A Mixmaster, a juicer, and a waffle iron were added to the pile. Sheila was running out of breath. She held a hand against her chest and sat down on one of the kitchen chairs. "Please, take whatever you want. I'd love to think you were using some of these old things."

Sam was doing the heavy lifting under her mother-in-law's strict direction. Sheila pointed to a set of Revere Ware in a lower cabinet, "Why don't you take those pots and pans? You and Ben never bought a proper set of cook ware." They had actually received several good pieces for their wedding, but Sheila was insistent. Sam finally took a large stock pot and a roaster, although she had absolutely no idea when she'd ever use such things.

When they were done, most of the cabinets were bare. Sheila kept four dishes, six glasses, a frying pan, a sauce pot, a can opener, two potholders, two dish towels, and a handful of utensils. Everything else was relegated to the trash, Goodwill, or the church.

Sam surveyed the empty kitchen, "Listen, Sheila, are you planning to move? It seems like you're clearing out the house to sell it or something."

"Yes, you might say that I'm planning to move. Or you might just say that I'm getting my house in order." Sheila seemed pleased with their work. "Would you help me load up the car so we can drop these things off and get them out of here?"

Sam watched with concern as Sheila hauled herself out of the chair and began wiping out the empty cupboards. *The woman isn't in her right mind and shouldn't be making any big changes or decisions.* "I'll finish that." Sam took the dust rag from Sheila. "Go sit down, you should be taking it easy. And why don't you wait a couple days before you give this stuff away. You might change your mind about some things."

"Why wait? You can't take it with you," Sheila chirped.

Sheila was like a runaway train, she had to be stopped. "You know what? I've changed my mind." Sam looked at the boxes and bags and piles of things covering the dining room table and overflowing onto the chairs and floor. "I think I might want a lot of this stuff after all. Let's take it all over to my house, okay?"

"Of course, that would be wonderful." The phone began to ring and Sheila got up to answer it. "Yes, this is Sheila Crawford." There was a long pause while Sheila appeared to be listening, then a longer pause while she stood motionless, her muscles sagging and her eyes closed. When she spoke, her voice was low and distorted like an audio tape being played back at the wrong speed. "Yes, I see. Yes, are you sure? Would you please say that again? How serious is that? Are you sure that's what the doctor said? No, no, I'm fine. My daughter-in-law's here with me. Of course, Friday the sixteenth would be fine. One o'clock. Thank you. Yes, thank you again. Good bye."

If Sam could have painted Sheila's portrait at that moment, she would have used nothing but shades of gray. Sheila's hair, her skin, her eyes had lost all their color. There was a control on a color television that you could twist until the screen turned black and white. Sheila looked as though someone had twiddled that knob and washed all the color from her face. She lowered herself back into her chair and sat there dry-eyed, not making a sound, not moving a muscle.

"Sheila," Sam put an arm around her mother-in-law's shoulders. "What did they say? How bad is it?" With a sigh like the sound of an old house settling, Sheila put her head down on the table. Sam could barely make out her words. "They didn't find anything."

"You mean the biopsy was negative, you don't have cancer?"

[handwritten margin note: simply like a screen, y]

[handwritten note at bottom: that you ett could change to b+w.]

Sheila nodded again; her eyes were open but didn't seem to see a thing.

"That's wonderful. What else did they tell you?" Sam was smiling, she wanted to give Sheila a hug, but her mother-in-law looked so devastated that Sam simply stood beside her, patting her on the back.

"Would you get me a glass of water? I feel a little faint." Sheila was bent over the kitchen table, holding her head in her hands. When Sam returned with the glass, she saw that Sheila's hands were shaking.

"What's the matter, Sheila? What did the doctor say?"

"The shadow on my lung is just an old scar from when I had pneumonia as a girl. There isn't any cancer. I probably have asthma."

"They can treat asthma. What a relief." She gave Sheila a big hug only to find that Sheila had become an inert lump. Undeterred, Sam continued, "I'm so happy that you're going to be alright."

"Mmm-hmmm." Sheila managed a little nod, but her face was a study in sorrow.

"You don't have cancer. Aren't you glad? Isn't that good news?" The tears running down Sheila's cheeks said that it wasn't.

"I thought I was going to see my boys. Dear God, I want to see my boys again."

"Sheila, please don't be like this. Be happy that you're going to live. Be happy for me. I couldn't bear to lose you." Now Sam was crying. *When had life gotten so crappy that they were crying over good news?*

"You'll have to stay here tonight. I'm not up to driving you home." Sheila stared at her denuded kitchen with sunken eyes. "I don't want any of my stuff back. I still want to give it all away."

"Sheila, it's your call, but why don't you go lie down now. You need time to figure things out."

Sheila hauled herself out of the chair like an old woman. Sam took her arm and helped her toward the stairs, "Is there anything I can do? Do you want a cup of tea or anything?"

"No, thank you, not right now. Oh, make a note on the calendar that I have to see the doctor on the sixteenth at one o'clock."

Tara was becoming anxious and restless. Sam knew that she couldn't tell time and that she didn't know one day of the week from another, but she wasn't stupid and she knew her routine. She knew that her father dropped her off at Sam's house every morning on his way to work, and that her mother picked her up every other afternoon—except that five days had passed and her mother hadn't shown up once.

It was a relief when Marcus came over with Billy just after lunch on Friday. Tara brightened the moment she saw their truck pull up beside the house. Billy was beaming too. "May I introduce you to a young man who has passed all his exams, turned in all his papers, and will be attending eighth grade at Seneca Rock Junior High in September. We got the official letter this morning."

"Seneca Rock? He's not going back to Buffalo?"

"He is not. He will be living with me and his Grandma for the foreseeable future." Billy placed his hand over Marcus's head.

"Congratulations, Marcus. Well done. I'm proud of you." She shook Marcus's hand with great formality. Tara didn't know what was going on, but she grinned and shook his hand as well.

"Also, I brought you a little something to thank you for letting us spend so much time in your barn these last few months. He presented her with a brown paper shopping bag as though it were a velvet box done up in a satin ribbon.

"Thank you." Sam took the bag expecting tomatoes or cucumbers from Billy's garden, but no, that couldn't be right. The bag was too light. Except for the faint rustling of tissue paper she'd have guessed it was empty. Tara watched expectantly as Sam pulled out a small package, gently pulled off the tape, and pulled back the paper, only to find an inner layer of flannel. Inside the flannel was an exquisite little bird whittled from a light wood and painted a delicious shade of blue with a white underbelly and an orange throat. Its legs clung to a hemlock branch that seemed to grow from the base of the little sculpture. Its head was cocked at an appraising angle as though it were sizing up the world through its small beaded eyes. This was a little bird that knew a thing or two and had a fine opinion of itself. Sam stroked the back of its neck with her finger. Each feather was individually carved, even the small downy feathers on its breast.

"Wow," she said. "You're a real artist, Billy." She turned it in her hand, examining the carving from all angles. "This is really beautiful." She bent down to show her gift to Tara, who was allowed to touch, but not to hold the small bird.

"Look at the bottom," Billy instructed her.

When she turned it over she saw the words, *Hope is the thing with feathers.*

She grinned up at him. Her handyman was not only an artist, he knew poetry. Impulsively, she gave him a kiss on the cheek. "Thank you. It's a beautiful gift. I didn't do anything to deserve anything this lovely, but thank you."

Surprised, and perhaps a bit alarmed, Billy took a step backward. "It's no big a thing," he said. "I make decoys for money but like I told you, these little birds are just a hobby. This one's an eastern bluebird; it's a kind of a thrush with a very pretty song. Marcus, do a bluebird song for the lady."

Marcus pretended to grab a microphone and take center stage like a rock star. But then, to Sam's astonishment, he produced the most convincing little warble that might indeed be the call of the eastern bluebird. Sam had no way of knowing, but it didn't matter. She laughed with pure delight.

"Where did you learn to do that?" she asked, completely charmed by his performance.

"Pop taught me; he can do all of them. Do you want to hear a vulture?"

"Not now, Marcus. We just stopped by to give you your present, and to let you know that I'll be picking Allis up next week. I've finally cleared out a spot for her and it's time that she came home."

"Of course, she's yours whenever you want to take her, but I'll miss having you around. Maybe I'll build an addition or something so you'll have to come back and see me."

"Where's Tara's mom?" Marcus asked out of the blue.

Sam looked down at him, disturbed by the question. "She couldn't come today. Why do you want to know?" Sam looked at Marcus who'd been sitting with Tara on the grass while she and Billy talked.

"Tara asked me, she did this," Marcus demonstrated two signs with his hands. "This one means 'where'—he wiggled his index finger back and forth with a furrowed brow. And this one means 'mom'—he touched his thumb to his chin with all of his fingers extended. 'Where's mom?' Can you tell her where her mom is?"

"No, I don't know how to tell her." Sam was ashamed to admit that she couldn't communicate with Tara as well as Marcus could. "Anyway, it's complicated. I don't think I could explain it to her even if she could talk."

"Don't you know where her mom is?" Marcus persisted.

"She's probably just at her own house. Her mother's fine, but she's not allowed to see Tara for awhile. Can you tell Tara that? Do you know how to say that in sign language?"

"I could say 'mom good' or 'mom in house.'" He produced various signs as he spoke, "But if I said 'mom in house' she'd probably think her mom was right here in your house. I don't know how to say that her mom's in her own house. Anyway, she's just learning how to talk with her hands. She probably wouldn't know what I was saying even if I knew how to say it."

"Yeah, I see what you mean." Six eyes turned and looked at Tara who looked back at them with eyes full of unanswered questions, not only unanswered, unasked. She wasn't even able to ask.

"You can't explain stuff to deaf kids with words, you have to show them." Marcus seemed to think that Sam had missed this obvious solution. "Why don't you just take her to her mom's motel so she can see that her mom's okay? I know where she lives. It's not that far."

"How do you know where her mom lives?"

"My grandma took me. They're old friends from a long time ago. We brought her a cherry pie."

Sam stared at him feeling completely betrayed. *Why shouldn't Marcus and his grandmother visit Margo and yet…*her stomach clenched. It took a moment to regain her composure but Sam finally said, "I can't take her. Tara's not allowed to see her mom for awhile." Sam saw the disbelief in Marcus's face and a wave of guilt washed over her. She wasn't at all sure that she and Jerry were doing the right thing. Was oral speech more important than seeing your mother? Besides, what did she really know about teaching a deaf child how to talk?

Marcus, on the other hand, had no doubts. "That's stupid. If Tara's mother is right in her motel, then her daughter should be able to see her."

"Young man, Mrs. Crawford didn't ask for your opinion. Now say goodbye to Tara because we've got to get going." He nodded at Sam, "I'll be back in a few days to pick up the tractor. I sold one of my John Deeres to make room for this one. As soon as my buyer picks up his tractor, I'll take this one home, probably sometime the middle of next week."

"Sure, no hurry. Thanks again for the blue bird. I just love it."

"My pleasure. Come on Marcus, let's get moving before your grandmother sets out looking for us." Billy tipped his cap in the manner of an old fashioned gentleman, and then he and his grandson climbed back in their truck and headed home.

CHAPTER 19

The summer's abundant rain and heat had turned Western New York into a veritable rain forest. Sam stood outside the barn and took a long, deep breath. It almost felt as though she were breathing under water. The air smelled distinctly green; its lush, verdant odor permeated the yard, the fields, the forest; it seeped into the house and saturated her clothes. She'd gotten up that morning half expecting to find a slick of fine moss growing over her tables and chairs. The plot of ground where she and Tara had ~~lovingly~~ planted beans, tomatoes, peas, and squash had become a jungle overrun with weeds. There was going to be a bumper crop, but it needed rescuing from the crab grass, dandelions, and wild mustard that had laid down roots between the neat rows of vegetables. She'd have sworn that it was only days since she'd stood admiring the first green shoots breaking through the soil, and now the ground was hardly visible beneath a heavy thatch of leaves. It was only early August but the garden was completely overgrown. *How did it away from me so quickly?* She turned around and went into the barn to search for a hoe.

By the time Jerry dropped Tara off at eight o'clock in the morning, two rows of beans were looking halfway respectable, although Samantha herself was a smudged and sweaty mess.

"Well, if it isn't the early bird," Jerry grinned. "Find any worms?"

"Plenty," Sam picked up a particularly juicy night crawler and dangled it in front of him. "Want one?"

"Thanks, but I've already eaten." He looked at the small hill of weeds piled up at Sam's feet, then out at the expanse of garden that still needed work. "This could take you all day. Why don't you hire a kid to help?"

"I have a kid to help me." Samantha pulled Tara toward her and gave her a big hug that left a muddy stain on her pink T-shirt.

"I was thinking of someone a little older."

"Great, are you volunteering? I have another hoe in the barn."

"Actually, I was thinking of Billy's grandson. I bet he'd be willing to help you out."

Samantha nodded her head in agreement, "You're right, he would, and Tara would love to see him again. I'll give him a call."

Jerry gave a little wave, then turned and left for work while Sam brushed the dirt from her jeans and headed into the house to use the phone.

As predicted, Marcus accepted the job and Billy dropped him off right after lunch. Although he'd been coming to her house for over two months, this was the first time he'd been there without his grandfather, and the first time he'd been hired to work on his own. This first business venture apparently meant something to him, and he meant to do it right. Sam watched with amusement as Marcus did a thorough survey of the garden, stopping periodically to tug at various weeds, calculating how much time and effort it would take to remove them. Sam had meant to work alongside Marcus, thinking of him more as company than labor, but Marcus clearly intended to take on the job himself. With an expression exactly like his grandfather's, Marcus put his hands in his pockets and said, "This job should take about five hours. Since I usually charge two dollars an hour, ten dollars would be a fair price. But since we're friends, I'm going to do it for nine if that's okay with you."

"That's more than fair, you've got the job." Samantha stuck out her hand and they sealed the deal.

Marcus didn't need much instruction. Once Sam was satisfied that he could tell the difference between a weed and a tomato, she left him with a shovel, a hoe and a thermos of cold water while she took Tara into the barn to do some art work. Sam was in the middle of a new self-portrait and was totally engrossed in her project. For awhile Tara was happy to paint page after page of water color flowers that bloomed into unpredictable shapes as the red and pink and purple pigments saturated her paper and spread across the page, but she eventually got bored and tugged on the apron Sam wore as a smock. Tara pointed toward the garden and Samantha nodded her approval. She watched Tara head toward Marcus who was diligently attacking the weeds before turning her attention back to her own canvas.

Sam was working on the most challenging self-portrait she'd ever attempted, a disturbing vision of *Alice Through the Looking Glass*. She'd sketched a young woman sitting at her dressing table wrapped in a white towel, staring at herself in the mirror, except that her reflection was facing away from her, in fact it was partly in the plane of the mirror, and partly emerging through it on the other side. The girl's side of the mirror was rendered realistically. The other side, the side where her reflection sat, appeared as a sort of cubist convergence of distorted space, each shape a separate plane, and each plane a different reality. At least that was the effect Sam was struggling to achieve. It was an ambitious work and way beyond her skill, but she wrestled with it valiantly until Marcus ran into the barn with the shovel and the hoe.

"It's starting to rain, but I'm almost finished. I can come back tomorrow and get the last part. You don't have to pay me until it's all done." His hair and shirt were already wet although the rain had just started. Looking past him toward the yard, Sam saw that the sky was the color of tarnished silver and that an ominous wind was blowing leaves and branches from the trees.

"Where's Tara? We'd better get inside the house; this looks like it's going to be a real gully washer."

"I don't know where Tara is. Isn't she in here with you?" Marcus looked around the art studio expecting to see Tara sitting at her workbench or hiding beneath the table.

"She went to help you in the garden. I saw her walking right toward you. You must have seen her." Sam's voice had raised an octave and sounded accusatory. *Not fair*, she told herself. *Calm down. I'm the idiot who let Tara wander off...it's not Marcus's fault.*

"Maybe she went back into the house to watch TV," Marcus offered.

"Good idea," A sudden crack of thunder made them both jump. "Run into the house and see if you can find her. I'm going to check around the yard. If you find her, just stay put. I'll be back as fast as I can."

Marcus nodded and took off at full speed. Sam grabbed the black oil cloth off Tara's art table and held it over her head as she searched between the house and barn. A few minutes later she stood dripping just inside the kitchen door. "No luck out there. Did Tara come home? Did you find her?" she called out to Marcus.

"Nope, she's not here, I looked everywhere." A crash of thunder was followed by the overhead light blinking out and the TV going silent in the living room.

"Damn it, now we've lost electricity." Sam was struggling to sound calm and in control when, in truth, she was on the verge of hysterics. "I'm going to check out a place in the woods where she sometimes goes." It was only four in the afternoon, but the sky was so black that Sam grabbed a flashlight from her gadget drawer.

"Where do you want me to look?" Marcus was clearly prepared to run back outside to help.

"You stay right where you are. This storm is getting fierce. Anyway, someone should be here in case Tara comes home." Sam turned

on the flashlight and headed toward the woods. The wind whipped
the table cloth behind her like an inverted umbrella. She struggled to
hang on to the black oil cloth, but it flew into the branches of a locust
tree where it flapped in the wind like the wings of a crazed vulture.

The wind had picked up such momentum that the rain was
slicing into her sideways and she was being pummeled with flying
twigs and trash. Holding her arms in front of her face to protect
herself from airborne branches, she continued on toward the clearing where she'd found Tara in the past. Simultaneously praying and
cursing, she kept expecting to see a drenched and dazed little girl
appear before her on the path, but her flashlight illuminated nothing
but fallen leaves, and rivulets of muddy water.

The thunder and lightning were becoming louder and closer.
A resounding boom made the ground tremble, turned the whole
world white, and shook her to the core. When her vision cleared she
found herself standing thirty feet from a pine tree blown apart by a
lightning strike. Her heart, which had been racing ever since Tara had
gone missing, now felt ready to explode. Wandering through a forest
in an electrical storm was madness, but she kept on past Whiskey
Road to the clearing where they'd first found the old transistor radio.
Her flashlight canvassed the bushes and the underbrush. She turned
its beam upwards and scanned the branches as though Tara might be
hiding in the tree tops. Nothing. Sam felt a wave of nausea wash
over her. Suppressing rising panic, she headed back toward the house
at a trot. She needed to call Jerry. She needed to call the police.

The wind was beginning to die down, but the rain continued at
a steady pace. She brushed strands of dripping hair off her forehead
as she squished her way back through the sodden muck as fast as she
could go. Emerging from the woods, she saw downed wires looping
through the trees and sparking along the grass. She gave the wires a
wide berth as she ran toward the house, clinging to a last hope that
Tara would be inside. "Are you all right? Did Tara come back?" It was
still late afternoon, but the house was unnaturally dark and silent.

"She's not here. We've got to go find her." Marcus sounded scared.

"We've got to call her dad and the police." Sam was already
reaching for the phone.

"You can't, the phones are out. I tried calling my granddad,
but there's no dial tone."

The receiver Sam was holding to her ear confirmed what
Marcus told her. Dead silence. She clicked the button up and down a
few times with no result, and then hung up the phone. Her mouth
was so dry it was difficult to talk.

"I guess we're going to have to find her ourselves. She wasn't in the woods. I don't even know where to start." Sam could hardly focus as her eyes raced around the kitchen looking for what? Clues? A crystal ball? Suddenly, it came to her. "Oh my God, I'm an idiot. Tara went to find her mother."

"I know where her mom lives. I could show you."

"Wait one minute, I want to get something." Sam ran upstairs and tore a blanket off her bed. The motel where Margo stayed was about three miles away. Did Tara even know the way, and if she did, could she have made it there before the storm? No chance, there just wasn't enough time.

"Where's your car?" Marcus asked, clearly anxious to get going.

"I don't have a car." Sam was instantly ashamed; the absence of a car suddenly seemed stupid, arrogant, and selfish. "Do you remember how to start the tractor?"

Sam and Marcus drove down Edison Road side by side on the tractor's bench seat at the Allis-Chalmers' maximum speed of nine miles per hour. Marcus had yelled at her when she'd tried to shift into a higher gear hoping to pick up speed. "Don't touch anything," he'd warned her. "You've got to stay in one gear while it's moving. You should let me drive." He was probably right. Sam hadn't driven for almost two years, and she was totally out of her element perched on top of a large piece of antique farm machinery, but she was the adult. This was her responsibility. "Turn to the right, to the right," Marcus leaned forward to grab the wheel before she steered them into the berm along the side of the road. Sam sat erect and kept the tractor on a straight course.

Everywhere they looked, fallen trees, broken branches, and hanging wires altered the familiar landscape. The late afternoon sun cast a thin gold light from behind banks of dark clouds. The storm had slowed to a steady downpour. Apart from the gravelly voice of the tractor motor and the occasional rumble of distant thunder, an unnatural silence added to the surreal quality of their trip; no cars passed them, no sirens wailed, no dogs barked. Neither of them said a word. Their full attention was focused on scanning the road, the yards, and empty fields for any sign of a small girl.

"What's that?" Marcus pointed to a large limb that had blown off a Norway spruce.

"What are you pointing at? I don't see anything."

"Under there. I see her. Come on." Marcus was out of his seat and running toward Tara before Sam had brought the tractor to a full stop.

Tara looked like a tattered rag doll under the fallen branch. Sam reached through the needles and gently touched her shoulder. She didn't move. "Marcus, we've got to get this tree off her. Can you help me lift it?"

Marcus nodded.

"Our best bet is to lift the trunk end as high as we can then pivot it off her. Don't push it or roll it. We have to really lift it or we'll scratch her up and make things worse. Can you help me do that?"

Marcus didn't say a word; he just squatted beside the heavy branch, positioning his hands beneath its trunk. She'd bet he didn't weigh a hundred pounds. She hoped he was stronger than he looked. Sam squatted beside him. The wet trunk was slippery and she prayed that they wouldn't lose their grip and drop it.

"On the count of three we lift it up and swing it around behind Tara. Don't let go until she's clear of the branches. Ready? One, two, three, lift."

The branch didn't budge. She tried again, putting her arms and shoulders into it, hanging on and forcing her legs to propel the branch upwards. The bark bit into Sam's flesh and the needles scratched her face but she found her center and kept lifting until she was standing almost upright. Holding the branch took all her strength, the idea that she could swing it backwards had been pure delusion. "Get Tara out from under there before I drop this thing. Now!"

Marcus disappeared under the drooping green needles and dragged the limp body out in a matter of seconds. Sam let the branch fall with a heavy thud then fell to her knees to examine Tara. She put her ear on Tara's chest and was rewarded with the sound of a strong steady heartbeat.

"Is she breathing?" Marcus was hardly breathing himself.

"Yeah, but we'd better get her to a hospital." Sam felt a surge of strength come back to her. "I left a blanket under the seat, would you go get it?"

They swaddled Tara in the blanket and lay her across their laps. Marcus cradled her head as Sam maneuvered the old tractor down Edison and made a left turn onto Grant. The rain had slowed to a soft drizzle and a few cars whizzed past them as Sam headed north toward Lake West Memorial Hospital. Sam and Marcus waved their arms trying to flag down one of the passing drivers. Most took no notice, a few waved back, misinterpreting their desperation for high spirits. The tractor was slow and cumbersome, but it plowed forward toward the main shopping strip. Up ahead, just past the grocery, Sam could see flashing lights, police cars and a fire truck. The cars that had sped ahead of her moments earlier were stopped in the road behind some sort of barrier. As she got closer, Sam saw that a telephone pole had fallen across the road blocking traffic in both directions.

"Shit." She stopped the tractor. Tara's eyes were open now and she was trying to sit up, but she was bruised, bleeding, and confused. Sam ran to the nearest police car. Its motor was running and a red light was rotating on the roof but there was no one inside. She turned, jogging down the row of idled vehicles toward an officer holding cars at bay at the center of the traffic jam.

He saw her approaching and blew his whistle, motioning for her to stay back. When she didn't even slow down he called out, "Get back in your car. Everyone needs to wait in their cars." As she kept on running straight toward him, she saw his hand go to his holster.

Sam called out, breathless but still moving, "I have an injured child. She needs to get to a hospital right away."

"Ma'am you need to stay in your car. We'll get someone to you as soon as we can." He looked as though he were still deciding whether or not to draw his gun. This was too much.

In a voice that sounded strangely like Aunt Harriet's she held her ground. "You'll call for emergency help right this minute. The child needs to be taken to the hospital now. We can hand lift her over the barrier into an ambulance. Don't stand there like an idiot, call someone." The officer hesitated, his hand shifting between his gun and his walkie-talkie.

By the time they arrived at the hospital, Tara was crying out in pain. The nurses and emergency technicians tried to soothe her with kind words asking again and again, "What happened? Where does it hurt?" Sam had to keep explaining that Tara was deaf and couldn't hear them and couldn't answer.

"Poor little thing, deaf and dumb," simpered one of the nurse's aides.

"Don't call her dumb," Marcus snapped. "She just can't hear, that's all."

A doctor tugged at Sam's sleeve, "Does she know sign language? Can you interpret for us?"

A blush crept up Sam's neck until her ears were warm. Why did it embarrass her that neither she nor Tara knew how to sign? "We're teaching her oral communication. She's learning to read lips and talk."

"Can you talk to her then? She doesn't understand a thing I'm saying."

"She doesn't understand me either." The doctor stared at her a moment, shook his head, and then walked back toward the examining room.

"Can we be in the room with her anyway? Sam called after him. "She needs to see a familiar face."

The doctor never turned around, but a large lady wearing a name tag that read, *Miss Hilda Schnell: Financial Services*, tapped Sam on the shoulder. "You can be with her in just a few minutes. First we have to fill out some paper work." She shepherded Sam and Marcus into a small office where she offered them seats on metal folding chairs.

"Now, let's start at the beginning. What's your daughter's name?"

"She's not my daughter. I'm her babysitter. Are your phones working?" Miss Schnell nodded. "Then we need to call her father right away."

Miss Schnell picked up the phone then paused, "And what about her mother?"

"Call her mother too," Marcus spoke for the first time, leaning forward in his chair. "Tell her Tara's in the hospital."

Chapter 20

In less than thirty minutes Jerry was sitting between Sam and Marcus in the hospital waiting room while the medical staff scanned, stitched, and x-rayed Tara's head. A kind orderly had draped warm blankets over Sam and Marcus, but Sam still shivered as she wiped her eyes with a crumpled tissue. Her other hand gripped Jerry's as she alternately apologized and berated herself for everything that had happened. Marcus, cocooned in his blanket, never took his eyes from the revolving door. Lost in her own misery, Sam barely noticed the old man reading the paper or the Amish couple sitting drawn and silent across the room, but she turned to look when Marcus sat up sharply, a broad smile spreading across his face.

Jerry let go of Samantha's hand as Margo walked toward them, gave them a quick once over, then strode past them toward the reception desk. As Margo stood at the desk talking with the clerk, Sam watched her with wary eyes. Beside her, Jerry seemed to be in the throes of an anxiety attack. He rubbed his hands back and forth across his thighs. He stood up, hesitated, and then sat down again two or three times. He was raking his fingers through his hair for the umpteenth time when Margo finally turned and walked over to them.

"Alright, it looks like you didn't actually kill her."

Despite her relief, Margo looked pissed. Sam tried to ease the tension. "Tara's going to be fine, she was alert and looking around before they wheeled her away." Sam wished Margo would stop staring at her as though she were an axe murderer. "There was a concussion, but they don't think there's any permanent brain damage. We're waiting for the results of the x-rays and CT scan right now."

"You know how Tara is." Jerry appeared small as he fumbled for words to appease the icy blue eyes glaring down at him. "I told you how she started running away after you left. I'd just blink and she'd be gone."

"Right, you know she runs away to look for me, so you take out a restraining order to make sure that I can't see her. What did you expect? What the hell were you thinking?"

Sam blew her nose into the damp tissue, "It was my fault. I thought she was in the garden with Marcus. I shouldn't have taken my eyes off her for a minute."

"You've got that right. Who the hell are you anyway?" Margo was steaming.

Sam didn't raise her voice but she stood up to face Margo, pulling the thin hospital blanket more tightly around her shoulders. "I'm the woman who's been taking care of your daughter since you've been too busy riding motorcycles, smoking pot, and getting your head together, or whatever it is you've been doing."

"Don't you dare throw that in my face. You don't know why I left or what I did while I was gone, and frankly, it's none of your business. You're not Tara's mother, I am."

"And I'm the father." Jerry's voice quavered, sounding more like a question than a statement.

"Like hell you are! My attorney is petitioning the court to have your name removed from Tara's birth certificate. Then maybe I'll get a restraining order against you and we'll see how you like it." The chairs where the Amish couple had been sitting were suddenly empty. The clerk at the reception desk shuffled papers on her desk pretending that she couldn't hear a thing.

Jerry's face fell and his eyes went flat. "That doesn't matter. You can do whatever you want with Tara's birth certificate. I'm still her father."

"You're not hearing me, you're *not* her father. I was pregnant before you ever got back from the service."

"Do I look like an idiot? Did you really think I couldn't figure that out?"

"You knew? You knew and you never said anything?" Margo's face seemed to be made of plasticine, her features molding and remolding themselves into various expressions as she and Jerry stared at one another and Sam tried to read the emotion in their eyes.

"Grandpop!" Marcus jumped up and ran toward the revolving doors to greet Billy who emerged carrying a pot of chrysanthemums. "Guess what? We drove the tractor."

Before Billy could reply, the door rotated again to reveal Sheila, who arrived breathless, agitated, and so distracted that she literally bumped into her old handyman.

"Billy, what are you doing here?"

"I came to pick up Marcus and to leave these for Tara. I hear the child took a bad blow to her head."

"That's what Sam told me. I got here as fast as I could."

"That was some storm; little twisters touched down all over the area. Trees and wires are down all over the place. You should see my old tool shed, the roof blew clear off." Billy removed his Buffalo Bills cap and brushed the rain from his coat.

"Thank God no one was killed," Sheila hurried toward her daughter-in-law, but Sam held up a hand to stop her.

"Sheila, give me a minute. I need to ask Margo something." Sam's heart was beating almost as fast as when she'd been searching for Tara in the storm. She didn't know where she got the nerve, but she had to know. "If Jerry's not Tara's father, was it Ben?"

Margo turned to Sam, "Ben? Who the hell is Ben?"

Jerry answered for her, "Ben Crawford, Joe's little brother. Sam's his widow." For the second time in as many minutes, Margo was speechless.

Sam went on, "Tara looks so much like Ben, and Jerry told me you dated him in high school. It made me wonder."

"I never dated Ben, he was just a kid in my class." Margo tilted her head to the side looking confused.

"But Jerry told me that Ben was your date for senior prom."

"Oh, for God's sake! Ben took me to prom as a favor since Joe was in the army and couldn't take me himself. I think Ben was supposed to babysit me, make sure I didn't get into any trouble. He did a great job. It was the most boring prom night on record."

Sheila sat down heavily in one of the molded plastic chairs. "You dated Joe? You were Joe's girlfriend?"

"Yeah, from my junior year in high school until, well until we knew he wasn't coming back. We snuck around, sure, but I'm sorry we never met. Joe knew how you felt about me."

"Tara is Joseph's daughter?" Sheila was gripping the chair as though she might fall off. Margo nodded.

"Damn." Billy shook his head in disbelief. The room went silent as they each calculated the implications of this news.

Sam felt as if she'd been slapped in the face. She could barely process the words and sounds around her. Somehow she found herself sitting in a chair on the far side of the room staring at the wall. *I wasn't crazy, only wrong. Tara looks like Ben because she's his niece, Sheila's granddaughter.* But was Tara anything to her? Did she have any claim on that sweet child? *Ben,* she called inside her heart. *Oh Ben.* But there was no reply.

"Mr. and Mrs. Michalski?" A nurse wearing a lab coat covered with smiley faces entered through a small door behind the reception desk.

"Doyle," Jerry corrected her.

"I'm sorry, Mr. and Mrs. Doyle." Jerry and Margo hesitated for an awkward moment, and then stepped forward. The nurse was smiling, a good sign. "The tests were all negative except for a small linear fracture just above her right temporal lobe. Linear fractures generally heal by themselves and shouldn't cause any long-term problems. Your daughter's pretty banged up and has some nasty cuts and bruises, but she's going to be fine. That kid has one hard head."

"She gets that from her mother," Jerry laid a hand on Margo's shoulder. Sam was disconcerted to see "Mr. and Mrs. Doyle" exchange tentative smiles.

"Can she come home?" Jerry asked.

"We'd like to keep her overnight for observation. If there are no further problems, she can go home in the morning. Would you like to see her now?" Sam, Marcus and Sheila all rose to their feet. "Sorry, only parents and immediate family are allowed." The nurse opened the door to the treatment rooms and Margo and Jerry followed her inside.

After the doors shut, and Jerry and Margo were out of sight, Sheila said, almost to herself, "I am immediate family. I'm her grandmother."

"Yes ma'am, it seems you've got yourself a grandbaby." The smile on Billy's face was pure sweetness. "God sure does work in mysterious ways." He took out a package of cigarettes and lit one, then offered the package to Sheila who shook her head, "I have to quit. I'm going to need good lungs to chase after a seven year old."

"Yes, you will. Yes, you will." He inhaled the tobacco then turned to look at Marcus. "Now what's this about my tractor?"

"Mrs. Crawford doesn't have a car so we had to drive your tractor to look for Tara. I started it for her because she didn't know how."

"Sam drove a tractor?" Sheila was incredulous. She stared at Marcus over the top of her glasses, disbelief clearly written in her face.

Sam stood up to find a seat beside her mother-in-law. "It wasn't that hard once Marcus showed me what to do. Luckily, I never had to change gears and I never had to back up." Sam shrugged nonchalantly as though this was nothing out of the ordinary.

"So it's true. You actually drove a tractor. I don't think my old heart could survive another day like this." Sheila had both her hands crossed over her chest. "I will never forget this day as long as I live."

"Where's my Allis? I didn't see her in the parking lot." Now that the crisis was past, Billy was worried about his tractor.

"I left her in the lot by the grocery. I guess she's still there. If you follow me and Sheila, we could pick her up on the way home."

Sheila patted Sam's hand, "Would you mind driving back with Billy? I think I'll stay here awhile. There's something that I need to do."

"Don't you mind about that tractor. It'll be okay overnight. I'll pick it up in the morning." Billy stood up and put his hat back on.

"Thanks. Would you mind dropping me off? I just want to go home, take a bath, and crawl into bed." She gave Sheila a hug. "Tell Jerry I'll call him in the morning."

"I will," Sheila returned her hug with crushing force. "I don't care what Margo says, I think you're a hero. God bless you for saving that child. Bless you for saving Joe's daughter."

The phone woke Sam the next morning. White curtains billowed in the morning light shining through the open window as she rolled over to pick up the receiver. "Hello, Jerry. No, it's fine, I'm up," she said stifling a yawn. "How's Tara? Have you called the hospital yet?" The digital clock read 8:03, which meant she'd been asleep for almost ten hours, but she felt as though she could use a couple more. "That's great. Sure, I'd love to drive over with you. Give me half an hour and I'll be waiting outside."

True to her word, Sam was standing in the driveway showered, dressed and munching on a piece of toast thirty minutes later. As they drove to the hospital they took turns pointing out the downed trees on every other lawn. One had fallen on a modern ranch house, collapsing part of the roof; another was blocking someone's drive. Fortunately, emergency crews had cleared the streets and they reached Lake West Memorial Hospital just before nine o'clock.

They were in a buoyant mood as they leaned against the patient information desk. Sam took Tara's Kermit the Frog puppet out of her purse and was fitting it on her hand while Jerry asked for Tara Michalski's room number.

"No, damn it!" Sam jumped as Jerry pounded his fist on the counter. "I have a restraining order for God's sake. Are you idiots? Do you just hand children out like stray kittens?"

"Of course not." The clerk put on the reading glasses that hung from a beaded chain around her neck and read from a clipboard. "The discharge was signed by Margo Michalski, mother. We discharged the child to her mother."

"But I'm the custodial parent. Margo had no right. We have a...damn!" Jerry pounded his fist on the desk again, but this time with less conviction. He knew he'd lost this round.

"What time did they leave?

The clerk checked the clipboard a second time. "Eight-fifteen. I'm sorry, we didn't know you were divorced, there's no record in the file...'

Jerry turned away from the desk without even a nod of acknowledgement. "Come on, Sam, we've got to go find them."

Kermit waved an apologetic farewell as Sam hurried after Jerry who, despite his bad leg, was already halfway to the parking lot.

"Where do we start?" she asked breathlessly once she'd caught up with him. She'd never seen a man move so fast, much less a man with a limp.

"The Wee Wan Chu Cottages. That's where she's been staying." The car motor was running before Sam opened the door. If he'd been driving a patrol car he'd have had the siren blaring and all the lights flashing. His face was grim and set like a rock. Neither of them said a word until they pulled into the parking lot of the small single story motel. "She's not here." Jerry's mouth was a thin taut line as he surveyed the property. "No car, no motorcycle. Where the hell did she go?" He raced off toward the motel office, without looking back to see if Sam was following him.

By the time Sam reached the office Jerry was already on his way out looking half crazed, "She checked out this morning and the deaf guy's been gone for two weeks. God damn it to Hell." He kicked at the garishly painted wooden Indian that stood outside the office door. "The bitch kidnapped my daughter."

"What do we do now?" Sam scanned the motel and saw nothing but two rows of identical windows and doors on either side of a small courtyard consisting of weeds and loose gravel.

"We call the department and put out an all points bulletin for a kidnapped child and a stolen car."

"Okay, but I'm not sitting at home waiting by the phone. We've got to keep looking for her too." Sam had no idea where to look, but she knew she'd lose her mind pacing around the kitchen waiting for the phone to ring.

"Look where?" Jerry turned toward her as though she might know something and wasn't telling him. "Any ideas?" Sam shook her head. Jerry sighed, "Me neither, I'm going back inside to use the phone."

By noon the police had contacted every hotel and motel within a hundred mile radius, and patrolmen in six counties were on the alert for a Blue Vega, New York State license SPL 2188. Sam and Jerry checked out local libraries, parks, and playgrounds, although Margo had probably left town and could be almost anywhere. Basically, they spent the morning driving in meaningless circles because moving was less painful than sitting still. Three hours later they were sitting in a booth at the Lighthouse Diner toying with food they couldn't eat.

"What goes through that broad's head? She's always been crazy, but this time she's gone too far." Jerry's face was pinched tight. His eyes and nose were streaked with small red veins. Sam must not have looked much better because Jerry looked into her face and said, "Hey, don't worry, the guys will find her. Tara sticks out like a sore thumb. Where does Margo think she can hide a red headed deaf kid anyway?"

Sam had been stirring her coffee for the last five minutes. Suddenly, she looked up and said softly, "In a school for the deaf."

"No way, you can't just drive up to a boarding school and drop a kid off like it's some kind of animal shelter. Margo might want Tara at one of those places, but it would take time to get her enrolled."

"But she's already filled out paper work for the school in Buffalo. They may have already accepted Tara."

"Do you remember the name of the school?" Jerry was reaching for the check.

"St. Francis de Sales. It's right downtown."

"It's a long shot, but what have we got to lose?" Jerry threw a couple of bills on the register as they headed out, their uneaten lunches still on their plates.

Buffalo was only ninety minutes away. If they didn't run into traffic they'd be there before three. "We should have called ahead to make sure they're open. A lot of schools close over the summer." Sam realized there was something crazy about their mission.

"Yeah," Jerry agreed, but he kept on driving. Once they reached Buffalo it was only a matter of stopping at a gas station to find the address, get directions, and wind their way through busy commercial streets to an aging residential neighborhood and a large Gothic building surrounded by a wrought iron fence. A discreet sign read, "St. Francis de Sales School for the Deaf—Anno Domini 1874." The open gate led to a parking lot with only a smattering of cars.

Jerry pulled in and turned off the ignition. "Say a prayer that she's in there."

The afternoon was uncomfortably warm and steamy after the previous day's storm. A neat brick path led to a pair of heavy oak doors that had been left open to let in some air. An office was immediately to the left as they entered the building where an attractive middle aged woman, whose hairstyle predated the Kennedy administration, was seated at a wooden desk talking on the phone. A large rotating fan riffled the papers on her desk but didn't budge a strand of her artfully combed and shellacked coiffure.

A textbook with a frayed cloth binding propped open a window through which Sam could see children playing in a side yard. They looked like children laughing and tussling on any playground anywhere, except that they made less noise and most of them wore hearing aids. Sam could hear laughter, a few grunts and giggles, but no chatter. However, these children were definitely communicating; their fingers flew and their faces were alive with expression. In fact, some gestures were so broad and exuberant that they seemed to be shouts. Sam watched through the window while she and Jerry waited for the woman to hang up the phone. Two little girls, not much older than Tara, were seated on a bench engaged in an animated conversation with their hands. Tara had never had a girlfriend, or a conversation. Sam turned away, her lips trembling.

"Sorry to keep you waiting, what may I do for you?" The woman hung up the phone and smiled up at them.

"I'm looking for a little girl, Tara Michalski, she's seven years old and has red hair. She may have been enrolled here today, possibly under another name." Jerry was using his most official Deputy Sheriff voice.

"Of course, Tara Michalski. Who could forget those adorable red curls? But she's not here now; we're not expecting her until September." The woman paused, a puzzled expression on her face, "Why would you think she enrolled here today?"

"There's a custody dispute and she's gone missing. We knew her mother wanted her to attend this school so we were just checking. Please, give me a call if you hear anything about her, anything at all." Jerry handed his card to the secretary.

She read the card then held out her hand. "Jerry Doyle. You're Tara's father. Margo told us about you." Her tone remained professional and cordial, but Sam wondered what she must be thinking. "I'm Jan Bender, the assistant principal. Ordinarily Mr. Walsh would speak with you, but he's at a conference in Albany today."

Jerry shook her hand, but Sam could tell that he had no interest in further conversation. If Tara wasn't here, he wanted to get back on the road. Mrs. Bender ignored the fact that Jerry's eyes moved from the clock on the wall to his wristwatch. "Would you like a tour of the school before you go?"

"Sorry, but we've got to get back to Kleiner. I can't rest until I know where Tara is."

"I understand how anxious you must be to find her, but if she's with her mother, I'm sure she's safe." Mrs. Bender walked over to the file cabinet behind her desk. "Margo is absolutely devoted to Tara. How many parents would learn sign, move to a new city, and look for a new job just to make sure their child got the best education possible?" She pulled a stiff manila folder out of the file and began looking through it. "I heard she's looking for work as a paralegal. Do you know if she found anything yet?"

Jerry looked pale; he was loosening the top button of his shirt as if he needed more air. "I don't know anything. I didn't know Margo was moving to Buffalo."

Mrs. Bender was reading from her file, "We have a local address for Margo Michalski effective the first of September. She wanted to be close to the school so that Tara could be admitted as a day student. We take children in residence as young as five, but we'd rather see the little ones at home with their parents."

"Did she tell you that she doesn't have custody?"

"Margo did say there was a problem, but she was pretty confident it would be cleared up in time for Tara to start school. She said the father, I guess that would be you, prefers a purely oral approach to Tara's education and that's been causing some problems. Is that right?"

Sam burst in, "He's been working with the special education department in Kleiner and they feel very strongly that children who use sign never learn to talk. They believe that learning oral language is the only hope deaf kids have to a full life in the hearing world."

The children outside the window had gathered around a young teacher who was talking while signing at the same time. One boy bounced a ball instead of paying attention and Sam could see the teacher scolding him. The two little girls she'd observed before signed something surreptitiously behind the teacher's back then dissolved in giggles. Mrs. Bender paused to observe the scene with Sam.

"Our kids live pretty full lives. Let me give you a quick tour, it will only take a minute. Maybe it will put your mind to rest."

Sam and Jerry followed her down the main corridor into a hallway lined with classrooms. The brown and tan linoleum tile floor was worn but clean. Between each classroom was a bulletin board displaying colorful art work or student essays. Sam paused before one board that was filled with pictures of people cut from magazines. There were photos of teachers, scientists, artists, attorneys, veterinarians, mechanics and carpenters under a stenciled heading that read, "Deaf People Can Do Anything."

"Did you know that St. Francis de Sales was a strictly oral school until about five years ago?" Sam and Jerry both shook their heads. Mrs. Bender went on, "There's been a revolution in deaf education over the past few years. I'm afraid the changes have been hard on the older teachers who've spent their whole careers committed to oralism. There was practically bloodshed in these hallways during the transition. It's a very emotional issue."

"Why did you make the switch?" Jerry seemed to have forgotten the time.

"What we're doing now isn't a switch exactly, we haven't given up on teaching oral skills, but the current research supports something called Total Communication. It uses sign in conjunction with oral language. It's made life so much easier for our children, especially for children like Tara who have profound hearing losses. Let me show you one of our hearing labs."

She opened the door to a classroom where twelve fourth graders sat in small desks arranged in a semicircle facing a teacher who was speaking into a microphone. "This room has been wired so that all the children hear the teacher's voice amplified through headsets. We haven't abandoned oral language, but we also make sure that no child is denied an education because of poor oral skills." Sam realized that the whole room functioned as a large auditory trainer, but the teacher wasn't asking the class to point to pies or peas, she was teaching a civics lesson on the three branches of government. The children listened attentively. Sometimes a hand would go up and a child would simultaneously speak and sign the answer to a question. Some spoke so clearly that it was hard to believe they couldn't hear. Others produced sounds that were unintelligible, but because they also signed their classmates knew exactly what they meant.

"What did you think?" Sam asked as they pulled back onto the road for the return trip to Kleiner.

"It looked like a nice school. The kids seemed pretty happy."

"Yeah, they did," Sam agreed. "What if Margo was right?"

"It won't matter who was right if we can't find Tara, at least it won't matter to me." Jerry headed for the entrance ramp to Interstate 90 East. "Do you really think Margo's planning to move to Buffalo? I always figured she'd move back to California and take Tara with her. That's what scared me the most—that she'd take Tara and I'd never see her again."

"It sure sounds as though she's moving to Buffalo. Why is Margo so sure that she's getting custody of Tara? You've been a perfect father while she disappeared with no forwarding address. Is she crazy—or am I missing something?" The visit to St. Francis de Sales had left Sam shaken. *Was I right about anything?*

"She's not crazy. She knows stuff about me that can't come out in court." Jerry was staring at the road, avoiding eye contact as he spoke.

Sam waited a couple of long minutes, but Jerry didn't elaborate. They passed a highway sign that said, Kleiner 68 miles. "What stuff?" she finally asked.

"After Ben was killed I started drinking this homemade hooch they sold in Vietnam...It was like fifty percent alcohol. My head was all messed up and I wasn't thinking straight."

"What happened?"

"I got really pissed, stole a jeep, and rolled it over on myself. That's how my leg got smashed. They wrote it up as an accident and sent me home with an honorable discharge, but there wasn't anything honorable about it. Margo and a couple of my army buddies are the only ones, besides you, who know the real story."

They were both silent as they sped past vineyards, a Stuckeys Restaurant, a trailer park, a plot of land with a sign that read, "For Sale—Will Build to Suit."

Jerry finally said, almost to himself, "She put up with a lot those first years after I got back home."

Sam squeezed his hand, "Stop at the next gas station and let's call the department, maybe they've already found Tara." They'd called three times in the past four hours, but Jerry started looking for an exit. Ten minutes later Jerry was hanging up the receiver in the phone booth just off the exit.

"No luck. No one's seen either of them since they left the hospital. Unless Margo's switched cars, she's not on the road." Jerry put his hand on Sam's knee and gave it a reassuring squeeze. "The Sheriff figures she's probably holed up with a friend somewhere in the area. He's pretty sure they'll find her."

"So, what do we do now? I'm out of ideas." Sam was exhausted physically and mentally, but too wired to go home and relax.

"My guess is that when Dan moved out of the motel he rented a house or an apartment and they're with him. If they are, the guys will track them down. Want to stop somewhere and get a drink?"

"I have a better idea." She put her hand over Jerry's and twined her fingers through his. "Let's pick up a bottle of wine and go back to my place."

"How about a six pack and I'll throw in a pizza?"

Sam would have preferred to unwind with a glass of Chardonnay, but she smiled and said, "Sure, that sounds great."

She and Jerry had known each other for four months. They'd fought and flirted and conspired together, but Sam realized, they'd never been alone—not totally alone in an empty house without a child, a mother-in-law, or a handyman lurking in the next room. A small shiver of anticipation made her hand shake as she fumbled with the key to the side door. Jerry stood so close behind her that she could feel his body heat radiating through her gauzy summer blouse. He moved closer, reaching around her with his free right arm to take the key as she struggled to keep a grip on the large white box from Mama Mia Pizza. The door swung open but Sam didn't move; she stood frozen to the spot as Jerry moved even closer. She let out a small gasp as she felt Jerry pressing against her and nuzzling her neck.

"I don't know how I would have gotten through today without you," he whispered in her ear. "You're amazing."

"Uhh, no. I…," Sam couldn't articulate a coherent word, much less a sentence. She stood in the doorway with the greasy pizza box in her hand not sure whether to step inside the house or to chicken out and say goodbye to Jerry where they stood, outside the door.

It was the pizza that finally settled it. In what she hoped was a friendly but business like tone she managed, "The pizza's getting cold." She willed her legs to move toward the kitchen where she put the carton on the table.

"I could sure use one of those beers," she said, ignoring the fact that Jerry had his arms around her waist and was nibbling on her ear. "Do the police know you're here? Do they have my number?"

"Mmm-hmm, I gave them all the numbers where they could reach me. If there's any news we'll hear about it."

His hands had moved up under her blouse and were cupping her breasts. *I didn't mean for things to go so fast. I'm not ready. I'm not sure about this at all.* His right hand was inside her panties, rubbing and probing places no one but Ben had ever touched. A small weak moan of surrender escaped as she turned to kiss him. Once they'd come up for breath, Jerry took her hand and led her toward the stairs.

"No, not the bedroom," she balked. "Follow me." She led Jerry to the big overstuffed couch in the living room. "It's really comfortable. I sleep here sometimes when it's too hot upstairs." It was comfortable. Deliciously comfortable in ways she'd almost forgotten.

The pizza was cold but the sun was still shining when they began sorting out the tangle of underwear, T-shirts and pants on the living room floor. Ben had been her second skin. She used to joke that she didn't know where her own body stopped and Ben's began, but with Jerry she felt awkward and self consciously naked. He handed her her bra and she turned her back to put it on and fasten it. The sex had felt delicious, but now she didn't know what to say or where to put her eyes. She decided she might as well be honest.

"That's the first time I've been with a man since my husband died. I guess that means I'm no longer a virgin." She gave Jerry an ironic smile. "It's been hard being alone all this time."

"Yeah, I know. I don't think I slept for a month after Margo left." He looked embarrassed, but in a confessional mode. "I used to spritz her cologne on my pillow."

"I thought I was the only one who did things like that. I used to wear Ben's pajamas to bed." A comradely smile passed between them. Maybe they could be friends. "I haven't slept with anyone in almost two years. I thought I'd never have sex again. How long has it been for you?"

Jerry blushed and shrugged as he buckled his belt. Sam persisted in a teasing tone, "Oh, go ahead, you can tell me."

"Alright, but it hasn't been that long, about a month." Jerry pulled his shirt on over his head and seemed to stay hidden inside it a moment or two longer than necessary.

"Really? I didn't know you'd been dating anyone. Who was she? Is she?" Sam noted that his revelation inspired only curiosity, not one bit of jealousy.

"We weren't dating and it's over. It was a mistake that I'll never make again. You can trust me on that one."

"So who was it? Someone from work? Someone you picked up in a bar? Where would you meet someone? You never go anywhere." Sam was in a playful mood and making idle chatter.

"It was Margo."

"Margo?" Sam repeated stupidly, not comprehending. "How could it be Margo? I thought you hated Margo, and anyway she has a boyfriend."

"Well, that's who it was. You asked so I told you, now let's forget it. It was a dumbass thing to do." Sam followed Jerry into the kitchen where he picked up a slice of cold pizza and stood wolfing it down over the box.

"My God, you're still in love with her. After everything that's happened, and everything she's done to you, you're still in love with her." Sam opened a warm beer and took a swig then handed it to Jerry.

"So what if I am, or was, what difference does it make?" He finished half the beer in one long swallow. "If she gave a crap about me, she wouldn't have kidnapped my daughter."

"Well, no. I guess not," Sam agreed.

"She told me that she'd changed, that she'd learned a lot while she was gone and I had this crazy fantasy that she'd come home, move back into the house, and everything would be all lovey-dovey. Then, when I found out she was planning to take Tara and put her in a boarding school in Buffalo I lost it. I took out the restraining order and the rest is history." He finished the beer and popped the cap off a second one.

"What about Dan? Does he know?" Sam had whisked the remaining pizza into the oven and was laying a couple plates on the table.

"She claims they're just friends. That probably means they're balling buddies. He supposedly came along for moral support because she was afraid of what I might do. What *I* might do? How do you like that?" Sam came over and stood behind Jerry's chair and began kneading the muscles in his shoulders. "Dan's divorced and has a hearing son back in California. He and Margo had a deal that he'd teach her how to raise a deaf kid if she taught him how to raise a hearing son. Oh, and he likes cross-country motorcycle rides so this was his idea of a vacation. Who knows, maybe some of it is true."

"Yeah, who knows?" Sam was working the muscles in Jerry's upper back when the phone rang.

Sam pounced on the phone then immediately looked up, covering the mouthpiece with one hand. "It's only Sheila," she mouthed the words to Jerry who slumped back in his chair. "Wait, she has Tara!" This time Sam was squealing with delight.

"Where are they? Let's go." Jerry was already on his feet.

"Wait a minute, I can't hear Sheila," Sam was making a shushing motion with her hands. "You're kidding? We've had the police in three states searching for them. Is she alright?" Sam gave Jerry a wide grin and a thumbs up. "We'll be over in two minutes. This is too crazy! Jerry isn't going to believe it." She hung up the phone and turned to Jerry. "You'd better phone the department and tell them to call off the hounds. Tara and Margo have been at Sheila's all day. She claims they've been trying to reach us since early this morning."

Sheila and Margo were sitting *tete-a-tete* at the dining room table over cups of tea and the remains of a peach pie. Tara was propped up on two pillows on the living room sofa happily rearranging Mr. Potato Head's face when Sam and Jerry walked through the front door. They stood there a moment taking in the scene, disconcerted by its tranquility after all their fears and fantasies.

Sheila stood up to greet them, "Well, where have you been? We were starting to get worried. Have you eaten? Do you want a slice of pie?"

Jerry's nostrils flared and his face turned red, "What do you mean, where have *we* been? We've been driving around like maniacs all day looking for Tara. We went all the way to Buffalo. We had the police in three states looking for her." Jerry was glaring at Margo. "You violated the restraining order. I could have you arrested."

"We tried calling, but you weren't at home. Sheila tried calling Sam, but she wasn't home either. What did you want us to do?" Margo was trying to project her usual tough persona, but her heart wasn't in it.

"I wanted you to...damn, what's the use? I wanted you to think about me, how I might feel when I went to pick up my daughter only to find she'd disappeared without a trace. Do you ever think about anyone but yourself?"

"Yes, she does. You'd be surprised how much she thinks about you and Tara." Sheila reached across the table and took Margo's hand. "She's made a lot of mistakes and she regrets them now, but Margo's never stopped caring about you both."

"Well, that's nice to know. She left town without a word of warning, didn't give a damn that her little girl was heartsick and confused, that she constantly ran away to search for her missing mommy. Never mind that she left me to raise a deaf child on my own. That she sent what—three postcards in two years without return addresses. But it's nice to know she cares. That really warms my heart."

Sam was surprised to see the formidable Margo slumped in her chair, chastened and diminished. Sheila took a firmer grip on Margo's hand. "There's more to the story than you know." She lowered her voice as though she were talking to an invalid or delivering bad news. "Do you want to tell them, Margo?"

"Could you do it?"

"It would mean more coming from you. Go ahead." She gave Margo's hand one more pat then let it go.

Margo picked up her tea cup and stared into it for a long time. All the bluster and bravado had gone out of her.

"Okay, what the hell? You asked, so here goes." Sam and Sheila both watched her intently, but she spoke only to Jerry. "You knew I drank a little too much and smoked weed when I could get it, but you didn't know I was drinking all day while you were at work. Mostly, I drank Vodka with orange juice or Kool-Aid. I'd always been a morning drinker, but it used to be just an eye-opener to get me going. After we found out about Tara, I figured it was my fault that she was deaf, and that really broke me up."

"Tara's a rubella baby," Jerry broke in. "She's deaf because you had German measles. You've made a mess of a lot of things, but Tara's deafness isn't your fault." Jerry was still standing, leaning against the archway that divided the dining room from the living room with his arms crossed. "The doctor explained that to us years ago."

"Maybe, but the doctor didn't know I dropped acid while I was pregnant. It was right at the beginning before I'd missed my period. I wouldn't have done it if I'd known." Jerry looked at her, not saying anything. "Anyway, after we found out Tara was deaf; I started to drink a little more. Tara would have her juice and I'd have mine, only mine was half Smirnoff. At first it wasn't so bad. I can drink a lot and never show it. I'd get the place straightened up, hide the bottle at the bottom of the trash, and have a nice dinner in the oven before you got home." Margo took a sip of her tea and went silent.

"Why don't the two of you come and sit down? How about some dessert?" Sheila cut a generous slice of the pie.

"No thanks." Jerry didn't move. His eyes were riveted on Margo who was studying the table cloth. "So, you were drinking. Big deal."

"It was a big deal. I wasn't thinking clearly and I was making mistakes. A couple of times I left my "juice" out where Tara could get it and she drank it and kind of passed out. Another time I got foggy and fell asleep while Tara was playing outside. A complete stranger rang the bell to tell me he'd missed running her over by inches. The guy threatened to report me for neglect, but I got lucky and he just drove away."

Jerry was standing with his jaw clenched, not saying a word. Sam stood beside him feeling awkward and out of place. Margo took another sip of tea then went on with her story, "Then I got the brilliant idea to take her on a picnic. I packed up fruit and sandwiches, her little swim suit and, of course, my bottle. We drove to Prendergast Point where I drank myself silly while she went swimming in the lake. By the time I came to, it was four o'clock and she'd disappeared. There was no point in calling her, so I just started running up and down the bank looking for her. It was a Tuesday afternoon and there was no one around except for a couple of old guys who were out fishing. They hadn't seen her, but they offered to help me look. They had some kind of spaniel with them, and it was really the dog that found her. Tara had walked about a half mile downstream to where the bank becomes really steep and it's all exposed shale and rock. The bottom falls off suddenly at that point so the water was over her head. She was huddled there, up to her neck in water and clinging to a big root, when the dog saw her and started barking.

Jerry and Sam both turned to look at Tara who'd fallen asleep on the couch. Her cherubic cheeks were surrounded by a halo of red curls, and a small bubble of spittle trembled on her lips. Mr. Potato Head stared back at them through googly plastic eyes.

"I figured it was only a matter of time before I killed her, so I left. If I wasn't such a coward I'd have told you what a shit I was and why I was going, but I couldn't do it. Could I have some more tea?" Sheila got up and carried Margo's cup into the kitchen.

"So, you left because you're a shit and almost killed Tara. The question is, why did you come back?" Jerry finally took a chair and sat down at the table. Sam remained standing, oddly out of place. She was in her mother-in-law's house, a place she'd visited a million times, but she felt like the outsider.

"Dan made me come back. He's a really good man."

"So, where is he now?" Jerry leaned forward in his chair.

"Probably back in Oakland by now. His vacation's over and he had to get back to work. He runs a service station with six bays, so he can't be gone that long. Anyway, his son visits for the month of August."

"I see." Jerry leaned back in his chair. "Why did he want you to come back here?"

"That was our deal from the beginning. He'd teach me how to take care of a deaf child if I'd help him with his hearing son. At first, we could only communicate through written notes; he's not a great lip reader. But he enrolled me in sign classes, and he practiced with me until I could carry on a pretty decent conversation with almost anyone who knows American Sign."

"How did you meet him?" This was the first thing Sam had said since they'd arrived.

"At a rest stop on Interstate 40 somewhere in Arizona. I saw him signing to one of his friends so I knew he was deaf and I just walked up and started asking him questions. I told him I had a deaf daughter and he sort of adopted me."

"It was like God sent her an angel. He got her to go to AA meetings just like I did, and she hasn't had a drink in how long?" Sheila put a cup of hot tea down in front of Margo.

"Twenty-one months."

"And she got a job as a legal assistant," Sheila went on.

"Legal secretary," Margo corrected.

"Legal secretary. And she's going to go back to college and become a lawyer. How about that?" Sheila was beaming.

"I have to get through college first, but that's what I want to do." Margo relaxed and Sam realized that she became a softer, less defensive person whenever Sheila was in the room.

"Did you plan on telling me any of this or did you think you could just grab Tara and write me out of the story? Why didn't you just talk to me like a normal person?"

"I figured you'd never let me near Tara, especially if you found out what I'd done. I tried telling you at the beginning. I thought we might even sort things out for a minute there." Margo looked up and held Jerry's gaze. "But then it turned out that you and this babysitter person," she nodded toward Sam, "were such fanatic oralists..." Sam bristled but kept her mouth shut. "It didn't seem that you had any interest in my opinion anymore. But everyone in the deaf community said to send her to St. Francis de Sales, so I just went ahead and made the arrangements without you."

"Jerry knows about St. Francis de Sales. He went there today looking for you." Sam said.

"So, what did you think?" Margo wanted to know.

"I liked it. The teachers seem to know what they're doing and the students look like regular, happy kids." Jerry and Margo's eyes were locked, engaged in a serious negotiation.

"Tara won't have to board there. I took an apartment so she can attend as a day student. She can see you on the weekends. You can have that in writing if you don't trust me." Margo was going to be a fine lawyer one day.

"I'm giving Margo a whole lot of stuff I won't be using any more so she'll have everything she needs to set up her new apartment." Sheila had to pause periodically to catch her breath, but her color looked better than it had it months. "Buffalo's only ninety minutes away so we'll be going back and forth all the time. I'll probably stay with Tara when her mother's taking night classes, and we'll all have to learn to talk with our hands."

Jerry was nodding his approval as Margo and Sheila made plans for the new apartment. Sam stood there listening for what felt like a very long time. Finally, she stood up and asked to use the phone. "It's a long distance call, but I'll reverse the charges." Sheila smiled and waved her into the kitchen.

Sam stood at the kitchen sink looking out into the night sky. It was mid August. Most schools wouldn't start for three more weeks.

A shooting star rocketed past the window. She blinked and another thin silvery trail blazed across the night and disappeared. *The Perseid meteor shower.* Sam stood mesmerized counting fifteen, sixteen, twenty shooting stars until the whole sky lit up. She'd never thought of painting the bridges of Providence, but why not? Who knew where those bridges might take her? She made a wish and picked up the phone.

"Hi Dad, listen, I want to drive up to Providence and I'm going to need a car."

draw it out
a bit more — the end.

It's too ↑ the words are too sudden
How does she feel
before & after she says
this?

ref. p. 184

① shorten or break up
the dialogue in places.
② fewer passive verbs "-ing"
★③ ending too abrupt
draw it out a bit more
★④ Did you consider other
titles. ⑤ p 227 Joe not Ben

About the Author

Patricia Averbach, a Cleveland native, is the former director of the Chautauqua Writers Center in Chautauqua, New York. She is the 2013 winner of the London-based Lumen/Camden Poetry Prize. As part of the prize, a poetry chapbook, *Missing Persons*, will be published late in 2013. Her previous work includes a memoir about her very early career as Anzia Yezierska's sixteen year old literary assistant, and an article about the Jewish community in a virtual world called Second Life. She holds a degree in speech pathology from Case Western Reserve University where she worked in a deaf nursery during the 1970s. She is married to attorney Mark Averbach and is the mother of two grown daughters, Ann and Elana. This is her first novel.

BOTTOM DOG PRESS

BOOKS IN THE HARMONY SERIES
Painting Bridges: A Novel
By Patricia Averbach, 234 pgs. $18
Ariadne & Other Poems
By Ingrid Swanberg, 120 pgs. $16
The Search for the Reason Why: New and Selected Poems
By Tom Kryss, 192 pgs. $16
Kenneth Patchen: Rebel Poet in America
By Larry Smith, Revised 2nd Edition, 326 pgs. Cloth $28
Selected Correspondence of Kenneth Patchen,
Edited with introduction by Allen Frost, Paper $18/ Cloth $28
Awash with Roses: Collected Love Poems of Kenneth Patchen
Eds. Laura Smith and Larry Smith
With introduction by Larry Smith, 200 pgs. $16

* * * *

HARMONY COLLECTIONS AND ANTHOLOGIES
d.a.levy and the mimeograph revolution
Eds. Ingrid Swanberg and Larry Smith, 276 pgs. $20
Come Together: Imagine Peace
Eds. Ann Smith, Larry Smith, Philip Metres, 204 pgs. $16
Evensong: Contemporary American Poets on Spirituality
Eds. Gerry LaFemina and Chad Prevost, 240 pgs. $16
America Zen: A Gathering of Poets
Eds. Ray McNiece and Larry Smith, 224 pgs. $16
Family Matters: Poems of Our Families
Eds. Ann Smith and Larry Smith, 232 pgs. $16

http://smithdocs.net

RECENT BOOKS BY BOTTOM DOG PRESS

Breathing the West: Great Basin Poems
By Liane Ellison Norman, 80 pgs. $16
Smoke: Poems By Jeanne Bryner, 96 pgs. $16
Maggot : A Novel By Robert Flanaga, 262 pgs. $18
Broken Collar: A Novel By Ron Mitchell, 234 pgs. $18
American Poet: A Novel By Jeff Vande Zande, 200 pgs. $18
The Pattern Maker's Daughter: Poems
By Sandee Gertz Umbach, 90 pages $16
The Way-Back Room: Memoir of a Detroit Childhood
By Mary Minock, 216 pgs. $18
The Free Farm: A Novel By Larry Smith, 306 pgs. $18
Sinners of Sanction County: Stories
By Charles Dodd White, 160 pgs. $17
Learning How: Stories, Yarns & Tales
By Richard Hague, 216 pgs. $18
Strangers in America: A Novel
By Erika Meyers, 140 pgs. $16
Riders on the Storm: A Novel
By Susan Streeter Carpenter, 404 pgs. $18
The Long River Home: A Novel
By Larry Smith, 230 pgs. Paper $16/ Cloth $22
Landscape with Fragmented Figures: A Novel
By Jeff Vande Zande, 232 pgs. $16
The Big Book of Daniel: Collected Poems
By Daniel Thompson, 340 pgs. Paper $18/ Cloth $22;
Reply to an Eviction Notice: Poems
By Robert Flanagan, 100 pgs. $15
An Unmistakable Shade of Red & The Obama Chronicles
By Mary E. Weems, 80 pgs. $15
Our Way of Life: Poems By Ray McNiece, 128 pgs. $15

http://smithdocs.net

CPSIA information can be obtained at www.ICGtesting.com
Printed in the USA
LVOW06s1359070114

368455LV00004B/169/P